Hans Christian Andersen (1805–75) was born in Odense, Denborn, Denmark. The young Andersen grew up solitary, dreamy, and enamored of literature and the thea.... urteen, armed with little e went to Copenhagen, patron-age of several pr ne for-mal schooling. In etches began to appear. *catore*, met with conside pub-lished his first col ...owed over the years by further creations in a genre he made singularly his own. His life was marked by extensive travels, enormous popularity, the friendship of many leading personalities of the era, and the highest honors of his native land. By the time of his death, this gauche, awkward figure, born in the humblest of circumstances, who set out alone to win fame and fortune had enjoyed a career that might well have come out of one of his most imaginative tales.

Poul Houe is professor of Scandinavian languages and literature at the University of Minnesota. He has lectured and/or taught at several European and American universities and presented at numerous other institutions and conferences in the U.S. and abroad. His research focuses on nineteenth- and twentieth-century Scandinavian literature and culture, specifically travel and exile literature in the context of modern European humanism, and his work has explored transnational issues and cultural transformation. His most recent books include a (Danish-language) collection of essays on Hans Christian Andersen and two co-edited (English-language) volumes on Søren Kierkegaard.

Joanne Greenberg was born in Brooklyn, New York, in 1932. She graduated from American University and presently teaches at the Colorado School of Mines. The author of many award-winning novels, including *I Never Promised You a Rose Garden* and *In This Sign*, she lives in Denver, Colorado.

ANDERSEN'S FAIRY TALES

HANS CHRISTIAN ANDERSEN

Translated by
Pat Shaw Iversen

With a New Introduction by
Poul Houe
and an Afterword by
Joanne Greenberg

Illustrated by
Sheila Greenwald

SIGNET CLASSICS

SIGNET CLASSICS
Published by the Penguin Group
Penguin Group (USA) Inc., 375 Hudson Street,
New York, New York 10014, USA
Penguin Group (Canada), 90 Eglinton Avenue East, Suite 700, Toronto,
Ontario M4P 2Y3, Canada (a division of Pearson Penguin Canada Inc.)
Penguin Books Ltd., 80 Strand, London WC2R 0RL, England
Penguin Ireland, 25 St. Stephen's Green, Dublin 2,
Ireland (a division of Penguin Books Ltd.)
Penguin Group (Australia), 707 Collins Street, Melbourne, Victoria 3008,
Australia (a division of Pearson Australia Group Pty. Ltd.)
Penguin Books India Pvt. Ltd., 11 Community Centre, Panchsheel Park,
New Delhi–110 017, India
Penguin Group (NZ), 67 Apollo Drive, Rosedale, Auckland 0632,
New Zealand (a division of Pearson New Zealand Ltd.)
Penguin Books (South Africa), Rosebank Office Park, 181 Jan Smuts Avenue,
Parktown North 2193, South Africa
Penguin China, B7 Jiaming Center, 27 East Third Ring Road North,
Chaoyang District, Beijing 100020, China

Penguin Books Ltd., Registered Offices:
80 Strand, London WC2R 0RL, England

Published by Signet Classics, an imprint of New American Library, a division of
Penguin Group (USA) Inc. This book previously appeared in a somewhat different form as *The Snow Queen and Other Tales*.

First Signet Classics Printing (New Edition), June 1987
First Signet Classics Printing (Houe Introduction), April 2013
10   9   8   7   6

Contents

Introduction

❖ ❖ ❖

No two anthologized editions of Andersen's fairy tales are alike—especially not in translation. The Andersen that emerges from different selections reflects different editorial, linguistic, and stylistic preferences; individual and epochal tastes and values; sociocultural circumstances. Like a mountain viewed differently from various angles, he is both the same and not the same. The simile brings to mind his own uncanny—and admittedly scary—ability to see into the hearts and minds of others, indeed to see the whole world from the point of view of its own phenomena, in much the way children do, instead of from the unifying viewpoint of most adults. One critic claims that Andersen urged the phenomena to speak to him—whenever it suited them.*

Leaving the issue of translation aside and considering only the volume's compositional makeup, *Andersen's Fairy Tales*, like most anthologies, draws upon the author's canon as well as his curio cabinet. Some anthologies are divided between tales for children and adults; folk and art tales; secular and religious tales; tales and so-called stories (Andersen's own distinction)—with each categorization having its own impact on readers' perceptions. Other anthologies—like this one—avoid subdivisions in favor of simple chronology. But how is the chronology weighted? The volume at hand offers a fairly equal distribution of tales (and stories) from all stages of Andersen's production, but underrepresents longer and more challenging specimens in favor of lesser known and lighter pieces.

That said, the question here is what constitutes the Andersen fairy tale (or story) that the anthology advances. How does its composition serve his artistic craft and socio-

---

*See Mogens Brøndsted, *"H. C. Andersens personlighedsproblem"* and Bo Hakon Jørgensen, *"At tænke i eventyr."* Both in Breitenstein, Jørgen et al., *H. C. Andersen og hans kunst i nyt lys* (Odense: Odense Universitetsforlag, 1976), pages 58–59 and 15, respectively; see also Søren Kassebeer's interview with Klaus P. Mortensen, *"'Verden er fuld af betydninger,'"* *Berlingske*, March 31, 2007.

cultural persona? For answers, it behooves us to reflect on the contents of *Andersen's Fairy Tales* in light of material not included between its covers.

What first meets the eye in several tales is a trademark of folk tales. "There was once" begin no fewer than ten of the texts included. If well begun is half done, this formula is good for starters—and good, too, are the volume's many happy endings, if they accord with the saying that all's well that ends well. However, compositions bookended by inclusive beginnings and comforting conclusions often destabilize both.

Take the semiautobiographical "The Ugly Duckling." It starts cheerfully: "It was so lovely out in the country—it was summer" (page 136) and ends even more so: "I never dreamed of so much happiness when I was the ugly duckling" (page 147). In between these hyperboles unfolds a *Bildungsreise*—a journey of personal edification—that is physically dramatic, but existentially a stasis. The feathered misfit was never a duckling but always a swan, and his many trials and tribulations did not grant him a new identity. Instead of suffering for real development, he does so for simply becoming who he was already. By inserting this precarious life story into a framework of endless happiness, the narrative only underscores how completely at risk selfhood is. "Being born in a duck yard doesn't matter if one has lain in a swan's egg" (page 146) are words of comfort that amount to nothing but a virtue made out of necessity. The excessive optimism in which the story wraps itself is self-contradictory.

Another tale that self-deconstructs is "The Snow Queen," the anthology's longest. Its subtitle, "An Adventure in Seven Tales," suggests yet another optimistic *Bildungsreise*. Indeed, its exit recalls "The Ugly Duckling's" entry: "And it was summer—the warm, glorious summer" (page 184). Gerda's grueling journey to rescue Kay from the Snow Queen's deadly embrace returns both children to their idyllic home. Thanks to her good heart, she, too, overcomes all obstacles which, by journey's end, confirms that developing or growing (up) means becoming who you are, i.e., becoming "as little children" in the biblical sense, or squaring the circle as the story does by having Kay and Gerda sit down, "grown up and yet children—children at heart" in their "little baby chairs" (page 184). Once again, the storyteller labors to put a positive spin on the existential drama of his characters, only to have his narrative reveal it as an art of the impossible.

It is a testament to Andersen's artistic integrity that his optimism unfailingly includes an account of the existential costs with which it comes. In "The Emperor's New Clothes," hope seems to be given the last word when a child spontaneously says the emperor "doesn't have anything on" (page 71). But the optimism drowns in the noise from the public shouting his words like copycats. Meanwhile, the emperor—after a moment's hesitation—regains his bearings: "Now I must go through with the procession" (page 71). Speaking truth to power proves useless, for even if it is recognized by all and sundry, such speech is short-lived.

"The Steadfast Tin Soldier" is about staying the course at the expense of one's better self. Overcompensating for being one-legged, the soldier stiffens his character precariously, so when this hapless victim of circumstance finally meets a "beautiful little dancer" who "was steadfast too," he is moved and "could have cried tears of tin," only it "wasn't proper"; it takes the oven, where he has been thrown and she has been blown, to pair them up. He melts into "a little tin heart" while she just "burn[s] as black as coal" (pages 76–77).

Andersen testifies repeatedly to love's simultaneous irresistibility and impossibility. "The Little Mermaid" sacrifices everything for a love she hopes will make her human—an effort in vain until hope in God's love may offer her reprieve. In "The Red Shoes," also about maturation, a child's self-indulgence collides with Christian criteria for salvation and adult "integrity." The youngster's behavior is reversed through a series of self-sacrifices culminating in death and atonement; heaven alone can break the spell of the red shoes that fettered her to bodily desires.

This type of chronic innocence comes to a head in "The Shepherdess and the Chimney Sweep," whose artificial couple gets engaged for purely logistical reasons. Facing the real world is above them, and their *Bildungsreise* ends in defeat and retreat. Traumatically bound to the past, they return to the china shelf with their harmonious concord in tatters. Much like "The Snow Queen's" Kay and Gerda, they have not moved beyond the limits of innocence.

In a few tales, most notably "The Nightingale," artificiality yields to the liberating spirit of nature. Like the emperor without clothes, this tale's ruler is caught up in the mock civilization of court and power. But unlike the former, he invites a live songbird into his world, and after its artificial replacement breaks down, it returns to save and enrich his life. "The Nightingale" is more wholesome than many of Andersen's tales.

In such powerful works as "The Shadow," "The Bog King's Daughter," and "Auntie Toothache," which are not included in this volume, the outlook is less forgiving. The learned man in "The Shadow" allows convention to govern his poetic imagination until the latter escapes into a shadowy life of its own and ends up destroying its former master. Complacent harmony breeds unrest.

In "The Bog King's Daughter," conflict ravages the daughter's inner being before divine intervention—barely—grants her redemption. Finally, in "Auntie Toothache," the narrator is a student with a poetic gift as restricted as that of the learned man in "The Shadow." When his aunt Millie prods him into poetic action, it awakens Auntie Toothache, Millie's fierce alter ego, who makes him suffer for falling for Millie's sweets. Gradually both illusion and reality are overpowered by the narration itself—until every character is gone for good.

While metatextual outcomes like this are rare in *Andersen's Fairy Tales*, other intrusions into characters' comfort zones—and disruptions of the familiar order—are in ample supply. Søren Kierkegaard, Andersen's contemporary and as much a fairy-tale buff as anyone, rebuked his fellow writer for lacking a coherent philosophy of life—and a novelist's integrity—a critique to which there is some truth. But if a weak artistic-philosophical backbone harmed Andersen's longer works, it stood him in good stead in his shorter prose and made him a "thinker in tales."

Critics agree that he shared in the discordant spirit of the younger romantics and that the fairy-tale genre's anarchistic dealing with society and its ways opened his mind to experiences "he had had as an underclass child playing the upper class's mascot."* While his novels may fluctuate sentimentally—between the writer's art and biography; pri-

---

*Jørgensen, page 56; the phrase "thinker in tales" is inspired by Jørgensen's title.

vate and artistic preferences; faith in providence and angst of death; self-confidence and feelings of inferiority—the fairy-tale format condenses such conflicts into revealing humor (and irony).

In his vacillation between social classes, Andersen destabilized conventions and foregrounded (post-)modern idioms. "My own heart is so changeable that only moments could be captured," he wrote to one friend, and "I almost believe that I myself am a disharmony in this world" to another.* It was his fairy tales' forte not to arrive at their insights by escaping reality but by getting to the bottom of it. The cost was shaky harmonies, the benefit a disarming appeal to readers of all ages—an altogether priceless balance.

How do lesser pieces in *Andersen's Fairy Tales* highlight his fairy-tale idiom? Several play with the notion of truth in writing. Although "Little Claus and Big Claus" begins by promising a "true story" (page 16), while "Cloddy Hans" ends by saying it's "not to be trusted" (page 248), they actually do the same thing, namely, toy with concepts of truth to enliven the conditions that make truth possible. The title "It's Quite True" pertains to the sentence that "one tiny feather can indeed turn into five hens" (page 226). Taken literally, it's the kind of truth, called lies, in which the tale's newspaper trades; but taken figuratively, it's an adage the tale itself vindicates.

When we then learn, in "The Princess on the Pea," that "she" is "black and blue all over" from having slept on a pea underneath "twenty eiderdown quilts" on top of "twenty mattresses" (pages 30–31), is the sensibility of royalty here being subserviently admired, or is such thin-skinned unworldliness found ridiculous? Or are the two conclusions different dimensions of a truly elusive humor? Certainly, the ending—"See, this was a true story!" (page 32)—identifies the story's truth with the story!

"The Little Match Girl" less buoyantly presents a character from the bottom of society. Yet she herself has dual sentiments—and literally ignites her own fantasies, which in turn take her mind from the depth of despair to the sum-

---

*Cited (in my translation) from *Breve fra H. C. Andersen*. Eds. C. St. A. Bille & Nicolaj Bøgh (1878; 2nd ed., Copenhagen: Aschehoug, 2005), pages 355 and 173, respectively.

mit of joy, showing both life at its peak and the costs of its ascendance. Andersen envisions a dash, not a period, between the world of mortals and an afterworld of bliss and rebirth; between the world of harsh realism and that of Christian idealism and Romantic pantheism. And New Year's Eve is the moment these irreconcilable worlds meet and part ways within his imagination.

On other occasions, his poetic sentiments collide in mutually assured destruction—as in "The Snail and the Rosebush," where the snail's condescending solipsism incessantly challenges the rosebush's graceful extroversion. In "The Gardener and the Lord and Lady" such disconnect is socially charged, and in "The Sweethearts," "The Swineherd," "The Butterfly," and "The Happy Family," social divisions separate potential lovers.

Two unsuccessful suitors live to watch the downfall of the superior objects they desired; a choosy butterfly winds up pinned down in a curio chest, as immobilized as the flowers he wouldn't court; and a declining family of snails in the burdocks around an old manor upholds its social illusions by insisting the manor must have collapsed; that's why the snails are not being cooked nor laid on "a silver dish" (page 218).

In many of Andersen's tales, a human desire to connect is obstructed by pompous reserve. The animals, plants, and various objects enacting these roles are not arbitrarily chosen. They employ a double vision, as in "The Darning Needle," who sees the human with a needle's eye.* This is how Andersen the animator approaches a world torn by human contradictions on its own terms. His strenuous mobility goes inward and outward, even upward, like a marsh plant's reach for the sun,† and his opposites blend, sometimes ironically, into one another's predators. Both basic and lofty, his imagination puts the reader in medias res or on other equal terms with the narrator, and *Andersen's Fairy Tales* captures its appeal to children at heart, old and young alike.

—Poul Houe

---

*Cf. Bo Grønbech, *H. C. Andersens eventyrverden* (1945; 2nd rev. ed., Copenhagen: Hans Reitzel, 1964), pages 50–51.
†See Brøndsted, pages 9–10; in Klaus P. Mortensen, *Svanen og Skyggen—historien om unge Andersen* (Copenhagen: Gad, 1989), the title concepts—the swan and the shadow—intimate the same polarity.

The Tinderbox

❖   ❖   ❖

A SOLDIER came marching along the highway: One, two! One, two! He had his knapsack on his back and a sword at his side, for he had been to war and now he was on his way home. Then he met an old witch on the highway. She was hideous, and her lower lip hung right down to her chest.

She said, "Good evening, soldier! My, what a pretty sword and a big knapsack you have! You're a real soldier! Now you shall have as much money as you'd like to have!"

"Thanks, old witch!" said the soldier.

"Do you see that big tree?" said the witch, and pointed to a tree beside them. "It's quite hollow inside. You're to climb up to the top. Then you'll see a hole you can slide through, and you'll come down way inside the tree! I'll tie a rope around your waist so I can pull you up again when you call me."

"What'll I do down in the tree, then?" asked the soldier.

"Fetch money!" said the witch. "Now I'll tell you: when you're down at the bottom of the tree, you'll find yourself in a great hall. It's quite light, for over a hundred lamps are burning there. Then you'll see three doors. You can open them: the keys are in them. If you go into the first chamber, you'll see a big chest in the middle of the floor. On top of it sits a dog with a pair of eyes as big as teacups.

But you needn't pay any attention to that. I'll give you my blue-checked apron, which you can spread out on the floor. Then go over quickly and get the dog, put him on my apron, open the chest, and take as many shillings as you like! They're all of copper. But if you'd rather have silver, then go into the next room. There sits a dog with a pair of eyes as big as mill wheels! But you needn't pay any attention to that. Put him on my apron and take the money. On the other hand, if you'd rather have gold, you can also have that, and as much as you can carry, if you just go into the third chamber. But the dog sitting on the money chest here has a pair of eyes each one as big as the Round Tower! That's a real dog, I'll have you know! But you needn't pay any attention to that. Just put him on my apron, so he won't do you any harm, and take as much gold as you like from the chest."

"There's nothing wrong with that!" said the soldier. "But what'll I get for you, old witch? For I daresay you want something too!"

"No," said the witch, "not a single shilling will I have! You can just bring me an old tinderbox, which my grandmother forgot the last time she was down there."

"Well, put the rope around my waist," said the soldier.

"Here it is," said the witch, "and here's my blue-checked apron."

Then the soldier climbed up into the tree, let himself drop down through the hole, and stood now, as the old witch had said, down in the great hall where the many hundreds of lamps were burning.

Now he unlocked the first door. Ugh! There sat the dog with eyes as big as teacups, and it glowered at him.

"You're a pretty fellow!" said the soldier; he put the dog on the witch's apron and then took as many copper shillings as he could get in his pocket. Then he closed the chest, put the dog on it again, and went into the second chamber. Yeow! There sat the dog with eyes as big as mill wheels.

"You shouldn't look at me so hard," said the soldier; "it might strain your eyes!" Then he put the dog on the witch's apron, but when he saw all the silver coins in the chest, he got rid of all the copper money he had and filled his pocket and his knapsack with silver only. Now he went into the third chamber! My, how hideous it was! The dog in there really did have two eyes each as big as the Round Tower, and they rolled around in his head like wheels!

"Good evening," said the soldier, and touched his cap, for he had never seen a dog like that before. But after he had looked at it for a while, he thought, "Now that's enough," and lifted it down to the floor and opened the chest. Well, heaven be praised! What a lot of gold there was! He could buy all of Copenhagen with it, and the sugar pigs of the cake wives, and all the tin soldiers and whips and rocking horses in the world! Yes, that was really a lot of money! Now the soldier threw away all the silver shillings in his pocket and knapsack and took gold instead. Yes, he filled all his pockets and his knapsack, and his cap and boots were so full that he could hardly walk! Now he had money! He put the dog on the chest, shut the door, and then shouted up through the tree: "Pull me up now, old witch."

"Do you have the tinderbox with you?" asked the witch.

"That's right," said the soldier. "I'd clean forgotten it." And then he went and got it. The witch pulled him up, and now he was standing on the highway again with his pockets, boots, knapsack, and cap full of money.

"What do you want that tinderbox for?" asked the soldier.

"That's none of your business!" said the witch. "Why, you've got the money now. Just give me the tinderbox!"

"Fiddlesticks!" said the soldier. "Tell me at once what you want it for, or I'll draw my sword and chop off your head!"

"No!" said the witch.

Then the soldier chopped off her head. There she lay! But he tied all his money in her apron, carried it like a pack on his back, put the tinderbox in his pocket, and went straight to the town.

It was a lovely town, and he put up at the finest inn and demanded the very best rooms and all the food he liked, for he was rich, now that he had so much money.

The servant who was to polish his boots thought, of course, that they were queer old boots for such a rich gentleman to have, for he hadn't bought any new ones yet. The next day he got boots to walk in and pretty clothes. Now the soldier had become a fine gentleman, and they told him about all the things to do in their town, and about their king, and what a lovely princess his daughter was.

"Where can she be seen?" asked the soldier.

"She can't be seen at all," they said. "She lives in a big copper castle with many walls and towers around it. No one but the king is allowed to go in and out, for it has been prophesied that she will be married to a common soldier, and the king can't stand that one bit!"

"I'd like to see her, all right," thought the soldier, but this he wasn't allowed to do at all.

Now he lived merrily and well, went to the theater, drove in the royal park, and gave lots of money away to the poor; and that was well done! He remembered very well from the old days how bad it was to be penniless! Now he was rich and had fine clothes and many friends, who all said what a nice fellow he was, a real cavalier; and the soldier certainly didn't mind hearing that. But as he spent money every day and didn't get any back at all, it happened that at last he had no more than two shillings left and had to move from the nice rooms where he had lived to a tiny little room way up under the roof, and he had to brush his boots himself and mend them with a needle; and none of his friends came to see him, for there were so many stairs to climb.

One evening it was quite dark and he couldn't buy even a candle, but then he remembered there was a little stub in the tinderbox he had taken out of the hollow tree where the witch had helped him. He took out the tinderbox and the candle stub, but just as he struck a light and the sparks flew from the flint, the door flew open and the dog with eyes as big as teacups, which he had seen down under the tree, stood before him and said, "What does my master command?"

"What's that?" said the soldier. "Why, this is a funny tinderbox if I can get whatever I like! Get me some money," he said to the dog. And whoops! It was gone! Whoops! It was back again, holding a bag full of coins in its mouth.

Now the soldier understood what a marvelous tinderbox it was. If he struck it once, the dog that sat on the chest full of copper money came; if he struck it twice, the one with the silver money came; and if he struck it three times, the one with the gold came. Now the soldier moved back down to the lovely rooms again, put on the fine clothing, and then all his friends knew him again right away, and they were so fond of him.

Then one day he thought: "Now, it's really quite odd that no one is allowed to see the princess. Everyone says she's supposed to be so lovely. But what's the good of it when she always has to sit inside that big copper castle with all the towers? Can't I even get to see her at all? Now, where's my tinderbox?" And then he struck a light, and whoops! There stood the dog with eyes as big as teacups.

"I know it's the middle of the night," said the soldier, "but I'd so like to see the princess, just for a tiny moment."

The dog was out of the door at once, and before the soldier had given it a thought, it was back again with the princess. She sat on the dog's back and was asleep, and she was so lovely that anyone could see that she was a real princess. The soldier couldn't resist; he had to kiss her, for he was a real soldier.

Then the dog ran back again with the princess. But in the morning, when the king and queen were having their tea, the princess said that she had dreamed such a remarkable dream last night about a dog and a soldier. She had ridden on the dog, and the soldier had kissed her.

"That was a pretty story, indeed!" said the queen.

Now, one of the old ladies-in-waiting was to keep watch by the princess' bed the next night to see if it really were a dream or what it could be.

The soldier wanted very much to see the lovely princess again, and so the dog came during the night, took her, and ran as fast as it could, but the old lady-in-waiting pulled on a pair of rubber boots and ran after it just as fast. When she saw that they disappeared inside a big house, she drew a big cross on the door with a piece of chalk. Then she went home and went to bed, and the dog came back with the princess. But when it saw that a cross had been made on the door, it also took a piece of chalk and made crosses on all the doors in the city, and that was wise, for now, of course, the lady-in-waiting couldn't find the right door when there was a cross on every single one.

Early the next morning the king and the queen, the old lady-in-waiting, and all the officers came to see where the Princess had been.

"There it is!" said the king when he saw the first door with a cross on it.

"No, *there* it is, my dear husband," said the queen, who saw the second door with a cross on it.

"But there's one and there's one!" they all said. No matter where they looked, there was a cross on the door. So then they could see that there was no use searching one bit.

But the queen was a very wise woman, who knew about more than just riding in the royal coach. She took her big golden scissors, cut up a large piece of silk, and sewed a lovely little bag. This she filled with small, fine grains of buckwheat, tied it to the princess' back, and when that was done, clipped a tiny hole in the bag so the grain could dribble out all along the way, wherever the princess went.

That night, the dog came again, took the princess on his back, and carried her straight to the soldier, who had fallen in love with her and gladly would have been a prince so he could make her his wife.

The dog didn't notice at all how the grains dribbled out all the way from the castle to the soldier's window, where it ran up the wall with the princess. In the morning the king and queen saw where their daughter had been, all right, and so they took the soldier and put him in jail. There he sat! Ugh! How dark and dreary it was! And then they said to him, "Tomorrow you're to be hanged!" That wasn't a nice thing to hear, and he had forgotten his tinderbox back at the inn. In the morning, through the bars in the tiny window, he could see the people hurrying out of the city to see him hanged. He heard drums and saw the soldiers marching. Everybody was rushing out, including a shoemaker's apprentice in his leather apron and slippers, who was in such a hurry that one of his slippers flew off and landed nearby the wall where the soldier sat peering out through the iron bars.

"Hey there, shoemaker's boy, you needn't be in such a hurry," said the soldier. "Nothing will happen until I get there. But if you'll run to my lodgings and fetch my tinderbox, you'll get four shillings. But then you must really run." The shoemaker's boy was only too glad to have four shillings, and he scurried away after the tinderbox and gave it to the soldier, and—yes, now we shall hear:

Outside the city a big gallows had been built; around it stood the soldiers and many hundreds of thousands of people. The king and the queen sat on a lovely throne right above the judge and the whole court. The soldier was already on the ladder, but as they were going to put the noose around his neck he said—oh, yes, a sinner is always granted one little innocent wish before he receives his punishment—he would so like to smoke a pipeful of tobacco. After all, it would be the last pipe he'd have in this world.

The king couldn't really say no to that, and so the soldier took out his tinderbox and struck a light: One! Two! Three! And there stood all the dogs: the first with eyes as big as teacups, the second with eyes as big as mill wheels, and the third with eyes each as big as the Round Tower.

"Help me now, so I won't be hanged!" said the soldier. And then the dogs flew right at the judge and the whole court, took one by the legs and one by the nose, and tossed them many miles up in the air so they fell down and broke into pieces.

"I won't!" said the king, but the biggest dog took both him and the queen and threw them after all the others. Then the soldiers were frightened, and all the people shouted: "Little soldier, you shall be our king and have the lovely princess!"

Then they put the soldier in the king's coach, and all three dogs danced in front and shouted, "Hurrah!" And all the boys whistled through their fingers, and the soldiers presented arms. The princess came out of the copper castle, and was made queen, and that she liked very well. The wedding party lasted eight days, and the dogs sat at the table and made eyes at everybody.

Little Claus
and Big Claus

❖   ❖   ❖

IN one town there were two men who had the very
same name: they were both called Claus, but one of
them owned four horses and the other only a single horse:
and so, in order to tell them apart, the one who had four
horses was called Big Claus, and the one who had only
one horse, Little Claus. Now we shall hear how the two
got along, for this is a true story!

All week long Little Claus had to plow for Big Claus and
lend him his one horse. Then Big Claus helped him in
return with all four of his horses, but only once a week,
and that was on Sunday. Huzzah! How Little Claus cracked
his whip over all five horses; after all, they were as good as
his on that one day. The sun was shining so delightfully,
and all the bells in the church tower were ringing for church.
People were all dressed up and walked by with their hymn
books under their arms, on their way to hear the parson
preach. And they looked at Little Claus, who was plowing
with five horses, and he was so contented that he cracked
his whip again and shouted: "Gee up, all my horses!"

"You mustn't say that," said Big Claus. "After all, only
one of the horses is yours!"

But when somebody went by again on the way to church,
Little Claus forgot that he mustn't say it, and so he shouted:
"Gee up, all my horses!"

"Well, now, I'm telling you to stop that!" said Big Claus. "If you say it just one more time, I'll strike your horse on the forehead so he'll be lying dead on the spot, and that'll be the end of him!"

"I certainly won't say it anymore," said Little Claus. But when people went by, nodding and saying, "Good day," he became so contented, thinking it looked so grand for him to have five horses to plow his field with, that he cracked his whip and shouted: "Gee up, all my horses!"

"I'll gee up your horse!" said Big Claus, and he took the tethering mallet and gave Little Claus's horse such a blow on the forehead that it fell down quite dead.

"Oh, woe! Now I haven't got any horse at all!" said Little Claus, and started to cry. Later he flayed the horse, took the hide, and let it dry well in the wind; and then, putting it in a bag that he carried on his back, he went to town to sell his horsehide.

He had such a long way to go, through a deep, dark forest, and now a terrible storm blew up; he completely lost his way, and before he had got back on the right path again it was evening and much too far both from town and from home to arrive at either before nightfall.

Close to the road stood a big farmhouse. The outside shutters were closed, but the light still shone out at the top. "I hope I'll be allowed to spend the night here," thought Little Claus, and went over to knock at the door.

The farmer's wife opened it, but when she heard what he wanted, she told him to be on his way. Her husband wasn't home, and she didn't take in strangers.

"Well, I'll have to sleep outside, then," said Little Claus, and the farmer's wife shut the door on him.

Nearby stood a big haystack, and between that and the house a little shed had been put up, with a flat thatched roof.

"I can lie up there," said Little Claus when he saw the roof. "After all, it's a lovely bed. I daresay the stork won't fly down and bite me in the legs!" For a real live stork was standing on the roof, where it had its nest.

Now Little Claus crawled onto the shed, where he lay twisting and turning in order to make himself comfortable. The wooden shutters in front of the windows didn't go all the way up to the top, and so he could see right into the parlor.

A big table had been laid with wine and a roast and such a delicious fish. The farmer's wife and the parish clerk were sitting at the table, and no one else at all was there. And she poured him a drink, and he prodded the fish, for that was something he liked.

"If only I could have some too!" said Little Claus, and stretched his head all the way over to the window. Heavens! What a lovely cake he could see standing there. That was quite a feast.

Now he heard someone riding along the road toward the house—it was the woman's husband who was coming.

He was such a good man, but he had the singular affliction of not being able to bear the sight of a parish clerk! If he laid eyes on a parish clerk, he would fly into a terrible rage. This was also the reason why the parish clerk had dropped in to pay his respects to the wife when he knew that the husband wasn't at home, and the good wife set before him the most delicious food she had. Now, when they heard the husband coming, they were so terrified that the wife bade the parish clerk crawl down inside a big empty chest that was standing over in the corner. This he did, for he knew, of course, that the poor husband couldn't bear the sight of a parish clerk! The wife quickly hid all the delicious food and wine in her oven, because if the husband had seen it, he certainly would have asked what it was all about.

"Oh, woe!" sighed Little Claus on the shed when he saw all the food disappear.

"Is there someone up there?" asked the farmer, and

peered up at Little Claus. "Why are you lying there? Come in the house with me instead!"

Then Little Claus told how he had lost his way, and he asked if he could spend the night there.

"Why, of course!" said the farmer. "But first we're going to have a bite to eat!"

The wife welcomed them both very warmly, laid a long table, and gave them a big bowl of porridge. The farmer was hungry and ate with a good appetite, but Little Claus couldn't stop thinking about the lovely roast and fish and cake that he knew were standing in the oven.

Under the table at his feet he had put his bag with the horsehide in it—for we know that he had brought it from home to sell in town. He wouldn't enjoy the porridge at all, and so he trod on his bag, and the dry hide inside gave out quite a loud creak.

"Hush!" said Little Claus to his bag, but trod on it again, making it creak louder than before.

"Why, what do you have in your bag?" asked the farmer.

"Oh, it's a sorcerer!" said Little Claus. "He says we shouldn't eat porridge; he's conjured the whole oven full of a roast and fish and cake."

"What's that?" said the farmer, and he quickly opened the oven and saw all the delicious food the wife had hidden, but which he now believed had been conjured up for them by the sorcerer in the bag. The wife dared not say a thing but put the food on the table at once, and then they both ate the fish and the roast and the cake. Without delay Little Claus trod on his bag again so the hide creaked.

"What does he say now?" asked the farmer.

"He says," said Little Claus, "that he has also conjured up three bottles of wine for us, and they're standing in the oven too!" Now the wife had to take out the wine she had hidden, and the farmer drank and became quite merry; he'd be only too willing to own a sorcerer like the one Little Claus had in his bag.

"Can he conjure up the devil too?" asked the farmer.
"I'd really like to see him, for now I feel so merry!"

"Yes," said Little Claus. "My sorcerer can do anything I
ask him to. Can't you?" he asked, and trod on the bag so it
creaked. "Can you hear? He says, 'Of course!' But the
devil looks so terrible that it's better not to look at him!"

"Oh, I'm not afraid at all. How do you think he'll look?"

"Well, he'll appear in the shape of a parish clerk!"

"Whew!" said the farmer. "That's awful! You've got to
know that I can't bear the sight of parish clerks! But no
matter! After all, I know it's the devil, so I guess I'll just
have to put up with it. I've got courage now! But he
mustn't come too close!"

"Now I'm going to ask my sorcerer," said Little Claus,
treading on the bag and holding his ear to it.

"What does he say?"

"He says that you can go over and open the chest
standing in the corner, and then you'll see the devil mop-

ing inside. But you've got to hold onto the lid so he doesn't get out!"

"Will you help me to hold it?" said the farmer, and went over to the chest where the wife had hidden the real parish clerk, who sat there scared to death.

The farmer lifted the lid a crack and peered in under it. "Yeow!" he shrieked, jumping back. "Yes, now I saw him; he looked just like our parish clerk! My, that was dreadful!"

They had to have a drink after this, and then they kept on drinking far into the night.

"You've got to sell that sorcerer to me!" said the farmer. "Ask whatever you like! Yes, I'll give you a whole bushel of money right away."

"No, I can't do that," said Little Claus. "Think of how much use that sorcerer is to me."

"Oh, I'd so like to have it," said the farmer, and kept on begging.

"Well," said Little Claus at last, "since you've been so kind as to put me up for the night, it's all right. You shall have the sorcerer for a bushel of money, but it has to be heaping full!"

"You shall have it!" said the farmer. "But you'll have to take that chest over there with you. I won't have it in the house another hour—you never can tell if he's still sitting in there."

Little Claus gave the farmer his bag with the dry hide inside, and was given a whole bushel of money—and heaping full, at that. And the farmer even gave him a big wheelbarrow on which to carry the money and the chest.

"Farewell!" said Little Claus, and then off he went with his money and the big chest with the parish clerk still sitting inside.

On the other side of the forest there was a big, deep river; it flowed so fast that one could hardly swim against the current. A large new bridge had been built across it. Little Claus stopped right in the middle of it and said quite loudly, so the parish clerk inside the chest could hear it: "Well, whatever am I going to do with that silly chest? It's as heavy as if it were full of stones. I'm getting quite tired of driving it any farther, so I'm going to throw it out in the river! If it sails home to me, then it's all very well; and if it doesn't, then it doesn't matter."

And taking hold of the chest with one hand, he lifted it up as if he were going to throw it in the water.

"No, stop! Don't do that!" shouted the parish clerk inside the chest. "Just let me come out!"

"Yeow!" said Little Claus, pretending to be afraid. "He's still sitting in there! I've got to throw it in the river right away so he can drown!"

"Oh, no! Oh, no!" shouted the parish clerk. "I'll give you a whole bushel of money if you don't!"

"Well, that's another story!" said Little Claus, and opened the chest. The parish clerk crawled out at once, shoved the empty chest into the water, and then went to his home, where Little Claus received a whole bushel of money—he had already gotten one from the farmer—and now his wheelbarrow was full of money.

"See, I got quite a good price for that horse," he said to himself when he came home to his cottage; then he emptied his bag in the middle of the floor and put all the money into a big pile. "That will annoy Big Claus when he finds out how rich I've become with my one horse. But I'm not going to tell him outright!"

Now he sent a boy over to Big Claus to borrow a bushel measure.

"I wonder what he wants that for!" thought Big Claus, and he smeared the bottom with tar so that a little of what was measured would stick fast. And so it did, too, for when he got the measure back, three new silver florins were stuck to it.

"What's this?" said Big Claus, and ran to Little Claus at once. "Where did you get all that money from?"

"Oh, that's for my horsehide. I sold it yesterday evening."

"I'll say you were well paid!" said Big Claus. He ran home, took an ax, struck all four of his horses on the forehead, flayed them, and drove to town with their hides.

"Hides! Hides! Who'll buy my hides?" he shouted through the streets.

All the shoemakers and tanners came running and asked how much he wanted for them.

"A bushel of money for each one!" said Big Claus.

"Are you mad!" they all said. "Do you think we have tons of money?"

"Hides! Hides! Who'll buy my hides?" he shouted again, but to everyone who asked what the hides cost he replied, "A bushel of money!"

"He's trying to make fun of us!" they all said, and then the shoemakers took their straps and the tanners their leather aprons and started to give Big Claus a thrashing.

"Hides! Hides!" they mimicked him. "Yes, we'll give you a hiding until you look like a flayed pig! Out of town with him!" they shouted, and Big Claus had to get moving as fast as he could. He'd never had such a thrashing before.

"Aha!" he said when he came back home. "I'll get even with Little Claus for this! I'm going to kill him!"

But meanwhile Little Claus's old grandmother had died at his home. To be sure, she had been quite shrewish and nasty to him, but he was still very sad, and taking the old woman, he laid her in his warm bed to see if he could bring her back to life again. She was to lie there all night while he was going to sit over in the corner and sleep on a chair, as he had done before.

Now as he was sitting there during the night the door opened, and Big Claus came in with his ax. He knew very well where Little Claus had his bed, and walking straight over to it, he struck the old grandmother on the forehead, thinking it was Little Claus.

"There now!" he said. "You're not going to fool me again!" And then he went back home again.

"Why, that nasty, wicked man!" said Little Claus. "He wanted to kill me! Still, it was a good thing old Granny was already dead, or else he'd have done away with her!"

Now he dressed old Granny in her Sunday best, borrowed a horse from his neighbor, hitched it to the wagon, and sat the old woman up in the back seat so she couldn't fall out when he was driving, and then they rolled away through the forest. When the sun came up they were outside a big inn. Here Little Claus stopped and went in to get a bite to eat.

The innkeeper had so very very much money; he was also a very good man but as hot-tempered as if he were full of pepper and snuff inside.

"Good morning," he said to Little Claus. "You're up early today in your Sunday best."

"Yes," said Little Claus. "I'm on my way to town with my old grandmother. She's sitting out there in the wagon. I can't get her to come inside. Won't you take a glass of mead out to her? But you'll have to speak quite loudly, as she can't hear very well."

"Indeed I shall," said the innkeeper, and poured out a big glass of mead, which he took out to the dead grandmother, who had been set up in the wagon.

"Here's a glass of mead from your grandson!" said the innkeeper, but the dead woman sat quite still and didn't say a word.

"Don't you hear!" shouted the innkeeper as loud as he could. "HERE'S A GLASS OF MEAD FROM YOUR GRANDSON!"

He shouted the same thing again, and once more after that, but when she didn't budge an inch he flew into a rage and threw the glass right in her face, so the mead ran down over her nose, and she fell over backward in the wagon, for she had only been propped up and not tied fast.

"GOOD LORD!" shouted Little Claus, running out of the door and grabbing the innkeeper by the collar. "You've killed my grandmother! Just look, there's a big hole in her forehead!"

"Oh, it was an accident!" cried the innkeeper, wringing his hands. "It's all because of my hot temper! Dear Little Claus, I'll give you a whole bushel of money if only you'll keep quiet about it, for otherwise they'll chop off my head, and that's so disgusting!"

So Little Claus got a whole bushel of money, and the innkeeper buried the grandmother as if she had been his own.

When Little Claus came back home with all the money, he sent his boy right over to Big Claus to ask if he could borrow a bushel measure.

"What's that?" said Big Claus. "Didn't I kill him? I'll have to go see for myself." And then he took the bushel measure to Little Claus.

"Why, where did you get all this money from?" he asked, his eyes opening wide at the sight of all this additional money that had come in.

"It was my grandmother and not me that you killed!" said Little Claus. "And now I've sold her for a bushel of money."

"You were really well paid!" said Big Claus, and hurrying home, he took an ax and killed his old grandmother straightaway; and putting her in the wagon, he drove off to town, where the apothecary lived, and asked if he wanted to buy a dead body.

"Whose is it, and where did you get it from?" asked the apothecary.

"It's my grandmother," said Big Claus. "I killed her for a bushel of money!"

"Good Lord!" said the apothecary. "You're talking non-

sense! But you mustn't say a thing like that, or you can
lose your head!" And then he told him what a really
wicked deed he had done, and what a terrible man he
was, and that he ought to be punished. Big Claus became
so terrified at this that he ran right out of the apothecary's
shop, right out to the wagon, whipped the horses, and
rushed home. But the apothecary and everybody else
thought he was mad, and so they let him drive wherever
he liked.

"I'll get even with you for that!" said Big Claus when he
was out on the highway. "Yes, I'll get even with you for
that, Little Claus!" And as soon as he came home he took
the biggest sack he could find, went to Little Claus, and
said, "Now you've fooled me again! First I killed my
horses and then my old grandmother! It's all your fault,
but you're never going to fool me again!" And then he
grabbed Little Claus by the waist, put him in his sack,
threw him on his back, and shouted, "Now I'm going to
drown you!"

He had a long way to go before he came to the river,
and Little Claus wasn't such a light burden. The road ran
by the church; the organ was playing and people were
singing so beautifully inside. Then Big Claus placed his
sack, with Little Claus in it, close to the church door, and
thought it would be a good idea to go in and listen to a
hymn first before he went on. After all, Little Claus couldn't
get out and everybody else was inside the church, so he
went in.

"Oh, woe! Oh, woe!" sighed Little Claus inside the
sack. He turned this way and that, but he couldn't open
the sack. At that very moment an old cattle drover, with
chalk-white hair and a big staff in his hand, came along.
He was driving a whole herd of cows and bulls ahead of
him; they ran against the sack in which Little Claus was
sitting, and it turned over.

"Oh, woe!" said Little Claus. "I'm so young, and I'm going to heaven already!"

"And I, poor soul," said the drover, "am so old and can't get there yet!"

"Open the sack!" shouted Little Claus. "Crawl in, in my place, and you'll get to heaven right away!"

"Yes, I'd be glad to!" said the drover, and untied the sack for Little Claus, who jumped out at once.

"Will you mind the cattle?" said the old man, and crawled down in the sack, which Little Claus tied up and then went on his way with all the cows and bulls.

A little later Big Claus came out of the church and put the sack on his back. Of course he thought it had grown lighter, for the old drover didn't weigh half as much as Little Claus did. "How light he's grown! Yes, I daresay it's because I've listened to a hymn!" Then he went over to the river, which was deep and wide, threw the sack with the old cattle drover in it, into the water, and shouted after him—for of course he thought it was Little Claus: "That's that! You're not going to trick me anymore!"

Then he started for home, but when he came to the crossroads he met Little Claus driving along all his cattle.

"What's that?" said Big Claus. "Didn't I drown you?"

"Yes indeed!" said Little Claus. "You threw me in the river not quite half an hour ago!"

"But where did you get all these fine cattle from?" asked Big Claus.

"They're sea cattle!" said Little Claus. "I'll tell you the whole story, and thanks for drowning me too! Now I'm on top! I'm really rich, I'll have you know! I was so frightened when I was lying in the sack, and the wind whistled about my ears when you threw me down from the bridge into that cold water. I sank straight to the bottom, but I didn't hurt myself, for down there grows the finest soft grass. There I fell, and at once the bag was opened, and the loveliest maiden, in chalk-white clothes and with a green garland on her wet hair, took me by the hand and said, 'Is that you, Little Claus? First of all, here's some cattle! A mile up the road is another herd, which I'm going to give you.' Then I saw that the river was a great highway for the sea people. On the bottom they walked and drove right up from the sea and all the way to land, where the river ends. The flowers there were so lovely and the grass so fresh, and the fish swimming in the water darted past my ears just the way the birds do up here in the air. What handsome people they were, and what a lot of cattle were walking by the fences and in the ditches!"

"But why did you come back up here so fast?" asked Big Claus. "I wouldn't have done that if it was so fine down there!"

"Oh, yes!" said Little Claus. "That was the shrewdest thing I could have done! You'll understand, of course, when I tell you: The mermaid said that about a mile up the road—and by the road she meant the river, of course, because she can't go anywhere else—another herd of cattle is waiting for me. But I know how the river twists and turns, first this way and then that. It's a long detour. Well, you can make it shorter by coming up here on land and driving straight across to the river again. Then I save almost half a mile and come to my sea cattle all the faster."

"Oh, you're a lucky man!" said Big Claus. "Do you think I would get some sea cattle if I went down to the bottom of the sea?"

"Oh, yes, I should think you would!" said Little Claus. "But I can't carry you to the river in the sack. You're too heavy for me. But if you'll walk over there yourself and then crawl into the sack, I'll throw you in with the greatest of pleasure!"

"Thank's a lot!" said Big Claus. "But if I don't get any sea cattle when I get down there, I'll give you a beating, I want you to know!"

"Oh, no! Don't be so mean!" And then they went to the

river. The cattle were thirsty, and when they saw the water they ran as fast as they could so as to have a drink.

"See how they hurry!" said Little Claus. "They're longing to go down to the bottom again!"

"Well, just help me first!" said Big Claus. "Or else you'll get a beating!" And then he crawled into the big sack, which had been lying across the back of one of the bulls. "Put a stone in it, or else I'm afraid I won't sink!" said Big Claus.

"You'll sink, all right!" said Little Claus, but nonetheless he put a big stone in the sack, tied it up tight, and then gave it a push. Plop! There was Big Claus in the water, and he sank to the bottom without delay.

"I'm afraid he won't find the cattle!" said Little Claus, and then he drove home what he had.

The Princess on the Pea

❖   ❖   ❖

THERE was once a prince. He wanted a princess, but it had to be a true princess! So he journeyed all around the world to find one, but no matter where he went, something was wrong. There were plenty of princesses, but whether or not they were true princesses he couldn't find out. There was always something that wasn't quite right. So he came home again and was very sad, for he wanted a true princess so very much.

One evening there was a terrible storm. The lightning flashed, the thunder boomed, and the rain poured down! It was really frightful! Then somebody knocked at the city gate, and the old king went out to open it.

A princess was standing outside, but heavens, how she looked from the rain and the bad weather! Water poured off her hair and clothes and ran in at the toe of her shoe and out at the heel, but she said she was a true princess!

"Well, we'll soon find that out!" thought the old queen, but she didn't say anything. She went into the bedroom, took off all the bedding, and put a pea on the bottom of the bed. Then she took twenty mattresses and laid them on top of the pea and then put twenty eiderdown quilts on top of the mattresses. There the princess was to sleep that night.

In the morning they asked her how she had slept.

"Oh, just miserably!" said the princess. "I've hardly closed my eyes all night! Heaven knows what was in my bed! I've been lying on something so hard that I'm black and blue all over! It's simply dreadful!"

Then they could tell that this was a true princess, because through the twenty mattresses and the twenty eiderdown quilts she had felt the pea. Only a true princess could have such delicate skin.

So the prince took her for his wife, for now he knew that he had a true princess, and the pea was put into the museum, where it can still be seen, if no one has taken it! See, this was a true story!

The Fable Alludes to You

❖ ❖ ❖

T HE Sages of Antiquity kindly invented a way of tell-ing people the truth without being rude to their faces: they held before them a singular mirror in which all kinds of animals and strange things came into view, and pro-duced a spectacle as entertaining as it was edifying. They called it "A Fable," and whatever foolish or intelligent thing the animals performed there, the human beings had but to apply it to themselves and thereby think: the fable alludes to you. Let us take an example.

There were two high mountains, and on the very top of each mountain stood a castle. Down in the valley a dog was running. It sniffed along the ground as if, to stay its hunger, it were searching for mice or partridges. Sud-denly, from one of the castles the trumpet sounded an-nouncing that dinner was ready. At once the dog started running up the mountain to get a little, too. But just as it had come halfway, the trumpeter stopped blowing, and a trumpet from the other castle began. Then the dog thought, "They will have finished eating here before I come, but over there they will have just begun." And so down it went and ran up the other mountain. But now the trum-pet at the first castle started blowing again, whereas the other had stopped. Once more the dog ran down one mountain and up the other, and he kept on in this way until both trumpets were at last silent and the meal would be at an end no matter to which place the dog came.

Guess now what the Sages of Antiquity wish to imply by this fable and which of us it alludes to, who wears himself out in this fashion without winning either here or there.

The Talisman

❖ ❖ ❖

A PRINCE and a princess were still on their honey-moon. They felt so extremely happy. Only one thought disturbed them; it was this: will we always be as happy as we are now? And so they wanted to own a talisman that would protect them against every disappointment in marriage.

Now, they had often heard of a man who lived in the forest, and who was held in high esteem by everyone for his wisdom. He knew how to give the best advice for every hardship and misery. The prince and the princess went to him and told him what was troubling them.

When the wise man had heard it, he replied, "Journey through all the lands in the world, and when you meet a truly contented married couple, ask them for a little piece of the linen they wear next to their skin. When you get it, always carry it with you. That is an effective remedy."

The prince and the princess rode off, and soon they heard of a knight who, with his wife, was said to live the happiest of lives. They came up to the castle and asked them, themselves, whether in their marriage they were as extremely happy as rumor would have it.

"Of course!" was the reply. "Except for one thing: we have no children!"

Here, then, the talisman was not to be found, and the

prince and the princess had to continue on their journey
to seek out the most perfectly contented married couple.

Next they came to a city in which, they heard, an
honest burgher lived with his wife in the greatest harmony
and contentment. They went to him, too, and asked whether
he really were as happy in his marriage as people said.

"Yes, indeed I am!" replied the man. "My wife and I
live the best of lives together. If only we didn't have so
many children. They cause us so much sorrow and anxiety!"

The talisman was not to be found with him, either, and
the prince and the princess journeyed on through the land
and inquired everywhere after contented married couples.

But not one came forward.

One day, as they were riding along fields and meadows,
they noticed a shepherd who was playing quite merrily on
a shawm. At the same time they saw a woman come over
to him with a child on her arm and leading a little boy by
the hand. As soon as the shepherd saw her, he went to

meet her. He greeted her and took the child, which he kissed and caressed. The shepherd's dog came over to the boy, licked his little hand, and barked and jumped up and down with joy. In the meantime the wife made ready the pot that she had brought with her and said, "Papa, come now and eat."

The man sat down and helped himself to the dishes. But the first bite went to the little child and he divided the second between the boy and the dog. All this the prince and the princess saw and heard. Now they went closer, talked with them, and said, "Are you truly what might be called a happy and contented married couple?"

"Yes, indeed we are!" replied the man. "Praise be to God! No prince or princess could be happier than we are."

"Then listen," said the prince. "Do us a favor that you will not come to regret. Give us a tiny piece of the linen that you wear next to your skin."

At this request the shepherd and his wife looked strangely at each other. At last he said, "Heaven knows we would gladly give it to you, and not just a tiny piece but the whole shirt and petticoat if only we had them. But we don't own a thread!"

So the prince and the princess continued on their journey without any success. At last they grew tired of this long, fruitless wandering, and so they headed for home. When they now came to the wise man's hut, they scolded him for having given them such poor advice. He listened to the whole story of their journey.

Then the wise man smiled and said, "Has your journey really been so fruitless? Didn't you come home rich in experience?"

"Yes," said the prince. "I have learned that contentment is a rare blessing on this earth."

"And I have learned," said the princess, "that in order to be content, you need nothing more than just that—to be content."

Then the prince gave the princess his hand. They gazed at each other with an expression of the deepest love. And the wise man gave them his blessing and said, "In your hearts you have found the true talisman. Guard it carefully, and never will the evil spirit of discontent gain power over you!"

The Little Mermaid

❖ ❖ ❖

FAR out to sea the water is as blue as the petals on the loveliest cornflower and as clear as the purest glass. But it is very deep, deeper than any anchor rope can reach. Many church steeples would have to be placed one on top of the other to reach from the bottom up to the surface of the water. Down there live the mermen.

Now, it certainly shouldn't be thought that the bottom is only bare and sandy. No, down there grow the strangest trees and plants, which have such flexible stalks and leaves that the slightest movement of the water sets them in motion as if they were alive. All the fish, big and small, slip in and out among the branches just the way the birds do up here in the air. At the very deepest spot lies the castle of the king of the sea. The walls are of coral, and the long tapering windows are of the clearest amber. But the roof is of mussel shells, which open and close with the flow of the water. The effect is lovely, for in each one there is a beautiful pearl, any of which would be highly prized in a queen's crown.

For many years the king of the sea had been a widower, and his old mother kept house for him. She was a wise woman and proud of her royal birth, and so she wore twelve oysters on her tail; the others of noble birth had to content themselves with only six. Otherwise she deserved

much praise, especially because she was so fond of the
little princesses, her grandchildren. They were six lovely
children, but the youngest was the fairest of them all. Her
skin was as clear and opalescent as a rose petal. Her eyes
were as blue as the deepest sea. But like all the others,
she had no feet. Her body ended in a fishtail.

All day long they could play down in the castle in the
great halls where living flowers grew out of the walls. The
big amber windows were opened, and then the fish swam
into them just as on land the swallows fly in when we open
our windows. But the fish swam right over to the little
princesses, ate out of their hands, and allowed themselves
to be petted.

Outside the castle was a large garden with trees as red
as fire and as blue as night. The fruit shone like gold, and
the flowers looked like burning flames, for their stalks and
leaves were always in motion. The ground itself was the
finest sand, but blue like the flame of brimstone. A strange
blue sheen lay over everything down there. It was more
like standing high up in the air and seeing only sky above
and below than like being at the bottom of the sea. In a
dead calm the sun could be glimpsed. It looked like a
purple flower from whose chalice the light streamed out.

Each of the little princesses had her own tiny plot in the
garden, where she could dig and plant just as she wished.
One made her flower bed in the shape of a whale. Another
preferred hers to resemble a little mermaid. But the youngest made hers quite round like the sun and had only
flowers that shone red the way it did. She was a strange
child, quiet and pensive, and while the other sisters decorated their gardens with the strangest things they had
found from wrecked ships, the only thing she wanted,
besides the rosy-red flowers that resembled the sun high
above, was a beautiful marble statue. It was a handsome
boy carved out of clear white stone, and in the shipwreck
it had come down to the bottom of the sea. By the pedes-

tal she had planted a rose-colored weeping willow. It grew magnificently, and its fresh branches hung out over the statue and down toward the blue, sandy bottom, where its shadow appeared violet and moved just like the branches. It looked as if the top and roots played at kissing each other.

Nothing pleased her more than to hear about the world of mortals up above. The old grandmother had to tell everything she knew about ships and cities, mortals and animals. To her it seemed especially wonderful and lovely that on the earth the flowers gave off a fragrance, since they didn't at the bottom of the sea, and that the forests were green and those fish that were seen among the branches there could sing so loud and sweet that it was a pleasure. What the grandmother called fish were the little birds, for otherwise the princesses wouldn't have understood her, as they had never seen a bird.

"When you reach the age of fifteen," said the grandmother, "you shall be permitted to go to the surface of the water, sit in the moonlight on the rocks, and look at the great ships sailing by. You will see forests and cities too."

The next year the first sister would be fifteen, but the others—yes, each one was a year younger than the other; so the youngest still had five years left before she might come up from the bottom of the sea and find out how it looked in our world. But each one promised to tell the others what she had seen on that first day and what she had found to be the most wonderful thing, for their grandmother hadn't told them enough—there was so much they had to find out.

No one was as full of longing as the youngest, the one who had to wait the longest and who was so quiet and pensive. Many a night she stood by the open window and looked up through the dark blue water where the fish flipped their fins and tails. She could see the moon and stars. To be sure, they shone quite pale, but through the water they looked much bigger than they do to our eyes. If it seemed as though a black shadow glided slowly under them, then she knew it was either a whale that swam over her or else it was a ship with many mortals on board. It certainly never occurred to them that a lovely little mermaid was standing down below stretching her white hands up toward the keel.

Now the eldest princess was fifteen and was permitted to go up to the surface of the water.

When she came back, she had hundreds of things to tell about. But the most wonderful thing of all, she said, was to lie in the moonlight on a sandbank in the calm sea and to look at the big city close to the shore, where the lights twinkled like hundreds of stars, and to listen to the music and the noise and commotion of carriages and mortals, to see the many church steeples and spires, and to hear the chimes ring. And just because the youngest sister couldn't go up there, she longed for all this the most.

Oh, how the little mermaid listened. And later in the evening, when she was standing by the open window and looking up through the dark blue water, she thought of the great city with all the noise and commotion, and then it seemed to her that she could hear the church bells ringing down to her.

The next year the second sister was allowed to rise up through the water and swim wherever she liked. She came up just as the sun was setting, and she found this sight the loveliest. The whole sky looked like gold, she said—and the clouds. Well, she couldn't describe their beauty enough. Crimson and violet, they had sailed over her. But even faster than the clouds, like a long white veil, a flock of wild swans had flown over the water into the sun. She swam toward it, but it sank, and the rosy glow went out on the sea and on the clouds.

The next year the third sister came up. She was the boldest of them all, and so she swam up a broad river that emptied into the sea. She saw lovely green hills covered with grapevines. Castles and farms peeped out among great forests. She heard how all the birds sang, and the sun shone so hot that she had to dive under the water to cool her burning face. In a little bay she came upon a whole flock of little children. Quite naked, they ran and splashed in the water. She wanted to play with them, but they ran away terrified. And then a little black animal came; it was a dog, but she had never seen a dog before. It barked at her so furiously that she grew frightened and made for the open sea. But never could she forget the great forests, the green hills, and the lovely children who could swim in the water despite the fact that they had no fishtails.

The fourth sister was not so bold. She stayed out in the middle of the rolling sea and said that this was the loveliest of all. She could see for many miles all around her, and the sky was just like a big glass bell. She had seen ships, but far away. They looked like sea gulls. The funny dolphins had turned somersaults, and the big whales had spouted water through their nostrils so it had looked like hundreds of fountains all around.

Now it was the turn of the fifth sister. Her birthday was in winter, so she saw what the others hadn't seen. The sea looked quite green, and huge icebergs were swimming all around. Each one looked like a pearl, she said, although they were certainly much bigger than the church steeples built by mortals. They appeared in the strangest shapes and sparkled like diamonds. She had sat on one of the biggest, and all the ships sailed, terrified, around where she sat with her long hair flying in the breeze. But in the evening the sky was covered with clouds. The lightning flashed and the thunder boomed while the black sea lifted the huge icebergs up high, where they glittered in the bright flashes of light. On all the ships they took in the sails, and they were anxious and afraid. But she sat calmly on her floating iceberg and watched the blue streaks of lightning zigzag into the sea.

Each time one of the sisters came to the surface of the water for the first time she was always enchanted by the new and wonderful things she had seen. But now that, as grown girls, they were permitted to go up there whenever they liked, it no longer mattered to them. They longed again for home. And after a month they said it was most beautiful down there where they lived and that home was the best of all.

Many an evening the five sisters rose up arm in arm to the surface of the water. They had beautiful voices, sweeter than those of any mortals, and whenever a storm was nigh and they thought a ship might be wrecked, they swam ahead of the ship and sang so sweetly about how beautiful it was at the bottom of the sea and bade the sailors not to be afraid of coming down there. But the sailors couldn't understand the words. They thought it was the storm. Nor were they able to see the wonders down there either, for when the ship sank, the mortals drowned and came only as corpses to the castle of the king of the sea.

Now, in the evening, when the sisters rose up arm in arm through the sea, the little sister was left behind quite alone, looking after them and as if she were going to cry. But a mermaid has no tears, and so she suffers even more.

"Oh, if only I were fifteen," she said. "I know that I will truly come to love that world and the mortals who build and dwell up there."

At last she too was fifteen.

"See, now it is your turn!" said her grandmother, the old dowager queen. "Come now, let me adorn you just like your other sisters." And she put a wreath of white lilies on her hair. But each flower petal was half a pearl. And the old queen had eight oysters squeeze themselves tightly to the princess' tail to who her high rank.

"It hurts so much!" said the little mermaid.

"Yes, you must suffer a bit to look pretty!" said the old queen.

Oh, how happy she would have been to shake off all this magnificence, to take off the heavy wreath. Her red flowers in her garden were more becoming to her, but she dared not do otherwise now. "Farewell," she said and rose as easily and as lightly as a bubble up through the water.

The sun had just gone down as she raised her head out of the water, but all the clouds still shone like roses and gold, and in the middle of the pink sky the evening star shone clear and lovely. The air was mild and fresh, and the sea was as smooth as glass. There lay a big ship with three masts. Only a single sail was up, for not a breeze was blowing, and around in the ropes and masts sailors were sitting. There was music and song, and as the evening grew darker hundreds of many-colored lanterns were lit. It looked as if the flags of all nations were waving in the air. The little mermaid swam right over to the cabin window, and every time the water lifted her high in the air she could see in through the glass panes to where many finely

dressed mortals were standing. But the handsomest by far
was the young prince with the big dark eyes, who was
certainly not more than sixteen. It was his birthday, and
this was why all the festivities were taking place. The
sailors danced on deck, and when the young prince came
out, more than a hundred rockets rose into the air. They
shone as bright as day, so the little mermaid became quite
frightened and ducked down under the water. But she
soon stuck her head out again, and then it was as if all the
stars in the sky were falling down to her. Never before
had she seen such fireworks. Huge suns whirled around,
magnificent flaming fish swung in the blue air, and everything was reflected in the clear, calm sea. The ship itself
was so lit up that every little rope was visible, not to
mention mortals. Oh, how handsome the young prince
was, and he shook everybody by the hand and laughed
and smiled while the wonderful night was filled with music.

It grew late, but the little mermaid couldn't tear her
eyes away from the ship or the handsome prince. The
many-colored lanterns were put out. The rockets no longer
climbed into the air, nor were any more salutes fired from
the cannons, either. But deep down in the sea it rumbled
and grumbled. All the while she sat bobbing up and down
on the water so she could see into the cabin. But now the
ship went faster, and one sail after the other spread out.
Now the waves were rougher, great clouds rolled up, and
in the distance there was lightning. Oh, there was going to
be a terrible storm, so the sailors took in the sails. The
ship rocked at top speed over the raging sea. The water
rose like huge black mountains that wanted to pour over
the mast, but the ship dived down like a swan among the
high billows and let itself be lifted high again on the
towering water. The little mermaid thought this speed was
pleasant, but the sailors didn't think so. The ship creaked
and cracked and the thick planks buckled under the heavy
blows. Waves poured in over the ship, the mast snapped

in the middle just like a reed, and the ship rolled over on its side while the water poured into the hold. Now the little mermaid saw they were in danger. She herself had to beware of planks and bits of wreckage floating on the water. For a moment it was so pitch black that she could not see a thing, but when the lightning flashed, it was again so bright that she could make out everyone on the ship. They were all floundering and struggling for their lives. She looked especially for the young prince, and as the ship broke apart she saw him sink down into the depths. At first she was quite pleased, for now he would come down to her. But then she remembered that mortals could not live in the water and that only as a corpse could he come down to her father's castle. No, die he mustn't! And so she swam among beams and planks that floated on the sea, quite forgetting that they could have crushed her. She dived deep down in the water and rose up high among the waves, and thus she came at last to the young prince, who could hardly swim any longer in the stormy sea. His arms and legs were growing weak; his beautiful eyes were closed. He would have died had the little mermaid not arrived. She held his head up above the water and thus let the waves carry them wherever they liked.

In the morning the storm was over. Of the ship there wasn't a chip to be seen. The sun climbed, red and shining, out of the water; it was as if it brought life into the prince's cheeks, but his eyes remained closed. The mermaid kissed his high, handsome forehead and stroked back his wet hair. She thought he resembled the marble statue down in her little garden. She kissed him again and wished for him to live.

Now she saw the mainland ahead of her, high blue mountains on whose peaks the white snow shone as if swans were lying there. Down by the coast were lovely green forests, and ahead lay a church or a convent. Which, she didn't rightly know, but it was a building. Lemon and orange trees were growing there in the garden, and in front of the gate stood high palm trees. The sea had made a little bay here, which was calm but very deep all the way over to the rock where the fine white sand had been washed ashore. Here she swam with the handsome prince and put him on the sand, but especially she saw to it that his head was raised in the sunshine.

Now the bells rang in the big white building, and many young girls came out through the gate to the garden. Then the little mermaid swam farther out behind some big rocks that jutted up out of the water, covered her hair and breast with sea foam so no one could see her little face, and then kept watch to see who came out to the unfortunate prince.

It wasn't long before a young girl came over to where he lay. She seemed to be quite frightened, but only for a moment. Then she fetched several mortals, and the mermaid saw that the prince revived and that he smiled at everyone around him. But he didn't smile out to her, for he didn't know at all that she had saved him. She was so unhappy. And when he was carried into the big building, she dived down sorrowfully in the water and found her way home to her father's castle.

She had always been silent and pensive, but now she was more so than ever. Her sisters asked about what she had seen the first time she was up there, but she told them nothing.

Many an evening and morning she swam up to where she had left the prince. She saw that the fruits in the garden ripened and were picked. She saw that the snow melted on the high mountains, but she didn't see the prince, and so she returned home even sadder than before. Her only comfort was to sit in the little garden and throw her arms around the pretty marble statue that resembled the prince. But she didn't take care of her flowers. As in a jungle, they grew out over the paths, with their long stalks and leaves intertwined with the branches of the trees, until it was quite dark.

At last she couldn't hold out any longer, but told one of her sisters. And then all the others found out at once, but no more than they, and a few other mermaids, who didn't tell anyone except their closest friends. One of them knew who the prince was. She had also seen the festivities on the ship and knew where he was from and where his kingdom lay.

"Come, little sister," said the other princesses, and with their arms around one another's shoulders they came up to the surface of the water in a long row in front of the spot where they knew the prince's castle stood.

It was made of a pale yellow, shiny kind of stone, with great stairways—one went right down to the water. Magnificent gilded domes soared above the roof, and among the pillars that went around the whole building stood marble statues that looked as if they were alive. Through the clear glass in the high windows one could see into the most magnificent halls, where costly silken curtains and tapestries were hanging, and all of the walls were adorned with large paintings that were a joy to behold. In the middle of the biggest hall splashed a great fountain. Streams of water shot up high toward the glass dome in the roof, through which the sun shone on the water and all the lovely plants growing in the big pool.

Now she knew where he lived, and many an evening and night she came there over the water. She swam much closer to land than any of the others had dared. Yes, she went all the way up the little canal, under the magnificent marble balcony that cast a long shadow on the water. Here she sat and looked at the young prince, who thought he was quite alone in the clear moonlight.

Many an evening she saw him sail to the sound of music in the splendid boat on which the flags were waving. She peeped out from among the green rushes and caught the wind in her long silvery white veil, and if anyone saw it, he thought it was a swan spreading its wings.

Many a night, when the fishermen were fishing by torchlight in the sea, she heard them tell so many good things about the young prince that she was glad she had saved his life when he was drifting about half dead on the waves. And she thought of how fervently she had kissed him then. He knew nothing about it at all, couldn't even dream of her once.

She grew fonder and fonder of mortals, wished more and more that she could rise up among them. She thought their world was far bigger than hers. Why, they could fly over the sea in ships and climb the high mountains way above the clouds, and their lands with forests and fields stretched farther than she could see. There was so much she wanted to find out, but her sisters didn't know the answers to everything, and so she asked her old grandmother, and *she* knew the upper world well, which she quite rightly called The Lands Above the Sea.

"If mortals don't drown," the little mermaid asked, "do they live forever? Don't they die the way we do down here in the sea?"

"Why, yes," said the old queen, "they must also die, and their lifetime is much shorter than ours. We can live to be three hundred years old, but when we stop existing here, we only turn into foam upon the water. We don't even have a grave down here among our loved ones. We have no immortal soul; we never have life again. We are like the green rushes: once they are cut they can never be green again. Mortals, on the other hand, have a soul, which lives forever after the body has turned to dust. It mounts up through the clear air to all the shining stars. Just as we come to the surface of the water and see the land of the mortals, so do they come up to lovely unknown places that we will never see."

"Why didn't we get an immortal soul?" asked the little mermaid sadly. "I'd gladly give all my hundreds of years just to be a mortal for one day and afterward to be able to share in the heavenly world."

"You mustn't go and think about that," said the old queen. "We are much better off than the mortals up there."

"I too shall die and float as foam upon the sea, not hear the music of the waves or see the lovely flowers and the red sun. Isn't there anything at all I can do to win an immortal soul?"

"No," said the old queen. "Only if a mortal fell so much in love with you that you were dearer to him than a father and mother; only if you remained in all his thoughts and he was so deeply attached to you that he let the priest place his right hand in yours with a vow of faithfulness now and forever; only then would his soul float over into your body, and you would also share in the happiness of mortals. He would give you a soul and still keep his own. But that never can happen. The very thing that is so lovely here in the sea, your fishtail, they find so disgusting up there on the earth. They don't know any better. Up there one has to have two clumsy stumps, which they call legs, to be beautiful!"

Then the little mermaid sighed and looked sadly at her fishtail.

"Let us be satisfied," said the old queen. "We will frisk and frolic in the three hundred years we have to live in. That's plenty of time indeed. Afterward one can rest in one's grave all the more happily. This evening we are going to have a court ball!"

Now, this was a splendor not to be seen on earth. Walls and ceiling in the great ballroom were of thick but clear glass. Several hundred gigantic mussel shells, rosy-red and green as grass, stood in rows on each side with a blue flame, which lit up the whole ballroom and shone out through the walls so the sea too was brightly illuminated. One could see the countless fish that swam over to the glass wall. On some the scales shone purple; on others they seemed to be silver and gold. Through the middle of the ballroom flowed a broad stream, and in this the mermen and mermaids danced to the music of their own lovely songs. No mortals on earth have such beautiful voices. The little mermaid had the loveliest voice of all, and they clapped their hands for her. And for a moment her heart was filled with joy, for she knew that she had the most beautiful voice of all on this earth and in the sea. But soon she started thinking again of the world above her. She couldn't forget the handsome prince and her sorrow at not possessing, like him, an immortal soul. And so she slipped out of her father's castle unnoticed, and while everything inside was merriment and song she sat sadly in her little garden. Then she heard a horn ring down through the water, and she thought: "Now he is sailing up there, the one I love more than a father or a mother, the one who remains in all my thoughts and in whose hand I would place all my life's happiness. I would risk everything to win him and an immortal soul. I will go to the sea witch. I have always been so afraid of her, but maybe she can advise and help me."

Now the little mermaid went out of her garden toward the roaring maelstroms behind which the sea witch lived. She had never gone that way before. Here grew no flowers, no sea grass. Only the bare, gray, sandy bottom stretched on toward the maelstroms, which, like roaring mill wheels, whirled around and dragged everything that came their way down with them into the depths. In between these crushing whirlpools she had to go to enter the realm of the sea witch, and for a long way there was no other road than over hot bubbling mire that the sea witch called her peat bog. In back of it lay her house, right in the midst of an eerie forest. All the trees and bushes were polyps—half animal, half plant. They looked like hundred-headed serpents growing out of the earth. All the branches were long slimy arms with fingers like sinuous worms, and joint by joint they moved from the roots to the outermost tips. Whatever they could grab in the sea they wound their arms around it and never let it go. Terrified, the little mermaid remained standing outside the forest. Her heart was pounding with fright. She almost turned back, but then she thought of the prince and of an immortal soul, and it gave her courage. She bound her long, flowing hair around her head so the polyps could not grab her by it. She crossed both hands upon her breast and then off she flew, the way the fish can fly through the water, in among the loathsome polyps that reached out their arms and fingers after her. She saw where each of them had something it had seized; hundreds of small arms held onto it like strong iron bands. Rows of white bones of mortals who had drowned at sea and sunk all the way down there peered forth from the polyps' arms. Ships' wheels and chests they held tightly, skeletons of land animals, and—most terrifying of all—a little mermaid that they had captured and strangled.

Now she came to a large slimy opening in the forest where big fat water snakes gamboled, revealing their ugly yellowish-white bellies. In the middle of the opening had been erected a house made of the bones of shipwrecked mortals. There sat the sea witch letting a toad eat from her mouth, just the way mortals permit a little canary bird to eat sugar. She called the fat, hideous water snakes her little chickens and let them tumble on her big spongy breasts.

"I know what you want, all right," said the sea witch. "It's stupid of you to do it. Nonetheless, you shall have your way, for it will bring you misfortune, my lovely princess! You want to get rid of your fishtail and have two stumps to walk on instead, just like mortals, so the young prince can fall in love with you, and you can win him and an immortal soul." Just then the sea witch let out such a loud and hideous laugh that the toad and the water snakes fell down to the ground and writhed there. "You've come just in the nick of time," said the witch. "Tomorrow, after the sun rises, I couldn't help you until another year was over. I shall make you a potion, and before the sun rises you shall take it and swim to land, seat yourself on the shore there, and drink it. Then your tail will split and shrink into what mortals call lovely legs. But it hurts. It is like being pierced through by a sharp sword. Everyone who sees you will say you are the loveliest mortal child he has ever seen. You will keep your grace of movement. No dancer will ever float the way you do, but each step you take will be like treading on a sharp knife so your blood will flow! If you want to suffer all this, then I will help you."

"Yes," said the little mermaid in a trembling voice, thinking of the prince and of winning an immortal soul.

"But remember," said the witch, "once you have been given a mortal shape, you can never become a mermaid again. You can never sink down through the water to your sisters and to your father's castle. And if you do not win the love of the prince so that for your sake he forgets his father and mother and never puts you out of his thoughts and lets the priest place your hand in his so you become man and wife, you will not win an immortal soul. The first morning after he is married to another, your heart will break and you will turn into foam upon the water."

"This I want!" said the little mermaid and turned deathly pale.

"But you must also pay me," said the witch, "and what I demand is no small thing. You have the loveliest voice of all down here at the bottom of the sea, and you probably think you're going to enchant him with it. But that voice you shall give to me. I want the best thing you have for my precious drink. Why, I must put my very own blood in it so it will be as sharp as a two-edged sword."

"But if you take my voice," said the little mermaid, "what will I have left?"

"Your lovely figure," said the witch, "your grace of movement, and your sparkling eyes. With them you can enchant a mortal heart, all right! Stick out your little tongue so I can cut it off in payment, and you shall have the potent drink!"

"So be it!" said the little mermaid, and the witch put her kettle on to brew the magic potion. "Cleanliness is a good thing," she said, and scoured her kettle with her water snakes, which she knotted together. Now she cut her breast and let the black blood drip into the kettle. The steam made strange shapes that were terrifying and dreadful to see. Every moment the witch put something new into the kettle, and when it had cooked properly, it was like crocodile tears. At last the drink was ready, and it was as clear as water.

"There it is," said the witch, and cut out the little mermaid's tongue. Now she was mute and could neither speak nor sing.

"If any of the polyps should grab you when you go back through my forest," said the witch, "just throw one drop of this drink on them and their arms and fingers will burst into a thousand pieces." But the little mermaid didn't have to do that. The polyps drew back in terror when they saw the shining drink that glowed in her hand like a glittering star. And she soon came through the forest, the bog, and the roaring maelstroms.

She could see her father's castle. The torches had been extinguished in the great ballroom. They were probably all asleep inside there, but she dared not look for them now that she was mute and was going to leave them forever. It was as though her heart would break with grief. She stole into the garden, took a flower from each of her sisters' flower beds, threw hundreds of kisses toward the castle, and rose up through the dark blue sea.

The sun had not yet risen when she saw the prince's castle and went up the magnificent marble stairway. The moon shone bright and clear. The little mermaid drank the strong, burning drink, and it was as if a two-edged sword were going through her delicate body. At that she fainted and lay as if dead. When the sun was shining high on the sea, she awoke and felt a piercing pain, but right in front of her stood the handsome prince. He fixed his coal-black eyes upon her so that she had to cast down her own, and then she saw that her fishtail was gone, and she had the prettiest little white legs that any young girl could have, but she was quite naked. And so she enveloped herself in her thick long hair. The prince asked who she was and how she had come there, and she looked at him softly yet sadly with her dark blue eyes, for of course she could not speak. Each step she took was, as the witch had said, like stepping on pointed awls and sharp knives. But she endured this willingly. At the prince's side she rose as easily as a bubble, and he and everyone else marveled at her graceful, flowing movements.

She was given costly gowns of silk and muslin to wear. In the castle she was the fairest of all. But she was mute; she could neither sing nor speak. Lovely slave girls, dressed in silk and gold, came forth and sang for the prince and his royal parents. One of them sang more sweetly than all the others, and the prince clapped his hands and smiled at her. Then the little mermaid was sad. She knew that she herself had sung far more beautifully, and she thought, "Oh, if only he knew that to be with him I have given away my voice for all eternity."

Now the slave girls danced in graceful, floating movements to the accompaniment of the loveliest music. Then the little mermaid raised her beautiful white arms, stood up on her toes, and glided across the floor. She danced as no one had ever danced before. With each movement, her beauty became even more apparent, and her eyes spoke more deeply to the heart than the slave girl's song.

Everyone was enchanted by her, especially the prince, who called her his little foundling, and she danced on and on despite the fact that each time her feet touched the ground it was like treading on sharp knives. The prince said she was to stay with him forever, and she was allowed to sleep outside his door on a velvet cushion.

He had boys' clothes made for her so she could accompany him on horseback. They rode through the fragrant forests, where the green branches brushed her shoulders and the little birds sang within the fresh leaves. With the prince she climbed up the high mountains, and despite the fact that her delicate feet bled so the others could see it, she laughed at this and followed him until they could see the clouds sailing far below them like a flock of birds on their way to distant lands.

Back at the prince's castle, at night while the others slept, she went down the marble stairway and cooled her burning feet by standing in the cold sea water. And then she thought of those down there in the depths.

One night her sisters came arm in arm. They sang so mournfully as they swam over the water, and she waved to them. They recognized her and told her how unhappy she had made them all. After this they visited her every night, and one night far out she saw her old grandmother, who had not been to the surface of the water for many years, and the king of the sea with his crown upon his head. They stretched out their arms to her but dared not come as close to land as her sisters.

Day by day the prince grew fonder of her. He loved her the way one loves a dear, good child, but to make her his queen did not occur to him at all. And she would have to become his wife if she were to live, or else she would have no immortal soul and would turn into foam upon the sea on the morning after his wedding.

"Don't you love me most of all?" the eyes of the little mermaid seemed to say when he took her in his arms and kissed her beautiful forehead.

"Of course I love you best," said the prince, "for you have the kindest heart of all. You are devoted to me, and you resemble a young girl I once saw but will certainly never find again. I was on a ship that was wrecked. The waves carried me ashore near a holy temple to which several young maidens had been consecrated. The youngest of them found me on the shore and saved my life. I only saw her twice. She was the only one I could love in this world. But you look like her and you have almost replaced her image in my soul. She belongs to the holy temple, and so good fortune has sent you to me. We shall never be parted!"

"Alas! He doesn't know that I saved his life!" thought the little mermaid. "I carried him over the sea to the forest where the temple stands. I hid under the foam and waited to see if any mortals would come. I saw that beautiful girl, whom he loves more than me." And the mermaid sighed deeply, for she couldn't cry. "The girl is consecrated to the holy temple, he said. She will never come out into the world. They will never meet again, but I am with him and see him every day. I will take care of him, love him, lay down my life for him!"

But now people were saying that the prince was going to be married to the lovely daughter of the neighboring king. That was why he was equipping so magnificent a ship. It was given out that the prince is to travel to see the country of the neighboring king, but actually it is to see his daughter. He is to have a great retinue with him.

But the little mermaid shook her head and laughed. She knew the prince's thoughts far better than all the rest. "I have to go," he had told her. "I have to look at the lovely princess. My parents insist upon it. But they won't be able to force me to bring her home as my bride. I cannot love her. She doesn't look like the beautiful girl in the temple, whom you resemble. If I should ever choose a bride, you would be the more likely one, my mute little foundling with the speaking eyes!" And he kissed her rosy mouth, played with her long hair, and rested his head upon her heart, which dreamed of mortal happiness and an immortal soul.

"You're not afraid of the sea, are you, my mute little child!" he said as they stood on the deck of the magnificent ship that was taking him to the country of the neighboring king. And he told her of storms and calms and of strange fish in the depths and of what the divers had seen down there. And she smiled at his story, for of course she knew about the bottom of the sea far better than anyone else.

In the moonlit night, when everyone was asleep—even the sailor at the wheel—she sat by the railing of the ship and stared down through the clear water, and it seemed to her that she could see her father's castle. At the very top stood her old grandmother with her silver crown on her head, staring up through the strong currents at the keel of the ship. Then her sisters came up to the surface of the water. They gazed at her sadly and wrung their white hands. She waved to them and smiled and was going to tell them that all was well with her and that she was happy, but the ship's boy approached and her sisters dived down, so he thought the white he had seen was foam upon the sea.

The next morning the ship sailed into the harbor of the neighboring king's capital. All the church bells were ringing, and from the high towers trumpets were blowing, while the soldiers stood with waving banners and glittering bayonets. Every day there was a feast. Balls and parties followed one after the other, but the princess had not yet come. She was being educated far away in a holy temple, they said; there she was learning all the royal virtues. At last she arrived.

The little mermaid was waiting eagerly to see how beautiful she was, and she had to confess that she had never seen a lovelier creature. Her skin was delicate and soft, and from under her long dark eyelashes smiled a pair of dark blue faithful eyes.

"It is you!" said the prince. "You, who saved me when I lay as if dead on the shore!" And he took his blushing bride into his arms. "Oh, I am far too happy," he said to the little mermaid. "The best I could ever dare hope for has at last come true! You will be overjoyed at my good fortune, for you love me best of all." And the little mermaid kissed his hand, but already she seemed to feel her heart breaking. His wedding morning would indeed bring her death and change her into foam upon the sea.

All the church bells were ringing. The heralds rode through the streets and proclaimed the betrothal. On all the altars fragrant oils burned in costly silver lamps. The priests swung censers, and the bride and bridegroom gave each other their hands and received the blessing of the bishop. The little mermaid, dressed in silk and gold, stood holding the bride's train, but her ears did not hear the festive music nor did her eyes see the sacred ceremony. She thought of the morning of her death, of everything she had lost in this world.

The very same evening the bride and bridegroom went on board the ship. Cannons fired salutes, all the flags were waving, and in the middle of the deck a majestic purple and gold pavilion with the softest cushions had been erected. Here the bridal pair was to sleep in the still, cool night. The breeze filled the sails, and the ship glided easily and gently over the clear sea.

When it started to get dark, many-colored lanterns were lighted and the sailors danced merrily on deck. It made the little mermaid think of the first time she had come to the surface of the water and seen the same splendor and festivity. And she whirled along in the dance, floating as the swallow soars when it is being pursued, and everyone applauded her and cried out in admiration. Never had she danced so magnificently. It was as though sharp knives were cutting her delicate feet, but she didn't feel it. The pain in her heart was even greater. She knew this was the last evening she would see the one for whom she had left her family and her home, sacrificed her beautiful voice, and daily suffered endless agony without his ever realizing it. It was the last night she would breathe the same air as he, see the deep sea and the starry sky. An endless night without thoughts or dreams awaited her—she who neither had a soul nor could ever win one. And there was gaiety and merriment on the ship until long past midnight. She laughed and danced, with the thought of death in her heart. The prince kissed his lovely bride and she played with his dark hair, and arm in arm they went to bed in the magnificent pavilion.

It grew silent and still on the ship. Only the helmsman stood at the wheel. The little mermaid leaned her white arms on the railing and looked toward the east for the dawn, for the first rays of the sun, which she knew would kill her. Then she saw her sisters come to the surface of the water. They were as pale as she was. Their long beautiful hair no longer floated in the breeze. It had been cut off.

"We have given it to the witch so she could help you, so you needn't die tonight. She has given us a knife; here it is. See how sharp it is? Before the sun rises, you must plunge it into the prince's heart! And when his warm blood spatters your feet, they will grow together into a fishtail, and you will become a mermaid again and can sink down into the water to us, and live your three hundred years before you turn into the lifeless, salty sea foam.

Hurry! Either you or he must die before the sun rises. Our old grandmother has grieved so much that her hair has fallen out, as ours has fallen under the witch's scissors. Kill the prince and return to us! Hurry! Do you see that red streak on the horizon? In a few moments the sun will rise, and then you must die!" And they uttered a strange, deep sigh and sank beneath the waves.

The little mermaid drew the purple curtain back from the pavilion and looked at the lovely bride asleep with her head on the prince's chest. She bent down and kissed his handsome forehead; looked at the sky, which grew rosier and rosier; looked at the sharp knife; and again fastened her eyes on the prince, who murmured the name of his bride in his dreams. She alone was in his thoughts, and the knife glittered in the mermaid's hand. But then she threw it far out into the waves. They shone red where it fell, as if drops of blood were bubbling up through the water. Once more she gazed at the prince with dimming eyes, then plunged from the ship down into the sea. And she felt her body dissolving into foam.

Now the sun rose out of the sea. The mild, warm rays fell on the deathly cold sea foam, and the little mermaid did not feel death. She saw the clear sun, and up above her floated hundreds of lovely transparent creatures. Through them she could see the white sails of the ship and the rosy clouds in the sky. Their voices were melodious but so ethereal that no mortal ear could hear them, just as no mortal eye could perceive them. Without wings, they floated through the air by their own lightness. The little mermaid saw that she had a body like theirs. It rose higher and higher out of the foam.

"To whom do I come?" she said, and her voice, like that of the others, rang so ethereally that no earthly music can reproduce it.

"To the daughters of the air," replied the others. "A mermaid has no immortal soul and can never have one unless she wins the love of a mortal. Her immortality depends on an unknown power. The daughters of the air have no immortal souls, either, but by good deeds they can create one for themselves. We fly to the hot countries, where the humid, pestilential air kills mortals. There we waft cooling breezes. We spread the fragrance of flowers through the air and send refreshment and healing. After striving for three hundred years to do what good we can, we then receive an immortal soul and share in the eternal happiness of mortals. Poor little mermaid, with all your heart you have striven for the same goal. You have suffered and endured and have risen to the world of the spirits of the air. Now by good deeds you can create an immortal soul for yourself after three hundred years."

And the little mermaid raised her transparent arms up toward God's sun, and for the first time she felt tears. On the ship there was again life and movement. She saw the prince with his lovely bride searching for her. Sorrowfully they stared at the bubbling foam, as if they knew she had thrown herself into the sea. Invisible, she kissed the bride's forehead, smiled at the prince, and with the other children of the air rose up onto the pink cloud that sailed through the air.

"In three hundred years we will float like this into the kingdom of God!"

"We can come there earlier," whispered one. "Unseen we float into the houses of mortals where there are children, and for every day that we find a good child who makes his parents happy and deserves their love, God shortens our period of trial. The child does not know when we fly through the room, and when we smile over it with joy a year is taken from the three hundred. But if we see a naughty and wicked child, we must weep tears of sorrow, and each tear adds a day to our period of trial!"

The Emperor's New Clothes

❖   ❖   ❖

MANY years ago there lived an emperor who was so exceedingly fond of beautiful new clothes that he spent all his money just on dressing up. He paid no attention to his soldiers, nor did he care about plays or taking drives in the woods except for the sole purpose of showing off his new clothes. He had a robe for every hour of the day, and just as it is said of a king that he is "in council," so they always said here: "The emperor is in the clothes closet!"

In the great city where he lived everybody had a very good time. Many visitors came there every day. One day two charlatans came. They passed themselves off as weavers and said that they knew how to weave the most exquisite cloth imaginable. Not only were the colors and the pattern uncommonly beautiful but also the clothes that were made from the cloth had the singular quality of being invisible to every person who was unfit for his post or else was inadmissably stupid.

"Well, these are some splendid clothes," thought the emperor. "With them on I could find out which men in my kingdom were not suited for the posts they have; I can tell the wise ones from the stupid! Yes, that cloth must be woven for me at once!" And he gave the two charlatans lots of money in advance so they could begin their work.

They put up two looms, all right, and pretended to be working, but they had nothing whatsoever on the looms. Without ceremony they demanded the finest silk and the most magnificent gold thread. This they put in their own pockets and worked at the empty looms until far into the night.

"Now I'd like to see how far they've come with the cloth!" thought the emperor. But it made him feel a little uneasy to think that anyone who was stupid or unfit for his post couldn't see it. Of course he didn't believe that he himself needed to be afraid. Nonetheless he wanted to send someone else first to see how things stood. The whole city knew of the remarkable powers possessed by the cloth, and everyone was eager to see how bad or stupid his neighbor was.

"I'll send my honest old minister to the weavers," thought the emperor. "He's the best one to see how the cloth looks, for he has brains and no one is better fitted for his post than he is!"

Now the harmless old minister went into the hall where the two charlatans sat working at the empty looms.

"Heaven help us!" thought the old minister, his eyes opening wide. "Why, I can't see a thing!" But he didn't say so.

Both the charlatans asked him to please step closer and asked if it didn't have a beautiful pattern and lovely colors. Then they pointed to the empty loom, and the poor old minister kept opening his eyes wider. But he couldn't see a thing, for there was nothing there.

"Good Lord!" he thought. "Am I supposed to be stupid? I never thought so, and not a soul must find it out! Am I unfit for my post? No, it'll never do for me to say that I can't see the cloth!"

"Well, you're not saying anything about it!" said the one who was weaving.

"Oh, it's nice! Quite charming!" said the old minister,

and peered through his spectacles. "This pattern and these colors! Yes, I shall tell the emperor that it pleases me highly!"

"Well, we're delighted to hear it!" said both the weavers, and now they named the colors by name and described the singular pattern. The old minister paid close attention so he could repeat it all when he came back to the emperor. And this he did.

Now the charlatans demanded more money for more silk and gold thread, which they were going to use for the weaving. They stuffed everything into their own pockets. Not a thread went onto the looms, but they kept on weaving on the empty looms as before.

Soon afterward the emperor sent another harmless official there to see how the weaving was coming along and if the cloth should soon be ready. The same thing happened to him as to the minister. He looked and he looked, but as there was nothing there but the empty looms, he couldn't see a thing.

"Well, isn't it a beautiful piece of cloth?" both the charlatans said, and showed and explained the lovely pattern that wasn't there at all.

"Well, I'm not stupid!" thought the man. "Then it's my good position that I'm unfit for? That is strange enough, but I must be careful not to show it!" And so he praised the cloth he didn't see and assured them how delighted he was with the beautiful colors and the lovely pattern. "Yes, it's quite charming!" he said to the emperor.

All the people in the city were talking about the magnificent cloth.

Now the emperor himself wanted to see it while it was still on the loom. With a whole crowd of hand-picked men, among them the two harmless old officials who had been there before, he went to where the two sly charlatans were now weaving with all their might, but without a stitch or a thread.

"Yes, isn't it *magnifique?*" said the two honest officials. "Will your majesty look—what a pattern, what colors!" And then they pointed to the empty looms, for they thought that the others were certainly able to see the cloth.

"What's this?" thought the emperor. "I don't see anything! Why, this is dreadful! Am I stupid? Am I not fit to be emperor? This is the most horrible thing that could happen to me!"

"Oh, it's quite beautiful!" said the emperor. "It has my highest approval!" And he nodded contentedly and regarded the empty looms. He didn't want to say that he couldn't see a thing. The entire company he had brought with him looked and looked, but they weren't able to make any more out of it than the others. Yet, like the emperor, they said, "Oh, it's quite beautiful!" And they advised him to have clothes made of the magnificent new cloth in time for the great procession that was forthcoming.

"It is *magnifique!* Exquisite! Excellent!" passed from mouth to mouth. And every one of them was so fervently delighted with it. Upon each of the charlatans the emperor bestowed a badge of knighthood to hang in his buttonhole, and the title of "Weaver-Junker."

All night long, before the morning of the procession, the charlatans sat up with more than sixteen candles burning. People could see that they were busy finishing the emperor's new clothes. They acted as if they were taking the cloth from the looms, they clipped in the air with big scissors, they sewed with needles without thread, and at last they said, "See, now the clothes are ready!"

With his highest gentlemen-in-waiting the emperor came there himself and both the charlatans lifted an arm in the air as if they were holding something and said, "See, here are the knee breeches! Here's the tailcoat! Here's the cloak!" And so on.

"It's as light as a spider's web! You'd think you had nothing on, but that's the beauty of it!"

"Yes," said all the gentlemen-in-waiting, but they couldn't see a thing, for there was nothing there.

"Now, if your majesty would most graciously consent to take off your clothes," said the charlatans, "we will help you on with the new ones here in front of the big mirror!"

The emperor took off all his clothes, and the charlatans

acted as if they were handing him each of the new garments that had supposedly been sewed. And they put their arms around his waist as if they were tying something on—that was the train—and the emperor turned and twisted in front of the mirror.

"Heavens, how well it becomes you! How splendidly it fits!" they all said. "What a pattern! What colors! That's a magnificent outfit!"

"They're waiting outside with the canopy that is to be carried over your majesty in the procession," said the chief master of ceremonies.

"Well, I'm ready!" said the emperor. "Isn't it a nice fit?"

And then he turned around in front of the mirror just one more time, so it should really look as if he were regarding his finery.

The gentlemen-in-waiting, who were to carry the train, fumbled down on the floor with their hands just as if they were picking up the train. They walked and held their arms high in the air. They dared not let it appear as if they couldn't see a thing.

And then the emperor walked in the procession under the beautiful canopy. And all the people in the street and at the windows said, "Heavens, how wonderful the emperor's new clothes are! What a lovely train he has on the robe! What a marvelous fit!" No one wanted it to appear that he couldn't see anything, for then of course he would have been unfit for his position or very stupid. None of the emperor's clothes had ever been such a success.

"But he doesn't have anything on!" said a little child.

"Heavens, listen to the innocent's voice!" said the father, and then the child's words were whispered from one to another.

"He doesn't have anything on! That's what a little child is saying—he doesn't have anything on!"

"He doesn't have anything on!" the whole populace shouted at last. And the emperor shuddered, for it seemed to him that they were right. But then he thought, "Now I must go through with the procession." And he carried himself more proudly than ever, and the gentlemen-in-waiting carried the train that wasn't there at all.

The Steadfast Tin Soldier

❖ ❖ ❖

THERE were once five-and-twenty tin soldiers; they were all brothers, for they had been born of an old tin spoon. They shouldered their arms, they faced straight ahead, and their uniforms—red and blue—were ever so lovely. The very first thing they heard in this world, when the lid was taken off the box in which they were lying, were the words: "Tin soldiers!" It was shouted by a little boy, and he clapped his hands. They had been given to him for his birthday, and now he was lining them up on the table. Each soldier looked exactly like the other. Only one was slightly different: he had but one leg, for he was the last one to be cast and there hadn't been enough tin. And yet he stood just as firmly on his one leg as the others did on their two, and he is the very one who turns out to be unique.

On the table where they had been lined up there were many other playthings, but the one that stood out most was a lovely paper castle. Through the tiny windows you could look right into the halls. Outside were tiny trees standing around a little mirror that was supposed to look like a lake. Wax swans were swimming on it and being reflected there. It was all lovely, and yet the loveliest of all was a little maiden who was standing in the open door of the castle. She too had been cut out of paper, but she was wearing a skirt of the sheerest lawn and a narrow ribbon over her shoulder just like a drapery; in the very center of it was a shining spangle as big as her whole face. The little maiden was stretching out both her arms, for she was a dancer, and then she had raised one leg so high in the air that the tin soldier couldn't find it at all, and he thought she had but one leg, just like himself.

"That's the wife for me!" he thought. "But she's very highborn. She lives in a castle and I have only a box, and then it must do for five-and-twenty of us—that's no place for her. Still, I must see about making her acquaintance!" And then he stretched out at full length behind a snuffbox that stood on the table. From here he could look right at the little highborn lady, who continued to stand on one leg without losing her balance.

Later in the evening all the other tin soldiers went back in their box, and the people of the house went to bed. Now the toys began to play—at "Visitors," waging war, and holding balls. The tin soldiers rattled in their box because they wanted to join in, but they couldn't get the lid off. The nutcracker turned somersaults, and the slate pencil did monkeyshines on the slate; there was such a racket that the canary bird woke up and joined in the talk—and in verse, at that! The only two who didn't budge an inch were the tin soldier and the little dancer. She held herself erect on the tip of her toe and with both arms outstretched; he was just as steadfast on his one leg and his eyes never left her for a moment.

Now the clock struck twelve, and crash! The lid of the snuffbox flew off, but there wasn't any snuff in there—no, but a little black troll, and that was quite a trick.

"Tin soldier!" said the troll. "Will you keep your eyes to yourself!"

But the tin soldier pretended not to hear.

"Well, wait until tomorrow!" said the troll.

Now, when it was morning and the children got up, the

tin soldier was placed over in the window; and whether it was caused by the troll or the draft, the window suddenly flew open and the tin soldier went headlong out from the third floor with a terrible speed. He turned his leg up in the air and landed on his cap, with his bayonet stuck between the paving stones.

The maid and the little boy went right down to look for him, but despite the fact that they nearly stepped on him, they couldn't see him. If the tin soldier had shouted "Here I am!" they would have found him, all right. But he didn't think it proper to shout when he was in uniform.

Now it started to rain; the drops fell thick and fast. It turned into a regular downpour. When it was over, two street urchins came along.

"Look!" said the first. "There's a tin soldier. He's going out sailing!"

And so they made a boat out of a newspaper and put the tin soldier in the middle of it, and now he sailed down the gutter. Both the boys ran alongside and clapped their hands. Heaven help us! What waves there were in that gutter and what a current! But, then, the rain had poured down. The paper boat bobbed up and down, and now and then it turned around, sending a shudder through the tin soldier. But he was just as steadfast, didn't bat an eyelash, looked straight ahead, and shouldered his gun.

All at once the boat drifted in under a long gutter plank; it was just as dark as if he were in his box.

"I wonder where I'm going now," he thought. "Well, well, it's the fault of the troll. Alas, if only the little maiden were sitting here in the boat, then it could be twice as dark for all I'd care!"

At the same moment a big water rat came along, who lived under the gutter plank.

"Do you have a passport?" asked the rat. "Hand over your passport!"

But the tin soldier remained silent and held the gun

even tighter. The boat flew away with the rat right behind it. Whew! How it gnashed its teeth and shouted to sticks and straws: "Stop him! Stop him! He hasn't paid the toll! He hasn't shown his passport!"

But the current grew stronger and stronger; the tin soldier could already see daylight ahead where the gutter plank ended, but he could also hear a roaring sound that was enough to frighten a brave man. Just think, where the gutter plank ended, the gutter poured right out into a big canal! It was just as dangerous for him as it would be for us to sail down a great waterfall.

Now he was already so close to it that he couldn't stop. The boat shot out; the poor tin soldier held himself as stiffly as he could. No one was going to say that he had blinked his eyes. The boat whirled around three or four times and filled with water right up to the edge. It had to sink. The tin soldier stood in water up to his neck. The boat sank deeper and deeper; the paper grew soggier and soggier. Now the water went over the tin soldier's head. Then he thought of the lovely little dancer, whom he would never see again, and in the ears of the tin soldier rang the song:

> Fare forth! Fare forth, warrior!
> Thou shalt suffer death!

Now the paper was torn to pieces and the tin soldier plunged through—but at the same moment he was gobbled up by a big fish.

My, how dark it was in there! It was even worse than under the gutter plank, and then too it was so cramped! But the tin soldier was steadfast and lay at full length, shouldering his gun.

The fish darted about; it made the most terrible movements. At last it was quite still. It was as if a flash of

lightning had streaked through it. The light was shining
quite brightly and someone shouted: "A tin soldier!"

The fish had been caught, taken to market, and sold,
and had ended up in the kitchen, where the maid had cut
it open with a big knife. With two fingers she picked the
tin soldier up by the middle and carried him into the
parlor, where they all wanted to see this remarkable man
who had journeyed about in the stomach of a fish. But the
tin soldier wasn't proud at all. They stood him up on the
table, and there—my, what strange things can happen in
this world! The tin soldier was in the very same room he
had been in before! He saw the very same children and the
playthings standing on the table, and the lovely castle with
the beautiful little dancer. She was still standing on one
leg and holding the other high in the air—she was steadfast too. The tin soldier was so moved that he could have
cried tears of tin, but it wasn't proper! He looked at her
and she looked at him, but they didn't say anything.

At the same moment one of the little boys took the tin soldier and threw him right into the tiled stove without giving any reason for doing so. It was decidedly the troll in the box who was to blame.

The tin soldier stood all aglow and felt the terrible heat—but whether it was from the real fire or from love, he didn't know. His colors were all gone, but whether that had happened on the journey or from sorrow, no one could tell. He looked at the little maiden, she looked at him, and he felt he was melting. But still he stood steadfast and shouldered his gun. Then a door opened, the wind took the dancer, and like a sylphid she flew right into the tiled stove to the tin soldier, blazed up, and was gone. Then the tin soldier melted to a clump, and when the maid took out the ashes the next day, she found him in the shape of a little tin heart. Of the dancer, on the other hand, only the spangle was left, and that was burned as black as coal.

The Garden of Paradise

❖　❖　❖

THERE was once a king's son. No one had so many or such beautiful books as he had. He was able to read about everything that had taken place in this world and see it depicted in magnificent pictures. He was able to learn about every nation and every land. But about where the Garden of Paradise was to be found there wasn't a word, and that was the very thing he thought of most.

When he was still quite young, but was going to start his schooling, his grandmother had told him that every flower in the Garden of Paradise was the sweetest cake, and the filaments were the choicest wine. On one flower was written "History," on another "Geography" or "Tables." You had only to eat cake and you knew your lesson. Indeed, the more you ate, the more history or geography or tables you knew.

He believed it then, but as he grew bigger and learned more and became much wiser he understood very well that there had to be far different delights in the Garden of Paradise.

"Oh, why did Eve pick from the Tree of Knowledge? Why did Adam partake of the forbidden fruit? It should have been me, then it would never have happened! Never would sin have entered the world!"

He said it then, and he was still saying it when he was seventeen. The Garden of Paradise filled his thoughts.

One day he went into the forest; he went alone, for that gave him the greatest pleasure.

It grew dark, the sky clouded over, and then it began to rain as if the whole sky were one big sluice from which the water was pouring. It was as dark as it usually is at night in the deepest well. Now he was slipping on the wet grass, now he was falling over the bare stones that jutted out of the rocky ground. Everything was wringing wet. There wasn't a dry stitch left on the unfortunate prince. He had to crawl up over huge blocks of stone, where the water seeped out of the deep moss. He was just about to drop when he heard a strange rushing sound, and ahead of him he saw a huge brightly lit cave. In the middle burned a fire big enough to roast a stag by, and this was being done too. The most magnificent stag, with its high antlers, had been stuck on a spit and was being slowly turned around between two felled fir trees. An elderly woman, tall and husky like a man in disguise, was sitting by the fire throwing on one piece of wood after another.

"Just come closer!" she said. "Sit by the fire so you can dry your clothes!"

"There's a terrible draft here!" said the prince, and sat down on the floor.

"It'll be even worse when my sons come home!" answered the woman. "You're in the Cave of the Winds; my sons are the Four Winds of the world. Can you grasp that?"

"Where are your sons?" asked the prince.

"Well, it's not so easy to give an answer when you ask a stupid question!" said the woman. "My sons are on their own. They're playing ball with the clouds up there in the parlor!" And then she pointed up in the air.

"Oh, is that so!" said the prince. "By the way, you speak

quite harshly and not so gently as the womenfolk I usually see about me."

"Well, as likely as not, they don't have anything else to do! I've got to be harsh if I'm to keep my boys under control! But I can do it, even if they are pigheaded! Do you see those four sacks hanging on the wall? They're just as afraid of them as you were of the rod behind the mirror. I can double the boys up, I'll have you know, and then into the sack they go. No fuss about it! There they sit, and they don't come out to go gallivanting until I see fit! But here comes one of them!"

It was the North Wind, who strode in with an icy chill. Huge hailstones bounced across the floor and snowflakes whirled about. He was clad in bearskin pants and jacket, a sealskin hood went down over his ears, long icicles hung from his beard, and one hailstone after another slid down from the collar of his jacket.

"Don't go over to the fire right away," said the prince. "You can easily get chilblains on your face and hands."

"Chilblains!" said the North Wind, and gave quite a loud laugh. "Chilblains! Why, that's just what I enjoy most! But what sort of a milksop are you? How did you get into the Cave of the Winds?"

"He's my guest!" said the old woman. "And if you don't like that explanation, you can just go in the sack! You're familiar with my judgment!"

See, it helped, and now the North Wind told where he had come from and where he had been for almost a whole month.

"I come from the Arctic Ocean," he said. "I've been on Bering Island with the Russian walrus hunters. I sat and slept at the helm when they sailed out from the North Cape. Now and then, when I woke up for a little while, the stormy petrel was flying about my legs. That's a funny bird: it gives a quick flap of the wings and then holds them outstretched, motionless, and now it has enough speed."

"Just don't make it so long-drawn-out!" said the Mother of the Winds. "And then you came to Bering Island!"

"It's lovely there! There's a floor to dance on as flat as a plate, half-thawed snow and moss, and sharp stones with skeletons of walruses and polar bears, lay there. They looked like the arms and legs of giants, moldy and green. You'd think the sun had never shone on them. I blew on the fog a little to get a glimpse of the hut. It was a house built of wreckage and covered with walrus hide, the fleshy side turned out—it was all red and green. A live polar bear was sitting on the roof growling. I went to the shore, looked at the birds' nests, looked at the bald nestlings shrieking and gaping. I blew into the thousands of throats, and they learned how to shut their mouths. Down below, the walruses were tumbling about like living entrails or giant maggots with heads of pigs and teeth a yard long!"

"You tell the story well, my boy," said the mother. "It makes my mouth water to listen to you."

"Then the hunt began! The harpoon was plunged into the breast of the walrus so the steaming jet of blood spurted onto the ice like a fountain. Then I also thought of my game. I started to blow and let my sailing ships—the icebergs as high as a cliff—crush the boats. Whew! How the men sniveled and how they shrieked, but I shrieked louder! They had to unload the whale carcasses, the chests, and the ropes onto the ice. I shook the snowflakes over them and let them drift south in the wedged-in vessels to have a taste of salt water. They'll never come back to Bering Island!"

"Then you've been up to mischief!" said the Mother of the Winds.

"The others can tell you of the good I've done," he said. "But there's my brother from the West. I like him best of all—he smacks of the sea and brings a heavenly chill along with him."

"Is that little Zephyrus?" asked the prince.

"Yes, that's Zephyrus, all right!" said the old woman. "But he's not so little after all. In the old days he was a handsome boy, but that's over now!"

He looked like a wild man, but he had on a baby's cap so as not to hurt himself. In his hand he carried a mahogany club, chopped down in the mahogany forests of America. It could be no less!

"Where do you come from?" asked his mother.

"From the forest wilderness," he said, "where the thorny lianas make a fence between each tree, where the water snake lies in the grass and mankind seems to be unnecessary."

"What were you doing there?"

"I was looking at the deep river and saw how it plunged down from the cliff, turned to spray, and flew up to the clouds to carry the rainbow. I was watching the wild buffalo swimming in the river, but the current dragged him along with it, and he drifted with a flock of wild ducks that flew in the air where the water went over the edge. The buffalo had to go over. I liked that, so I blew up a storm so the ancient trees went sailing and were dashed to shavings."

"And you haven't done anything else?" asked the old woman.

"I've been turning somersaults in the savannas, and I've been patting the wild horse and shaking down coconuts. Oh, yes, I've got stories to tell, but one shouldn't tell everything one knows. You're well aware of that, old lady!" And then he gave his mother such a kiss that she almost fell over backward. He was really a wild boy.

Now the South Wind came in, wearing a turban and a flowing burnoose.

"It's mighty cold in here!" he said, throwing a log on the fire. "It's easy to tell that North Wind has come first."

"It's hot enough to roast a polar bear in here!" said the North Wind.

"You're a polar bear yourself!" said the South Wind.

"Do you want to be put in the sack?" asked the old woman. "Sit down on that stone and tell us where you've been."

"In Africa, Mother!" he replied. "I was hunting lions with the Hottentots in the land of the Kaffirs. My, what grass is growing on the plain there, as green as an olive! There the gnu was dancing and the ostrich ran races with me, but I'm still more nimble-footed. I came to the desert, to the golden sand that looks like the bottom of the sea. I met a caravan. They were butchering their last camel to get water to drink, but they got only a little. The sun blazed up above, and the sand roasted down below. The vast desert has no boundaries. Then I frolicked about in the fine loose sand and whirled it up into tall pillars! What a dance that was! You should have seen how dispiritedly the dromedary stood and how the merchant drew his caftan over his head. He prostrated himself before me, as before Allah, his god. Now they're buried. A pyramid of sand stands over them all. Someday, when I blow it away, the sun will bleach their bones. Then the travelers will be able to see that people have been here before; otherwise you wouldn't think so in the desert!"

"Then you've just been doing harm too!" said the mother. "March into the sack!" And before he knew it, she had the South Wind by the middle and into the sack! It rolled about on the floor, but she sat on it and then it had to lie still.

"You've got some lively boys here, I must say!" said the prince.

"Yes, so I have," she replied, "but I know how to handle them! There's the fourth!"

It was the East Wind. He was clad like a Chinese.

"So, you've come from that direction!" she said. "I thought you'd been to the Garden of Paradise."

"I'm not flying there until morning. It'll be a hundred

years tomorrow since I was there! Now I've just come from China, where I've been dancing on the porcelain tower so all the bells tinkled. Down in the street the officials were being flogged. Bamboo poles were being worn out on their shoulders, and they were people from the first to the ninth rank. They shrieked, "Many thanks, my fatherly benefactor!" But they didn't mean a thing by it; and I tinkled the bells and sang 'Tsing tsang tsu!' "

"You're a wild one!" said the old woman. "It's a good thing you're going to the Garden of Paradise tomorrow. That always improves your manners. Drink deeply of the Spring of Wisdom, and bring home a little flaskful for me."

"That I'll do!" said the East Wind. "But why did you put my brother from the South down in the sack? Out with him! He's going to tell me about the Phoenix. The princess in the Garden of Paradise always wants to hear about that bird when I pay a visit every hundred years. Open the sack, that's my sweet mother, and I'll make you a present of two pocketsful of tea, as green and fresh as it was on the spot where I picked it."

"Well, for the sake of the tea and because you're mother's darling, I'll open the sack!" And so she did! And the South Wind crawled out, but he looked quite crestfallen because the strange prince had seen it.

"Here's a palm leaf for you to give to the princess!" said the South Wind. "That leaf has been given to me by the old Phoenix, the only one in the world. With his beak he has scratched on it the whole account of his life, the hundred years he has lived; now she can read it for herself. I saw how the Phoenix himself set fire to his nest, sat on it, and burned up like the Hindu's widow. My, how the dry branches crackled, what smoke and fragrance there was! At last it all went up in flames. The old Phoenix turned to ashes, but his egg lay red in the fire. It cracked with a loud bang and the youngster flew out. Now he's the ruler of all the birds and the only Phoenix in the world. He has bitten a hole in the palm leaf I gave you. That's his greeting to the princess."

"What about a bit to eat!" said the Mother of the Winds, and then they all sat down to dine on the roasted stag. The prince sat beside the East Wind, and thus they soon became good friends.

"Listen, tell me now," said the prince, "just who is this princess there has been so much talk about, and where is the Garden of Paradise?"

"Ho! Ho!" said the East Wind. "If you'd like to go there, just fly with me tomorrow. But otherwise I'd better tell you that no mortal has been there since the time of Adam and Eve. I daresay you know about them from your Scriptures!"

"Yes, of course!" said the prince.

"At the time they were driven out, the Garden of Paradise sank into the earth. But it kept its warm sunshine, its gentle breeze, and all its splendor. The queen of the fairies dwells there. There lies the Isle of Bliss, where Death never comes; it's a delightful place to be. Sit on my back tomorrow and I'll take you with me. I daresay it can be done! But now you mustn't talk anymore, for I want to go to sleep!"

And then they all went to sleep.

Early in the morning the prince woke up, and he was not a little dumbfounded to find himself already high above the clouds. He was sitting on the back of the East Wind, who was holding onto him quite squarely. They were so high in the sky that forests and fields, rivers and lakes, looked like an enormous illustrated map.

"Good morning," said the East Wind. "You could just as well have slept a little longer; there's not much to look at on the flatland beneath us unless you like to count churches! They stand out like pricks of chalk on the green board down there." The fields and meadows were what he called "the green board."

"It was very impolite of me not to say good-bye to your mother and your brothers," said the prince.

"Allowances are made for one who's sleeping," said the East Wind, and then they flew faster than ever. You could tell by the treetops in the forest that they were rushing over them: all the leaves and branches rustled; you could tell by the seas and lakes, for wherever they flew, the waves rolled higher and the great ships curtsied deep down in the water like floating swans.

Toward evening, as it was growing dark, the big cities were a delight to behold: the lights were burning, now here, now there—just as when someone burns a piece of paper and sees the myriads of tiny sparks, like children on their way from school! And the prince clapped his hands, but the East Wind told him to stop that and hang on tight instead, or else he could easily fall down and find himself hanging on a church spire.

The eagle from the dark forest flew quite easily, but the East Wind flew easier still. The cossack on his horse dashed along over the steppes, but the prince was dashing along in another fashion.

"Now you can see the Himalayas!" said the East Wind. "They're the highest mountains in Asia. We should be coming to the Garden of Paradise soon!" Then they veered in a more southerly direction, and soon there was the scent of spices and flowers. Figs and pomegranates were growing wild, and the wild grapevines had blue and red grapes. Here they both came down and stretched out in the soft grass, where the flowers nodded to the wind as if they wanted to say, "Welcome back!"

"Are we in the Garden of Paradise now?" asked the prince.

"No, not at all!" replied the East Wind. "But we should be there soon. Do you see that wall of rock there, and the big grotto with the grapevines hanging around it like a huge green curtain? We're going in through there! Wrap yourself up in your cloak. The sun is scorching hot here, but one step away and it's as cold as ice. The bird that sweeps past that grotto has one wing out here in the heat of summer and the other in there in the cold of winter!"

"So that's the way to the Garden of Paradise?" asked the prince.

Now they went into the grotto. Whew! How icy cold it was! But it didn't last long. The East Wind spread out his wings, and they shone like the brightest fire. My, what a grotto that was! Huge blocks of stone, from which water dripped, hung over them in the most fantastic shapes. Now the grotto was so narrow that they had to crawl on their hands and knees; now it was as high and spacious as if they were out in the open. It looked like a sepulchral chapel with mute organ pipes and petrified banners.

"I daresay we're taking the Road of Death to the Garden of Paradise," said the prince, but the East Wind didn't answer a word; he pointed ahead, and the loveliest blue light was shining at them. The blocks of stone overhead were fading more and more into a haze that at last was as bright as a white cloud in the moonlight. Now they were in the loveliest gentle breeze, as refreshing as in the mountains, as fragrant as in a valley of roses.

A river was flowing there, as clear as the air itself, and the fish were like silver and gold. Violet eels, which shot off blue sparks at every turn, were frolicking down in the water, and the broad leaves of the water lily were the colors of the rainbow. The flower itself was a reddish-yellow burning flame, which was fed by the water, just as oil constantly keeps the lamp burning. A massive bridge of marble—but as remarkably and delicately carved as if it were of lace and glass beads—spanned the water to the Isle of Bliss, where the Garden of Paradise was blooming.

The East Wind took the prince in his arms and carried him across. There the flowers and leaves were singing the most beautiful songs from his childhood, but in swelling tones more delightful than any human voice can sing.

Were they palm trees or huge water plants that were growing here? The prince had never seen such lush and enormous trees before. There, in long garlands, hung the most remarkable twining vines, such as are to be found only in gold and color in the margins of the ancient books about the saints or threading in and out of the initial letters. It was the strangest combination of birds, flowers, and flourishes. Nearby, in the grass, stood a flock of peacocks with outspread, iridescent tails. Of course, that's just what they were! But no, when the prince touched them, he realized that they weren't animals but plants; they were huge dock plants that were as radiant here as the peacock's lovely tail. The lion and tiger were gamboling about like supple cats among the green hedges, which had a fragrance of olive blossoms, and the lion and the tiger were tame. The wild wood pigeon, as lustrous as the most beautiful pearl, flapped the lion's mane with its wings and the antelope, which is usually so timid, stood nodding its head as if it too wanted to join in the play.

Now the Fairy of Paradise came; her raiment shone like the sun and her face was as mild as that of a happy mother whose child has brought her joy. She was so young and fair, and attending her were the loveliest maidens, each with a shining star in her hair.

The East Wind gave her the inscribed leaf from the Phoenix, and her eyes sparkled with joy. She took the prince by the hand and led him into her castle, where the walls were the color of the most magnificent tulip petal when held up to the sun; the ceiling itself was one big lustrous flower, and indeed, the more you stared into it, the deeper its calyx seemed to be. The prince stepped over to the window and looked through one of the panes.

Then he saw the Tree of Knowledge with the serpent, and Adam and Eve were standing nearby. "Weren't they driven out?" he asked. And the Fairy smiled and explained to him that Time had thus burned its picture onto every pane, but not the way one usually saw it. No, there was life in it, the leaves on the trees moved. The people came and went, as in a reflected image. And he looked through another pane, and there was Jacob's dream, with the ladder going straight up to heaven, and the angels with big wings were hovering up and down. Yes, everything that had happened in this world was living and moving in the panes of glass. Time alone could burn such remarkable pictures.

The Fairy smiled and led him into a huge, lofty hall. Its walls seemed to be transparent paintings, with each face lovelier than the next. There were millions of happy faces that smiled and sang until it blended into a single melody. The ones at the very top were so tiny that they appeared to be tinier than the tiniest rosebud when it is drawn as a dot on the paper. And in the middle of the hall stood a huge tree, with luxuriant, hanging branches; golden apples, big and small, hung like oranges among the green leaves. This was the Tree of Knowledge, of whose fruit Adam and Eve had partaken. From each leaf dripped a glistening red drop of dew! It was as if the tree were crying tears of blood.

"Now let us get the boat," said the Fairy. "There we will enjoy refreshments out on the billowing water. The boat rocks, and yet it doesn't budge from the spot. But all the lands of the world will glide past our eyes." And it was strange to see how the whole coast moved. Here came the high snow-capped Alps, with clouds and black fir trees. The horn rang out, deep and melancholic, and the shepherd yodeled prettily in the valley. Now the banana trees bent their long drooping branches over the boat, coal-black swans were swimming on the water, and the most curious animals and flowers came into sight on the shore. This was New Holland, the fifth continent, that was gliding past and offering a view of the blue mountains; you could hear the chants of the priests and see the wild men dance to the sound of drums and bone pipes. The pyramids of Egypt, soaring to the clouds, and overturned columns and sphinxes half buried in the sand sailed past. The Aurora Borealis blazed over the glaciers of the North; it was a display of fireworks that none could match. The prince was so blissful. And indeed, he saw a hundred times more than we have described here.

"And can I stay here always?" he asked.

"That depends on yourself!" answered the Fairy. "If you don't, like Adam, allow yourself to be tempted to do what is forbidden, then you can always stay here."

"I won't touch the apples on the Tree of Knowedge!" said the prince. "Why, there're thousands of fruits here as lovely as they are."

"Test yourself, and if you're not strong enough, then go back with the East Wind, who brought you; he is flying back now and won't be coming here again for a hundred years. The time here in this place will pass for you as though it were only a hundred hours, but that's a long time for temptation and sin. Every evening, when I leave you, I must call out to you: 'Follow me!' I must beckon to you with my hand—but remain where you are. Don't come with me, for with every step your yearning will increase. You will enter the hall where the Tree of Knowledge grows. I sleep beneath its fragrant, drooping boughs. You will bend over me and I must smile. But if you press one kiss upon my lips, Paradise will then sink deep into the earth and be lost to you. The biting wind of the desert will whistle around you, the cold rain will drip from your hair. Trial and tribulation will be your lot."

"I'm staying here!" said the prince. And the East Wind kissed his forehead and said, "Be strong, and we'll meet here again in a hundred years. Farewell! Farewell!" And the East Wind spread out his mighty wings; they shone like heat lightning in the summer, or the Northern Lights in the cold winter. "Farewell! Farewell!" came the echo from flowers and trees. Storks and pelicans flew in rows like fluttering streamers and accompanied him to the boundary of the garden.

"Now our dance begins," said the Fairy. "At the end, when I dance with you, you will see me beckoning to you as the sun goes down; you will hear me calling you: 'Follow me!' But don't do it! For a hundred years I must repeat it every evening. Every time that hour is past you will gain more strength; at last you will never think of it again. This evening is the first time. Now I have warned you."

And the Fairy led him into a great hall of white transparent lilies. The yellow filament of each was a tiny harp of gold, which rang out with the sound of strings and flutes. The most beautiful maidens, graceful and willowy, clad in billowing gauze that revealed their lovely limbs, hovered in the dance and sang of how delightful it is to live, of how they would never die, and of how the Garden of Paradise would bloom in all eternity.

As the sun went down the entire sky turned a golden hue that tinged the lilies like the loveliest roses. And the prince drank of the sparkling wine handed to him by the maidens, and he felt a bliss he had never known before. He saw how the back of the hall opened, and the Tree of Knowledge stood in a radiance that blinded his eyes! The song coming from it was soft and lovely, like his mother's voice, and it was as if she were singing, "My child, my beloved child!"

Then the Fairy beckoned and called so affectionately, "Follow me! Follow me!" And he plunged toward her, forgetting his vow, forgetting it already on the very first evening. And she beckoned and smiled. The fragrance,

the spicy fragrance all around, grew headier; the harps
rang out far more beautifully; and the millions of smiling
heads in the hall where the tree was growing seemed to
be nodding and singing: "One should know everything!
Man is the lord of the earth!" And they were no longer
tears of blood that fell from the leaves of the Tree of
Knowledge; they were red, twinkling stars, it seemed to
him. "Follow me! Follow me!" echoed the tremulous strains,
and at every step the prince's cheeks burned hotter and
his blood flowed faster. "I must!" he said. "Why, that's no
sin. It can't be! Why not follow beauty and happiness! I
will look at her asleep. After all, nothing is lost as long as I
don't kiss her, and I won't do that, I am strong! I have a
strong will!"

And the Fairy let drop her dazzling raiment, bent back
the branches, and a moment later was hidden inside.

"I haven't sinned yet!" said the prince. "And I'm not

going to, either." And then he drew the branches aside. She was already asleep, as lovely as only the Fairy in the Garden of Paradise can be. She smiled in her dreams. He bent over her and saw the tears welling up between her eyelashes.

"Are you crying over me?" he whispered. "Don't cry, you lovely woman! Only now do I comprehend the happiness of Paradise! It pours through my blood and through my thoughts. I can feel the might of cherubs and of eternal life in my mortal limbs! Let there be everlasting night for me; one moment such as this is riches enough!" And he kissed the tears away from her eyes, and his lips touched hers. . . .

Then there was a thunderclap louder and more dreadful than had ever been heard before, and everything fell down: the lovely Fairy and the blossoming Paradise sank. It sank so deep, so deep. The prince saw it sink in the black night; like a tiny gleaming star, it sparkled far away. A deathly chill went through his limbs; he closed his eyes and lay as if dead for a long time.

The cold rain was falling on his face and the biting wind was blowing about his head when he regained his thoughts. "What have I done?" he sighed. "I have sinned like Adam! Sinned so that Paradise has sunk deep down there!" And he opened his eyes. He could still see the star in the distance, the star that twinkled like the sunken Paradise—it was the Morning Star in the sky.

He got up and found that he was in the great forest close to the Cave of the Winds, and the Mother of the Winds was sitting by his side. She looked angry, and she lifted her arm in the air. "Already on the very first evening!" she said. "I thought as much! Yes, if you were my boy, you'd go down in the sack now!"

"That's where he's going," said Death; he was a strong old man with a scythe in one hand and with huge black wings. "He'll be laid in a coffin, but not now. I'll just mark him and then let him wander about the world for a while, atone for his sin, grow better and improve! I'll come one day. When he least expects it, I'll put him in the black coffin, place it on my head, and fly up toward the star. The Garden of Paradise is blooming there too. And if he is good and pious, he shall enter there; but if his thoughts are evil and his heart is still full of sin, he will sink in the coffin deeper than Paradise sank and only once every thousand years will I fetch him up again, so that he may sink deeper or remain on the star, the twinkling star on high!"

The Flying Trunk

❖   ❖   ❖

THERE was once a merchant; he was so rich that he could pave the whole street, and most of a little alleyway too, with silver money. But he didn't do it; he knew of other ways to use his money. If he spent a shilling, he got back a daler. That's the sort of merchant he was—and then he died.

Now the son got all this money, and he lived merrily—going to masquerade balls every night, making paper kites out of rixdaler bills, and playing ducks and drakes on the lake with golden coins instead of stones. So I daresay the money could go, and go it did. At last he had no more than four shillings left, and he had no other clothes than a pair of slippers and an old bathrobe. His friends no longer bothered about him now, as, indeed, they couldn't walk down the street together. But one of them, who was kind, sent him an old trunk and said, "Pack it!" Now, that was all very well, but he had nothing to pack, and so he seated himself in the trunk.

It was a funny trunk. As soon as you pressed the lock, the trunk could fly—and fly it did! Whoops! It flew up through the chimney with him, high above the clouds, farther and farther away. The bottom creaked, and he was afraid it would go to pieces, for then he would have made quite a big *jolt!* Heaven help us! And then he came to the land of the Turks. He hid the trunk in the woods under the dried leaves and then went into the town. He could do this easily, for among the Turks everyone, of course, walked around like he did, in a bathrobe and slippers. Then he met a nurse with a baby.

"Listen, you Turkish nurse," he said, "what big castle is this close to the city? The windows are so high!"

"The king's daughter lives there!" she said. "It has been prophesied that a sweetheart is going to make her very unhappy, so no one can come in to see her unless the king and the queen are there!"

"Thanks!" said the merchant's son. And then he went out in the woods, seated himself in his trunk, flew up on the roof, and crawled in through the window to the princess.

She was lying on the sofa asleep. She was so lovely that the merchant's son had to kiss her. She woke up and was quite terrified, but he said that he was the God of the Turks, who had come down to her through the air, and she liked that very much.

Then they sat next to each other, and he told her tales about her eyes: they were the loveliest dark pools, and her thoughts swam about there like mermaids. And he told her about her forehead: it was a snow-capped mountain with the most magnificent halls and pictures. And he told her about the stork that brings the sweet little babies.

Yes, those were some lovely tales! Then he proposed to the princess, and she said yes right away.

"But you must come here on Saturday," she said. "Then the king and the queen will be here with me for tea! They will be very proud that I am getting the God of the Turks. But see to it that you know a really lovely story, for my parents are especially fond of them. My mother likes it to be moral and decorous, while my father likes it jolly, so you can laugh!"

"Well, I'm bringing no other wedding present than a story!" he said, and then they parted. But the princess gave him a saber that was encrusted with golden coins—and he could particularly use those.

Now he flew away, bought himself a new bathrobe, and then sat out in the woods and started making up a story. It had to be ready by Saturday, and that's not at all easy.

Then he was ready, and then it was Saturday.

The king and the queen and the whole court were waiting with tea at the princess'. He was given such a nice reception!

"Now, will you tell a story!" said the queen. "One that is profound and imparts a moral."

"But one that can still make you laugh!" said the king.

"Yes, of course!" he said, and started his tale. And now you must listen very carefully.

"There was once a bunch of matches that were so exceedingly proud of their high descent. Their family tree—that is to say, the big fir tree of which each one was a tiny stick—had been a huge old tree in the forest. The matches were now lying on the shelf between a tinderbox and an old iron pot, and they were telling them about their youth.

" 'Yes, when we lived high on the green branch,' they said, 'we were really living high! Every morning and evening, diamond tea—that was the dew. All day we had sunshine—when the sun was shining—and all the little birds had to tell us stories. We were very well aware that we were rich too, for the leafy trees were clad only in the summer, but our family could afford green clothes both summer and winter. But then came the woodcutters—that was the Great Revolution—and our family was split up. The head of the family was given a post as the mainmast on a splendid ship that could sail around the world—if it wanted to. The other branches ended up in other places, and it is now our task to provide light for the rank and file. That's why people of rank like ourselves happen to be in the kitchen.'

" 'Well, it's been different with me!' said the iron pot, which was lying beside the matches. 'Ever since I came out into the world, I've been scoured and boiled many times! I attend to the substantial things, and as a matter of fact, I really come first in this house. My only joy—next to the table—is to lie nice and clean on the shelf and carry on a sensible chat with my companions. But—with the exception of the water pail, which occasionally goes down in the yard—we always live indoors. Our only news bringer is the market basket, but it talks so alarmingly about the government and the people. Yes, the other day an elderly pot was so upset by it all that it fell down and broke to bits! That's liberalism, I tell you!'

" 'Now you're talking too much!' said the tinderbox, and the steel struck the flint so the sparks flew. 'Weren't we going to have a cheerful evening?'

" 'Yes, let's talk about which of us is the most aristocratic!' said the matches.

" 'No, I don't enjoy talking about myself!' said the earthenware pot. 'Let's have an evening's *divertissement*. I'll begin. I'm going to tell about the sort of thing each one of us has experienced; you can enter into it so nicely, and that's such a delight. On the Baltic Sea, by the Danish beeches! . . .'

" 'That's a delightful beginning!' said all the plates. 'This is decidedly going to be the kind of story I like!'

" 'Well, there I spent my youth with a quiet family. The furniture was polished, the floors washed; clean curtains were put up every fourteen days!'

" 'My, what an interesting storyteller you are!' said the mop. 'You can tell right away that it's being told by a lady. Such cleanliness pervades!'

" 'Yes, you can feel it!' said the water pail, and then it gave a little hop for joy, so it went splash on the floor.

"And the pot went on with the story, and the end was just as good as the beginning.

"All the plates rattled with delight, and the mop took green parsley out of the sand bin and crowned the pot with it, for it knew this would irritate the others. 'And if I crown her today,' it said, 'then she'll crown me tomorrow!'

" 'Well, I want to dance,' said the fire tongs, and dance she did. Yes, heaven help us, how she could lift one leg up in the air! The old chair cover over in the corner split just from looking at it. 'May I be crowned too?' said the fire tongs, and then she was.

" 'All the same, they're only rabble!' thought the matches.

"Now the samovar was to sing, but it had a cold, it said—it couldn't unless it was boiling. But that was plain snobbishness; it wouldn't sing except when it was standing on the table in the room with the family.

"Over in the window sat an old quill pen, which the maid usually wrote with. There was nothing exceptional about it except that it had been dipped too far down in the inkwell. But because of this it now put on airs. 'If the samovar won't sing,' it said, 'then it needn't. Hanging outside in a cage is a nightingale. It can sing. To be sure, it hasn't been taught anything, but we won't malign it this evening!'

" 'I find it highly improper,' said the tea kettle, who was a kitchen singer and half sister to the samovar, 'that such an alien bird is to be heard! Is that patriotic? I'll let the market basket be the judge!'

" 'I'm simply vexed!' said the market basket. 'I'm as deeply vexed as anyone can imagine! Is this a fitting way to spend an evening? Wouldn't it be better to put the house to rights? Then everyone would find his place, and I'd run the whole caboodle! Then there'd be another song and dance!'

" 'Yes, let's raise a rumpus!' they all said. At the same moment the door opened. It was the maid, and so they stood still. There wasn't a peep out of anyone. But there wasn't a pot there that didn't know what it was capable of doing or how distinguished it was.

" 'Yes, if only I'd wanted to,' each thought, 'it really would have been a lively evening!'

"The maid took the matches and made a fire with them! Heavens, how they sputtered and burst into flames!

" 'Now,' they thought, 'everyone can see that we're the first! What a radiance we have! What a light!' And then they were burned out."

"That was a delightful story!" said the queen. "I felt just as if I were in the kitchen with the matches! Yes, now thou shalt have our daughter!"

"Certainly!" said the king. "Thou shalt have our daughter on Monday!" They said "thou" to him now that he was going to be one of the family.

And thus the wedding was decided; on the evening before, the entire city was illuminated. Buns and cakes were thrown out to be scrambled for. The street urchins stood on tiptoe, shouted "Hurrah!" and whistled through their fingers.

It was truly magnificent.

"Well, I guess I'd better see about doing something too," thought the merchant's son, and then he bought rockets, torpedoes, and all the fireworks you can imagine, put them in his trunk, and flew up in the air with them.

SWOOOOOOOOSH! How they went off! And how they popped!

It made all the Turks hop in the air so their slippers flew about their ears. They'd never seen a vision like this before. Now they could tell that it was the God of the Turks himself who was going to marry the princess.

As soon as the merchant's son had come back down in the forest again with his trunk, he thought, "I'll just go into the city to find out how it looked!" And of course it was only reasonable that he wanted to do that.

My, how people were talking! Every last person he asked had seen it, in his own fashion, but they all thought it had been delightful!

"I saw the God of the Turks himself!" said one. "He had eyes like shining stars and a beard like frothy water!"

"He flew in a fiery robe!" said another. "The loveliest cherubs were peeking out from among the folds!"

Indeed, those were delightful things he heard, and on the following day he was to be married.

Now he went back to the forest to seat himself in the trunk—but where was it?

The trunk had burned up! A spark from the fireworks had remained and set it on fire, and the trunk was in ashes. No longer could he fly, no longer could he come to his bride.

She stood all day on the roof and waited. She's waiting still while he's wandering about the world telling stories. But they're no longer as gay as the one he told about the matches.

The Rose Elf

❖ ❖ ❖

IN the middle of a garden there grew a rosebush. It was quite full of roses, and in one of these, the most beautiful of them all, there dwelled an elf. He was so teeny-weeny that no human eye could see him; behind each petal of the rose he had a bedchamber. He was as well shaped and delightful as any child could be, and he had wings from his shoulders all the way down to his feet. Oh, what a fragrance there was in his chamber, and how bright and lovely were the walls! After all, they were the pale red, delicate rose petals.

All day long he amused himself in the warm sunshine flying from flower to flower, dancing on the wings of the fluttering butterfly, and counting the number of steps he had to take to run across all the highways and paths to be found on a single linden leaf. He regarded what we call the veins of the leaf as highways and paths, and indeed they were endless roads to him. Before he had finished, the sun had gone down, but then he had started so late.

It grew so cold; the dew was falling and the wind was blowing. The best thing to do now was to go home! He hurried as fast as he could, but the rose had closed and he wasn't able to come in—not a single rose was open; the poor little elf became so frightened, for he had never been out at night before and had always slept so soundly behind the sheltered rose petals. Oh, this would certainly be the death of him!

At the other end of the garden, he knew, there was a bower of lovely honeysuckle. The flowers looked like big painted horns; he would climb into one of these and sleep until morning.

He flew there. Shhhh! Two people were inside: a hand-

some young man and the loveliest of maidens. They were sitting side by side, wishing that they would never be parted. They were so much in love with each other, much more than the best of children can love his father and mother.

"And yet we must part!" said the young man. "Your brother has it in for us, so he's sending me on an errand far away over the mountains and seas! Farewell, my sweet bride, for that is what you are to me!"

And then they kissed each other, and the young maiden

wept and gave him a rose. But before she handed it to him she pressed so firm and fervent a kiss upon it that the flower opened. Then the little elf flew inside and leaned his head against the delicate, fragrant walls. But he could hear very well that they were saying: "Farewell! Farewell!" And he could feel the rose being placed at the young man's breast. Oh, how his heart was pounding inside! The little elf couldn't fall asleep, it was pounding so!

The rose didn't remain at the young man's breast long. He took it off, and as he walked alone through the dark forest he kissed the flower so often and so fervently that the little elf came close to being crushed to death. He could feel through the petals how the young man's lips were burning, and the rose had opened as in the heat of the strongest noonday sun.

Now came another man, dark and angry. He was the lovely maiden's evil brother. He drew a big sharp knife, and as the other was kissing the rose the evil man stabbed him to death, cut off his head, and buried it with the body in the soft earth under a linden tree.

"Now he's gone and forgotten!" thought the evil brother. "He'll never come back again. He was going to take a long journey over mountains and seas. Then it's easy to lose one's life, and so he has! He won't be back, and my sister will never dare to ask me about him!"

Then with his foot he scattered withered leaves over the upturned earth and went back home in the dark night. But he didn't go alone as he thought—the little elf went with him. He was sitting in a withered, curled-up linden leaf that had fallen on the hair of the evil man as he was digging the grave. The hat had been placed over him now. It was so dark in there, and the elf was trembling with fright and rage at that odious deed.

The evil man came home at daybreak; he took off his hat and went into his sister's bedroom. There lay the lovely maiden, in the bloom of youth, dreaming about the one she loved so much, and who she now thought was going over mountains and through forests. And the evil brother leaned over her, laughing nastily as only a devil can laugh. Then the withered leaf fell out of his hair and onto the cover, but he didn't notice it and went out, to get a little sleep in the early-morning hours. But the elf popped out of the withered leaf, went into the sleeping girl's ear, told her—as if in a dream—about the horrible murder, described the spot to her where the brother had killed him and left his body, told about the blossoming linden tree close by, and said, "So that you do not think what I have told you is a dream, you will find a withered leaf on your bed." And this is what she found when she awoke.

Oh, how she cried salt tears now! And she dared not confide her grief in anyone. The window stood open all day; the little elf could easily have gone out into the garden to the roses and all the other flowers, but he didn't have the heart to leave the grief-stricken girl. In the window was standing a bush of monthly roses. He seated himself in one of the flowers and looked at the poor girl. Her brother came into the room many times, and he was merry and evil, but she dared not say a word about her broken heart.

As soon as it was night she slipped out of the house, went into the forest to the spot where the linden tree stood, swept the leaves away from the dirt, dug down in it, and found at once the one who had been killed. Oh, how she wept and prayed to the Lord to let her die soon.

She wanted to take the body home with her, but she wasn't able to do it. But then she picked up the pale head with the closed eyes, kissed the cold lips, and shook the dirt out of his beautiful hair.

"I want this!" she said, and after covering the dead body with dirt and leaves, she took home with her the head and a little twig of the jasmine that blossomed in the forest where he had been killed.

As soon as she was in her room, she fetched the biggest flowerpot she could find, and putting the dead man's head in it, she covered it with earth and then planted the twig of jasmine in the pot.

"Farewell! Farewell!" whispered the little elf. He could no longer bear to see so much grief, and so he flew out into the garden to his rose. But it had withered, and only a few pale petals were hanging to the green hip.

"Alas, how soon everything that is beautiful and good comes to an end!" sighed the elf. At last he found another rose. This became his dwelling, behind its delicate, fragrant petals he could stay.

Every morning he flew over to the window of the unfortunate girl, and she was always standing there crying by the flowerpot. The salt tears fell on the jasmine branch, and for every day that she grew paler and paler, the branch became fresher and greener; one shoot after the other grew out; little white buds turned into blossoms and she kissed them. But the evil brother scolded her and asked if she weren't being silly; he didn't like it, nor could he know whose eyes had been closed and whose red lips had turned to dust. And she rested her head against the flowerpot, and the little elf from the rose found her dozing there. Then he climbed into her ear and told her about the evening in the bower, about the fragrance of the roses, and the love of the elves. She had such a sweet dream, and as she was dreaming her life faded away. She had died a peaceful death; she was in heaven with the one she loved.

And the jasmine blossoms opened their big white bells and shed a strange fragrance; this was their only way of weeping for the dead.

But the evil brother looked at the beautiful flowering tree and took it for himself as an inheritance. He put it in his room next to his bed, for it was so lovely to look at and the fragrance was so sweet and delicious. The little rose elf went along too, flying from blossom to blossom. In each one dwelled a tiny soul, and he told them all about the murdered young man, whose head had now turned to dust, and about the evil brother and the unfortunate sister.

"We know it," said all the souls in the blossoms. "We know it! Haven't we sprung forth from the dead man's eyes and lips? We know it! We know it!" And they nodded their heads in such a curious fashion.

The rose elf couldn't understand how they could remain so calm, and he flew out to the bees, who were gathering honey, and told them the story about the evil brother. And the bees told their queen, who ordered them all to kill the murderer the next morning.

But that night—it was the first night after the sister's death—as the brother was sleeping in his bed next to the fragrant jasmine tree, each flower opened its cup; and invisible, but with a poisonous spear, each flower soul climbed out. First they sat by his ear and told him bad dreams, and then they flew over his lips and stuck his tongue with the poisonous spears. "Now we have avenged the dead!" they said, and returned to the jasmine's white bells.

In the morning, when the window to the bedroom was suddenly thrown open, the rose elf and the queen bee with the whole swarm of bees flew in to kill him.

But he was already dead. People were standing around the bed, and they said, "The jasmine odor has killed him!"

Then the rose elf understood the revenge of the flowers. And he told the queen bee, and she and the whole swarm flew buzzing around the flowerpot. The bees were not to be ousted. Then a man took the flowerpot away, but one of the bees stung him on the hand, making him drop the pot, and it broke.

Then they saw the white skull and knew that the dead man in the bed was a murderer.

And the queen bee buzzed in the air and sang about the revenge of the flowers and about the rose elf, and that behind each tiny petal there dwells one who knows how to reveal and to avenge evil.

The Evil Prince
(A Legend)

❖ ❖ ❖

THERE was once an evil and overbearing prince whose only thought was to conquer all the lands of the world and strike terror with his name; he fared forth with fire and sword; his soldiers trampled down the grain in the field; they set fire to the farmer's house and saw the red flame lick the leaves from the trees and the fruit hang scorched on the black, charred branches. Many a poor mother hid with her naked, nursing babe behind the smoking wall, and the soldiers hunted for her; and if they found her and the child, their fiendish pleasures began. Evil spirits could not have behaved worse; but the prince thought that this was just as it should be. Day by day his power grew; his name was feared by everyone and success followed him in all his deeds. From the conquered cities he took gold and great treasures. In his royal residence were amassed riches, the like of which was nowhere to be found. Now he had erected magnificent castles, churches, and arches, and everyone who saw these splendors said, "What a great prince!" They did not think of the misery he had brought upon other lands; they did not hear the sighs and the wails that went up from the scorched cities.

The prince looked at his gold, looked at his magnificent buildings, and thought, as the mob, "What a great prince! But I must have more! Much more! No power must be mentioned as equal to mine, much less greater!" And he went to war against all his neighbors and conquered them all. He had the vanquished kings fettered to his carriage with golden chains as he drove through the streets, and when he sat down at the table, they had to lie at his feet and at the feet of his courtiers and take the pieces of bread that were thrown to them.

Now the prince had his statue erected in the squares and in the royal palace. Yes, he even wanted it to stand in the churches before the altar of the Lord. But the priests said, "Prince, you are mighty, but God is mightier. We dare not do it."

"Well," said the evil prince, "then I am going to conquer God too!" And with overweening pride and folly in his heart, he had a remarkable ship built that he could fly through the air with. It was as brightly colored as the tail of a peacock and appeared to be encrusted with a thousand eyes. But each eye was the barrel of a gun. The prince sat in the middle of the ship; he had only to push a spring and a thousand bullets flew out, and the guns were again loaded as before. A hundred strong eagles were attached to the front of the ship, and in this fashion he flew up toward the sun. The earth lay far below; at first, with its mountains and forests, it resembled a plowed-up field where the green peeps forth from the overturned turf. Then it looked like a flat map, and soon it was quite hidden in fog and clouds. Higher and higher flew the eagles. Then God dispatched a single one of his myriads of angels, and the evil prince let fly a thousand bullets at him. But the bullets fell off the angel's shining wings like hail. A drop of blood—only a single one—dripped from the wing feather, and this drop fell on the ship in which the prince was sitting. It burned itself fast; it was as heavy as a thousand hundredweights of lead and swept the ship down toward the earth at breakneck speed. The strong wings of the eagles were broken, the wind rushed around

the prince's head, and the clouds that were all around—
after all, they were from the burned cities—took on threat-
ening shapes, like mile-long crayfish that stretched out
their strong claws after him, like rolling boulders or fire-
spouting dragons. Half dead, he lay in the ship, which was
caught at last among the thick branches of the forest.

"I will vanquish God!" he said. "I have sworn it; my will
shall be done!" And for seven years he had remarkable
ships constructed that would fly through the air. He had
thunderbolts forged from the hardest steel, because he
wanted to blow up the fortress of heaven. From all his
lands he gathered a great army, which covered a radius of
several miles when the men stood lined up. They climbed
into the remarkable ships. The prince himself was ap-
proaching his when God sent out a swarm of mosquitoes, a

little swarm of mosquitoes. They buzzed around the prince and bit him on the face and hands. In a rage he drew his sword, but struck out at the empty air. He couldn't touch the mosquitoes. Then he ordered costly carpets to be brought. They were to be wrapped around him—no mosquito could penetrate them with its sting—and this was done as he ordered. But a single mosquito was sitting on the innermost carpet. It crawled into the prince's ear and bit him there. It seared like fire; the poison surged up to his brain. He tore himself loose, yanked off the carpets, ripped his clothes to shreds, and danced naked in front of the brutal, barbarous soldiers that were now mocking the mad prince, who wanted to pester God and was vanquished by a single little mosquito.

The Swineherd

❖　❖　❖

THERE was once a poor prince. He had a kingdom that was quite small, but then it was big enough to get married on, and marry he would.

Now it was, of course, a bit presumptuous of him to dare to say to the emperor's daughter: "Will you have me?" But that he dared, all right, for his name was known far and wide, and there were hundreds of princesses who would have been glad to have him. But see if she was!

Now we shall hear.

On the grave of the prince's father there grew a rosebush. Oh, such a lovely rosebush! It bore flowers every fifth year, and then only a single rose. But it was a rose that smelled so sweet that by smelling it one forgot all one's cares and woes. And then he had a nightingale that could sing as though all the lovely melodies in the world were in its little throat. That rose and that nightingale the princess was to have, and so they were put into two big silver cases and sent to her.

The emperor had them brought in before him to the great hall, where the princess was playing "Visitors" with her ladies-in-waiting—they had nothing else to do—and when she saw the big cases with the presents inside, she clapped her hands for joy.

"If only it were a little pussycat!" she said—but then out came the lovely rose.

"My, how nicely it has been made!" said all the ladies-in-waiting.

"It is more than nice," said the emperor, "it is beautiful!"

But the princess touched it, and then she was on the verge of tears.

"Fie, Papa!" she said. "It's not artificial! It's real."

"Fie!" said all the ladies-in-waiting. "It's real!"

"Now, let us first see what is in the other case before we lose our tempers," thought the emperor, and then the nightingale came out. It sang so sweetly that to begin with no one could find fault with it.

"Superbe! Charmante!" said the ladies-in-waiting, for they all spoke French, each one worse than the other.

"How that bird reminds me of the late-lamented empress' music box," said one old courtier. "Ahhh yes, it is quite the same tune, the same rendering."

"Yes," said the emperor, and then he cried like a little baby.

"I should hardly like to think that it's real," said the princess.

"Why, yes, it is a real bird," said the people who had brought it.

"Well, then, let that bird go!" said the princess, and she would in no way permit the prince to come.

But he didn't lose heart. He stained his face brown and black, and pulling his cap down over his eyes, he knocked at the door.

"Good morning, Emperor!" he said. "Can't you take me into your service here at the palace?"

"Well, there are so many who apply here," said the emperor. "But—let me see—I need someone to keep the pigs, for we have a lot of them."

And so the prince was hired as the imperial swineherd. He was given a wretched little room down by the pigsty,

and there he had to stay. But the whole day he sat
working, and by the time it was evening he had made a
pretty little pot. Around it were bells, and as soon as the
pot boiled they started ringing delightfully and played an
old tune:

> *Ach, du lieber Augustin,*
> *Alles ist weg! Weg! Weg!*[1]

But the most curious thing of all, however, was that anyone holding his finger in the steam from the pot could
smell at once what food was cooking on every stove in the
town, so that was certainly a far cry from a rose.

Now the princess came walking along with all her ladies-
in-waiting, and when she heard the tune, she stood still
and looked very pleased, for she could also play "Ach, du
lieber Augustin." It was the only tune she knew, and she
played it with one finger.

"Why, that's the tune I can play!" she said. "This must
be a cultivated swineherd! Listen! Go in and ask him what
that instrument costs."

And then one of the ladies-in-waiting had to run in, but
she put on wooden shoes.

"What will you have for that pot?" said the lady-in-waiting.

"I want ten kisses from the princess," said the swineherd.

"Heaven help us!" said the lady-in-waiting.

"Well, it can't be less," said the swineherd.

"Now! What does he say?" asked the princess.

"That I really can't tell you!" said the lady-in-waiting.
"It is too horrible!"

"Then you can whisper!" And so she whispered.

"Why, how rude he is!" said the princess, and left at
once. But when she had gone a little way, the bells tinkled
so prettily:

[1] Ah, dear Augustine,
   All is over and done! Done! Done!

Ach, du lieber Augustin,
Alles ist weg! Weg! Weg!

"Listen," said the princess. "Ask him if he will take ten kisses from my ladies-in-waiting."

"No, thanks!" said the swineherd. "Ten kisses from the princess, or else I keep the pot."

"How really vexatious!" said the princess. "But then you must stand around me so that no one sees it."

And the ladies-in-waiting lined up in front of her and spread out their skirts, and then the swineherd got the ten kisses and she got the pot.

Oh, what fun they had! All that evening and the next day the pot had to boil. They knew what was cooking on every stove in the whole town, whether at the chamberlain's or at the shoemaker's. The ladies-in-waiting danced and clapped their hands.

"We know who's going to have fruit soup and pancakes! We know who's going to have porridge and meatballs! Oh, how interesting!"

"Extremely interesting," said the mistress of the robes.

"Yes, but keep it a secret, for I am the emperor's daughter!"

"Heaven help us!" they all said.

The swineherd—that is to say, the prince, but they didn't know, of course, that he was anything but a real swineherd—didn't let the next day pass before he had made something else, and this time he made a rattle. Whenever anyone swung it around, it played all the waltzes and quadrilles and polkas that were known since the creation of the world.

"But that is *superbe!*" said the princess as she went by. "I have never heard a lovelier composition! Listen, go in and ask what that instrument costs. But no kissing!"

"He wants a hundred kisses from the princess!" said the lady-in-waiting who had been inside to ask.

"I do believe he's mad!" said the princess. And then she left. But after she had gone a little way, she stopped. "One should encourage the arts!" she said. "I *am* the emperor's daughter. Tell him he shall get ten kisses just like yesterday. The rest he can take from my ladies-in-waiting."

"Yes, but not unless we have to!" said the ladies-in-waiting.

"That's just talk!" said the princess. "If I can kiss him, then you can too! Remember, I give you board and wages!" And then the lady-in-waiting had to go in to him again.

"One hundred kisses from the princess," he said, "or else each keeps what he has!"

"Stand in front!" she said. So all the ladies-in-waiting lined up in front of her, and then he started kissing.

"What can all that commotion be down by the pigsty?" said the emperor, who had stepped out onto the balcony. He rubbed his eyes and put on his glasses. "Why, it's the ladies-in-waiting! They're up to something. I certainly must go down to them!" And then he pulled his slippers up in back, for they were shoes that he had worn down at the heel.

My, how he hurried!

As soon as he came down into the courtyard he walked quite softly, and the ladies-in-waiting were so busy counting the kisses to make sure there was fair play—so he shouldn't get too many, but not too few, either—that they didn't notice the emperor at all. He stood up on tiptoe.

"What on earth!" he said when he saw them kissing, and then he hit them on the head with his slipper just as the swineherd got the eighty-sixth kiss. *"Heraus!"*[2] said the emperor, for he was furious, and both the swineherd and the princess were put out of his empire.

There she stood now and cried, the swineherd swore, and the rain poured down.

[2] "Get out!"

"Ohhhh, what a miserable soul I am," said the princess. "If only I'd taken that lovely prince! Ohhhh, how unhappy I am!"

And the swineherd went behind a tree, wiped away the brown and black from his face, threw away the ugly clothes, and stepped forth in his prince's clothing, looking so handsome that the princess had to curtsy to him.

"I have come to despise you," he said. "You wouldn't have an honest prince! You didn't understand about the rose and the nightingale, but you could kiss the swineherd for a mechanical music box! Now it serves you right!"

And then he went into his kingdom and closed and bolted the door, so she really could stand outside and sing:

> "*Ach, du lieber Augustin,*
> *Alles ist weg! Weg! Weg!*"

The Nightingale

❖　❖　❖

IN China, you know of course, the emperor is Chinese, and everyone he has around him is Chinese too. Now this happened many years ago, but that is just why the story is worth hearing, before it is forgotten. The emperor's palace was the most magnificent in the world. It was made entirely of fine porcelain, so precious and so fragile and delicate that one really had to watch one's step. In the garden the most unusual flowers were to be seen, and the most beautiful had fastened to them silver bells that tinkled so that no one would go past without noticing them. Yes, everything had been very well thought out in the emperor's garden, and it stretched so far that even the gardener didn't know where it stopped. If one kept on walking, one came to the loveliest forest with great trees and deep lakes. The forest stretched all the way down to the sea, which was blue and so deep that great ships could sail right in under the branches. And in these branches lived a nightingale that sang so sweetly that even the poor fisherman, who had so many other things to keep him busy, lay still and listened when he was out at night pulling in his net.

"Good heavens! How beautiful!" he said. But then he had to look after his net and forgot the bird, although the next night, when it sang again and the fisherman came out there, he said the same thing: "Good heavens! How beautiful!"

From every land in the world travelers came to the emperor's city. They admired the city, the palace, and the garden. But when they heard the nightingale, they all said: "But this is really the best thing of all!" And the travelers told about it when they got home, and scholars wrote many books about the city, the palace, and the garden. But they didn't forget the nightingale—it was given the highest place of all. And those who were poets wrote the loveliest poems, each one about the nightingale in the forest by the sea.

These books went around the world, and once some of them came to the emperor. He sat in his golden chair, reading and reading and nodding his head, for he was pleased by the lovely descriptions of the city, the palace, and the garden. "But the nightingale is really the best thing of all"—there it stood in print.

"What's that?" said the emperor. "The nightingale? Why, I don't know anything about it! Is there such a bird in my empire, in my very own garden? I have never heard of it before! Fancy having to find this out from a book!"

And then he summoned his chamberlain, who was so grand that if anyone of lower rank dared speak to him or ask about something, he would only say: "P!" And that doesn't mean anything at all.

"There is supposed to be a highly remarkable bird here called a nightingale!" said the emperor. "They say it's the very best thing of all in my great kingdom! Why hasn't anyone ever told me about it?"

"I have never heard it mentioned before!" said the chamberlain. "It has never been presented at court!"

"I want it to come here this evening and sing for me," said the emperor. "The whole world knows what I have, and I don't!"

"I have never heard it mentioned before!" said the chamberlain. "I shall look for it! I shall find it!"

But where was it to be found? The chamberlain ran up and down all the stairs, through great halls and corridors. But no one he met had ever heard of the nightingale, and the chamberlain ran back again to the emperor and said it was probably a fable made up by the people who write books. "Your Imperial Majesty shouldn't believe what is written in them. They are inventions and belong to something called black magic!"

"But the book in which I read it was sent to me by the mighty emperor of Japan, so it cannot be false. I will hear the nightingale! It shall be here this evening! I bestow my highest patronage upon it! And if it doesn't come, I'll have the whole court thumped on their stomachs after they have eaten supper!"

"Tsing-pe!" said the chamberlain, and again ran up and down all the stairs and through all the great halls and corridors. And half the court ran with him, for they weren't at all willing to be thumped on their stomachs. They asked and asked about the remarkable nightingale that was known to the whole world but not to the court.

Finally they met a little peasant girl in the kitchen. She said, "The nightingale? Heavens! I know it well. Yes, how it can sing! Every evening I'm permitted to take a few scraps from the table home to my poor sick mother—she lives down by the shore. And on my way back, when I'm tired and stop to rest in the forest, I can hear the nightingale sing. It brings tears to my eyes. It's just as though my mother were kissing me."

"Little kitchen maid!" said the chamberlain. "You shall have a permanent position in the kitchen and permission to stand and watch the emperor eating if you can lead us to the nightingale. It has been summoned to appear at court this evening."

And so they all set out for the part of the forest where

the nightingale usually sang. Half the court went with them. As they were walking along at a fast pace a cow started mooing.

"Oh!" said a courtier. "There it is! Indeed, what remarkable force for so tiny an animal. I am certain I have heard it before."

"No, that's the cow mooing," said the little kitchen maid. "We're still quite a long way from the spot."

Now the frogs started croaking in the marsh.

"Lovely," said the Chinese imperial chaplain. "Now I can hear her. It's just like tiny church bells."

"No, that's the frogs!" said the little kitchen maid. "But now I think we'll soon hear it."

Then the nightingale started to sing.

"That's it!" said the little girl. "Listen! Listen! There it sits!" And then she pointed to a little gray bird up in the branches.

"Is it possible?" said the chamberlain. "I had never imagined it like this. How ordinary it looks! No doubt seeing so many fine people has made it lose its *couleur!*"

"Little nightingale," shouted the little kitchen maid quite loud, "our gracious emperor would so like you to sing for him!"

"With the greatest pleasure," said the nightingale, and sang in a way to warm one's heart.

"It is just like glass bells!" said the chamberlain. "And look at that tiny throat. How it vibrates! It's remarkable that we have never heard it before. It will be a great success at court."

"Shall I sing for the emperor again?" said the nightingale, who thought the emperor was there.

"My enchanting little nightingale," said the chamberlain, "it gives me the greatest pleasure to command you to appear at a court celebration this evening, where you will delight his High Imperial Eminence with your *charmante* song!"

"It sounds best out of doors," said the nightingale, but it followed them gladly when it heard it was the emperor's wish.

The palace had been properly polished up. Walls and floors, which were of porcelain, glowed from the lights of thousands of golden lamps. The loveliest flowers, which really could tinkle, had been lined up in the halls. There was such a running back and forth that it caused a draft that made all the bells tinkle so one couldn't hear oneself think.

In the middle of the great hall, where the emperor sat, a golden perch had been placed for the nightingale to sit on. The whole court was there, and the little kitchen maid had been given permission to stand behind the door, for now she really did have the title of kitchen maid. Everyone was wearing his most splendid attire. They all looked at the little gray bird, to which the emperor was nodding.

And the nightingale sang so sweetly that tears came to the emperor's eyes and rolled down his cheeks. And then the nightingale sang even more sweetly. It went straight to one's heart. And the emperor was so pleased that he said the nightingale was to have his golden slipper to wear around its neck. But the nightingale said no, thank you—it had been rewarded enough.

"I have seen tears in the emperor's eyes. To me, that is the richest treasure. An emperor's tears have a wondrous power. Heaven knows I have been rewarded enough!" And then it sang again with its sweet and blessed voice.

"That is the most adorable *coquetterie* I know of," said the ladies standing around. And then they put water in their mouths so they could gurgle whenever anyone spoke to them, for now they thought that they were nightingales too. Yes, even the lackeys and chambermaids let it be known that they were also satisfied, and that was saying a lot, for they are the hardest to please. Yes indeed, the nightingale had really been a success.

Now it was to remain at court and have its own cage as well as freedom to take a walk outside twice during the day and once at night. It was given twelve servants, too, each one holding tightly to a silken ribbon fastened to its leg. That kind of walk was no pleasure at all.

The whole city talked about the remarkable bird, and whenever two people met, the first merely said "Night!" and the other said "Gale!" And then they sighed and understood each other! Yes, eleven shopkeepers' children were named after it, but not one of them could ever sing a note in his life!

One day a big package came for the emperor. On the outside was written "Nightingale."

"Here's a new book about our famous bird," said the emperor. But it was no book, it was a little work of art in a case: an artificial nightingale made to resemble the real one, except that it was encrusted with diamonds and rubies and sapphires! As soon as the artificial bird was wound up it could sing one of the melodies the real one sang, and then its tail bobbed up and down, glittering with gold and silver. Around its neck hung a ribbon, and on it was written: "The emperor of Japan's nightingale is poor compared to the emperor of China's."

"How lovely!" said everyone. And the person who had brought the artificial nightingale immediately had the title of chief-imperial-nightingale-bringer bestowed upon him.

"Now they must sing together! What a duet that will be!"

And then they had to sing together, but it didn't really come off because the real nightingale sang in its own way and the artificial bird worked mechanically.

"It is not to blame," said the music master. "It keeps time perfectly and according to the rules of my own system!" Then the artificial bird had to sing alone. It was as much of a success as the real one, and besides, it was so much more beautiful to look at: it glittered like bracelets and brooches.

Thirty-three times it sang one and the same melody, and still it wasn't tired. People were only too willing to hear it from the beginning again, but the emperor thought that now the living nightingale should also sing a little. But where was it? No one had noticed it fly out of the open window, away to its green forest.

"But what kind of behavior is that?" said the emperor. And all the courtiers berated it and said the nightingale was a most ungrateful bird.

"We still have the best bird," they said, and again the artificial bird had to sing. And it was the thirty-fourth time they had heard the same tune, but they didn't know it all the way through yet, for it was so hard. And the music master praised the bird very highly—yes, even assured them that it was better than the real nightingale, not only as far as its clothes and the many diamonds were concerned, but internally as well.

"You see, my lords and ladies, and your Imperial Majesty above all! You can never figure out what the real nightingale will sing, but with the artificial bird everything has already been decided. This is the way it will be, and not otherwise. It can be accounted for; it can be opened up to reveal the human logic that has gone into the arrangement of the works, how they operate and how they turn one after the other!"

"Those are my thoughts precisely!" they all said. And on the following Sunday the music master was allowed to show the bird to the people. They were also going to hear it sing, said the emperor. And they heard it and were as happy as if they had all drunk themselves merry on tea, for that is so very Chinese. And then they all said "Oh" and held their index fingers high in the air and nodded. But the poor fisherman, who had heard the real nightingale, said: "It sounds pretty enough, and it is similar too. But something is missing. I don't know what it is."

The real nightingale was banished from the land.

The artificial bird had its place on a silken pillow close to the emperor's bed. All the gifts it had received, gold and precious stones, lay around it, and its title had risen to high-imperial-bedside-table-singer. It ranked Number One on the left, for the emperor considered the side where the heart lies to be the most important. And the heart of an emperor is on the left side too. The music master wrote a treatise in twenty-five volumes about the artificial bird. It was very learned and very long and contained the biggest Chinese words, and all the people said they had read and understood it, for otherwise they would have been considered stupid and would have been thumped on their stomachs.

It went on like this for a whole year. The emperor, the

court, and all the other Chinese knew every little "cluck" in the song of the artificial bird by heart. But this is why they prized it so highly now: they could sing along with it themselves, and this they did! The street boys sang "Zizizi! Cluck-cluck-cluck!" And the emperor sang it too. Yes, it was certainly lovely.

But one evening, as the artificial bird was singing away and the emperor was lying in bed listening to it, something went "Pop!" inside the bird. "Whirrrrrrrrrrrr!" All the wheels went around, and then the music stopped.

The emperor sprang out of bed and had his personal physician summoned. But what good was he? Then they summoned the watchmaker, and after much talk and many examinations of the bird he put it more or less in order again. But he said it must be used as sparingly as possible. The cogs were so worn down that it wasn't possible to put in new ones in a way that would be sure to make music. What a great affliction this was! Only once a year did they dare let the artificial bird sing, and even that was hard on it. But then the music master made a little speech, with big words, and said it was just as good as new, and then it *was* just as good as new.

Five years passed, and then a great sorrow fell upon the land. They were all fond of their emperor, but now he was sick and it was said he could not live. A new emperor had already been picked out, and people stood out in the street and asked the chamberlain how their emperor was.

"P!" he said, and shook his head.

Cold and pale, the emperor lay in his great magnificent bed. The whole court thought he was dead, and they all ran off to greet the new emperor. The lackeys ran out to talk about it, and the chambermaids had a big tea party. Cloths had been put down in all the halls and corridors to deaden the sound of footsteps. And now it was so quiet, so quiet. But the emperor was not yet dead. Stiff and pale, he lay in the magnificent bed with the long velvet curtains and the heavy gold tassels. High above him a window stood open, and the moon shone in on the emperor and the artificial bird.

The poor emperor could hardly breathe. It was as though something heavy were sitting on his chest. He opened his eyes and then he saw that Death was sitting on his chest. He had put on his golden crown and was holding the emperor's golden sword in one hand and his magnificent banner in the other. All around from the folds of the velvet curtains strange faces were peering out. Some were quite hideous, others so kindly and mild. These were all the emperor's good and wicked deeds that were looking at him now that Death was sitting on his heart.

"Do you remember that?" whispered one after the other. "Do you remember that?" And then they told him so much that the sweat stood out on his forehead.

"I never knew that!" said the emperor. "Music! Music! The big Chinese drum!" he shouted. "So I don't have to hear all the things they're saying!"

But they kept it up, and Death nodded, just the way the Chinese do, at everything that was being said.

"Music! Music!" shrieked the emperor. "Blessed little golden bird, sing now! Sing! I've given you gold and costly presents. I myself hung my golden slipper around your neck. Sing now! Sing!"

But the bird kept silent. There was no one to wind it up, so it didn't sing. But Death kept on looking at the emperor out of his big empty sockets, and it was so quiet, so terribly quiet.

Suddenly the loveliest song could be heard close to the window. It was the little real nightingale sitting on the branch outside. It had heard of the emperor's need and had come to sing him comfort and hope. And as it sang the face became paler and paler, and the blood started flowing faster and faster in the emperor's weak body, and Death himself listened and said, "Keep on, little nightingale, keep on!"

"If you will give me the magnificent golden sword! If you will give me the rich banner! If you will give me the emperor's crown!"

And Death gave each treasure for a song, and the nightingale kept on singing. And it sang about the quiet churchyard where the white roses grow and the scent of the elder tree perfumes the air and where the fresh grass is watered by the tears of the bereaved. Then Death was filled with longing for his garden and drifted like a cold, white mist out of the window.

"Thank you, thank you!" said the emperor. "Heavenly little bird, I know you, all right. I have driven you out of my land and empire, and still you have sung the bad visions away from my bed and removed Death from my heart! How can I reward you?"

"You have already rewarded me!" said the nightingale. "You gave me the tears from your eyes the first time I sang. I will never forget that. Those are the jewels that do a singer's heart good. But sleep now, and get well and strong. I shall sing for you."

And it sang, and the emperor fell into a sweet sleep, which was calm and beneficial.

The sun was shining in on him through the windows when he awoke, refreshed and healthy. None of his servants had returned yet, for they thought he was dead, but the nightingale still sat there and sang.

"You must always stay with me," said the emperor. "You shall sing only when you yourself want to, and I shall break the artificial bird into a thousand bits!"

"Don't do that!" said the nightingale. "Why, it has done what good it could. Keep it as before. I cannot build my nest and live at the palace, but let me come whenever I want to. Then in the evening I will sit on the branch here by the window and sing for you. I shall sing about those who are happy and those who suffer. I shall sing of good and evil, which is kept hidden from you. The little songbird flies far, to the poor fisherman, to the farmer's roof, to everyone who is far from you and your court. I love your heart more than your crown, and yet your crown has an odor of sanctity about it. I will come. I will sing for you. But you must promise me one thing!"

"Everything!" said the emperor, standing there in his imperial robe, which he himself had put on, and holding the heavy golden sword up to his heart.

"One thing I beg of you. Tell no one that you have a little bird that tells you everything! Then things will go even better!"

And then the nightingale flew away.

The servants came in to have a look at their dead emperor. Yes, there they stood, and the emperor said, "Good morning!"

The Sweethearts
(The Top and the Ball)

❖ ❖ ❖

THE top and the ball were lying in a drawer together
among other playthings, and so the top said to the
ball, "Shouldn't we be sweethearts, as long as we're lying
in a drawer together?"

But the ball, who had been sewn of morocco leather and
who put on just as many airs as a fashionable young lady,
would not reply to such a thing.

The next day the little boy who owned the playthings
came. He painted over the top red and gold, and ham-

mered a brass nail right in the middle. It was a magnificent sight when the top spun around.

"Look at me!" he said to the ball. "What do you say now? Shouldn't we be sweethearts? We go so well together. You spring and I dance! Happier than we no two could ever be!"

"So that's what you think!" said the ball. "I daresay you're unaware that my father and mother have been morocco leather slippers and that I have a cork inside!"

"Yes, but I am made of mahogany wood!" said the top. "And the bailiff himself has turned me out! He has his own lathe, and it afforded him great pleasure!"

"Indeed! Can I rely on that?" said the ball.

"May I never be whipped again if I'm lying!" said the top.

"You speak up quite well for yourself," said the ball, "but I can't, all the same. I'm as good as half engaged to a swallow. Every time I go up in the air he sticks his head out of the nest and says, 'Will you? Will you?' And now I've said yes to myself, and that's as good as being half engaged. But I promise I shall never forget you!"

"Well, that'll be a great help!" said the top, and then they stopped speaking to each other.

The next day the ball was taken out. The top saw how she flew high up in the air, just like a bird. At last she couldn't be seen at all. She came back again every time, but she always made a high jump when she touched the ground. And this came either from longing or because she had a cork inside. The ninth time the ball disappeared and didn't come back again. The boy searched and searched, but gone she was.

"I know where she is, all right," sighed the top. "She's in the swallow's nest and is married to the swallow!"

Indeed, the more the top thought about it, the more infatuated he became with the ball. Just because he couldn't have her, love began. And the queer thing about it was the fact that she had taken another! And the top danced and spun around, but he was always thinking of the ball, who, in his imagination, grew lovelier and lovelier. Thus many years passed—and then it was an old love affair.

And the top was no longer young! But one day he was gilded over. Never had he looked so lovely! Now he was a golden top, and he whirled until he hummed. Indeed, that was something! But all at once he whirled too high, and gone he was!

They searched and searched, even down in the cellar, but still he was nowhere to be found.

Where was he?

He had hopped up into the trash can, where all kinds of things were lying: cabbage stalks, sweepings, and rubble that had fallen down from the drainpipe.

"A fine place for me to be lying in, I must say! The gilding will soon come off. And what sort of rabble have I come among?" And then it stole a look at a long cabbage stalk that had come much too close and at a strange round thing that looked like an old apple. But it wasn't an apple. It was an old ball that had been lying in the drainpipe for many years, and through which the water had been oozing.

"Heaven be praised! Here comes one of my own kind that I can talk to!" said the ball, and regarded the gilded top. "I'm really of morocco leather, sewn by the hands of a maiden, and I have a cork inside! But no one can tell that by looking at me! I was just going to marry a swallow when I fell in the drainpipe, and there I've been lying for five years oozing water. For a maiden that's a long time, believe me!"

But the top didn't say a thing! He was thinking of his old sweetheart. And indeed, the more he listened, the more certain he became that this was she.

Then the serving girl came to empty the trash can. "Hey, now! There's the gold top!" she said.

And the top came back in the house, to high esteem and

honor. But no one heard anything about the ball, and the top never spoke about his old sweetheart again. That goes over when the sweetheart has been lying in a drainpipe oozing water for five years. Indeed, you never recognize her again if you meet her in the trash can!

The Ugly Duckling

❖ ❖ ❖

IT was so lovely out in the country—it was summer. The wheat stood golden, the oats green. The hay had been piled in stacks down in the green meadows, and there the stork went about on his long red legs and spoke Egyptian, for that is the language he had learned from his mother. Around the fields and meadows were great forests, and in the midst of the forests were deep lakes. Yes, it really was lovely out there in the country.

Squarely in the sunshine stood an old manor house with a deep moat all around it, and from the walls down to the water grew huge dock leaves that were so high that little children could stand upright under the biggest. It was as dense in there as in the deepest forest, and here sat a duck on her nest. She was about to hatch out her little ducklings, but now she had just about had enough of it because it was taking so long and she seldom had a visitor. The other ducks were fonder of swimming about in the moat than of running up and sitting under a dock leaf to chatter with her.

Finally one egg after the other started cracking.

"Cheep! Cheep!" they said. All the egg yolks had come to life and stuck out their heads.

"Quack! Quack!" she said, and then they quacked as hard as they could and peered about on all sides under the green leaves. And their mother let them look about as much as they liked, for green is good for the eyes.

"My, how big the world is!" said all the youngsters, for now, of course, they had far more room than when they were inside the eggs.

"Do you think this is the whole world?" said the mother. "It stretches all the way to the other side of the garden, right into the parson's meadow. But I've never been there! Well, you're all here now, aren't you?" And then she got up. "No, I don't have them all! The biggest egg is still there. How long will it take? Now I'll soon get tired of it!" And then she settled down again.

"Well, how's it going?" said an old duck who had come to pay her a visit.

"One egg is taking so long!" said the duck who was hatching. "It won't crack! But now you shall see the others. They're the prettiest ducklings I've seen. They all look just like their father, the wretch! He doesn't even come to visit me."

"Let me see that egg that won't crack!" said the old duck. "You can be certain it's a turkey egg! I was fooled like that myself once. And I had my sorrows and troubles with those youngsters, for they're afraid of the water, I can tell you! I couldn't get them out in it! I quacked and I snapped, but it didn't help! Let me have a look at that egg! Yes, it's a turkey egg, all right. You just let it lie there and teach the other children how to swim."

"Oh, I still want to sit on it a little longer," said the duck. "I've been sitting on it for so long that I can just as well wait a little longer!"

"Suit yourself!" said the old duck, and then she left.

Finally the big egg cracked. "Cheep! Cheep!" said the youngster, and tumbled out. He was very big and ugly. The duck looked at him.

"Now, that's a terribly big duckling!" she said. "None of the others looks like that! Could he be a turkey chick after all? Well, we'll soon find out. Into the water he'll go if I have to kick him out into it myself!"

The next day the weather was perfect. The sun shone on all the green dock leaves. The mother duck came down to the moat with her whole family. Splash! She jumped into the water. "Quack! Quack!" she said, and one duckling after the other plumped in. The water washed over their heads, but they came up again at once and floated splendidly. Their feet moved of themselves, and they were all out in the water. Even the ugly gray youngster was swimming too.

"That's no turkey," she said. "See how splendidly he uses his legs, how straight he holds himself. That's my own child! As a matter of fact, he is quite handsome when one looks at him in the right way. Quack! Quack! Now come with me, and I'll take you out in the world and present you to the duck yard. But always keep close to me so that no one steps on you. And keep an eye out for the cat!"

And then they came to the duck yard. There was a terrible commotion, for two families were fighting over an eel's head, and then the cat got it, of course.

"See, that's the way it goes in this world," said the mother duck, and smacked her bill, for she would have liked to have had the eel's head herself. "Now use your legs," she said. "See if you can't step lively and bow your necks to that old duck over there. She's the most aristocratic of anyone here: she has Spanish blood in her veins. That's why she's so fat. And see? She has a red rag around her leg. That is something very special and is the highest honor any duck can receive. It means that no one wants to get rid of her and that she is to be recognized by animals and men! Be quick! Out with your toes! A well-brought-up duck places his feet wide apart, just like his father and mother. Now, then! Bow your necks and say 'Quack!'"

This they did, but the other ducks all around looked at

them and said quite loudly, "Look there! Now we're to have one more batch, as if there weren't enough of us already! And fie, how that duckling looks! We won't put up with him!" And at once a duck flew over and bit him in the neck.

"Leave him alone!" said the mother. "He's not bothering anyone."

"Yes, but he's too big and queer!" said the duck who had bitten him. "So he has to be pushed around."

"Those are pretty children the mother has," said the old duck with the rag around her leg. "They're all pretty except that one; he didn't turn out right. I do wish she could make him over again."

"That can't be, your grace," said the mother duck. "He's not pretty, but he has an exceedingly good disposition, and he swims as well as any of the others; yes, I might venture to say a bit better. I do believe he'll grow prettier or in time a little smaller. He's lain in the egg too long, so he hasn't got the right shape!" And then she ruffled his feathers and smoothed them down. "Besides, he's a drake, so it doesn't matter very much. I think he'll grow much stronger. He'll get along all right."

"The other ducklings are lovely," said the old duck. "Just make yourselves at home, and if you can find an eel's head, you may bring it to me!"

And so they made themselves quite at home.

But the poor duckling, who had been the last one out of the egg and looked so ugly, was bitten and shoved and ridiculed by both the ducks and the hens. "He's too big!" they all said. And the turkey cock, who had been born with spurs on and so believed himself to be an emperor, puffed himself up like a ship in full sail, went right up to him, and gobbled until he got quite red in the face. The poor duckling didn't know whether to stay or go. He was miserable because he was so ugly and was the laughingstock of the whole duck yard.

So the first day passed, but afterward it grew worse and worse. The poor duckling was chased by everyone. Even his brothers and sisters were nasty to him and were always saying: "If only the cat would get you, you ugly wretch!" And his mother said, "If only you were far away!" And the ducks bit him, and the hens pecked him, and the girl who fed the poultry kicked at him.

Then he ran and flew over the hedge. The little birds in the bushes flew up in fright. "It's because I'm so ugly!" thought the duckling, and shut his eyes, but he still kept on running. Then he came out into the big marsh where the wild ducks lived. He was so exhausted and unhappy that he lay there all night.

In the morning the wild ducks flew up and looked at their new comrade. "What kind of a duck are you?" they asked, and the duckling turned from one side to the other and greeted them as best he could.

"How ugly you are!" said the wild ducks. "But it makes no difference to us as long as you don't marry into our family!"

Poor thing! He certainly wasn't thinking about marriage. All he wanted was to be allowed to lie in the rushes and to drink a little water from the marsh.

There he lay for two whole days, and then there came two wild geese, or rather two wild ganders, for they were both males, not long out of the egg, and therefore they were quite saucy.

"Listen, comrade!" they said. "You're so ugly that you appeal to us. Want to come along and be a bird of passage? In another marsh close by are some sweet lovely wild geese, every single one unmarried, who can say 'Quack!' You're in a position to make your fortune, ugly as you are!"

Bang! Bang! Shots suddenly rang out above them, and both the wild geese fell down dead in the rushes, and the water was red with blood. Bang! Bang! It sounded again, and whole flocks of wild geese flew up out of the rushes, and the guns cracked again. A great hunt was on. The hunters lay around the marsh. Yes, some were even sitting up in the branches of the trees that hung over the water. The blue smoke drifted in among the dark trees and hovered over the water. Into the mud came the hunting dogs. Splash! Splash! Reeds and rushes swayed on all sides. The poor duckling was terrified. He turned his head to put it under his wing and at the same moment found himself standing face to face with a terribly big dog! Its tongue was hanging way out of its mouth, and its eyes gleamed horribly. It opened its jaws over the duckling, showed its sharp teeth, and—splash!—went on without touching him.

"Oh, heaven be praised!" sighed the duckling. "I'm so ugly that even the dog doesn't care to bite me!"

And then he lay quite still while the buckshot whistled through the rushes and shot after shot resounded.

Not until late in the day did it become quiet, but even then the poor duckling didn't dare get up. He waited several hours before he looked around, and then he hurried out of the marsh as fast as he could. He ran over field and meadows, and there was such a wind that the going was hard.

Toward evening he came to a wretched little house. It was so ramshackle that it didn't know which way to fall, and so it remained standing. The wind blew so hard around the duckling that he had to sit on his tail to keep from blowing away. Then he noticed that the door was off one of its hinges and hung so crookedly that he could slip into the house through the crack, and this he did.

Here lived an old woman with her cat and her hen. And the cat, whom she called Sonny, could arch his back and purr, and he even gave off sparks, but only if one stroked him the wrong way. The hen had quite short tiny legs, so she was called Chicky Low Legs. She laid good eggs, and the old woman was as fond of her as if she were her own child.

In the morning the strange duckling was noticed at once, and the cat started to purr and the hen to cluck.

"What's that?" said the old woman, and looked around, but she couldn't see very well, so she thought the duckling was a fat duck that had lost its way. "Why, that was a fine catch!" she said. "Now I can get duck eggs, if only it's not a drake. That we'll have to try!"

So the duckling was accepted on trial for three weeks, but no eggs came. And the cat was master of the house, and the hen madam. And they always said, "We and the world," for they believed that they were half of the world, and the very best half, at that. The duckling thought there might be another opinion, but the hen wouldn't stand for that.

"Can you lay eggs?" she asked.

"No!"

"Then keep your mouth shut!"

And the cat said, "Can you arch your back, purr, and give off sparks?"

"No!"

"Well, then keep your opinion to yourself when sensible folks are speaking."

And the duckling sat in the corner in low spirits. Then he started thinking of the fresh air and the sunshine. He had such a strange desire to float on the water. At last he couldn't help himself; he had to tell it to the hen.

"What's wrong with you?" she asked. "You have nothing to do. That's why you're putting on these airs! Lay eggs or purr, then it'll go over."

"But it's so lovely to float on the water!" said the duckling. "So lovely to get it over your head and duck down to the bottom."

"Yes, a great pleasure, I daresay!" said the hen. "You've gone quite mad. Ask the cat, he's the wisest one I know, if *he* likes to float on the water or duck under it. Not to mention myself. Ask our mistress, the old woman; there is no one wiser than she in the whole world. Do you think she wants to float and get water over her head?"

"You don't understand me," said the duckling.

"Well, if we don't understand you, who would? Indeed, you'll never be wiser than the cat and the old woman, not to mention myself. Don't put on airs, my child! And thank your Creator for all the good that has been done for you. Haven't you come into a warm house, into a circle from which you can learn something? But you're a fool, and it's no fun associating with you! Believe you me! When I tell you harsh truths it's for your own good, and this way one can know one's true friends. See to it now that you start laying eggs or learn to purr and give off sparks."

"I think I'll go out into the wide world!" said the duckling.

"Yes, just do that!" said the hen.

So the duckling went out. He floated on the water and dived down to the bottom, but he was shunned by all the animals because of his ugliness.

Now it was autumn. The leaves in the forest turned golden and brown. The wind took hold of them and they danced about. The sky looked cold, and the clouds hung heavy with hail and snow. A raven stood on the fence and shrieked "Off! Off!" just from the cold. Merely thinking of it could make one freeze. The poor duckling was really in a bad way.

One evening as the sun was setting in all its splendor, a great flock of beautiful large birds came out of the bushes. The duckling had never seen anything so lovely. They were shining white, with long supple necks. They were swans, and uttering a strange cry, they spread their splendid broad wings and flew away from the cold meadows to warmer lands and open seas. They rose so high, so high, and the ugly little duckling had such a strange feeling. He moved around and around in the water like a wheel, stretching his neck high in the air after them and uttering a cry so shrill and strange that he frightened even himself. Oh, he couldn't forget those lovely birds, those happy birds; and when he could no longer see them, he dived right down to the bottom, and when he came up again he was quite beside himself. He didn't know what those birds were called or where they were flying, but he was fonder of them than he had ever been of anyone before. He didn't envy them in the least. How could it occur to him to wish for such loveliness for himself? He would have been glad if only the ducks had tolerated him in their midst—the poor ugly bird.

And the winter was so cold, so cold. The duckling had to swim about in the water to keep from freezing. But each night the hole in which he swam became smaller and smaller; it froze so the crust of the ice creaked. The duckling had to keep his legs moving so the hole wouldn't close, but at last he grew tired, lay quite still, and froze fast in the ice.

Early in the morning a farmer came along. He saw the duckling, went out and made a hole in the ice with his wooden shoe, and then carried him home to his wife. There he was brought back to life.

The children wanted to play with him, but the duckling thought they wanted to hurt him, and in his fright he flew into the milk dish so the milk splashed out in the room. The woman shrieked and waved her arms. Then he flew into the butter trough and down into the flour barrel and out again. My, how he looked now! The woman screamed and hit at him with the tongs, and the children knocked each other over trying to capture him, and they laughed and shrieked. It was a good thing the door was standing open. Out flew the duckling among the bushes, into the newly fallen snow, and he lay there as if stunned.

But it would be far too sad to tell of all the suffering and misery he had to go through during that hard winter. He was lying in the marsh among the rushes when the sun began to shine warmly again. The larks sang—it was a beautiful spring.

Then all at once he raised his wings. They beat more strongly than before and powerfully carried him away. And before he knew it, he was in a large garden where the apple trees were in bloom and the fragrance of lilacs filled the air, where they hung on the long green branches right

down to the winding canal. Oh, it was so lovely here with the freshness of spring. And straight ahead, out of the thicket came three beautiful swans. They ruffled their feathers and floated so lightly on the water. The duckling recognized the magnificent birds and was filled with a strange melancholy.

"I will fly straight to them, those royal birds, and they

will peck me to death because I am so ugly and yet dare approach them. But it doesn't matter. Better to be killed by them than to be bitten by the ducks, pecked by the hens, kicked by the girl who takes care of the poultry yard, or suffer such hardships during the winter!" And he flew out into the water and swam over toward the magnificent swans. They saw him and hurried toward him with ruffled feathers.

"Just kill me," said the poor creature, and bowed down his head toward the surface of the water and awaited his death. But what did he see in the clear water? Under him he saw his own reflection, but he was no longer a clumsy, grayish-black bird, ugly and disgusting. He was a swan himself!

Being born in a duck yard doesn't matter if one has lain in a swan's egg!

He felt quite happy about all the hardships and suffering he had undergone. Now he could really appreciate his happiness and all the beauty that greeted him. And the big swans swam around him and stroked him with their bills.

Some little children came down to the garden and threw bread and seeds out into the water, and the smallest one cried, "There's a new one!" And the other children joined in, shouting jubilantly, "Yes, a new one has come!" And they all clapped their hands and danced for joy and ran to get their father and mother. And bread and cake were thrown into the water, and they all said, "The new one is the prettiest! So young and lovely!" And the old swans bowed to him.

Then he felt very shy and put his head under his wing—he didn't know why. He was much too happy, but not proud at all, for a good heart is never proud. He thought of how he had been persecuted and ridiculed, and now he heard everyone saying that he was the loveliest of all the lovely birds. And the lilacs bowed their branches right down to the water to him, and the sun shone so warm and bright. Then he ruffled his feathers, lifted his slender neck, and from the depths of his heart said joyously:

"I never dreamed of so much happiness when I was the ugly duckling."

The Snow Queen
(An Adventure in Seven Tales)

❖ ❖ ❖

FIRST TALE:
WHICH IS ABOUT THE MIRROR
AND THE FRAGMENTS

SEE, there! Now we're going to begin. When we come to the end of the tale, we'll know more than we do now, because of an evil troll! He was one of the worst of all, he was the "Devil." One day he was in a really good humor because he had made a mirror that had the quality of making everything good and fair that was reflected in it dwindle to almost nothing, but whatever was worthless and ugly stood out and grew even worse. The loveliest landscapes looked like boiled spinach in it, and the best people became nasty or stood on their heads without stomachs; the faces became so distorted that they were unrecognizable, and if you had a freckle, you could be certain that it spread over nose and mouth. "That was highly entertaining," said the Devil. Now, if a person had a good, pious thought, a grin would appear in the mirror, and the troll Devil had to laugh at his curious invention. Everyone who went to the troll school—for he ran a school for trolls—spread the word that a miracle had occurred: now, for the first time, they believed, you could see how the world and mortals really looked. They ran about with the mirror, and at last there wasn't a land or a person that hadn't been distorted in it. Now they also wanted to fly up to Heaven itself, to make fun of the angels and Our Lord. Indeed, the higher they flew with the mirror, the harder it grinned! They could hardly hold onto it. Higher and higher they flew, nearer to God and the angels. Then the mirror quivered so dreadfully in its grin that it shot out of their hands and plunged down to the earth, where it broke into a hundred million billion—and even more—fragments. And now it did much greater harm than before, for some of the fragments were scarcely bigger than a grain of sand; and these flew about in the wide world, and wherever they got into someone's eyes, they remained there; and then these people saw everything wrong or had eyes only for what was bad with a thing—for each tiny particle of the mirror had retained the same power as the whole mirror. Some people even got a little fragment of the mirror in their hearts, and this was quite horrible—the heart became just like a lump of ice. Some of the fragments of the mirror were so big that they were used as windowpanes, but it wasn't advisable to look at one's friends through those panes. Other fragments came into spectacles, and when people put these spectacles on, it was hard to see properly or act fairly. The Evil One laughed until he split his sides, and that tickled him pink.

But outside tiny fragments of glass were still flying about in the air. Now we shall hear!

SECOND TALE:
A LITTLE BOY AND A LITTLE GIRL

In a big city—where there are so many houses and people that there isn't enough room for everyone to have a little garden, and where most of them have to content themselves with flowers in pots—there were two poor children, however, who did have a garden somewhat bigger than a flowerpot. They weren't brother and sister, but they were just as fond of each other as if they had been. Their parents lived next to each other; they lived in two garrets; there, where the roof of one house adjoined the other, and the gutter ran along the eaves, from each house a tiny window faced the other. One had only to step over the gutter to go from one window to the other.

Outside, the parents each had a big wooden box, and in it grew potherbs, which they used, and a little rosebush; there was one in each box, and they grew so gloriously. Now, the parents hit upon the idea of placing the boxes across the gutter in such a way that they almost reached from one window to the other, and looked just like two banks of flowers. The pea vines hung down over the boxes, and the rosebushes put forth long branches, twined about the windows, and bent over toward each other. It was almost like a triumphal arch of greenery and flowers. As the boxes were quite high, and the children knew that they mustn't climb up there, they were often allowed to go out to each other and sit on their little stools under the roses, and here they played quite splendidly.

During the winter, of course, this pleasure was at an end. The windows were often frozen over completely; but then they warmed up copper coins on the tiled stove, placed the hot coin on the frozen pane, and thus there would be a wonderful peephole as round as could be. Behind it peeped a lovely, gentle eye, one from each window. It was the little boy and the little girl. He was called Kay and she was called Gerda. In summer they could come to each other at one jump; in winter they first had to go down the many flights of stairs and then up the many flights of stairs; outside the snow was drifting.

"The white bees are swarming," said the old grandmother.

"Do they have a queen bee too?" asked the little boy, for he knew that there was one among the real bees.

"So they have!" said the grandmother. "She flies there where the swarm is thickest! She's the biggest of them all, and she never remains still on the earth. She flies up again into the black cloud. Many a winter night she flies through the city streets and looks in at the windows, and then they freeze over so curiously, as if with flowers."

"Yes, I've seen that!" said both the children, and then they knew it was true.

"Can the Snow Queen come in here?" asked the little girl.

"Just let her come," said the boy. "I'll put her on the hot stove and then she'll melt."

But the grandmother smoothed his hair and told other tales.

In the evening, when little Kay was back home and half undressed, he climbed up on the chair by the window and peeped out through the tiny hole. A few snowflakes were falling out there, and one of these, the biggest one of all, remained lying on the edge of one of the flower boxes. The snowflake grew and grew, and at last it turned into a complete woman, clad in the finest white gauze, which seemed to be made up of millions of starlike flakes. She was so beautiful and grand, but of ice—dazzling, gleaming ice—and yet she was alive. Her eyes stared like two clear stars, but there was no peace or rest in them. She nodded to the window and motioned with her hand. The little boy became frightened and jumped down from the chair. Then it seemed as if a huge bird flew past the window.

The next day there was a clear frost—and then a thaw set in—and then came the spring. The sun shone, green sprouts appeared, the swallows built nests, windows were opened, and again the little children sat in their tiny garden way up high in the gutter above all the floors.

The roses bloomed so wonderfully that summer; the

little girl had learned a hymn and there was something about roses in it, and these roses made her think of her own; and she sang it to the little boy, and he sang it along with her:

> "Roses growing in the dale
> Where the Holy Child we hail."

And the children took each other by the hand, kissed the roses, and gazed into God's bright sunshine and spoke to it as if the Infant Jesus were there. What glorious summer days these were, how wonderful it was to be out by the fresh rosebushes, which never seemed to want to stop blooming.

Kay and Gerda sat looking at a picture book of animals and birds. It was then—the clock in the big church tower had just struck five—that Kay said, "Ow! Something stuck me in the heart! And now I've got something in my eye!"

The little girl put her arms around his neck; he blinked his eyes. No, there wasn't a thing to be seen.

"I guess it's gone," he said. But it wasn't gone. It was one of those fragments of glass that had sprung from the mirror, the troll mirror. I daresay we remember that loathsome glass that caused everything big and good that was reflected in it to grow small and hideous, whereas the evil and wicked duly stood out, and every flaw in a thing was noticeable at once. Poor Kay! He had got a particle right in his heart. Soon it would be just like a lump of ice. It didn't hurt anymore now, but it was there.

"Why are you crying?" he asked. "You look so ugly! There's nothing wrong with me after all! Fie!" he suddenly cried. "That rose there is worm-eaten! And look, that one there is quite crooked! As a matter of fact, that's a nasty batch of roses! They look just like the boxes they're standing in!" And then he gave the box quite a hard kick with his foot and pulled out the two roses.

"Kay! What are you doing!" cried the little girl. And when he saw how horrified she was, he yanked off yet another rose and then ran in through his window away from dear little Gerda.

When she came later with the picture book, he said it was for babies! And if grandmother told stories, he would always come with a "But—" Yes, if he got a chance to, he would walk behind her, put on glasses, and talk just the way she did. It was exactly like her, and he made people laugh. Soon he could copy the voice and gait of everyone on the whole street. Everything queer or not nice about them Kay knew how to imitate, and then people said, "He's certainly got an excellent head on him, that boy!" But it was the glass he had got in his eye, the glass that sat in his heart; and that is why he even teased little Gerda, who loved him with all her heart.

His games were now quite different from what they had been, they were so sensible; one winter's day, as the snowflakes piled up in drifts, he took a big burning glass, and holding out a corner of his blue coat, he let the snowflakes fall on it.

"Now look in the glass, Gerda!" he said. Each snowflake became much bigger and looked like a magnificent flower or a ten-sided star. It was a delight to behold.

"Do you see how funny it is?" said Kay. "That's much more interesting than real flowers! And there isn't a single flaw in them; they're quite accurate as long as they don't melt."

A little later Kay appeared in big gloves and with his sled on his back. He shouted right in Gerda's ear: "I've been allowed to go sledding in the big square where the others are playing." And off he went.

Over in the square the most daring boys often tied their sleds to the farmer's wagon, and then they rode a good distance with it. It was lots of fun. As they were playing there a big sleigh came up. It was painted white, and there was someone sitting in it, swathed in a fleecy white fur and wearing a white fur cap. The sleigh drove twice around the square, and Kay quickly managed to tie his little sled to it, and now he was driving along with it. It went faster and faster, straight into the next street. The driver turned his head and gave Kay a kindly nod; it was just as if they knew each other. Every time Kay wanted to untie his little sled, the person would nod again and Kay remained seated. They drove straight out through the city gate. Then the snow began tumbling down so thickly that the little boy couldn't see a hand in front of him as he rushed along. Then he quickly let go of the rope in order to get loose from the big sleigh, but it was no use. His little vehicle hung fast, and it went like the wind. Then he gave quite a loud cry, but no one heard him; and the snow piled up in drifts and the sleigh rushed on. Now and then it gave quite a jump, as if he were flying over ditches and fences. He was scared stiff; he wanted to say the Lord's Prayer, but the only thing he could remember was the Big Multiplication Table.

The snowflakes grew bigger and bigger; at last they looked like huge white hens; suddenly they sprang aside. The big sleigh stopped, and the one who was driving it stood up—the furs and cap were all of snow. It was a lady, so tall and straight, so shining white. It was the Snow Queen.

"We've made good progress," she said. "But is it freezing? Crawl into my bearskin." And then she seated him in the sleigh with her and wrapped the fur around him; it was as if he were sinking into a snowdrift.

"Are you still freezing?" she asked, and then she kissed him on the forehead. Ugh! That was colder than ice; it went straight to his heart, which of course was half a lump of ice already. He felt as if he were going to die—but only for a moment, then it only did him good; he no longer felt the cold around him.

"My sled! Don't forget my sled!" Only then did he remember it, and it was tied to one of the white hens. And it flew along behind with the sled on its back. The Snow Queen kissed Kay once again, and by then he had forgotten little Gerda and grandmother and all of them at home.

"Now you're not getting any more kisses," she said, "or else I'd kiss you to death!"

Kay looked at her; she was so very beautiful. A wiser, lovelier face he couldn't imagine; and now she didn't seem to be of ice, as she had seemed that time she had sat outside his window and motioned to him. In his eyes she was perfect, nor did he feel afraid at all. He told her that he knew how to do mental arithmetic, and with fractions, at that; and he knew the square mileage of the countries and "how many inhabitants." And she always smiled. Then it occurred to him that what he knew still wasn't enough. And he looked up into the vast expanse of sky. And she flew with him, flew high up on the black cloud; and the storm whistled and roared—it was like singing the old lays. They flew over forests and lakes, over sea and land; down below the icy blast whistled, the wolves howled, the snow sparkled. Over it flew the black screeching crows, but up above the moon shone so big and bright; and Kay looked at it all through the long winter night. By day he slept at the Snow Queen's feet.

THIRD TALE: THE FLOWER GARDEN OF THE WOMAN WHO WAS VERSED IN SORCERY

But how did little Gerda get on when Kay didn't come back again? Where was he after all? Nobody knew. Nobody could send word. The boys related only that they had seen him tie his little sled to a beautiful big sleigh,

which drove into the street and out of the city gate. Nobody knew where he was; many tears flowed and little Gerda cried hard and long. Then they said that he was dead, that he had fallen in the river that flowed close by the city. Oh, what truly long dark winter days they were.

Now the spring came and warmer sunshine.

"Kay is dead and gone!" said little Gerda.

"I don't think so!" said the sunshine.

"He's dead and gone!" she said to the swallows.

"I don't think so," they replied, and at last little Gerda didn't think so, either.

"I'm going to put on my new red shoes," she said early one morning, "the ones that Kay has never seen, and then I'll go down to the river and ask it too!"

It was quite early. She kissed the old grandmother, who was sleeping, put on the red shoes, and walked quite alone out of the gate to the river.

"Is it true that you've taken my little playmate? I'll make you a present of my red shoes if you'll give him back to me again!"

And it seemed to her that the billows nodded so strangely. Then she took her red shoes, the dearest things she owned, and threw them both out into the river. But they fell close to the shore, and the little billows carried them back on land to her right away. It was just as if the river didn't want to take the dearest things she owned. Then it didn't have little Kay after all. But now she thought she hadn't thrown the shoes out far enough, and so she climbed into a boat that was lying among the rushes. She went all the way out to the farthest end and threw the shoes, but the boat wasn't tied fast, and her movement made it glide from land. She noticed it and hastened to get out, but before she reached the back of the boat, it was more than an alen out from shore and now it glided faster away.

Then little Gerda became quite frightened and started to cry, but nobody heard her except the sparrows, and they couldn't carry her to land. But they flew along the shore and sang, as if to comfort her: "Here we are! Here we are!" The boat drifted with the stream. Little Gerda sat quite still in just her stockings; her little red shoes floated along behind, but they couldn't catch up with the boat, which gathered greater speed.

It was lovely on both shores, with beautiful flowers, old trees, and slopes with sheep and cows, but not a person was to be seen.

"Maybe the river is carrying me to little Kay," thought Gerda, and this put her in better spirits. She stood up and gazed at the beautiful green shores for many hours. Then she came to a big cherry orchard, where there was a little house with curious red and blue windows and—come to think of it—a thatched roof and two wooden soldiers outside who shouldered arms to those who sailed by.

Gerda shouted to them—she thought they were alive—but naturally they didn't answer; she came close to them, for the boat drifted right in to shore.

Gerda shouted even louder, and then out of the house came an old old woman leaning on a crooked staff. She was wearing a big sun hat, which had the loveliest flowers painted on it.

"You poor little child!" said the old woman. "However did you come out on that great strong stream and drift so far out into the wide world?" And then the old woman went all the way out in the water, hooked the boat with her staff, pulled it to land, and lifted little Gerda out.

And Gerda was glad to be on dry land, but, all the same, a little afraid of the strange old woman.

"Come, now, and tell me who you are and how you came here," she said.

And Gerda told her everything, and the old woman shook her head and said, "Hm! Hm!" And when Gerda had told her everything and asked if she hadn't seen little Kay, the old woman said that he hadn't come by, but he'd be along, all right; she just shouldn't be grieved, but should taste her cherries and look at her flowers—they were prettier than any picture book and each one could tell a complete story. Then she took Gerda by the hand; they went into the little house and the old woman locked the door.

The windows were so high up, and the panes were red, blue, and yellow. The daylight shone in so strangely there with all the colors, but on the table stood the loveliest cherries, and Gerda ate as many as she liked, for this she dared to do. And while she ate, the old woman combed her hair with a golden comb, and the yellow hair curled and shone so delightfully around the lovely little face, which was so round and looked like a rose.

"I've been really longing for such a sweet little girl!" said the old woman. "Now you shall see how well we two are going to get along!" And as she combed little Gerda's hair Gerda forgot her playmate, little Kay. For the old woman was versed in sorcery, but she wasn't a wicked sorceress, she only did a little conjuring for her own pleasure, and now she so wanted to keep little Gerda. And so she went out in the garden and held out her crooked staff at all the rosebushes, and no matter how beautifully they were blooming, they sank down into the black earth, and no one could see where they had stood. The old woman was afraid that when Gerda saw the roses, she would think of her own and then remember little Kay and run away.

Now she led Gerda out in the flower garden. My, how fragrant and lovely it was here! Every conceivable flower, for every season of the year, stood here blooming magnificently. No picture book could be gayer or lovelier. Gerda sprang about for joy and played until the sun went down behind the tall cherry trees. Then she was given a lovely bed with red silken coverlets; they were stuffed with blue violets, and she slept there and dreamed as delightfully as any queen on her wedding day.

The next day she could again play with the flowers in the warm sunshine—and so many days passed. Gerda knew every flower, but no matter how many there were, it still seemed to her that one was missing. But which one it was she didn't know. Then one day she was sitting, looking at the old woman's sun hat with the painted flowers on it, and the prettiest one of all was a rose. The old woman had forgotten to take it off the hat when the other flowers had sunk down in the ground. But that's the way it goes when one is absentminded.

"What?" said Gerda. "Aren't there any roses here?" And she ran in among the flower beds, searching and searching; but her hot tears fell on the very spot where a rosebush had sunk, and as the warm tears moistened the ground the tree suddenly shot up as full of blossoms as when it had sunk. And Gerda threw her arms around it, kissed the roses, and thought of the lovely roses at home and of little Kay.

"Oh, how I've been delayed!" said the little girl. "Why, I was going to find Kay! Don't you know where he is?" she asked the roses. "Do you think he's dead and gone?"

"He's not dead," said the roses. "To be sure, we've been in the ground, where all the dead are, but Kay wasn't there."

"Thank you!" said little Gerda, and she went over to the other flowers and looked into their chalices and asked: "Don't you know where little Kay is?"

But each flower was standing in the sunshine and dreaming of its own fairy tale or history; little Gerda was told so very many of these, but no one knew anything about Kay.

And then what did the tiger lily say?

"Do you hear the drum? Boom! Boom! There are only two notes—always 'Boom! Boom!' Listen to the dirge of the women! Listen to the cry of the priests! In her long red kirtle, the Hindu wife stands on the pyre, as the flames leap up about her and her dead husband. But the Hindu wife is thinking of the one still alive here in the ring, the one whose eyes burn hotter than the flames, the one whose burning eyes come closer to her heart than the flames that will soon burn her body to ashes. Can the flames of the heart die in the flames of the pyre?"

"I don't understand that at all!" said little Gerda.

"That's my story!" said the tiger lily.

What does the convolvulus say?

"Overhanging the narrow mountain trail is an old baronial castle; the thick periwinkles grow up around the ancient red walls, leaf for leaf about the balcony, and there stands a lovely girl. She leans out over the balustrade and peers at the road. No rose hangs fresher on its branch than she. No apple blossom borne by the wind from the tree is more graceful than she; how the magnificent kirtle rustles! 'Isn't he coming after all!' "

"Is it Kay you mean?" asked Little Gerda.

"I'm speaking only about my tale, my dream," replied the convolvulus.

What does the little snowdrop say?

"Between the trees the long board is hanging by ropes; it is a swing. Two lovely little girls—their dresses are as white as snow, long green silken ribbons are fluttering from their hats—sit swinging. Their brother, who is bigger than they are, is standing up in the swing. He has his arm around the rope to hold on with, for in one hand he has a little bowl and in the other a clay pipe; he is blowing soap bubbles; the swing is moving and the bubbles are soaring with lovely changing colors. The last one is still hanging to the pipe stem and bobbing in the wind; the swing is moving. The little black dog, as lightly as the bubbles, stands up on its hind legs and wants to get on the swing; it soars, the dog tumbles down with an angry bark, it is teased, the bubbles burst—a swinging board, a picture of flying lather, is my song."

"It may be that what you tell is beautiful, but you tell it so sorrowfully and make no mention of Kay at all. What do the hyacinths say?"

"There were three lovely sisters, so ethereal and fine: one's kirtle was red, the second's was blue, the third's was all white. Hand in hand they danced by the calm lake in the bright moonlight. They were not elfin maidens, but mortal children. There was such a sweet fragrance, and the maidens vanished in the forest. The fragrance grew stronger: three coffins—in them lay the three lovely girls— glided from the forest thicket across the lake. Fireflies flew twinkling about, like tiny hovering candles. Are the dancing maidens asleep or are they dead? The fragrance of the flowers says they are corpses. The evening bell is tolling for the dead!"

"You make me miserable," said little Gerda. "You have such a strong fragrance. It makes me think of the dead maidens. Alas, is little Kay really dead, then? The roses have been down in the ground, and they say no!"

"Dingdong," rang the hyacinth bells. "We're not ringing for little Kay; we don't know him. We're just singing our song, the only one we know!"

And Gerda went over to the buttercup, which shone out among the glistening green leaves. "You're a bright little sun!" said Gerda. "Tell me, if you know, where I shall find my playmate."

And the buttercup shone so prettily and looked back at Gerda. Which song, by chance, could the buttercup sing? That wasn't about Kay, either.

"In a little yard Our Lord's sun was shining so warmly on the first day of spring. The beams glided down along the neighbor's white wall; close by grew the first yellow flowers, shining gold in the warm sunbeams. Old granny was out in her chair; the granddaughter—the poor, beautiful serving maid—was home on a short visit. She kissed her grandmother. There was gold, a heart of gold in that blessed kiss. Gold on the lips, gold on the ground, gold in the morning all around. See, that's my story!" said the buttercup.

"My poor old grandmother!" sighed Gerda. "Yes, she's probably grieving for me, just as she did for little Kay. But I'm coming home again, and then I'll bring little Kay with me. There's no use my asking the flowers. They know only their songs; they're not telling me anything." And then she tucked up her little dress, so as to be able to run faster, but the narcissus tapped her on the leg as she jumped over it. Then she stopped, looked at the tall flower, and asked, "Do you, by any chance, know something?" And she stooped all the way down to it. And what did it say?

"I can see myself! I can see myself!" said the narcissus. "Oh! Oh! How I smell! Up in the tiny garret, half dressed, stands a little dancer. Now she's standing on one leg, now on two! She kicks out at the whole world. She's only an optical illusion. She pours water from the teapot onto a piece of cloth she's holding. It's her corset. Cleanliness is a good thing. The white dress hanging on the peg has also been washed in the teapot and dried on the roof; she puts it on and the saffron-yellow kerchief around her neck. Then the dress shines even whiter. Leg in the air! See how she rears up on a stalk! I can see myself! I can see myself!"

"I don't care at all about that!" said Gerda. "That's not anything to tell me!" And then she ran to the edge of the garden.

The gate was locked, but she wiggled the rusty iron hook, then it came loose and the gate flew open. And then little Gerda ran barefooted out into the wide world. She looked back three times, but no one came after her. At last she couldn't run anymore, and sat down on a big stone. And when she looked around her, summer was at an end. It was late autumn. You couldn't tell this at all inside the lovely garden, where the sun was always shining and flowers of every season were blooming.

"Heavens! How I've held myself up!" said little Gerda. "Why, it's autumn! I dare not rest!" And she got up to go.

Oh, how sore and tired her little feet were, and on all sides it looked cold and raw. The long willow leaves were quite yellow and dripping wet in the fog: one leaf fell after the other. Only the blackthorn bore fruit, but so sour that it puckered the mouth. Oh, how gray and bleak it was in the wide world!

FOURTH TALE:
PRINCE AND PRINCESS

Gerda had to rest again. Then a huge crow hopped on the snow right in front of where she sat. For a long time it had been sitting looking at her and wagging its head. Now it said, "Caw! Caw! Go da! Go da!" It wasn't able to say it any better. But it meant well by the little girl and asked where she was going all alone out in the wide world. Gerda understood the word "alone" very well and felt rightly all that it implied. And so she told the crow the whole story of her life and asked if it hadn't seen Kay.

And the crow nodded quite thoughtfully and said, "Could be! Could be!"

"What? Do you think so?" cried the little girl, and nearly squeezed the crow to death, she kissed it so.

"Sensibly! Sensibly!" said the crow. "I think it could be little Kay. But now he's probably forgotten you for the princess!"

"Is he living with a princess?" asked Gerda.

"Yes, listen!" said the crow. "But it's hard for me to

speak your language. If you understand crow talk, then I can tell it better."

"No, I haven't learned that," said Gerda. "But grandmother could, and she knew Double Dutch too. If only I'd learned it."

"No matter!" said the crow. "I'll tell you as well as I can, but it'll be bad all the same." And then it told what it knew.

"In the kingdom where we are sitting now, there dwells a princess who is exceedingly wise. But then she has read all the newspapers there are in the world and forgotten them—so wise is she. The other day she was sitting on the throne—and that's not so much fun after all, they say. Then she started humming a song, the very one that goes: 'Why shouldn't I wed . . .'

" 'Listen, there's something to that!' she said, and then she wanted to get married. But she wanted a husband who was ready with an answer when he was spoken to. One who didn't just stand there looking aristocratic, because that's so boring. Now she got all her ladies-in-waiting together, and when they heard what she wanted, they were so pleased.

" 'I like that!' they said. 'That's just what I was thinking the other day!' You can believe every word I say is true," said the crow. "I have a tame sweetheart who walks freely about the castle, and she has told me everything!"

Naturally this was a crow too, for birds of a feather flock together, and one crow always picks another.

"The newspapers came out right away with a border of hearts and the princess' monogram. You could read for yourself that any young man who was good-looking was free to come up to the castle and talk to the princess. And the one who talked in such a way that you could hear he was at home there, and talked the best, he was the one the princess would take for a husband! Well, well!" said the crow. "You can believe me, it's as true as I'm sitting here, people came in swarms. There was a jostling and a scurrying, but it didn't prove successful, neither on the first day nor on the second. They could all talk well when they were out in the street, but when they came in the castle gate and saw the guards in silver and the lackeys in gold up along the stairs, and the great illuminated halls, then they were flabbergasted. And if they stood before the throne where the princess was sitting, they didn't know of a thing to say except for the last word she had said, and she didn't think much of hearing that again. It was just as if people in there had swallowed snuff and fallen into a trance until they were back out in the street. Yes, then they were able to speak. There was a line all the way from the city gate to the castle. I was inside to look at it myself!" said the crow. "They became both hungry and thirsty, but from the castle they didn't get so much as a glass of lukewarm water. To be sure, some of the smartest had taken sandwiches with them, but they didn't share with their neighbor. They thought, 'Only let him look hungry, then the princess won't take him!'"

"But Kay! Little Kay!" said Gerda. "When did he come? Was he among the multitude?"

"Give me time! Give me time! Now we're just coming to him. It was the third day. Then a little person, without horse or carriage, came marching dauntlessly straight up to the castle. His eyes shone like yours; he had lovely long hair, but shabby clothes."

"That was Kay!" Gerda shouted jubilantly. "Oh, then I've found him!" And she clapped her hands.

"He had a little knapsack on his back!" said the crow.

"No, that was probably his sled," said Gerda, "for he went away with the sled!"

"That's very likely!" said the crow. "I didn't look at it so closely! But I do know from my tame sweetheart that when he came in through the castle gate and saw the bodyguard in silver and the lackeys in gold up along the stairs, he didn't lose heart a bit. He nodded and said to them, 'It must be boring to stand on the steps, I'd rather go inside!' There the halls were ablaze with light. Privy councillors and excellencies were walking about barefoot, carrying golden dishes. It was enough to make one solemn. His boots were creaking so terribly loudly, but still he didn't become frightened."

"That certainly is Kay!" said Gerda. "I know he had new boots. I've heard them creaking in Grandmother's parlor."

"Well, creak they did!" said the crow. "But nothing daunted, he went straight in to the princess, who was sitting on a pearl as big as a spinning wheel. And all the ladies-in-waiting, with their maids and maids' maids, and all the gentlemen-in-waiting, with their menservants and menservants' menservants who kept a page boy, stood lined up on all sides. And indeed the closer they stood to the door, the haughtier they looked. And the menservants' menservants' boy, who always goes about in slippers, is hardly to be looked upon at all, so haughtily does he stand in the door."

"That must be horrible!" said little Gerda. "And yet Kay has won the princess?"

"If I hadn't been a crow, I'd have taken her—despite the fact that I'm engaged. He's supposed to have spoken just as well as I speak when I speak crow talk. I have that from my tame sweetheart. He was dauntless and charming; he hadn't come to woo at all, only to hear the princess' wisdom; and he found that to be good, and she found him to be good in return."

"Of course! That was Kay!" said Gerda. "He was wise. He could do Mental Arithmetic with fractions! Oh, won't you take me into the castle?"

"Well, that's easily said," said the crow, "but how are we going to do it? I shall speak to my tame sweetheart about it. I daresay she can advise us, although I must tell you that a little girl like you will never be allowed to come in the proper way."

"Oh, yes, so I will!" said Gerda. "As soon as Kay hears I'm here he'll come right out and fetch me."

"Wait for me by the stile there!" said the crow, wagging its head, and it flew away.

Not until it was late in the evening did the crow come back again. "Rah! Rah!" it said. "She asked me to give you her love! And here's a little loaf for you. She took it from the kitchen, and there's bread enough there, and you're probably hungry. It's impossible for you to come into the castle. Why, you're barefoot. The guard in silver and the lackeys in gold wouldn't allow it, but don't cry. You'll come up there after all. My sweetheart knows of a little back stairway that leads to the royal bedchamber, and she knows where to get hold of the key!"

And they went into the garden, into the great avenue where the leaves fell one after the other; and when the lights were put out in the castle, one after the other, the crow led little Gerda over to a back door that stood ajar.

Oh, how little Gerda's heart was pounding with fear and longing! It was just as if she were going to do something wrong, and yet she only wanted to know whether it was little Kay. Indeed, it had to be him; she could picture vividly to herself his wise eyes, his long hair. She could clearly see the way he smiled, as he did when they sat at home under the roses. Of course he would be glad to see her, and he would want to hear what a long way she had walked for his sake and learn how miserable everyone at home had been when he hadn't come back. Oh, how frightened and glad she was.

Now they were on the stairs; there was a little lamp burning on a cupboard. In the middle of the floor stood the tame crow, turning its head on all sides and regarding Gerda, who curtsied the way her grandmother had taught her.

"My fiancé has spoken so nicely about you, my little miss," said the tame crow. "Your vita, as it is called, is also very touching! If you will take the lamp, then I will lead the way. We go here as the crow flies, so we don't meet anyone!"

"It seems to me that someone is coming right behind me!" said Gerda, and something swished past her; it was just like shadows along the wall, horses with flowing manes and thin legs, grooms, and ladies and gentlemen on horseback.

"It's only the dreams!" said the tame crow. "They come to fetch the royal thoughts out hunting. It's a good thing, for then you can have a better look at them in bed. But if you do come into favor, see to it then that you reveal a grateful heart!"

"Why, that's nothing to talk about!" said the crow from the woods.

Now they entered the first hall. The walls were covered with rose-red satin and artificial flowers. Here the dreams were already sweeping past them, but they went so fast that Gerda didn't catch a glimpse of the royal riders. Each hall was more magnificent than the last—indeed it was enough to made one astonished—and now they were in the bedchamber. The ceiling in here was like an enormous palm tree with leaves of glass, costly glass. And in the middle of the floor, hanging from a stalk of gold, were two beds that looked like lilies. One of them was white and in it lay the princess. The other was red, and it was in this one that Gerda was to look for little Kay. She bent one of the petals aside, and then she saw the nape of a brown neck. Oh, it was Kay! She shouted his name quite loudly and held the lamp up to him. The dreams on horseback rushed into the room again—he awoke, turned his head, and . . . it wasn't little Kay.

Only the prince's nape of the neck resembled little Kay's, but he was young and handsome. And from the white lily bed the princess peeped out and asked what was wrong. Then little Gerda cried and told her whole story and all that the crows had done for her.

"You poor little thing!" said the prince and princess. And they praised the crows and said that they weren't angry at them at all. But still they weren't to do it often. In the meantime they were to be rewarded.

"Do you want to fly away free?" asked the princess. "Or would you rather have permanent posts as Court Crows—with everything that falls off in the kitchen?"

And both the crows curtsied and asked for permanent positions, for they were thinking of their old age, and said, "It's good to have something for a rainy day," as they called it.

And the prince got out of his bed and let Gerda sleep in it, and he could do no more. She folded her little hands and thought, "Indeed, how good people and animals are." And then she closed her eyes and slept so delightfully. All the dreams came flying back in, looking like God's angels, and they pulled a little sled and on it Kay sat and nodded. But they were only reveries, and for that reason they were gone again as soon as she woke up.

The next day she was clad from top to toe in silk and velvet. She was invited to stay at the castle and be in clover, but all she asked for was a little cart with a horse in front, and a pair of tiny boots. And then she wanted to drive out into the wide world and find Kay.

And she was given both boots and a muff. She was dressed so beautifully. And when she was ready to go, a new coach of pure gold was standing at the door. The coat of arms of the prince and princess shone from it like a star, and the coachman, footmen, and outriders—for there were outriders too—sat wearing golden crowns. The prince and princess themselves helped her into the coach and wished her all good fortune. The crow from the woods, who was now married, accompanied her the first twelve miles. It sat beside her, for it couldn't stand to ride backward. The other crow stood in the gate and flapped its wings. It didn't go with them as it suffered from headaches, since it had been given a permanent post and too much to eat. The inside of the coach was lined with sugared pretzels, and in the seat were fruits and gingersnaps.

"Farewell! Farewell!" shouted the prince and princess. And little Gerda cried and the crow cried—thus the first miles passed. Then the crow also said farewell, and that was the hardest leave-taking of all.

It flew up into a tree and flapped its black wings as long as it could see the coach, which shone like the bright sunshine.

FIFTH TALE:
THE LITTLE ROBBER GIRL

They drove through the dark forest, but the coach shone like a flame; it hurt the eyes of the robbers and they couldn't stand that.

"It's gold! It's gold!" they cried, and rushing out, they grabbed hold of the horses, killed the little outriders, the coachman, and the footmen, and then they dragged little Gerda out of the coach.

"She's fat! She's sweet! She's been fattened on nut kernels!" said the old robber crone, who had a long bristly beard and eyebrows that hung down over her eyes. "That's as good as a little fat lamb. Oh, how good she'll taste!" And then she pulled out her burnished knife—and it glittered so horribly.

"Ow!" said the crone at the same moment; she had been bitten in the ear by her own little daughter, who hung on her back and was so wild and naughty that it was a joy to behold. "You nasty brat!" said the mother, and didn't have time to slaughter Gerda.

"She shall play with me!" said the little robber girl. "She shall give me her muff, her pretty dress, and sleep with me in my bed!" And then she bit her again, so the robber crone hopped in the air and whirled around, and all the robbers laughed and said, "See how she's dancing with her young!"

"I want to get in the coach!" said the little robber girl, and she would and must have her own way, for she was so spoiled and so willful. She and Gerda seated themselves inside, and then they drove, over stubble and thickets, deeper into the forest. The little robber girl was the same size as Gerda, but stronger, with broader shoulders and darker skin. Her eyes were quite black, and they looked almost mournful. She put her arm around little Gerda's waist and said, "They're not going to slaughter you as long as I don't get angry with you. I expect you're a princess?"

"No," said little Gerda, and told her everything she had gone through and how fond she was of little Kay.

The robber girl looked at her quite gravely, nodded her head a little, and said, "They're not going to slaughter you even if I do get angry with you—then I'll do it myself." And then she dried little Gerda's eyes and put both her hands in the beautiful muff that was so soft and so warm.

Now the coach came to a standstill. They were in the middle of the courtyard of a robber's castle. It had cracked from top to bottom. Ravens and crows flew out of the open holes, and huge ferocious dogs—each one looking as if it could swallow a man—jumped high in the air. But they didn't bark, for that was forbidden.

In the big old sooty hall a huge fire was burning in the middle of the stone floor. The smoke trailed along under the ceiling and had to see about finding its way out itself. Soup was cooking in an enormous brewing vat, and both hares and rabbits were turning on spits.

"You shall sleep here tonight with me and all my little pets!" said the robber girl. They got something to eat and drink and then went over to a corner, where straw and rugs lay. Overhead nearly a hundred pigeons were sitting on sticks and perches; they all seemed to be sleeping, but still they turned a bit when the little girls came.

"They're all mine," said the little robber girl, and quickly grabbed hold of one of the nearest, held it by the legs, and shook it so it flapped its wings. "Kiss it!" she cried, and beat Gerda in the face with it. "There sit the forest rogues!" she went on, pointing behind a number of bars that had been put up in front of a hole in the wall high above. "They're forest rogues, those two! They fly away at once if you don't lock them up properly. And here stands my old sweetheart, baa!" And she pulled a reindeer by the horns. It had a bright copper ring around its neck and was tied up. "We always have to keep hold of him, or else he'll run away from us! Every single evening I tickle his neck with my sharp knife—he's so afraid of it!" And the little girl drew a long knife out of a crack in the wall and ran it along the reindeer's neck. The poor animal lashed out with its legs, and the robber girl laughed and then pulled Gerda down into the bed with her

"Do you want to take the knife along when you're going to sleep?" asked Gerda, and looked at it a bit uneasily.

"I always sleep with a knife!" said the little robber girl. "One never knows what may happen. But tell me again now, what you told before about little Kay, and why you've gone out into the wide world." And Gerda told from the beginning, and the wood pigeons cooed up there in the cage; the other pigeons were asleep. The little robber girl put her arm around Gerda's neck, held the knife in her other hand, and slept so you could hear it. But Gerda couldn't shut her eyes at all: she didn't know whether she was going to live or die. The robbers sat around the fire, singing and drinking, and the robber crone turned somersaults. Oh, it was quite a horrible sight for the little girl to look upon.

Then the wood pigeons said, "Coo! Coo! We have seen little Kay. A white hen was carrying his sled. He was sitting in the Snow Queen's carriage, which rushed low over the forest when we were in the nest. She blew on us squabs, and all died save the two of us. Coo! Coo!"

"What are you saying up there?" cried Gerda. "Where did the Snow Queen go? Do you know anything about that?"

"As likely as not she journeyed to Lappland. There's always snow and ice there. Just ask the reindeer, who stands tied with the rope."

"That's where the ice and snow are; that's a glorious and a grand place to be," said the reindeer. "That's where you can spring freely about in the great shining valleys. That's where the Snow Queen has her summer tent, but her permanent castle is up near the North Pole on the island they call Spitzbergen!"

"Oh, Kay, little Kay!" sighed Gerda.

"Now you're to lie still!" said the robber girl. "Or else you'll get the knife in your belly!"

In the morning Gerda told her everything that the wood pigeons had said, and the robber girl looked quite grave, but nodded her head and said, "No matter! No matter! Do you know where Lappland is?" she asked the reindeer.

"Who should know that better than I do?" said the animal, and its eyes danced in its head. "That's where I was born and bred; that's where I frolicked on the snowy wastes."

"Listen!" said the robber girl to Gerda. "You see that all our menfolk are away, but Mama's still here, and she's staying. But a little later in the morning she'll have a drink from the big bottle, and afterwards she'll take a little nap upstairs. Then I'm going to do something for you." Now she jumped out of the bed, flung herself on her mother's neck, yanked her moustache, and said, "My own sweet nanny goat, good morning!" And her mother tweaked her nose so it turned both red and blue, but it was all out of pure affection.

Now, when the mother had taken a drink from her bottle and was having a little nap, the robber girl went over to the reindeer and said, "I'd so like to keep on tickling you a lot more with that sharp knife, for then you're so funny. But no matter. I'm going to untie your knot and help you outside so you can run to Lappland. But you're to take to your heels and carry this little girl for me to the Snow Queen's castle, where her little playmate is. I daresay you've heard what she said, for she talked loud enough and you eavesdrop."

The reindeer jumped high for joy. The robber girl lifted little Gerda up and was prudent enough to tie her fast—yes, even give her a little pillow to sit on. "No matter," she said. "There are your fleecy boots, for it's going to be cold. But I'm keeping the muff, it's much too lovely! Still, you won't freeze. Here are my mother's big mittens; they reach up to your elbows. Put them on! Now your hands look just like my nasty mother's!"

And Gerda wept for joy.

"I can't stand your sniveling!" said the little robber girl. "Now you should looked pleased! And here are two loaves and a ham for you so you can't starve." Both were tied to the reindeer's back. The little robber girl opened the door, called in all the big hounds, and then cut through the rope with her knife and said to the reindeer, "Now run! But take good care of the little girl!"

And Gerda stretched out her hands in the big mittens to the robber girl and said farewell, and then the reindeer flew away, over bushes and stubble, through the great forest, over marsh and steppes, as fast as it could. The wolves howled and the ravens screeched. "Sputter! Sputter!" came from the sky. It was just as if it sneezed red.

"They're my old Northern Lights!" said the reindeer. "See how they shine!" And then it ran on even faster, night and day. The loaves were eaten, the ham too, and then they were in Lappland.

SIXTH TALE:
THE LAPP WIFE AND THE FINN WIFE

They came to a standstill by a little house; it was so wretched. The roof went down to the ground, and the door was so low that the family had to crawl on their stomachs when they wanted to go out or in. There was nobody home except an old Lapp wife, who stood frying fish over a train-oil lamp. And the reindeer told her Gerda's whole story, but first its own, for it thought that was more important, and Gerda was so chilled that she couldn't speak.

"Alas, you poor wretches!" said the Lapp wife. "You've still got a long way to run! You have to go hundreds of miles into Finnmark, for that's where the Snow Queen stays in the country and burns blue lights every single evening. I'll write a few words on a piece of dried cod—I don't have paper. I'll give it to you to take to the Finn wife up there; she can give you better directions than I can!"

And now, when Gerda had warmed up and had something to eat and drink, the Lapp wife wrote a few words on a piece of dried cod, told Gerda to take good care of it, and tied her onto the reindeer again, and away it sprang. "Sputter! Sputter!" it said up in the sky. All night the loveliest blue Northern Lights were burning—and then they came to Finnmark and knocked on the Finn wife's chimney, for she didn't even have a door.

It was so hot in there that the Finn wife herself went about almost completely naked. She was small and quite swarthy. She loosened little Gerda's clothing at once, took off the mittens and the boots (or else she would have been too hot), put a piece of ice on the reindeer's head, and then read what was written on the dried cod. She read it three times, and then she knew it by heart and put the fish in the food caldron, for it could be eaten and she never wasted anything.

Now the reindeer told first its own story and then little Gerda's. And the Finn wife blinked her wise eyes, but didn't say a thing.

"You're so wise," said the reindeer. "I know that you can bind all the Winds of the World with a sewing thread. When the skipper unties one knot, he gets a good wind; when he unties the second, a keen wind blows; and when he unties the third and fourth, there's such a storm that the forest falls down. Won't you give the little girl a draft so she can gain the strength of twelve men and overpower the Snow Queen?"

"The strength of twelve men!" said the Finn wife. "Indeed, that'll go a long way!" And then she went over to a shelf and took a big, rolled-up hide, and this she unrolled. Curious letters were written on it, and the Finn wife read it until the water poured down her forehead.

But again the reindeer begged so much for little Gerda, and Gerda looked with such beseeching tearful eyes at the Finn wife, that the latter started to blink her eyes again and drew the reindeer over in a corner, where she whispered to it while she put fresh ice on its head.

"Little Kay is with the Snow Queen, to be sure, and finds everything there quite to his liking and believes it's the best place in the world. But that's because he's got a fragment of glass in his heart and a tiny grain of glass in his eye. They have to come out first, or else he'll never become a man and the Snow Queen will keep him in her power."

"But can't you give little Gerda something to take so she can gain power over it all?"

"I can't give her greater power than she already has. Don't you see how great it is? Don't you see how mortals and animals have to serve her, how, in her bare feet, she has come so far in the world? She mustn't be made aware of her power by us. It's in her heart, it's in the fact that she is a sweet, innocent child. If she herself can't come in to the Snow Queen and get the glass out of little Kay, then we can't help! About ten miles from here the garden of the Snow Queen begins. You can carry the little girl there and put her down by the big bush with red berries that's standing in the snow. Don't linger to gossip, but hurry back here!" And then the Finn wife lifted little Gerda up onto the reindeer, which ran with all its might.

"Oh, I didn't get my boots! I didn't get my mittens!" cried little Gerda. She could feel that in the stinging cold, but the reindeer dared not stop. It ran until it came to the big bush with the red berries. There it put little Gerda down and kissed her on the mouth, and big shining tears ran down the animal's cheeks, and then it ran back again with all its might. There stood poor Gerda, without shoes, without gloves, in the middle of the dreadful, ice-cold Finnmark.

She ran forward as fast as she could; then along came a whole regiment of snowflakes. But they didn't fall down from the sky, for it was quite clear and shone with the Northern Lights. The snowflakes ran along the ground, and indeed, the nearer they came, the bigger they grew. Gerda probably remembered how big and queer they had looked that time she had seen the snowflakes through the burning glass. But here, of course, they were much much bigger and more horrible—they were alive. They were the Snow Queen's advance guard. They had the strangest shapes. Some looked like huge loathsome porcupines, others like whole knots of snakes that stuck forth their heads, and others like little fat bears with bristly hair—all shining white, all living snowflakes.

Then little Gerda said the Lord's Prayer, and the cold was so intense that she could see her own breath; it poured out of her mouth like smoke. Her breath grew denser and denser until it took the shape of little bright angels that grew bigger and bigger when they touched the ground. And they all had helmets on their heads and spears and shields in their hands. More and more of them appeared, and when Gerda had finished her prayers there was a whole legion of them. And they hacked at the horrible snowflakes with their spears until they flew into hundreds of pieces, and little Gerda walked on quite safely and fearlessly. The angels patted her feet and hands, and then she didn't feel the cold so much, and walked quickly on toward the Snow Queen's castle.

But now we should first see how Kay is getting along. To be sure, he wasn't thinking of little Gerda, and least of all that she was standing outside the castle.

SEVENTH TALE:
WHAT HAPPENED IN THE SNOW QUEEN'S CASTLE AND WHAT HAPPENED AFTERWARD

The castle walls were of the driven snow, and the windows and doors of the biting winds. There were more than a hundred halls, according to the way the snow drifted; the biggest stretched for many miles, all lit up by the intense Northern Lights; and they were so big, so bare, so icy cold, and so sparkling. Never was there any merriment here, not even so much as a little ball for the bears, where the storm could blow up and the polar bears could walk on their hind legs and put on fancy airs. Never a little game party, with muzzle tag and touch paw; never the least little bit of gossiping over coffee by the white lady-foxes; empty, big, and cold it was in the halls of the Snow Queen. The Northern Lights flared up so punctually that you could figure out by counting when they were at their highest and when they were at their lowest. In the middle of that bare, unending snow hall there was a frozen sea. It had cracked into a thousand fragments, but each fragment was so exactly like the next that it was quite a work of art. And in the middle of it sat the Snow Queen—when she was at home—and then she said that she was sitting on the Mirror of Reason and that it was the best and the only one in this world.

Little Kay was quite blue with cold, yes, almost black; but still he didn't notice it, for after all she had kissed the shivers out of him, and his heart was practically a lump of ice. He went about dragging some sharp, flat fragments of ice, which he arranged in every possible way, for he wanted to get something out of it—just as the rest of us have small pieces of wood and arrange these in patterns, and this is called the "Chinese Puzzle." Kay also made patterns, a most curious one; this was the "Ice Puzzle of Reason." To his eyes the pattern was quite excellent and of the utmost importance. This was due to the grain of glass that was sitting in his eye! He arranged whole figures that made up a written word, but he could never figure out how to arrange the very word he wanted: the word "eternity." And the Snow Queen had said, "If you can arrange that pattern for me, then you shall be your own master, and I shall make you a present of the whole world and a pair of new skates." But he wasn't able to.

"Now I'm rushing off to the warm countries!" said the Snow Queen. "I want to have a look down in the black caldrons!" Those were the volcanoes Etna and Vesuvius, as they are called. "I'm going to whiten them a bit; that's customary; it does good above lemons and wine grapes!" And then the Snow Queen flew off, and Kay sat quite alone in the big bare hall of ice many miles long, and looked at the pieces of ice, and thought and thought until he creaked. He sat quite stiff and still—you'd have thought he was frozen to death.

It was then that little Gerda came into the castle through the huge doors of the biting winds; but she said an evening prayer, and then the winds abated as if they were going to sleep, and she stepped into the big bare cold hall. Then she saw Kay. She recognized him, flung her arms around his neck, held him so tight, and cried, "Kay! Sweet little Kay! So I've found you, then!"

But he sat quite still, stiff, and cold. Then little Gerda cried hot tears. They fell on his chest, they soaked into his heart, they thawed out the lump of ice, and ate away the little fragment of mirror that was in there. He looked at her and she sang the hymn:

> "Roses growing in the dale
> Where the Holy Child we hail."

Then Kay burst into tears. He cried until the grain of the mirror rolled out of his eye. He knew her and shouted jubilantly, "Gerda! Sweet little Gerda! Where have you been all this time? And where have I been?" And he looked about him. "How cold it is here! How empty and big!" And he clung to Gerda, and she laughed and cried for joy. It was so wonderful that even the fragments of ice danced for joy on all sides. And when they were tired and lay down, they arranged themselves in the very letters the Snow Queen had said he was to find, and then he would be his own master and she would give him the whole world and a pair of new skates.

And Gerda kissed his cheeks and they blossomed; she kissed his eyes and they shone like hers; she kissed his hands and feet and he was well and strong. The Snow Queen was welcome to come home if she liked. His release stood written there in shining pieces of ice.

And they took each other by the hand and wandered out of the big castle; they talked about Grandmother and about the roses up on the roof. And wherever they walked, the winds abated and the sun broke through. And when they came to the bush with the red berries, the reindeer was standing there waiting. It had with it another reindeer, whose udder was full, and it gave the little ones its warm milk and kissed them on the mouth. Then they carried Kay and Gerda, first to the Finn wife, where they warmed themselves in the hot room, and were told about the journey home, and then to the Lapp wife, who had sewed new clothes for them and put her sleigh in order.

And the reindeer and the young reindeer sprang alongside and accompanied them all the way to the border of the country, where the first green sprouts were peeping forth. There they took leave of the reindeer and the Lapp wife.

"Farewell!" they all said.

And the first little birds began to twitter; the forest had

green buds; and out of it, riding on a magnificent horse, which Gerda recognized (it had been hitched to the golden coach), came a young girl with a blazing red cap on her head and pistols in front. It was the little robber girl, who had become bored with staying at home and now wanted to go North first and later in another direction if she weren't content.

She recognized Gerda at once, and Gerda recognized her! They were delighted.

"You're a funny one to go traipsing about!" she said to little Kay. "I'd really like to know whether you deserve someone running to the ends of the earth for your sake!"

But Gerda patted her on the cheek and asked about the prince and princess.

"They've gone away to foreign lands," said the robber girl.

"But the crow?" asked little Gerda.

"Well, the crow is dead!" she replied. "The tame sweetheart has become a widow and goes about with a bit of woolen yarn around her leg. She complains pitifully, and it's all rubbish! But tell me now how you've fared and how you got hold of him!"

And Gerda and Kay both told her.

"And snip, snap, snee, go on a spree!" said the robber girl, and taking them both by the hand, she promised that if she ever came through their city, she would come and pay them a visit.

And then she rode out into the wide world. But Kay and Gerda walked hand in hand. It was a lovely spring, with flowers and greenery. The church bells rang, and they recognized the high towers, the big city. It was the one in which they lived, and they went into it and over to Grandmother's door, up the stairs into the room where everything stood in the same spot as before, and the clock said, "Ticktock!" and the hands went around. But as they went through the door they noticed that they had become grown people. The blooming roses from the gutter were coming in through the open window, and there stood the little baby chairs. And Kay and Gerda sat on their own chairs and held each other by the hand. They had forgotten the cold, empty splendor of the Snow Queen's castle like a bad dream. Grandma was sitting in God's clear sunshine and reading aloud from the Bible: "Except ye become as little children, ye shall not enter into the Kingdom of Heaven."

And Kay and Gerda gazed into each other's eyes, and they understood at once the old hymn:

> Roses growing in the dale
> Where the Holy Child we hail.

And they both sat, grown up and yet children—children at heart. And it was summer—the warm, glorious summer.

The Darning Needle

❖ ❖ ❖

THERE was once a darning needle who put on such a lot of airs that she fancied she was a sewing needle.

"Now, just mind what you're holding!" said the darning needle to the fingers that took her out. "Don't drop me! If I fall on the floor I'm capable of never being found again, I'm so fine!"

"Well, I wouldn't go so far!" said the fingers, and then they squeezed her around the middle.

"Do you see, here I come with a suite!" said the darning needle, and then she drew a long thread after her—though it didn't have a knot.

The fingers guided the needle straight at the kitchen maid's slipper, where the vamp had been torn and was now going to be sewn together.

"That is degrading work!" said the darning needle. "I'll never go through. I'm breaking! I'm breaking!" And then she broke. "What did I tell you!" said the darning needle. "I'm too fine!"

"Now she's no good for anything," thought the fingers, but still they had to hold her tight. The kitchen maid dripped sealing wax on her, and then stuck her in the front of her kerchief.

"See, now I'm a brooch!" said the darning needle. "I knew very well that I would come into favor. When one is

185

something, one always becomes something." And then she laughed deep down inside, for you can never tell from the outside that a darning needle is laughing. There she sat now, as proud as if she were driving in a carriage, and looked around on all sides.

"May I have the honor of inquiring whether you are of gold?" she asked the pin who was her neighbor. "You're lovely to look at, and you have your very own head. But it is small! You must see to it that it grows out, because not everyone can have sealing wax dripped on his end!" And then the darning needle drew herself up so proudly that she fell out of the kerchief and into the sink just as the kitchen maid was rinsing it out.

"Now we're going on a journey!" said the darning needle. "As long as I don't get lost!" But so she did.

"I'm too fine for this world!" she said as she sat in the gutter. "I'm fully aware of it, and that's always a slight pleasure!" And then the darning needle held herself erect and didn't lose her good spirits.

All sorts of things were sailing over her: sticks, straws, pieces of newspaper. "See how they sail!" said the darning needle. "Little do they know what's behind it all. I'm behind it all! I'm sitting here. See, there goes a stick now. It thinks of nothing but 'sticks,' and it is one itself. There floats a straw—see how it whirls, see how it twirls! Don't think about yourself so much, you'll bump against the paving stones! There floats a newspaper; everything in it is forgotten and still it spreads! I sit patiently and quietly! I know what I am, and this I shall remain."

One day something nearby shone prettily, and so the darning needle thought it was a diamond, but it was a fragment of a broken bottle. And as it was shining, the darning needle spoke to it and presented herself as a brooch. "I daresay you're a diamond, aren't you?" "Well, something like that." And then each one thought the other was quite costly, and so they talked about the arrogance of the world.

"Yes, I lived in a box belonging to a maiden," said the darning needle. "And that maiden was a kitchen maid. On each hand she had five fingers, but I've never known anything as conceited as those five fingers, and yet they existed for the sole purpose of holding me, taking me out of the box, and putting me in the box."

"Did they shine?" asked the bottle fragment.

"Shine? No," said the darning needle. "No. That was arrogance for you! They were five brothers, born 'fingers' all of them. They carried themselves erect, side by side, although they were of different lengths. The outermost one, Thumbkin, was short and fat. He went outside the row, and then he had but one joint in his back and could bow only once. But he said that if he were chopped off of somebody, then the whole of the person was ruined for military duty. Lick Pan made its way into sweet and sour alike, pointed at the sun and moon, and he's the one who squeezed when they wrote. Longman looked over the heads of the others. Ringman wore a golden ring around his belly, and Little Per didn't do a thing and was proud of it. Boast they did and boast they always will, so I went in the sink!"

"And now we're sitting here, glittering!" said the fragment of glass. At the same moment more water came into the gutter; it overflowed, dragging the bottle fragment along with it.

"See, now it has been promoted!" said the darning needle. "I'll stay where I am; I'm too fine, but I'm proud of it, and that is worthy of respect!" And then she held herself erect and thought of many things.

"I'm inclined to believe I was born of a sunbeam, I'm so fine! And then too, the sun always seems to seek me out under the water. Alas, I'm so fine that my own mother can't find me! If only I had my one eye that broke off, I think I could cry—even though I wouldn't do it, crying just isn't done!"

One day some street urchins were poking about in the gutter, where they found old nails, shillings, and the like. It was a messy pastime, but they enjoyed it.

"Ow!" said one, sticking himself on the darning needle. "There's a fellow for you!"

"I'm not a fellow, I'm a miss!" said the darning needle, but nobody heard it. The sealing wax had come off and she had turned black. But black is slimming, and so she thought she was finer than ever.

"Here comes an eggshell sailing along!" said the boys, and then they stuck the darning needle firmly in the shell.

"White walls, and black myself!" said the darning needle. "That's becoming! At least I can be seen! If only I don't become seasick, for then I'll throw up!" But she didn't become seasick, and she didn't throw up.

"It's good for seasickness to have a stomach of steel and to remember that one is a little more than a human being. Now mine has passed over. Indeed, the finer one is, the more one can endure!"

"Crack!" said the eggshell as a loaded cart went over it. "My, how it squeezes!" said the darning needle. "Now I'm going to be seasick all the same! I'm breaking! I'm breaking!" But she didn't break, even though a whole cart load had gone over her. She was lying at full length—and there she can stay!

The Red Shoes

❖   ❖   ❖

T HERE was once a little girl, so delicate and fair; but in summer she always had to go barefoot, because she was poor, and in winter she wore big wooden shoes, so her little insteps turned quite red—and horribly red at that.

In the middle of the village lived old Mother Shoemaker; she sat and sewed, as well as she could, out of strips of old red cloth, a pair of little shoes. They were quite clumsy, but they were well meant, and the little girl was to have them. The little girl was named Karen.

On the very day her mother was buried she was given the red shoes, and had them on for the first time. To be sure, they weren't the sort of thing to mourn in, but she had no others, and so she walked barelegged in them behind the poor straw coffin.

At that very moment a big old carriage came up, and in it sat a big old lady. She looked at the little girl and felt sorry for her, and so she said to the parson, "Listen here, give that little girl to me and I will be good to her!"

And Karen thought it was all because of the red shoes. But the old lady said they were horrid, and they were burnt. But Karen was given clean, neat clothes to wear; she had to learn to read and sew, and people said she was pretty, but the mirror said, "You're much more than pretty, you're lovely!"

Once the queen journeyed through the land, and she took with her, her little daughter, who was a princess. People streamed to the castle, and Karen was there too. And the little princess stood at a window, dressed in white, and showed herself; she wore neither a train nor a golden crown, but she had on lovely red morocco-leather shoes. To be sure, they were prettier by far than the ones old Mother Shoemaker had made for little Karen. After all, there was nothing in the world like red shoes!

Now Karen was old enough to be confirmed. She was given new clothes, and she was to have new shoes too. The rich shoemaker in the city measured her little foot at home in his own parlor, and there stood big glass cases full of lovely shoes and shiny boots. It was a pretty sight, but the old lady couldn't see very well, and so it gave her no pleasure. In the middle of all the shoes stood a pair of red ones, just like the shoes the princess had worn. How beautiful they were! The shoemaker said that they had been made for the daughter of an earl, but they didn't fit.

"I daresay they're of patent leather!" said the old lady. "They shine!"

"Yes, they shine!" said Karen. And they fit and they were bought, but the old lady had no idea that they were red, for she would never have permitted Karen to go to confirmation in red shoes. But that is exactly what she did.

Everybody looked at her feet, and as she walked up the aisle to the chancel it seemed to her that even the old pictures on the tombs—the portraits of parsons and parsons' wives, in stiff ruff collars and long black robes—fixed their eyes on her red shoes. And she thought only of these when the parson laid his hand upon her head and spoke of the holy baptism, of the covenant with God, and said that now she was to be a grown-up Christian. And the organ played so solemnly, and the beautiful voices of children sang, and the old choirmaster sang. But Karen thought only of the red shoes.

By afternoon the old lady had been informed by everyone that the shoes had been red, and she said it was shameful! It wasn't done! And after this, when Karen went to church, she was always to wear black shoes, even if they were old.

Next Sunday was communion, and Karen looked at the black shoes and she looked at the red ones—and then she looked at the red ones again and put the red ones on. It was beautiful sunny weather. Karen and the old lady took the path through the cornfield, and it was a bit dusty there.

By the door of the church stood an old soldier with a crutch and a curious long beard. It was more red than white, for it was red. And he bent all the way down to the ground and asked the old lady if he might wipe off her shoes. And Karen stretched out her little foot too. "See what lovely dancing shoes!" said the soldier. "Stay put when you dance!" And then he struck the soles with his hand.

The old lady gave the soldier a shilling, and then she went into the church with Karen.

And all the people inside looked at Karen's red shoes, and all the portraits looked at them, and when Karen knelt before the altar and lifted the golden chalice to her lips, she thought of nothing but the red shoes; and it seemed to her that they were swimming about in the chalice, and she forgot to sing her hymn, forgot to say the Lord's Prayer.

Now everybody went out of the church, and the old lady climbed into her carriage. Karen lifted her foot to climb in behind her, when the old soldier, who was standing nearby, said: "See what lovely dancing shoes!" And Karen couldn't help it, she had to take a few dancing steps! And once she had started, her feet kept on dancing. 't was just as if the shoes had gained control over them.

She danced around the corner of the church; she couldn't stop! The coachman had to run after her and grab hold of her, and he lifted her up into the carriage. But the feet kept on dancing, giving the old lady some terrible kicks. At last they got the shoes off, and the feet came to rest.

At home the shoes were put up in a cupboard, but Karen couldn't stop looking at them.

Now the old lady was ill in bed. They said she couldn't live. She had to be nursed and taken care of, and Karen was the proper person to do it. But over in the city there was a great ball. Karen had been invited. She looked at the old lady, who wasn't going to live after all, she looked at the red shoes, and she didn't think there was anything sinful in that. She put the red shoes on, too; surely she could do that—but then she went to the ball, and then she started to dance.

But when she wanted to go to the right, the shoes danced to the left, and when she wanted to go up the floor, the shoes danced down the floor, down the stairs, through the street, and out of the city gate. Dance she did and dance she must—straight out into the gloomy forest.

Then something was shining up among the trees, and she thought it was the moon, for it was a face. But it was the old soldier with the red beard. He sat and nodded, and said, "See what lovely dancing shoes!"

Now she became terrified and wanted to throw away the red shoes, but they stayed put; and she ripped off her stockings, but the shoes had grown fast to her feet. And dance she did and dance she must, over field and meadow, in rain and sunshine, by night and by day. But the nighttime was the most horrible.

She danced into the graveyard, but the dead there didn't dance; they had something better to do than dance. She wanted to sit down on the pauper's grave where the bitter tansy grew, but there was no peace or rest for her. And when she danced over toward the open door of the church, she saw an angel there in a long white robe, with wings that reached from his shoulders down to the ground. His face was hard and grave, and in his hand he held a sword, so broad and shining.

"Dance you shall!" he said. "Dance in your red shoes until you turn pale and cold! Until your skin shrivels up like a skeleton! Dance you shall from door to door, and where there are proud and vain children, you shall knock so they will hear you and fear you! Dance you shall, dance!"

"Mercy!" cried Karen. But she didn't hear the angel's reply, for the shoes carried her through the gate, out in

the field, over roads, over paths, and she had to keep on
dancing.

One morning she danced past a door she knew well.
The sound of a hymn came from inside, and they carried
out a coffin decorated with flowers. Then she knew that the
old lady was dead, and she felt that she had been abandoned by everyone and cursed by God's angel.

Dance she did and dance she must. Dance in the dark
night. The shoes carried her off through thorns and stubble, and she scratched herself until the blood flowed; she

danced on, over the heath, to a lonely little house. She knew that the executioner lived here, and she knocked on the pane with her finger and said, "Come out! Come out! I can't come in because I'm dancing!"

And the executioner said, "You probably don't know who I am, do you? I chop the heads off wicked people, and I can feel my ax quivering!"

☞ "Don't chop off my head," said Karen, "for then I can't repent my sin! But chop off my feet with the red shoes!"

And then she confessed all her sins, and the executioner chopped off her feet with the red shoes. But the shoes danced away with the tiny feet, over the field and into the deep forest. ☜

And he carved wooden feet and crutches for her and taught her a hymn that sinners always sing; and she kissed the hand that had swung the ax, and went across the heath.

"Now I've suffered enough for the red shoes!" she said. "Now I'm going to church so they can see me!" And she walked fairly quickly toward the church door. But when she got there, the red shoes were dancing in front of her, and she grew terrified and turned back.

All week long she was in agony and cried many heavy tears. But when Sunday came she said: "That's that! Now I've suffered and struggled enough. I daresay I'm just as good as many of those who sit there in church putting on airs!" And then she went bravely enough, but she got no farther than the gate. Then she saw the red shoes dancing ahead of her, and she grew terrified and turned back, and deeply repented her sin.

And she went over to the parsonage and begged to be taken into service there; she would work hard and do anything she could. She didn't care about the wages, only that she might have a roof over her head and stay with good people. And the parson's wife felt sorry for her and took her into her service. And she was diligent and pensive. She sat quietly and listened when the parson read aloud from the Bible in the evening. All the little ones were quite fond of her, but when they talked of finery and dressing up, and of being as lovely as a queen, she would shake her head.

The next Sunday they all went to church, and they asked her if she wanted to come with them. But she looked miserably at her crutches with tears in her eyes, and so they went to hear the word of God while she went in her little chamber alone. It was just big enough for a bed and a chair, and here she sat with her hymn book; and as she was piously reading in it the wind carried the strains of the organ over to her from the church. And with tears in her eyes, she lifted up her face and said, "O God, help me!"

Then the sun shone brightly, and right in front of her stood the angel of God in the white robe, the one she had seen that night in the door of the church. He was no longer holding the sharp sword, but a lovely green branch full of roses. And with it he touched the ceiling, and it rose high; and where he had touched it there shone a golden star. And he touched the walls, and they expanded, and she saw the organ that was playing; she saw the old pictures of the parsons and the parsons' wives. The congregation was sitting in the ornamented pews and singing from the hymn books; for the church itself had come home to the poor girl in the tiny, narrow chamber, or else she had come to it. She was sitting in the pew with the rest of the parson's family, and when they had finished singing the hymn and looked up, they nodded and said, "It was right of you to come, Karen."

"It was by the grace of God!" she said.

And the organ swelled, and the voices of the children in the choir sounded so soft and lovely. The bright sunshine streamed in through the window to the pew where Karen sat. Her heart was so full of sunshine and contentment and happiness that it broke. Her soul flew on the sunshine to God, and there was no one there who asked about the red shoes.

The Jumpers

❖ ❖ ❖

THE flea, the grasshopper, and the skipjack once wanted to see which of them could jump the highest, and so they invited the whole world—and anybody else who wanted to come—to see the fun. And they were three proper jumpers who came together in the room.

"Well, I'm giving my daughter to the one who jumps the highest!" said the king. "For it's poor consolation that those persons should jump for nothing!"

The flea stepped forward first. He had genteel manners and bowed on every side, for he had spinster blood in his veins and was used to associating with people. And that, after all, means a lot.

The grasshopper came next. He, of course, was considerably bigger, but still he had quite good manners. He was wearing a green uniform, which he had been born with. What's more, this personage said that he came of a very old family in the land of Egypt, and that back home he was prized very highly. He had been taken right out of the field and put in a house of cards, three stories high—all face cards, with the colored side turned in. It had both doors and windows that had been cut out of the waist of the Queen of Hearts.

"I sing so well," he said, "that sixteen local crickets, who have been chirping ever since they were small and have not yet been given a house of cards, were so vexed that they became even thinner after listening to me sing."

Both of them—the flea and the grasshopper—thus gave a good accounting of who they were and why they thought they could indeed wed a princess.

The skipjack said nothing, but it was said that he thought all the more; and the court hound sniffed at him alone because he recognized that the skipjack came of a good family. The old alderman, who had been given three orders for keeping silent, maintained that the skipjack had the gift of prophecy: one could tell from his back whether the winter would be mild or severe, and one can't even tell that from the back of the man who writes the Almanac.

"Well, I'm not saying a thing," said the old king, "but then I always did go about this way and keep my thoughts to myself!"

Now the jumping was to begin. The flea jumped so high

that no one could see him, and so they contended that he hadn't jumped at all. And this was unfair.

The grasshopper only jumped half as high, but he landed right in the king's face, so the king said that was revolting!

The skipjack stood still and meditated for a long time. At last they thought he couldn't jump at all.

"If only he hasn't become indisposed!" said the court hound, and then he sniffed at him again: SWOOOOOOOOSH! The skipjack jumped a tiny, wobbly jump right into the lap of the princess, who was sitting on a low golden stool.

Then the king said, "The highest jump is to jump up to my daughter, for that's the very point! But a head is needed to hit upon such a thing, and the skipjack has shown that he has a head. He has legs in his forehead!"

And so he got the princess.

"Nonetheless I jumped the highest!" said the flea. "But it doesn't matter. Just let her have that contraption of pegs and wax. I jumped the highest! But in this world one needs a body if one is to be seen."

And then the flea went abroad to the wars, where it is said he was killed.

The grasshopper sat down in a ditch and thought over the way of the world as it really is. And then he also said, "What's needed is a body! What's needed is a body!"

And then he sang his own melancholy song, and this is where we have taken the story from. But it could very well be a lie, even if it has appeared in print.

The Shepherdess and
the Chimney Sweep

❖ ❖ ❖

H AVE you ever seen a really old wooden cupboard,
quite black with age and carved with scrolls and foliage? Just such a cupboard was standing in a parlor. It had
been inherited from a great-grandmother and was carved
with roses and tulips from top to bottom. There were the
most curious scrolls, and here and there among them tiny
stags were sticking out their antler-covered heads. But in
the middle of the cupboard had been carved a whole man;
just looking at him was enough to make you grin. And grin
he did—you couldn't call it laughing. He had the legs of a
billy goat, tiny horns in his forehead, and a long beard.
The children of the house called him "Billygoatlegs
Chiefandsubordinategeneralwarcommandersergeant," for it
was a hard name to say, and there aren't many who
receive that title. But to have him carved out was also
something! Yet there he stood! He was always staring over
at the table under the mirror, for there stood a lovely little
shepherdess of porcelain. Her shoes were gilded, her
dress was daintily tucked up with a red rose, and she had
a golden hat and a shepherd's crook. She was delightful!
Close by her side stood a little chimney sweep, as black as
coal, but of porcelain too, for that matter. He was just as
clean and handsome as anybody else—a chimney sweep
was only something he was supposed to be. The porcelain-

maker could just as well have made him a prince, it made
no difference.

There he stood so nicely with his ladder, and with a face
as rosy and as fair as a girl's. And this was really a mistake,
for at least he could have been made a little black. He
stood quite close to the shepherdess. They had both been
placed where they were standing, and as they had been
placed like this, they had become engaged. After all, they
were well suited to each other: they were young, they

were both made of the same porcelain, and they were equally as fragile.

Close by them stood yet another doll, which was three times as big. This was an old Chinaman who could nod. He was also made of porcelain and said he was the little shepherdess' grandfather. But he certainly couldn't prove it! He insisted that he had authority over her, and this is why he nodded to Billygoatlegs Chiefandsubordinategeneralwarcommandersergeant, who had been courting the little shepherdess.

"You'll be getting a man there!" said the old Chinaman. "A man I'm almost certain is made of mahogany. He can make you 'Mrs. Billygoatlegs Chiefandsubordinategeneralwarcommandersergeant,' and he has the whole cupboard full of silver—in addition to what he has in secret drawers."

"I won't go inside that dark cupboard!" said the little shepherdess. "I've heard it said that he has eleven porcelain wives in there!"

"Then you can be the twelfth!" said the Chinaman. "Tonight, as soon as the old cupboard starts to creak, the wedding will be held—as sure as I'm Chinese." And then he nodded his head and fell asleep.

But the little shepherdess cried and looked at her dearly beloved, the porcelain chimney sweep.

"I do believe I will ask you," she said, "to go out into the wide world with me, for we can't stay here!"

"I'll do anything you wish!" said the little chimney sweep. "Let us go right away; I daresay I can support you by my profession!"

"If only we were safely down off the table!" she said. "I won't be happy until we're out in the wide world!"

And he comforted her and showed her where to place her little foot on the carved edges and the gilded foliage down around the table leg. He also used his ladder, and then they were down on the floor. But when they looked over at the old cupboard, there was quite a commotion!

All the carved deer were thrusting out their heads even farther and raising their antlers and craning their necks. Billygoatlegs Chiefandsubordinategeneralwarcommandersergeant hopped high in the air and shouted to the old Chinaman, "There they run! There they run!"

This frightened them a little, and they quickly jumped up into the drawer of the dais. Here lay three or four packs of cards that weren't complete and a little toy theater that had been set up as well as possible. A play was being performed, and all the queens—diamonds and hearts, clubs and spades—were sitting in the first row, fanning themselves with their tulips. And behind them stood all the jacks and showed that they had heads both right side up and upside down, the way playing cards do. The play was about two sweethearts who couldn't have each other, and it made the shepherdess cry, for it was just like her own story.

"I cannot bear it!" she said. "I must get out of the drawer!" But when they were down on the floor and looked up at the table, the old Chinaman was awake and his whole body was rocking—for his lower half was a single lump.

"Now the old Chinaman is coming!" screamed the little shepherdess, and she was so miserable that she fell right down on her procelain knees.

"I've got an idea!" said the chimney sweep. "Let's crawl down in the big potpourri crock that stands in the corner. There we could lie on roses and lavender and throw salt in his eyes when he comes."

"That would never do," she said. "And besides, I know that the old Chinaman and the potpourri crock were once engaged, and there's always a little feeling left when you've been on such terms. No, there's nothing left to do but to go out into the wide world!"

"Do you really have enough courage to go out into the wide world with me?" asked the chimney sweep. "Have you ever thought of how big it is and that we could never come back here again?"

"I have!" she said.

Then the chimney sweep gave her a steady look and said, "My way goes through the chimney. Do you really have enough courage to crawl with me through the tiled stove, through both the drum and the flue? Then we come out in the chimney, and from there I know what to do. We'll climb so high that they can't reach us. And at the very top there is a hole out to the wide world."

And he led her to the door of the tiled stove.

"It looks black!" she said, but still she went with him, through the drum and through the flue, where it was as black as pitch.

"Now we're in the chimney!" he said. "And look! Look! The loveliest star is shining up above!"

And there in the sky was a real star that shone all the way down to them, as if it wanted to show them the way. And they crawled and they crept—it was a terrible way—so high, so high! But he lifted her and he helped her; he held her and pointed out the easiest places for her to put her tiny porcelain feet. Then they came all the way up to the edge of the chimney. And there they sat down, for they were really tired—and so they should be too.

The sky with all its stars was overhead, and the city with all its rooftops lay down below. They could see far around them, so far out into the world. The poor shepherdess had never imagined it was like this. She lay her little head against her chimney sweep, and then she cried so hard that the gold popped off her sash.

"It's much too much!" she said. "I cannot bear it! The world is much too big! If only I were back there again. I have followed you out into the wide, wide world, so now you can just follow me home again if you have any feelings for me!"

And the chimney sweep tried to talk sense into her. He

talked about the old Chinaman, and about Billygoatlegs Chiefandsubordinategeneralwarconmandersergeant. But she sobbed so bitterly, and kissed her little chimney sweep so, that the only thing he could do was to do as she said, even though it was wrong.

And so with considerable difficulty they crawled back down through the chimney, and they crept through the flue and the drum—it wasn't at all pleasant. And then they were standing in the dark stove, eavesdropping behind the door to find out how things stood in the room. It was quite still. They peeked out. Alas! There in the middle of the floor lay the old Chinaman. He had fallen down off the table while trying to go after them, and lay broken in three pieces. His back had come off in one piece, and his head had rolled over in a corner. Billygoatlegs Chiefandsubordinategeneralwarcommandersergeant stood where he always stood, thinking everything over.

"It's gruesome!" said the little shepherdess. "Old grandfather is smashed to bits, and we're to blame! I can never live it down!" And then she wrung her teeny-weeny hands.

"He can still be riveted," said the chimney sweep. "He can be riveted very well. Don't carry on so! After they glue his back and put a good rivet in his neck, he'll be just as good as new and be able to tell us many unpleasantries!"

"Do you think so?" she said. And then they crawled back up on the table where they had stood before.

"See how far we've come!" said the chimney sweep. "We could have spared ourselves all that bother!"

"If only old grandfather were riveted," said the shepherdess. "Can it be too expensive?"

And he was riveted. The family had his back glued, and a good rivet was put in his neck. He was just as good as new, but he couldn't nod.

"You've certainly become high and mighty since you were broken!" said Billygoatlegs Chiefandsubordinategeneralwarcommandersergeant. "Although I don't think that's anything to be so proud of! Am I to have her or am I not?"

And the chimney sweep and the little shepherdess gave the old Chinaman such a piteous look. They were afraid he was going to nod. But he couldn't. And it was unpleasant for him to have to tell a stranger that he would always have a rivet in his neck. So the porcelain people remained together, and they gave grandfather's rivet their blessing and loved each other until they broke into bits.

The Little Match Girl

❖   ❖   ❖

IT was so bitterly cold. It was snowing, and the evening was growing dark. It was also the last evening of the year: New Year's Eve. In this cold and in this darkness a poor little girl was walking along the street. Her head was uncovered and her feet were bare. To be sure, she had been wearing slippers when she left home, but what was the good of that? The slippers were quite big; her mother had used them last, they were so big. And the little girl had lost them when she hurried across the street, just as two carriages went rushing past at a frightful speed. One slipper was nowhere to be found, and a boy had run off with the other. He said he could use it for a cradle when he had children of his own.

There walked the little girl now on her tiny bare feet, which were red and blue with the cold. In an old apron she had a lot of matches, and she carried a bunch in her hand. No one had bought any from her the whole day. No one had given her a single shilling. Hungry and frozen, she looked so cowed as she walked along, the poor little thing. The snowflakes fell on her long golden hair, which curled so prettily about her neck. But of course she didn't think about anything as fine as that. The lights were shining out from all the windows, and there in the street was such a delicious odor of roast goose. After all, it was New Year's Eve. Yes, she did think about that.

Over in a corner between two houses—one of them jutted a little farther out in the street than the other—she sat down and huddled. She tucked her tiny legs under her, but she froze even more, and she dared not go home. She hadn't sold any matches, hadn't received a single shilling. Her father would beat her, and then too it was cold at home. They had only the roof above them, and the wind whistled in even though the biggest cracks had been stuffed with straw and rags. Her tiny hands were almost numb with cold. Alas! One little match would do so much good! Did she dare to pull just one out of the bunch, strike it against the wall and warm her fingers? She pulled one out. Scratch! How it spluttered, how it burned! It was a warm clear flame, just like a tiny candle when she held her hand around it. It was a strange light. It seemed to the little girl that she was sitting before a huge iron stove, with shining brass knobs and a brass drum. The fire burned so wonderfully, was so warming. No, what was that? The little girl was already stretching out her feet to warm them too when the flame went out. The stove disappeared. She sat with a little stump of the burnt-out match in her hand.

A new one was struck. It burned, it shone, and where the light fell on the wall it became transparent like gauze. She looked right into the room where the table was set with a gleaming white cloth, fine china, and a splendid, steaming roast goose stuffed with prunes and apples. And what was even more splendid, the goose hopped down from the platter and waddled across the floor with a fork and a knife in its back. Right over to the poor girl it came. Then the match went out, and only the thick cold wall could be seen.

She lit a new match. Now she was sitting under the loveliest Christmas tree. It was even bigger and had more decorations on it than the one she had seen through the glass door of the rich merchant's house last Christmas. A thousand candles were burning on the green branches, and gaily colored pictures—like the ones that decorate shop windows—looked down at her. The little girl stretched out both hands in the air. Then the match went out; the many Christmas candles went higher and higher; she saw that they were now bright stars. One of them fell and made a long fiery streak in the sky.

"Now someone is dying!" said the little girl, for her old grandmother—the only one who had ever been good to her, but now was dead—had said that when a star falls, a soul goes up to God.

Again she struck a match against the wall. It shone around her, and in the glow stood the old grandmother, so bright and shining, so blessed and mild.

"Grandma!" cried the little one. "Oh, take me with you! I know you'll be gone when the match goes out, gone just like the warm stove, the wonderful roast goose, and the big, heavenly Christmas tree!" And she hastily struck all the rest of the matches in the bunch. She wanted to keep her grandmother with her. And the matches shone with such a radiance that it was brighter than the light of day. Never before had grandmother been so beautiful, so big. She lifted up the little girl in her arms, and in radiance and rejoicing they flew so high, so high. And there was no cold, no hunger, no fear—they were with God.

But in a corner by the house, in the early-morning cold, sat the little girl with rosy cheeks and a smile on her face—dead, frozen to death on the last evening of the old year. The morning of the New Year dawned over the little body sitting with the matches, of which a bunch was almost burned up. She had wanted to warm herself, it was said. No one knew what lovely sight she had seen or in what radiance she had gone with her old grandmother into the happiness of the New Year.

The Drop of Water

❖ ❖ ❖

YOU are familiar, of course, with a magnifying glass, a round spectacle lens that makes everything a hundred times larger than it is. When you hold it up to your eye and look at a drop of water from the pond, you can see more than thousand strange creatures that are otherwise never seen in the water; but they are there and it is real. It looks almost like a saucer full of shrimps frisking about one another, and they are so gluttonous that they tear arms and legs and bottoms and edges off one another—and yet they are happy and contented in their own fashion.

Now, there was once an old man whom everyone called Wiggle-Waggle, for that was his name. He always wanted the best of everything, and when he couldn't get it, he used magic.

One day he was sitting there, holding his magnifying glass to his eye and looking at a drop of water that had been taken from a puddle in the ditch. My, what a wiggling and a waggling there was! All the thousands of tiny creatures were jumping about, stepping on one another and taking bites out of one another.

"Why, how abominable that is!" said old Wiggle-Waggle. "Can't they be made to live in peace and quiet, and each one mind his own business?" And he thought and he thought, but it wouldn't work. And then he had to start conjuring. "I must give them color so they can be seen plainly," he said, and then he poured something resembling a tiny drop of red wine into the drop of water. But it was witch's blood, the very best sort at two shillings. Then all the strange creatures turned a rosy-red all over their bodies. It looked like a whole city of naked wild men.

"What have you there?" asked an old troll who had no name, and that was what was so fine about him.

"Well, if you can guess what it is," said Wiggle-Waggle, "I shall make you a present of it. But it's not so easy to find out as long as you don't know."

And the troll who had no name looked through the

magnifying glass. It really did look like a whole city, where all the people ran about with no clothes on! It was frightful, but it was even more frightful to see how each one shoved and jostled the other, how they nipped and nibbled at one another and dragged one another forth. The ones at the bottom had to be at the top, and the ones at the top had to be at the bottom. "See! See! His leg is longer than mine! Biff! Away with it! There's one who has a tiny pimple behind his ear, a wee little innocent pimple, but it plagues him, and so it shall not plague him anymore!" And they hacked at it and they tugged at him and they ate him for the sake of that tiny pimple. One was sitting there so still, like a little maiden, and desired only peace and quiet, but the maiden had to come forth, and they tugged at her and they pulled at her and they ate her up!

"It's extremely amusing!" said the troll.

"Yes, but what do you think it is?" asked Wiggle-Waggle. "Can you figure it out?"

"Why, that's easy to see," said the other. "It's Copenhagen, of course, or another big city. They all resemble one another, to be sure. A big city it is!"

"It's water from a ditch!" said Wiggle-Waggle.

The Happy Family

❖ ❖ ❖

THE biggest green leaf here in the land is, to be sure, a dock leaf. If you hold it in front of your little tummy, it's just like a whole apron; and if you put it on your head, then in rainy weather it's almost as good as an umbrella, for it's so terribly big. A dock plant never grows alone. No, where one grows, there grow more. It's a great delight, and all that delightfulness is food for snails—those big white snails that fashionable people, in the old days, had made into a fricassee, ate, and said, "Yum! How good it tastes!" because they thought it tasted so delicious. The snails lived on dock leaves, and for that reason the dock plants were sown.

Now there was an old manor house where snails were no longer eaten; they were quite extinct. But the dock plants were not extinct. They grew and grew over all the paths and all the beds. It was no longer possible to cope with them. There was a whole forest of dock plants. Here and there stood an apple tree or a plum tree, otherwise you would never have thought it was a garden. Everything was dock plants, and in there lived the last two exceedingly old snails.

They themselves didn't know how old they were; but they could well remember that there had been many more, that they belonged to a family from foreign parts, and that the entire forest had been planted for them and theirs. They had never been beyond it, but they knew that there was one thing more in the world, called The Manor House. And up there you were cooked and then you turned black and then you were placed on a silver platter. But what happened next no one knew. For that matter they couldn't imagine how it felt to be cooked and lie on a silver platter, but it was supposed to be delightful and particularly distinguished. Neither the cockchafer, the toad, nor the earthworm, whom they asked about it, could give them any information. None of them had ever been cooked or placed on a silver platter.

The old white snails were the most aristocratic in the world, they knew; the forest existed for their sakes, and the manor house existed so that they could be cooked and laid on a silver platter.

They now lived quite happily and secluded, and as they had no children themselves, they had adopted an ordinary little snail, which they reared as their own. But the little one wouldn't grow, for he was ordinary. Yet the old folks, especially Mama—Mama Snail—still thought they could see that he was progressing. And she asked Papa, in case he couldn't see it, to feel the little shell. And so he felt it and found out that Mama was right.

One day there was a heavy downpour.

"Listen to how it rub-a-dub-dubs on the dock leaves!" said Papa Snail.

"Drops are coming in too!" said Mama Snail. "Why, it's running right down the stalks! You'll see how wet it's going to be here! I'm so glad we have our good houses, and the little one has his too! More has certainly been done for us than for any other creatures. It's plain to see that we're the Lords and Masters of the world! We have a house from birth, and the dock forest has been sown for our sakes. I'd so like to know how far it stretches and what is beyond it."

"There's nothing beyond it!" said Papa Snail. "There can be no better place than here where we are, and I have nothing else to wish for!"

"Oh, yes," said Mama. "I'd so like to come up to the manor house and be cooked and laid on a silver platter. All our ancestors have, and you can imagine there's something special about that."

"It's possible the manor house may have fallen down," said Papa Snail. "Or else the dock forest has grown up over it so the people can't come out. There's no need to be in such a hurry, either. But you're always in such a terrible rush, and now the little one is starting too. For three days he's been crawling up that stalk. It gives me a headache when I look up at him!"

"Now, you mustn't fuss!" said Mama Snail. "He's crawling so steadily; he'll be a great joy to us, all right, and we old folks have nothing else to live for! But have you thought of where we're going to find a wife for him? Don't you think that far, far inside the dock forest there might be some of our own kind?"

"I daresay there are plenty of black slugs!" said the old snail. "Black slugs without a house. But that would be such a comedown—and they put on airs! But we could commission the ants to look into it. They scurry back and forth as if they had something to do. They certainly must know of a wife for our little snail!"

"Of course, we know of the loveliest one!" said the ants. "But we're afraid it won't do, for she's a queen!"

"That doesn't matter!" said the old snails. "Does she have a house?"

"She has a castle!" said the ants. "The loveliest ant castle, with seven hundred halls!"

"No, thank you!" said Mama Snail. "Our son is not going into an ant hill! If you haven't got better sense, we'll give the commission to the white gnats. They fly far and wide, in sunshine and in rain. They know the dock forest inside and out."

"We have a wife for him!" said the gnats. "A hundred human paces from here, sitting on a gooseberry bush, is a little snail with a house. She is quite alone and old enough to get married. It's only a hundred human paces."

"Well, let her come to him," said the old snails. "He has a forest of dock plants; she has only a bush!"

And so they fetched the little snail maiden. It took eight days for her to get there, but that was just what was so nice about it—one could tell she belonged to the same species.

And then the wedding was held. Six glow worms shone as well as they could, but otherwise it all proceeded quietly, for the old snails couldn't stand carousing and merry-making. But a lovely speech was made by Mama Snail—Papa couldn't, he was so moved. And then they passed on the entire forest of dock plants to them and said what they had always said: that it was the best forest in the world, and as long as they led honest and unpretentious lives and multiplied, then they and their children would one day come to the manor house, be cooked black, and laid on a silver dish.

And after that speech had been made, the old folks crawled into their houses and never came out again; they had gone to sleep. The young snail couple reigned in the forest and had a huge progeny. But they were never cooked, and they never came onto a silver dish. And from this they concluded that the manor house had fallen down, and that all the people in the world were extinct. And as no one contradicted them, it was true, of course. And the rain beat upon the dock leaves to make music for their sakes, and the sun shone on the dock forest to give color for their sakes. And they were very happy, and the whole family was happy. Indeed it was!

The Collar

❖   ❖   ❖

T HERE was once a fashionable cavalier whose entire inventory consisted of a bootjack and a comb. But he had the finest collar in the world, and it is about the collar that we are going to hear a tale.

Now, the collar was so old that he was thinking of getting married, and then it happened that he was put in the wash along with a garter.

"My!" said the collar. "I've never seen anyone so slender and so elegant, so soft and so cuddly! May I ask your name?"

"I'm not saying!" said the garter.

"Where do you belong?" asked the collar.

But the garter was shy and thought this was an odd question to reply to.

"I daresay you're a waistband!" said the collar. "One of those waistbands that are worn underneath! I can see very well that you're both useful and decorative, little maid!"

"You mustn't talk to me!" said the garter. "I don't think I've given you any occasion to!"

"Oh, yes! When anyone's as lovely as you are," said the collar, "then it's occasion enough!"

"Stop coming so close to me!" said the garter. "You look so masculine!"

"I'm a fashionable cavalier too!" said the collar. "I have a bootjack and a comb!" Now that, of course, wasn't true. It was his master who had them, but he was bragging.

"Don't come near me!" said the garter. "I'm not used to it!"

"Prude!" said the collar, and then he was taken out of the wash. He was starched, hung on a chair in the sunshine, and then placed on an ironing board. Along came the hot iron.

"Madame!" said the collar. "Little widow lady! I'm turning quite warm! I'm becoming quite another! I'm losing my creases! You're burning a hole in me! Ugh—I'm proposing to you!"

"Rag!" said the iron, and went arrogantly over the collar; for it imagined it was a steam engine that was on its way to the railroad to pull carriages.

"Rag!" it said.

The collar was a little frayed at the edges, and so the scissors came to clip off the fuzz.

"Oh!" said the collar. "I daresay you're the prima ballerina! My, how you can stretch your legs! That's the most adorable sight I've ever seen! No human being can ever equal you!"

"I know that!" said the scissors.

"You deserve to be a countess!" said the collar. "All I

have is a fashionable cavalier, a bootjack, and a comb! If only I had an estate!"

"He's proposing!" said the scissors, growing angry. And then it gave him a proper clip, and so he was discarded.

"I daresay I must propose to the comb!" said the collar. "It's incredible the way you keep all your teeth, little miss! Haven't you ever thought of becoming engaged?"

"I'll say I have!" said the comb. "I'm engaged to the bootjack!"

"Engaged!" said the collar. Now there were no more to propose to, and so he scorned proposing.

A long time passed. Then the collar ended up in a box at the paper mill. The rags were having a party, the finer ones for themselves, the rougher ones for themselves—just as it should be. They all had a lot to tell, but the collar had the most—he was a real braggart!

"I've had such a lot of sweethearts!" said the collar. "I was never left in peace! But then I was a fashionable cavalier—with starch! I had both a bootjack and a comb, which I never used! You should have seen me then, seen me when I lay on my side! I'll never forget my first sweetheart! She was a waistband, so fine, so soft, so cuddly! She threw herself into a tub of water on my account! Then there was a widow lady who became red hot, but I let her stand there and turn black! Then there was that prima ballerina, she gave me the scar that I still carry. She was so wild! But my heart bleeds most for the garter—I mean the waistband—who ended up in the tub of water. I have so much on my conscience. It's time I turned into white paper."

And so he was—all the rags turned into white paper. But the collar was made into the very piece of white paper we are looking at here. And that was because he bragged so dreadfully about all the things he had never been. And we should keep this in mind, so that we don't carry on in the same way. For we never can tell if we too won't end up in the rag box and be made into white paper—and have our whole story printed on it, even the most secret, and have to go about and relate it ourselves, just like the collar.

It's Quite True

❖ ❖ ❖

IT'S a frightful affair!" said a hen, and this was over on
the side of town where the business hadn't taken place.
"It's a frightful affair in a hen house! I dare not sleep alone
tonight! It's a good thing there are a lot of us on the roost
together!" And then she went on to tell, and the feathers
of the other hens stood on end and the cock dropped his
comb! It's quite true!

But we will begin at the beginning, and that was in a
hen house on the other side of town. The sun went down
and the hens flew up. One of them—she had white feathers and bandy legs—laid her prescribed number of eggs
and, as a hen, was respectable in every way. When she
came to the roost she preened herself with her beak, and
then a tiny feather fell out.

"There it went," she said. "Indeed, the more I preen
myself, the more beautiful I become!" Now, it was said in
jest, for of all those hens she had the merriest disposition,
but otherwise, as has been said, she was quite respectable. And then she went to sleep.

It was dark all around. Hen sat beside hen, and the one
who sat next to her did not sleep. She heard and she
didn't hear, as indeed you should in this world if you are
to have peace of mind. But still she had to tell it to her
other neighbor. "Did you hear what was said here? I'm

not naming any names, but there's a hen who wants to pluck out all her feathers just to look good. If I were a cock, I'd despise her!"

And right above the hens sat the owl, with owl-husband and owl-children. They had sharp ears in that family. They heard every word the neighbor hen said. And they rolled their eyes, and Mama Owl fanned herself with her wings.

"Just don't pay any attention! But I daresay you heard what was said? I heard it with my own ears, and it'll take a lot before *they* fall off. One of the hens has forgotten what is proper for a hen, to such an extent that she's sitting there plucking out all her feathers and letting the cock look on!"

"*Prenez garde aux enfants!*" said Papa Owl. "That's not for the children!"

"I just want to tell the owl across the way. It's such a worthy owl to associate with." And away Mama flew.

"Whoooo! Hooooo! Whoooo! Hooooo!" they both hooted right down to the doves in the neighboring dovecote.

"Have you heard? Have you heard? Whoooo! Hoooo! There's a hen who's plucked out all her feathers for the cock's sake. She's freezing to death, if she hasn't already! Whoooo! Hoooo!"

"Where? Where?" cooed the doves.

"In the hen yard across the way! I've as good as seen it myself! It's almost an improper story to tell, but it's quite true!"

"Believe! Believe every last word!" said the doves. Then they cooed down to their own hen yard: "There's a hen— yes, some say there are two who have plucked out all their feathers so as not to look like the others, and thus attract the attention of the cock. It's a risky game. You can catch a cold and die of a fever, and they're both dead!"

"Wake up! Wake up!" crowed the cock, and flew up on the fence. Sleep was still in his eyes, but he crowed all the same: "Three hens have died of unrequited love for a cock! They have plucked out all their feathers. It's a dreadful affair! I don't want to keep it! Let it go on!"

"Let it go on!" squeaked the bats. And the hens clucked and the cocks crowed: "Let it go on! Let it go on!" And so the story flew from hen house to hen house, and at last it came back to the spot from which it had originally gone out.

"There are five hens," so it went, "who have all plucked out their feathers to show which of them had grown the shinniest because of an unhappy love affair with the cock! And then they hacked at one another until the blood flowed, and fell down dead, to the shame and disgrace of their families, and a great loss to the owner!"

And the hen who had lost the tiny loose feather naturally did not recognize her own story again. And as she was a respectable hen, she said, "I despise those hens! But there are more of that sort! Such a thing should not be hushed up, and I will do my best to see to it that the story appears in the newspaper. Then it will be known throughout the land. Those hens have deserved it, and their families too!"

And the story did appear in the newspaper; it was printed. And it's quite true: one tiny feather can indeed turn into five hens!

In a Thousand Years

❖ ❖ ❖

YES, in a thousand years they'll come on wings of steam, through the air and across the ocean! America's young inhabitants will visit old Europe. They will come to the ancient monuments here and to places falling to ruin, just as we in our day journey to the smoldering splendors of southern Asia.

In a thousand years they'll come!

The Thames, the Danube, the Rhine, are rolling still: Mont Blanc is standing with a snowy cap; the Aurora Borealis is shining over the lands of the North. But generation after generation has turned to dust, rows of the mighty of the moment are forgotten, like those who already slumber in the mound, where the prosperous flour merchant, on whose land it is, makes himself a bench on which to sit and look out across the flat, rippling fields of grain.

"To Europe!" is the cry of America's young generation. "To the land of our fathers, the lovely land of memory and imagination, Europe!"

The airship comes. It is overcrowded with travelers, for the speed is faster than by sea. The electromagnetic thread under the ocean has already telegraphed how large the air caravan is. Europe is already in sight—it is the coast of Ireland—but the passengers are still asleep. They are not to be awakened until they are over England; there they will set foot on European soil in the Land of Shakespeare, as it is called by the sons of the intellect; the Land of Politics or the Land of Machinery is what others call it.

The sojourn here lasts a whole day; so much time the busy generation has for the great England and Scotland.

On they speed through the Channel Tunnel to France, the land of Charlemagne and Napoleon. Molière is mentioned, the learned speak of a Classical and a Romantic school in the far-distant past, and there is jubilation over heroes, bards, and men of science unknown to our time, but who will be born on the crater of Europe: Paris.

The airship flies on, over the land where Columbus sailed forth, where Cortez was born, and where Calderón sang dramas in flowering verse. Lovely dark-eyed women still dwell in the flowering vale, and ancient songs tell of El Cid and the Alhambra.

Through the air, across the sea to Italy, where ancient Eternal Rome once lay; it has been wiped out, the Campagna is a wilderness. Of St. Peter's Church, only the remains of a solitary wall are shown, but its authenticity is doubted.

To Greece, in order to sleep for one night at the luxurious hotel high on the top of Mount Olympus—just to say they've been there. The journey continues to the Bosporus, to get a few hours' rest and see the spot where Byzantium lay. Poor fishermen spread their nets where legend tells of the harem garden in the time of the Turks.

Remains of mighty cities by the foaming Danube, cities our age never knew, are crossed in flight; but here and there—places rich in memory, those still to come, those yet unborn—the air caravan alights only to take off again.

Down there lies Germany, once encircled by the tightest network of railways and canals—the land where Luther spoke and Goethe sang, and where Mozart in his day wielded the scepter of music. Great names shine out in science and art, names unknown to us. A one-day stop for Germany, and one day for Scandinavia, the native lands of Ørsted and Linnaeus, and Norway, the land of the ancient heroes and the young Norwegians. Iceland is taken on the homeward journey; geysers no longer boil, Hekla is extinguished, but, as an eternal monument to the Sagas, the rocky island stands firm in the roaring sea.

"There's a lot to see in Europe!" says the young American. "And we have seen it in eight days. And it can be done, as the great traveler"—the name of a contemporary is mentioned—"has shown in his famous work: *Europe Seen in Eight Days.*"

The Nisse at
the Sausagemonger's

❖ ❖ ❖

THERE was a real student; he lived in a garret and
owned nothing. There was a real sausagemonger; he
lived on the ground floor and owned the whole house. And
the nisse stuck to him, for here every Christmas Eve he
received a dish of porridge with a big lump of butter in
it—the sausagemonger could afford it. And the nisse remained in the shop, and that was quite instructive.

One evening the student came in the back door to buy
himself candles and cheese. He had no one to send, so he
came himself. He got what he ordered and paid for it, and
the sausagemonger and the missus nodded "good evening." And that was a woman who could do more than
nod: she had the gift of gab! And the student nodded back
and then stood there, engrossed in reading the leaf of
paper that had been wrapped about the cheese. It was a
page torn out of an old book that should not have been
torn to pieces, an old book full of poetry.

"There's more of it lying about," said the sausagemonger.
"I gave an old woman some coffee beans for it. If you'll
give me eight shillings, you can have the rest."

"Thanks," said the student. "Let me have that instead
of the cheese! I can eat the bread and butter plain. It
would be a sin for the whole book to be torn to shreds
and tatters. You're a splendid man, a practical man, but

230

you don't understand any more about poetry than that tub!"

And that was a rude thing to say, especially about the tub. But the sausagemonger laughed, and the student laughed. It was said, of course, as a kind of joke. But it annoyed the nisse that anyone dared to say such a thing to a sausagemonger who was a landlord and who sold the best butter.

When it was night, and the shop was closed and everyone was in bed except the student, the nisse went in and took the missus' gift of gab. She didn't use it when she was asleep. And no matter which object in the room he put it on, it acquired speech and language; it could express its thoughts and feelings just as well as the missus. But only one could have it at a time, and that was a blessing, for otherwise they would have been speaking all at once.

And the nisse put the gift of gab on the tub in which the old newspapers lay. "Is it really true," he asked, "that you don't know what poetry is?"

"Of course I know," said the tub. "That's the sort of thing that stands at the bottom of the page in the newspaper and is clipped out. I should think I have more of that in me than the student, and I'm only a lowly tub compared to the sausagemonger."

And the nisse put the gift of gab on the coffee grinder. My, how it chattered! And he put it on the butter measure and on the till. They were all of the same opinion as the tub, and what the majority agrees upon must be respected.

"Now the student's going to catch it!" And then the nisse went softly up the backstairs to the garret where the student lived. There was a light inside, and the nisse peeped through the keyhole and saw that the student was reading the tattered book from below. But how bright it was in there! From the book shone a clear ray of light that turned into the trunk of a mighty tree that soared so high and spread its branches far out over the student. Every leaf was so fresh, and each blossom was the head of a lovely maiden—some with eyes so dark and radiant, others with eyes so blue and wondrously clear. Each fruit was a twinkling star, and a wonderfully lovely song rang out.

No, the little nisse had never imagined such splendor, much less seen or experienced it. And so he remained standing on tiptoe, peeping and peeping until the light inside went out. The student probably blew out his lamp and went to bed. But the nisse stood there all the same, for the song could still be heard so softly and sweetly—a lovely lullaby for the student who had lain down to rest.

"How wonderful!" said the little nisse. "I never expected that! I believe I'll stay with the student." And he thought—and thought quite sensibly—and then he sighed: "The student has no porridge!" And so he went—yes, he went back down to the sausagemonger. And it was a good thing he came, for the tub had used up almost all the missus' gift of gab by declaring on one side all the things it contained. And now it was just on the point of turning, in order to repeat the same thing on the other side, when the nisse came and brought the gift of gab back to the missus. But from then on, all the inhabitants of the whole shop, from the till to the kindling wood, were of the same opinion as the tub, and so high was their esteem and so great was their confidence in it that from then on, whenever the sausagemonger read the "Art and Theater Reviews" in his *Times*, the evening one, they believed it came from the tub.

But the little nisse no longer sat quietly and listened to all the wisdom and intelligence down there. No, as soon as the light shone from the chamber in the garret, the rays were like a strong anchor rope that dragged him up there, and he had to go and peep through the keyhole. And a feeling of grandeur engulfed him, such as we feel on the rolling sea when God strides across it in the storm. And he burst into tears. He didn't know himself why he was crying, but there was something so refreshing in those tears. How wonderfully delightful it must be to sit with the student under that tree! But that could never happen. He was happy at the keyhole. He was still standing there on the cold landing when the autumn wind blew down from the trap door in the loft, and it was so cold, so cold. But the little fellow didn't feel it until the light was put out in the garret room and the tones died before the wind. Brrrrr! Then he froze, and he crept back down to his sheltered corner where it was so cozy and warm. And when the Christmas porridge came with the big lump of butter in it, well, then the sausagemonger was master.

But in the middle of the night the nisse was awakened by a terrible commotion at the shutters. People were pounding outside! The night watch was blowing his whistle! There was a big fire; the whole street was ablaze! Was it here in the house or at the neighbor's? Where? It was terrifying! The sausagemonger's missus was so upset that she removed her golden earrings and put them in her pocket, just to have something to save! The sausagemonger ran to get his bonds, and the serving maid ran to get her silk mantilla. And the little nisse ran too. In a couple of bounds he was up the stairs and in the room of the student, who was standing quite calmly at the open window, watching the fire in the house across the way. The little nisse grabbed the wonderful book on the table, put it in his red cap, and held onto it with both hands. The greatest treasure of the house was saved! And then he rushed all the way out on the roof, all the way up to the chimney. And there he sat, lit up by the burning house right in front of him. And with both hands he held onto his red cap with the treasure in it. Now he knew where his heart lay, to whom he really belonged. But then, when the fire had been put out and he had regained his composure—well, "I'll divide myself between them!" he said. "I can't give up the sausagemonger completely for the sake of the porridge!"

And that was quite human! The rest of us also go to the sausagemonger—for the porridge!

Two Virgins

❖ ❖ ❖

HAVE you ever seen a virgin? That is to say, what the street pavers call a virgin: something to pound down the cobblestones with. She is solid wood, broad at the bottom with iron rings all around, and small at the top with a stick for her arms.

Two such virgins stood in the tool yard. They stood among shovels, cordwood measures, and wheelbarrows, and it had been rumored there that the virgin was no longer going to be called a virgin, but a "stamper" instead. And this is the latest and only correct term in the street-paver language for what, in days gone by, we all called a virgin.

Now, among us mortals there exist "emancipated females," among which are included headmistresses of institutions, midwives, dancers (who, by virtue of their office, can stand on one leg), modistes, and night nurses; and behind these ranks of "The Emancipated," the two virgins in the tool yard also ranged themselves. They were Virgins of the Highway Authority, and under no circumstances were they going to give up their good old name and allow themselves to be called stampers!

"Virgin is a human name," they said, "but a stamper is a thing, and we will not allow ourselves to be called a thing. That is the same as being called names."

"My fiancé is capable of breaking up with me," said the youngest, who was engaged to a pile driver, one of those big machines that drives down piles and consequently does on a large scale what the virgin does on a small one. "He will have me as a virgin, but he might not as a stamper, and so I cannot permit them to rechristen me."

"Yes, I'd sooner have my two arms broken off!" said the eldest.

The wheelbarrow, on the other hand, was of another opinion, and the wheelbarrow regarded itself as one-fourth a cart because it went on one wheel.

"I must indeed tell you that to be called a virgin is fairly commonplace, and not nearly as fine as being called a stamper; for in being called by that name one joins the rank of the signets, and think of the Signet of the Law. This is what affixes the judicial seal. In your place I would give up the virgin!"

"Never! I am too old for that!" said the eldest.

"You are certainly not aware of something called 'The European Necessity,' " said the honest old cordwood measure. "One must be kept within bounds, subordinate oneself; one must yield to time and necessity. And if there is a law that the virgin is to be called a stamper, then she must be called a stamper. Everything has a standard by which it is measured."

"Then if worst comes to worst," said the youngest, "I would sooner allow myself to be called 'Miss' instead. Miss smacks a little of virgin."

"But I would rather let myself be chopped into kindling wood!" said the old virgin.

Now they went to work. The virgins were driven; they were put on the wheelbarrow, and that was always fine treatment. But they were called stampers.

"Vir——!" they said as they stamped against the cobblestones. "Vir——!" And they were just about to say the whole word "Virgin"! But they bit the word off short.

They caught themselves in time, for they found that they needn't once bother to answer. But among themselves they always addressed one another by the name virgin and praised The Good Old Days, when everything was called by its right name and one was called a virgin when one *was* a virgin. And virgins they remained—both of them—for the pile driver, the great machine, really *did* break off with the youngest. He would not have anything to do with a stamper!

The Piggy Bank

❖ ❖ ❖

THERE were such a lot of playthings in the nursery;
on the top of the cupboard stood the bank. It was
made of clay in the shape of a pig. It had a natural crack in
its back, and the crack had been made bigger with a knife
so that silver dalers could also go in. And two had gone in,
in addition to lots of shillings. The piggy bank was stuffed
so full that he could no longer rattle, and that is the
utmost a piggy bank can do. There he stood now, on top of
the shelf, and looked down on all the things in the room.

He knew very well that with what he had in his stomach he could buy it all, and that is what is known as being well aware of oneself.

The others thought about it too, even if they didn't say so. Indeed, there were other things to talk about. The bureau drawer stood halfway open, and a big doll could be seen. She was quite old, and her neck had been riveted. She looked out and said, "Shall we play at being people? At least that's something!"

Now there was a commotion! Even the pictures turned around on the wall to show that there was another side to them too. But it was not done to be contrary.

It was the middle of the night. The moon shone in through the window and provided free illumination. Now the game was to begin, and all the things had been invited—even the baby buggy, who was really one of the heavier playthings.

"There is some good in everyone!" he said. "We can't all be of noble birth. Somebody has to make himself useful, as the saying goes."

The piggy bank was the only one who had received a written invitation. They thought he stood too high up to hear it by word of mouth. Nor did he send a reply that he was coming, for he didn't come. If he was to take part, he would have to enjoy it from home. They could suit themselves accordingly, and so they did.

The little toy theater was immediately set up so he could look right into it. They were going to begin with a play, and then there would be tea and intellectual exercise. But they started with this first. The rocking horse talked about training and thoroughbreds, the baby buggy about railroads and steam power. Indeed, it all had something to do with their professions, which they could talk about. The clock talked about politic-tic-tics! It knew the hour had struck! But it was said that it did not keep the correct time! The rattan cane stood, and was proud of his ferrule and his silver knob, for, indeed, he was capped above and below. On the sofa lay two embroidered pillows—they were beautiful and dumb. And now the play could begin.

They all sat and watched, and they were asked to crack and smack and rumble, all according to how pleased they were. But the riding whip said he never cracked for the aged, only for those who were not engaged.

"I crack for everything!" said the firecracker.

"After all, one has to be somewhere," thought the cuspidor.

Indeed, this was everyone's idea in attending a play. The play was no good, but it was well acted. All the players turned their painted sides out; they could be looked at only from one side—not the wrong side—and they all performed excellently, all the way out in front of the theater. Their strings were too long, but this made them all the more noticeable. The riveted doll was so moved that her rivet came loose; and the piggy bank was so impressed by it, in his fashion, that he decided to do something for one of them: include him in his testament as the one who was to lie buried with him when the time came.

It was such a treat that the tea was abandoned, and they went on with the intellectual exercise. It was called "Playing People." There was no malice intended, for they were only playing; and each one thought of himself and of what the piggy bank was thinking. And the piggy bank thought the most. He, of course, was thinking about the testament and the funeral, and when it was to be held—always before one expects it. CRASH! He fell down from the cupboard and lay on the floor in bits and pieces, and the coins danced and sprang. The smallest spun, the biggest rolled—especially one of the silver dalers. He really wanted to go out into the world, and so he did! And so did every last one of them! And the fragments of the piggy bank ended up in the basket. But the next day, on the cupboard stood a new piggy bank made of clay. There wasn't a shilling in it yet, and so it couldn't rattle, either! In this he resembled the other. It was always a beginning, and with that we shall end.

Cloddy Hans

❖ ❖ ❖

O UT in the country there was an old manor, and in it
lived an old squire who had two sons. They were so
witty that they were too witty by half. They wanted to
propose to the king's daughter, and this they dared to do
because she had proclaimed that she would take for a
husband the one she found who could best speak up for
himself.

Now the two made their preparations for eight days.
This was all the time they had for it, but it was enough.
They had previous learning, and that is useful. One of
them knew the whole Latin dictionary by heart and the
city newspaper for three years—both forward and backward. The other had acquainted himself with all the Guild
Articles and what every alderman should know. So he was
able to discuss Affairs of State, he thought. And what's
more, he also knew how to embroider suspenders, for he
had delicate hands and was clever with his fingers.

"I'm going to win the king's daughter!" they both said,
and so their father gave them each a splendid horse; the
one who knew the dictionary and the newspapers by heart
was given a coal-black horse, and the one who knew about
aldermen and did embroidery got a milk-white steed. And
then they smeared the corners of their mouths with cod-
liver oil to make them more flexible. All the servants were

down in the yard to see them mount their steeds. At the same moment the third brother came up—for there were three of them, but no one counted him as a brother because he didn't have the same kind of learning as the other two, and they only called him "Cloddy Hans"!

"Where are you off to, since you're wearing your Sunday best?" he asked.

"To court to talk the princess into marrying us! Haven't you heard what's being proclaimed throughout the land?" And then they told him.

"My word! Then I've got to come along too!" said Cloddy Hans, but the brothers laughed at him and rode off.

"Father, let me have a horse!" shouted Cloddy Hans. "I'd so like to get married. If she'll take me, she'll take me; and if she won't, I'll take her all the same!"

"That's just twaddle!" said the father. "I'm not giving any horse to you! Why, you don't know how to talk! No, your brothers are real gentlemen."

"Well, if I can't have a horse," said Cloddy Hans, "I'll just take the billy goat! It's mine, and it can carry me very well!" And then he straddled the billy goat, dug his heels into its sides, and rushed off down the highway. Whew! How he flew!

"Here I come!" said Cloddy Hans, and then he sang so the forest rang.

But the brothers rode ahead quite silently. They didn't utter a word. They had to think over all the clever retorts they were going to make, for it had to be so well thought out.

"Hey hallo!" shouted Cloddy Hans. "Here I come! Look what I found on the highway!" And then he showed them a dead crow he had found.

"Clod!" they said. "What do you want with that?"

"I'm going to present it to the king's daughter!"

"Yes, just do it!" they said, and laughed and rode on.

"Hey hallo! Here I come! Look what I found now! You don't find this on the highway every day!"

And the brothers turned around to see what it was. "Clod!" they said. "Why, it's an old wooden shoe that has lost its top. Is the king's daughter going to have that too?"

"Yes, indeed!" said Cloddy Hans. And the brothers laughed and rode until they were way ahead of him.

"Hey hallo! Here I am!" shouted Cloddy Hans. "My! Now it's getting worse and worse! Hey hallo! It can't be beat!"

"What have you found now?" said the brothers.

"Oh," said Cloddy Hans, "it's nothing to speak of! How happy the king's daughter will be!"

"Ugh!" said the brothers. "Why, it's just mud that's been thrown up out of the ditch!"

"Yes, so it is!" said Cloddy Hans. "And it's the finest sort! You can't hold it!" And then he filled his pocket.

But the brothers rode as hard as they could, and they came to the city gates a whole hour ahead of him. There the suitors were given numbers as they arrived and were placed in rows six abreast—so close together that they couldn't move their arms. And it was just as well, for otherwise they would have stabbed one another in the back, just because one was standing in front of the other.

The rest of the populace was standing around the castle, right up to the windows, to see the king's daughter receive the suitors. But just as each one came into the room, his eloquence failed him.

"Won't do!" said the king's daughter. "Scram!"

Now came the brother who knew the dictionary by heart. But while standing in line he had clean forgotten it. And the floor creaked, and the ceiling was of mirrors so he saw himself upside down on his head. And at each window stood three scribes and an alderman, who wrote down everything that was said, so it could go right into the newspaper and be sold for two shillings on the corner. It was terrible! And then they had made up such a roaring fire that the stove was red hot.

"It's pretty warm in here!" said the suitor.

"That's because my father's roasting cockerels today!" said the king's daughter.

Bah! There he stood. He hadn't expected that speech. He didn't know a word to say, for he had wanted to say something amusing! Bah!

"Won't do!" said the king's daughter. "Scram!" And then he had to go. Now the second brother came.

"It's terribly hot here!" he said.

"Yes, we're roasting cockerels today!" said the king's daughter.

"I beg your . . . I beg! . . ." he said, and all the scribes wrote: "I beg your. . . . I beg! . . ."

"Won't do!" said the king's daughter. "Scram!"

Now Cloddy Hans came. He rode the billy goat straight into the hall.

"Well, this is a scorcher!" he said.

"That's because I'm roasting cockerels!" said the king's daughter.

"Well, now, that is strange!" said Cloddy Hans. "Then maybe I can roast a crow!"

"Indeed you can, quite well!" said the king's daughter. "But do you have anything to roast it in? For I have neither a pot nor a pan!"

"Oh, I have!" said Cloddy Hans. "Here's a cooker with a tin cramp!" And then he pulled out the old wooden shoe and put the crow in the middle of it.

"That's enough for a whole meal," said the king's daughter, "but where will we get the drippings from?"

"I've got that in my pocket!" said Cloddy Hans. "I've got so much that I can dribble some on." And then he poured a little mud out of his pocket.

"Now you're talking!" said the king's daughter. "Why, you know how to answer! And you know how to talk!

You're the one I'll have for my husband! But do you know that every word we're saying and have said is being writ-ten down and will appear in the newspaper tomorrow! At each window you can see three scribes and an old alderman. And the alderman is the worst of all because he doesn't understand a thing." Now, she said this just to frighten him. And all the scribes snickered and threw blots of ink on the floor.

"Those are the high and mighty, all right!" said Cloddy Hans. "Then I must give the best to the alderman." And then he turned out his pockets and gave him the mud right in his face!

"That was well done!" said the king's daughter. "I couldn't have done it, but I'm certainly going to learn how!"

And so Cloddy Hans became king and got a wife and a crown and a throne of his own. And we got it straight from the alderman's newspaper—but that's not to be trusted.

Soup from a Sausage Peg

❖   ❖   ❖

T HAT was an excellent dinner yesterday!" said an old
     she-mouse to one who hadn't been to the banquet. "I
sat number twenty-one from the old Mouse King; that's
not so bad, after all! Now, shall I tell you the courses?
They were put together very well: moldy bread, bacon
rind, tallow candles, and sausage, and then the same thing
all over again. It was as good as getting two meals. There
was a convivial atmosphere and a delightful twaddling, as
in a family circle. Not a bit was left except the sausage
pegs, and so we talked about them, and then the making
of soup from a sausage peg came up. Everybody, of course,
had heard about it, but no one had tasted the soup, much
less knew how to make it. A charming toast was proposed
for the inventor: he deserved to be Purveyor to the Needy!
Wasn't that witty? And the old Mouse King stood up and
promised that the young mouse who could make the soup
in question the tastiest would become his queen. They
were to have a year and a day to think it over in."

"That wasn't so bad, considering!" said the other mouse.
"But how do you make the soup?"

"Yes, how do you make it?" They asked about that too,
all the she-mice young and old. They all wanted to be
queen, but they didn't want to take the trouble of going
out into the wide world to learn how, and that'll probably

be necessary! But, then, it isn't everyone who can leave his family and the old nooks and crannies too. One doesn't go out every day on a cheese rind and the smell of bacon. No, one can end up starving—yes, perhaps be eaten alive by a cat.

I daresay these thoughts also frightened most of them out of sallying forth after knowledge; only four mice—young and pretty, but poor—presented themselves for departure. Each of them wanted to go to one of the four corners of the earth, so it was a question of which one of them Dame Fortune would follow. They each took a sausage peg with them, as a reminder of what they were traveling for; it was to be their pilgrim's staff.

Early in May they set out, and early in May the following year they came back—but only three of them. The fourth one didn't turn up and didn't send any word, and now the day of decision was at hand.

"There always has to be something sad bound up with one's greatest pleasures!" said the Mouse King, but gave orders to invite all the mice for miles around; they were to gather in the kitchen. The three traveling mice stood in a row, by themselves. For the fourth, who was missing, a sausage peg with black crepe around it had been put up. No one dared speak his mind before the three of them had spoken—and the Mouse King had said what more there was to be said.

Now we shall hear!

WHAT THE FIRST LITTLE MOUSE HAD SEEN AND LEARNED ON THE JOURNEY

"When I went out into the wide world," said the little mouse, "I thought, like so many of my age, that I knew everything. But one doesn't; it takes a year and a day before that happens. I went to sea at once; I went with a

ship that was going to the North. I had heard that at sea
the cook has to look after himself, but it's easy to look after
oneself when one has plenty of sides of bacon, barrels of
salt provisions, and flour full of mites. The food is delicious, but one doesn't learn anything that can produce
soup from a sausage peg. We sailed for many days and
nights; we were subjected to a rolling and a drenching.
Then, when we came to where we should, I left the
vessel. That was far up in the North.

"It's strange to come away from home, from your own
nook and cranny, to go by ship—which is also a kind of
nook and cranny—and then suddenly be more than a
hundred miles away and stand in a foreign land! There
were trackless forests of fir and birch! They gave off such a
strong odor! I'm not fond of it! The wild herbs had such a
spicy fragrance that I sneezed; it made me think of sausage! There were big forest lakes; close at hand the water
looked clear, but seen from a distance as black as ink.
White swans were floating there—I took them for foam,
they were lying so still. But I saw them fly and I saw them
walk, and then I recognized them. They belong to the
goose family; you can certainly tell by the gait. No one can
repudiate one's kinship! I kept to my own kind; I attached
myself to the field and meadow mice, who, for that matter, know exceedingly little—especially as far as treating is
concerned. And that, of course, is what I journeyed abroad
for. That soup could be made from a sausage peg was such
an extraordinary thought to them that it spread through
the entire forest at once. But that the problem could be
solved they relegated to the impossible. Least of all did I
think then that here and on that very same night I was to
be initiated in the making of it. It was midsummer, and
that was why the forest gave off such a strong odor, they
said; that was why the herbs were so spicy, the lakes so
clear and yet so dark with the white swans on them. At
the edge of the forest, between three or four houses, a

pole as high as a mainmast had been set up, and from the top of it hung garlands and ribbons: it was the Maypole. Lads and lasses were dancing around it and singing to it, vying with the fiddler's violin. Things got lively at sundown and in the moonlight, but I didn't join in. What business has a little mouse at a forest ball? I sat in the soft moss and held onto my sausage peg. The moon shone on one spot in particular where there was a tree, and moss as fine—yes, I daresay as fine as a Mouse King's hide! But it was of a green color that was a balm to the eyes. All at once the loveliest little people, who reached no higher than my knee, came marching up; they looked like human beings, but were better proportioned. They called themselves 'elves' and had delicate garments of flower petals, with fly- and gnat-wing trimmings—not bad at all. Right away they seemed to be looking for something, I didn't know what, but then a couple of them came over to me. The noblest of them pointed to my sausage peg and said, 'That's just the kind we use! It has been carved out, it's excellent!' And he became more and more delighted as he looked at my pilgrim's staff.

" 'Borrow, of course, but not keep!' " I said.

" 'Not keep!' they all said. And taking hold of the sausage peg, which I released, they danced over to the fine mossy spot and set up the sausage peg right there in the open. They wanted to have a Maypole too, and it was as if the one they had now had been carved out for them. Now it was decorated, yes, then it was a sight to behold.

"Tiny spiders spun threads of gold around it, and hung up fluttering veils and banners so finely woven and bleached so snowy white in the moonlight that it dazzled my eyes. They took colors from the wings of butterflies and sprinkled them on the white linen, and flowers and diamonds were sparkling there. I didn't recognize my sausage peg anymore. I daresay a Maypole like the one it had turned into was nowhere to be found in the world. And not until then did the really great company of elves arrive. They were quite without clothes; it could be no finer. And I was invited to look at the doings—but from a distance, as I was too big for them.

"Now the playing began! It was as if a thousand glass bells were ringing out so loud and strong; I thought it was the swans that were singing. Indeed, it seemed to me that I could also hear the cuckoo and thrush. At last it was as if the entire forest were resounding along with it; there were children's voices, the sound of bells and the song of birds— the sweetest melodies. And all that loveliness rang out from the Maypole of the elves. It was a whole carillon, and it was my sausage peg. Never had I believed that so much could come out of it, but I daresay it depends on whose hands it falls into. I was really quite moved. I cried, as only a little mouse can cry, for pure joy.

"The night was all too short! But, indeed, it isn't any longer up there at that time of the year. At daybreak a breeze sprang up, rippling the mirrored surface of the forest lake; all the delicate, fluttering veils and banners blew away in the air; the swaying gossamer pavilions, suspension bridges, and balustrades—or whatever they're called—that had been erected from leaf to leaf blew away at once. Six elves came and brought me my sausage peg, asking as they did so whether I had any wish they could grant. Then I asked them to tell me how soup from a sausage peg is made.

" 'The way we go about it!' said the noblest of them, and laughed. 'Yes, you saw that just now! I daresay you hardly recognized your sausage peg again!'

" 'You mean in that fashion?' I said, and told outright why I was on a journey and what was expected of it at home. 'Of what advantage is it to the Mouse King, and the whole of our mighty kingdom, that I have seen this magnificence? I can't shake it out of the sausage peg and say:

"See, here's the peg, now comes the soup! Still, it was a course of sorts when one was full!" '

"Then the elf dipped his little finger down in a blue violet and said to me, 'Take care, I'm stroking your pilgrim's staff, and when you come home to the Mouse King's castle, touch your staff at the king's warm breast. Then violets will spring out all over the staff, even in the coldest wintertime. See, there's something for you to take home with you and a little more besides.' "

But before the little mouse said what this little more could be, she touched her staff at the king's breast, and the loveliest bouquet of flowers really did spring out. It had such a strong odor that the Mouse King ordered the mice standing closest to the chimney to stick their tails into the fire right away, in order that there might be a slight smell of something burning, for that odor of violets was unbearable. That wasn't the sort of thing one set store by.

"But what was that 'little more besides' you mentioned?" asked the Mouse King.

"Well," said the little mouse, "I daresay that's what is called 'the effect'!" And then she gave the sausage peg a turn, and then there were no more flowers. She was holding only the bare peg, and she raised it just like a baton.

"Violets are for Sight, Smell, and Touch, the elf told me, but Hearing and Taste still remain!" And then she beat time: there was music, not the way it resounded in the forest during the festivities of the elves, no, but as it can be heard in the kitchen. My, what a to-do! It came suddenly, just as if the wind were whistling through all the flues. Kettles and pots boiled over; the fire shovel pounded on the brass kettle. And then, all at once, it was quiet. You could hear the subdued song of the teapot. So strange, you couldn't tell at all whether it was stopping or starting; and the little pot bubbled and the big pot bubbled; one took no heed of the other. It was as if there wasn't a thought in the pot. And the little mouse swung her baton, wilder and wilder—the pots foamed, bubbled, boiled over; the wind whistled; the chimney squeaked. Hey! Hey! It was so dreadful that the little mouse even dropped the baton.

"That was quite a soup!" said the old Mouse King. "Doesn't the main course come now?"

"That was all!" said the little mouse, and curtsied.

"All! Well, then, let us hear what the next one has to say!" said the Mouse King.

WHAT THE SECOND LITTLE MOUSE RELATED

"I was born in the castle library," said the second mouse. "I, and others of my family there, have never had the good fortune of coming into the dining room, not to mention the larder; only when I journeyed out, and now here today, did I see a kitchen. We often suffered real hunger and privation in the library, but we acquired much knowledge. Up there the rumor reached us about the royal prize that had been offered for making soup from a sausage peg, and it was then that my old grandmother pulled out a manuscript. She couldn't read it, but she had heard it read. On it was written: 'If one is a poet, then one knows how to cook soup from a sausage peg!' She asked me if I were a poet. My conscience was clear, but then she said that I had to go and see about becoming one. But what was needed for that, I asked. For it was just as difficult for me to find that out as it was to make the soup. But Grandma had listened to reading; she said that three main components were needed: 'Intelligence, fantasy, and feeling! If you can go and get those inside you, you're a poet, and then I daresay you'll find that out about the sausage peg!'"

"And so I headed West, out into the wide world to become a poet.

"I knew that in all things intelligence is the most important; the two other components are not held in the same esteem. And accordingly I set out after intelligence. Well, where does it dwell? 'Go to the ant and be wise,' a great king in the Holy Land is supposed to have said. This I knew from the library, and I didn't stop until I came to the first big anthill. There I lay in wait, in order to be wise.

"The ants are quite a respectable race; they are all brain. Everything about them is like a correctly worked problem in arithmetic that comes out right. Working and laying eggs, they say, is the same as living in the present and providing for the future, and that is just what they do. They divide themselves into the clean ants and the dirty ants. Rank consists of a number; the ant queen is number one, and her opinion is the only correct one. She knows everything, and that was essential for me to find out. She said so much that was so wise that I thought it was stupid. She said that their anthill was the tallest thing in the world. But close to the anthill stood a tree. It was taller, much taller; that couldn't be denied and so it wasn't mentioned at all. One evening an ant had strayed over there and crawled up the trunk, not even to the top, and yet higher than any ant had ever been before. And when it had turned around and made its way home, it told in the mound about something taller outside. But all the ants found this to be an insult to the entire society, and so the little ant was sentenced to wear a muzzle, and to everlasting solitude. But shortly afterward another ant came to the tree and made the same journey and discovery, and talked about it, as it is said, with deliberation and articulation. And, as it was an esteemed ant into the bargain—one of the clean ants—they believed it. And when it died, they put up an eggshell to it as a monument to the venerated sciences.

"I saw," said the little mouse, "that the ants perpetually ran about with their eggs on their backs. One of them dropped hers. She did her utmost to get it up again, but without success. Then two others came and helped with all their might, so they very nearly dropped their own eggs. But then they stopped at once, for one has to look after oneself. And concerning this, the ant queen said that both heart and intelligence had been displayed here. 'The two establish us ants as the highest of the rational beings. Intelligence must and should predominate, and I have the most!' And then she stood up on her hind legs; she was so recognizable that I couldn't make a mistake! And I swallowed her. Go to the ant and be wise! Now I had the queen!

"Now I went closer to the big tree in question. It was an oak, it had a tall trunk and a mighty crown, and was very old. I knew that a living creature dwelled here, a woman. She is called a 'dryad' and is born with the tree and dies with it. I had heard about that in the library. Now I was looking at such a tree, looking at such an oak maiden. She let out a terrible shriek when she saw me so close. Like all females, she had a great fear of mice, but then she had more of a reason than the others: for I could gnaw through the tree, and therein, of course, hung her life. I talked to her, kindly and sincerely, and gave her courage, and she picked me up in her delicate hand; and when she found out why I had gone out into the wide world, she promised that, perhaps the same evening, I should obtain one of the two treasures for which I was still looking. She told me that Phantasus was her very good friend, that he was as beautiful as the God of Love, and that many a time he had rested here under the leafy branches of the tree, which rustled even louder above them both. He called her his dryad, she said, the tree his tree. The gnarled, mighty,

beautiful oak was just to his liking. The roots spread
deeply and firmly down in the ground; the trunk and the
crown soared high in the fresh air, and felt the drifting
snow and the biting wind the way they should be felt. Yes,
this is the way she spoke: 'The birds sing up there and tell
about the foreign lands! And on the only dead limb the
stork has built a nest; that's a good trimming, and one can
hear a little from the land of the pyramids. Phantasus likes
it all very well. But even that is not enough for him; I
must tell him about life in the forest from the time I was
small and the tree was tiny enough to be hidden by a
nettle, and up to now, when it has grown so big and
mighty. Now, if you just sit over there under the woodruff
and pay close attention, when Phantasus comes I daresay
I'll have a chance to tweak him in his wing and yank out a
little feather. Take it; no poet ever received a better one.
Then you'll have enough!'

"And Phantasus came, the feather was yanked out, and
I grabbed it," said the little mouse. "I kept it in water
until it became soft! It was still quite hard to digest, but I
managed to gnaw it up! It's not at all easy to gnaw oneself
into a poet, there's so much that has to be taken in. . . .
Now I had the two: intelligence and fantasy, and through
them I knew now that the third was to be found in the
library. For a great man has said and written that there
are novels that are produced for the sole purpose of releas-
ing mankind from superfluous tears; that is to say, they are
a kind of sponge in which to absorb emotions. I remembered a couple of these books; they had always looked
quite appetizing to me—they were so well read, so greasy;
they must have absorbed an unending flood.

"I went home to the library, immediately ate practically
a whole novel—that is to say, the soft part, the novel
proper; the crust, on the other hand, the binding, I left
alone. Now, when I had digested that and one more, I was
already aware of the way it was stirring inside me. I ate a

little of the third, and then I was a poet. I said so to myself, and the others said so along with me. I had a headache, a bellyache—I don't know all the aches I had. Now I thought of the stories that might be connected with sausage pegs, and then so many pegs came to my mind— the ant queen had had exceptional intelligence. I remembered the man who'd been taken down a peg; I thought of old beer with a peg in it; standing on one's pegs; a peg for hanging a claim on; and then the pegs to one's coffin. All my thoughts were wrapped up in pegs! And it should be possible to make up something about them as long as one is a poet. And that's what I am, that's what I've struggled to be. Thus, every day in the week, I'll be able to serve you a peg—a story. Well, that's my soup!"

"Let us hear the third," said the Mouse King.

"Squeak! Squeak!" it said in the kitchen door, and a little mouse—it was the fourth, the one they thought was dead—scurried in. It bowled over the big sausage peg with the band of mourning on it. It had been running night and day; it had gone by rail, on a freight train when the opportunity presented itself, and still had come almost too late. It pushed its way forward, looking disheveled; it had lost its sausage peg but not its voice. It started talking right away, just as if everyone had been waiting for it alone and only wanted to listen to it. Everything else was of no concern to the world. It spoke at once and said what it had to say. It came so unexpectedly that no one had time to take exception to it or to its speech while it was talking. Now we shall hear!

WHAT THE FOURTH MOUSE—
WHO SPOKE BEFORE THE THIRD—HAD TO RELATE

"I went right away to the biggest city," it said. "I don't remember the name. I'm not good at remembering names. I came from the train to the City Hall along with confiscated goods, and there I ran to the jailer. He told about his prisoners, especially about one who had let fall rash words. These words, in turn, had been commented on, and now he'd been given a dressing down. 'The whole business is soup from a sausage peg!' he said. 'But that soup can cost him his neck!' This made me interested in that prisoner," said the little mouse, "and I seized the opportunity and slipped in to him. There's always a mousehole behind locked doors. He looked pale, had a great beard and big flashing eyes. The lamp smoked, and the walls were used to it—they grew no blacker. The prisoner scratched both pictures and verse, white on black. I didn't read them. I think he was bored. I was a welcome guest. He coaxed me with bread crumbs, with whistling, and with kind words. He was so happy because of me; I trusted him, and so we became friends. He shared bread and water with me, gave me cheese and sausage; I was living in great style, but, I must say, it was really the good company in particular that kept me there. He let me run on his hand and arm, all the way up in his sleeve. He let me crawl in his beard, called me his little friend. I grew really fond of him; I daresay that sort of thing is mutual. I forgot my errand out in the wide world, forgot my sausage peg in a crack in the floor; it's lying there still. I wanted to stay where he was; if I went away, the poor prisoner would have no one at all, and that's not enough in this world. I stayed, he didn't. He talked to me so sorrowfully that last time, gave me twice as much bread and cheese rinds, then blew kisses to me; he left and never came back. I don't know his story. 'Soup from a sausage peg!'

the jailer said, and I went to him. But I shouldn't have believed him. To be sure, he picked me up in his hand, but he put me in a cage, on a treadmill. That's dreadful! You run and run, you come no farther, and you only make a fool of yourself.

"The jailer's grandchild was a lovely little thing, with golden curls, the happiest eyes, and a laughing mouth. 'Poor little mouse!' she said, and peered into my nasty cage, and pulled away the iron peg—and I leaped down onto the windowsill and out into the gutter. Free! Free! I thought of that alone, and not of the journey's goal.

"It was dark, night was falling. I took shelter in an old tower. There lived a nightwatch and an owl. I didn't trust either of them, least of all the owl. It looks like a cat, and has the great shortcoming that it eats mice. But one can be mistaken, and I was. This was a respectable, exceedingly well-bred old owl; she knew more than the nightwatch and just as much as I did. The owlets found fault with everything. 'Don't make soup from a sausage peg!' she said. That was the harshest thing she could say here, she was so devoted to her own family. I gained such confidence in her that I said 'Squeak!' from the crack where I was sitting. She found that confidence to her liking and assured me that I would be under her protection. No creature would be allowed to do me harm. She herself would do that in winter, when food became scarce.

"She was wise about each and every thing. She convinced me that the nightwatch couldn't hoot except through a horn that hung loosely at his side. 'He puts on such terrible airs because of that; he thinks he's an owl in the tower! That's supposed to be grand, but it's only a little. Soup from a sausage peg!'

"I asked her for the recipe, and then she explained it to me: 'Soup from a sausage peg is only a human way of talking, and can be interpreted in various ways. And each one thinks that his way is the most correct, but the whole thing is really much ado about nothing!'

" 'Nothing!' I said. It struck me! The truth isn't always pleasant, but the truth is the highest. The old owl said so too. I thought it over and realized that when I brought the highest, then I was bringing much more than soup from a sausage peg. And so I hurried off in order to come back home in time and bring the highest and the best: the truth. The mice are an enlightened race, and the Mouse King is above them all. He is capable of making me queen for the sake of the truth."

"Your truth is a lie!" said the mouse who hadn't yet been allowed to speak. "I can make the soup, and so I shall!"

HOW IT WAS MADE

"I didn't go on a journey," said the fourth mouse. "I remained in the land; that's the proper thing to do. One doesn't need to travel; one can get everything here just as well. I remained. I haven't learned what I did from supernatural beings, or eaten my way to it, or talked with owls. I've thought it out all by myself. Now, if you'll just have the kettle put on and fill it all the way up with water! Make a fire under it! Let it burn; let the water come to a boil—it has to boil furiously! Now throw in the peg! Now if the Mouse King will be so kind as to stick his tail down in the bubbling water and stir. Indeed, the longer he stirs, the stronger the soup will be. It doesn't cost a thing. No additions are needed—just stir!"

"Can't someone else do it?" asked the Mouse King.

"No," said the mouse, "the stock is in the tail of the Mouse King alone!"

And the water bubbled furiously, and the Mouse King took his stand close to it—it was nearly dangerous—and he stuck out his tail the way the mice do in the dairy when they skim the cream from a dish and afterward lick their tails. But he only got it into the hot steam, then he jumped down at once.

"Naturally you are my queen!" he said. "We'll wait with the soup until our Golden Wedding Anniversary. Then the needy in my kingdom will have something to look forward to—and a protracted pleasure!"

And so the wedding was held. But when they came home, several of the mice said, "You couldn't very well

call that 'soup from a sausage peg'; it was more like 'soup from a mouse's tail'!"

They found that one thing or another, of what had been said, had been presented quite well, but the whole thing could have been different. "Now, *I* would have told it like this and like that! . . ."

That was the criticism, and that's always so wise—afterward!

And the story went around the world. Opinions about it were divided, but the story itself remained intact. And that is what is best—in matters great and small—in soup from a sausage peg. It's just that one shouldn't expect thanks for it!

The Girl Who Trod
on the Loaf

❖   ❖   ❖

Y OU'VE probably heard of the girl who trod on the loaf
so as not to soil her shoes, and of how badly she fared. It
has been written down and printed as well.

She was a poor child, vain and overbearing; she had an
ornery disposition, as they say. As quite a little child she
delighted in catching flies and picking off their wings to
make crawling things out of them. She took the cockchafer
and the dung beetle, stuck them each on a pin, and then
held a green leaf or a tiny scrap of paper up to their feet.
The wretched creatures would thereby cling to it, twisting
and turning it, to get off the pin.

"Now the cockchafer's reading!" said little Inger. "See
how it's turning the page!"

As she grew she became worse, if anything, instead of
better. But she was pretty, and that was her undoing, or
else in all likelihood she would have been given a good
many more cuffs than she was.

"It'll take a desperate remedy to cure your ailment!" her
own mother would say. "As a child you've often trod on
my apron. I'm afraid when you're older you'll often come
to tread on my heart."

And that is precisely what she did.

Now she went out in the country to enter the service of
a gentle family. They treated her as if she had been their

very own child and dressed her in the same fashion. She looked good, and her arrogance increased.

She had been out there for a year when her mistress said, "Really, you should pay your parents a visit one day, little Inger!"

She went too, but only to show off. They were to see how grand she had become. But when she came to the village gate and saw the maidens and young lads gossiping by the pond—and her mother was sitting right there, resting with a bundle of twigs that she had gathered in the forest—Inger turned around. She was ashamed that she, who was so finely dressed, should have such a ragamuffin for a mother, who went about gathering sticks. She didn't regret turning back at all, she was merely irritated.

Now another half year passed.

"Really, you should go home for a day and see your old parents, little Inger!" said her mistress. "Here's a big loaf of white bread for you; you can take it to them. They'll be delighted to see you."

And Inger put on her best finery and her new shoes, and she lifted her skirts and walked so carefully in order to keep her feet nice and clean—and she couldn't be blamed for that. But when she came to where the path went over boggy ground, and a long stretch of it was wet and muddy, she tossed the loaf into the mud so as to tread on it and get across dry-shod. But as she was standing with one foot on the bread and lifting the other, the bread sank with her, deeper and deeper, until she had disappeared completely, and only a black, bubbling pool was to be seen.

That's the story.

But where did she come to? She came down to the Marsh Wife, who was brewing. The Marsh Wife is paternal aunt to the elfin maidens—they're well enough known: ballads have been written about them and pictures have been painted of them. But the only thing people know about the Marsh Wife is that when the meadows are

steaming in the summertime, the Marsh Wife is brewing.
It was down into her brewery that Inger sank, and you
can't stand being there for long. The cesspool is a bright,
elegant salon compared with the Marsh Wife's brewery!
The stink from each vat is enough to make people swoon,
and then too the vats are jammed so close together. And if
there is a little opening somewhere through which you
could squeeze, you can't because of all the wet toads and
fat snakes that become matted together here. Down here
sank little Inger; all that loathsome, writhing matting was
so freezing cold that she shivered in every limb; indeed,
she became more and more rigid. She stuck to the loaf,
and it dragged her just as an amber button drags a bit of
straw.

The Marsh Wife was at home. That day the brewery
was being inspected by the Devil and his great-grandma,

and *she's* a most virulent old female, who's never idle. She never goes out unless she has her needlework with her, and she had it along here too. She sewed unrest to put in people's shoes so they couldn't settle down; she embroidered lies and crocheted thoughtless remarks that had fallen to the ground—anything to cause harm and corruption. Oh, yes, great-grandma really knew how to sew, embroider, and crochet!

She saw Inger, held her eyeglass up to her eye, and had another look at her. "That's a girl with aptitude!" she said. "Give her to me as a token of my visit here! She'll be a suitable pedestal in my great-grandchild's anteroom!"

And she got her. And this is how little Inger came to Hell. People don't always rush straight down there, but they can get there by a roundabout way—when they have aptitude!

It was an anteroom that went on forever. It made you dizzy to look ahead and dizzy to look back; and here stood a miserable host waiting for the Door of Mercy to be opened, and they would have a long wait! Big fat waddling spiders spun thousand-year webs over their feet, and these webs clamped like footscrews and held like copper chains. And added to this was an eternal unrest in every soul, a tormenting unrest; there was the miser who had forgotten the key to his moneybox, and he knew it was sitting in the lock. Indeed, it would be too long-winded to rattle off all the various torments and tortures that were endured here. It was a dreadful feeling for Inger to stand as a pedestal; it was as if she had been toggled to the loaf from below.

"That's what you get for wanting to keep your feet clean!" she said to herself. "See how they glower at me!" Indeed, they were all looking at her. Their evil desires flashed from their eyes and spoke without a sound from the corners of their mouths. They were dreadful to behold.

"It must be a pleasure to look at me!" thought little Inger. "I have a pretty face and good clothes." And now she turned her eyes—her neck was too stiff to move. My, how dirty she had gotten in the Marsh Wife's brewery. She hadn't thought of that! It was as if one big blob of slime had been poured over her clothes. A snake had got caught in her hair and was flapping down the back of her neck. And from every fold of her dress a toad was peering out, croaking like a wheezy pug dog. It was quite unpleasant. "But the others down here look just as horrible," she consoled herself.

Worst of all, however, was the dreadful hunger she felt. Couldn't she even bend down and break off a piece of the bread she was standing on? No, her back had stiffened, her arms and hands had stiffened; her entire body was like a pillar of stone. She could turn only her eyes in her head, turn them completely around so they could see backward— and that was a terrible sight, that was. And then the flies came. They crawled over her eyes, back and forth. She blinked her eyes, but the flies didn't fly away—they couldn't. Their wings had been picked off; they had turned into crawling things. That was a torment. And then there was the hunger—at last it seemed to her as if her entrails were devouring themselves, and she became so empty inside, so horribly empty.

"If this keeps up for long, I won't be able to stand it," she said. But she had to stand it, and it did keep up.

Then a burning tear fell on her head; it trickled down her face and breast, straight down to the loaf. Yet another tear fell, and many more. Who was crying over little Inger? Didn't she have a mother up on earth? The tears of grief that a mother sheds over her child always reach it, but they don't redeem it, they burn. They only add to the torment. And now this excruciating hunger, and not being able to reach the loaf she was treading with her foot! At last she had a feeling that everything inside her must have devoured itself. She was like a thin hollow tube that sucked every sound into it. She heard clearly everything

up on earth that concerned her, and what she heard was
ill-natured and harsh. To be sure, her mother wept deeply
and sorrowfully, but she added, "Pride goes before a fall!
That was your undoing, Inger! How you have grieved your
mother!"

Her mother and everyone else up there knew about her
sin: that she had trod on the loaf and sunk down and
disappeared. The cowherd had told about it; he had seen
it himself from the hillside.

"How you have grieved your mother, Inger!" said the
mother. "But then I always thought you would!"

"If only I'd never been born!" thought Inger. "Then I'd
have been much better off. My mother's sniveling can't be
of any help now."

She heard how her master and mistress, those gentle
souls who had been like parents to her, spoke: "She was a
sinful child," they said. "She paid no heed to the gifts of
the Lord, but trod them under her feet. The Door of
Mercy will be hard for her to open."

"They should have minded me better," thought Inger,
"cured me of my whims—if I had any!"

She heard that a whole ballad had been written about
her: "The arrogant lass who trod on the loaf in order to
have pretty shoes!" And it was sung throughout the land.

"Imagine hearing so much about it and suffering so
much for it!" thought Inger. "I daresay the others ought to
be punished for what they've done too! Yes, then there'd
be a lot to punish! Ugh, how tormented I am!"

And her soul grew even harder than her shell.

"One won't grow any better in this company! And I
don't want to grow any better! See how they glower!"

And her heart was filled with wrath and spite for
everybody.

"Well, now they have something to tell up there! Ugh,
how tormented I am!"

And she heard that they told her story to the children,

and the little ones called her "Ungodly Inger." "She was so nasty," they said, "so wicked! She really ought to be tormented!"

There were always hard words against her on the children's lips.

Yet one day, as resentment and anger were gnawing at her hollow shell, and she was hearing her name being mentioned and her story being told to an innocent child, a little girl, she became aware that the little one burst into tears at the story of the arrogant Inger who loved finery.

"But is she never coming up again?" asked the little girl.

And the reply came: "She is never coming up again!"

"But if she were to ask forgiveness and never do it again?"

"But she will never ask forgiveness," they said.

"I'd so like for her to do it!" said the little girl, and was quite inconsolable. "I'll give my doll's wardrobe if only she can come up! It's so gruesome for poor Inger."

And those words reached all the way down to Inger's heart; they seemed to do her good. It was the first time that anyone had said "Poor Inger!" without adding the least little thing about her shortcomings. A tiny innocent child was crying and praying for her. It made her feel so strange; she would have gladly cried, but she couldn't cry. And that was also a torment.

As the years went by there was no change down below; she seldom heard sounds from above, and less was said about her. Then one day she was aware of a sigh: "Inger, Inger, how you have grieved me! But I always said you would!" It was her mother, who had died.

Now and then she heard her name mentioned by her old master and mistress, and the mildest words the housewife said were: "Will I ever see you again, Inger? One never knows where one is going."

But Inger realized very well that her gentle mistress would never be able to come to where she was.

Thus another long and bitter time elapsed.

Then Inger again heard her name being mentioned and saw something shining above her like two bright stars. They were two mild eyes that were closing on earth. So many years had gone by since the time the little girl had cried inconsolably over "poor Inger" that the child had become an old woman whom the Lord now wanted to call up to himself. And at that very moment, when the thoughts from her whole life rose before her, she also remembered how bitterly she had cried as a little girl on hearing the story of Inger. The time and the impression appeared so lifelike to the old woman in the hour of her death that she exclaimed aloud, "Lord, my God, haven't I too, like Inger, often trod on your blessed gifts without a thought? Haven't I too gone with pride in my heart? But you, in your mercy, didn't let me sink. You held me up. Don't desert me in my final hour!"

And the eyes of the old woman closed, and the eyes of her soul opened to what is hidden; and as Inger had been so vivid in her last thoughts, she saw her, saw how far down she had been dragged. And at the sight the pious soul burst into tears. In the Kingdom of Heaven she was standing like a child and crying for poor Inger. Those tears and those prayers rang out like an echo in the hollow, empty shell that encased the imprisoned, tortured soul. It was overwhelmed by all this unthought-of love from above; one of God's angels was crying over her! Why was this being granted to her? It was as if the tortured soul collected in its thoughts every deed it had performed in its earthly life, and it shook with tears such as Inger had never been able to cry. She was filled with anguish for herself; she felt that the Door of Mercy could never be opened for her. But as she acknowledged this with a broken heart, at the same moment a beam of light shone

down into the abyss. The beam was stronger than the
sunbeam that thaws the snowman put up in the yard by
the boys. And then, much faster than the snowflake falling
on the warm mouth of the child melts away to a drop,
Inger's petrified figure faded away. A tiny bird, zigzagging
like lightning, soared up to the world of mortals. But it
was afraid and wary of everything around it; it was ashamed
of itself and ashamed to face all living creatures, and
hurriedly sought shelter in a dark hole it found in the
decayed wall. Here it sat huddled, trembling all over. It
couldn't utter a sound—it had no voice. It sat for a long
while before it was calm enough to look at and be con-
scious of all the magnificence out there. Yes, it was magnificent: the air was so fresh and mild, the moon shone so
brightly, trees and bushes gave off such a fragrance; and
then too it was so pleasant there where it sat. Its feathered
kirtle was so clean and fine. My, how all creation had been
borne along in love and glory! All the thoughts that were
stirring in the breast of the bird wanted to vent themselves in song, but the bird was unable to do it. It would
gladly have sung like the cuckoo and nightingale in spring.
The Lord, who also hears the worm's silent hymn of
praise, was here aware of the hymn of praise that soared in
chords of thought, the way the Psalm resounded in Da-
vid's breast before it was given words and music.

For weeks these silent songs grew and swelled in its
thoughts; they had to burst forth at the first flap of the
wings in a good deed; such a deed had to be performed.

Now the holy celebration of Christmas was at hand.
Close to the wall the farmer set up a pole and tied an
unthreshed sheaf of oats to it so the birds of the air could
also have a joyous Christmas and a gratifying meal at this
time of the Savior's.

The sun came up on Christmas morning and shone on
the sheaf of oats, and all the twittering birds flew about
the feeding pole. Then a "cheep-cheep" rang out from the

wall as well! The swelling thoughts had turned into sound; the feeble cheeping was a complete hymn of rejoicing. An idea for a good deed had awakened, and the bird flew out from its shelter. In the Kingdom of Heaven they knew very well what kind of bird this was.

Winter set in with a vengeance, the waters were frozen deep. The birds and animals of the forest had a hard time finding food. The little bird flew along the highway, searching in the tracks of the sleighs, and here and there it found a grain of corn; at the resting places it found a few bread crumbs. Of these it ate only a single one, but called to all the other starving sparrows that they could find food here. It flew to the cities and scouted about, and wherever a loving hand had strewn bread by a window for the birds, it ate but a single crumb itself and gave everything to the others.

In the course of the winter the bird had gathered and given away so many bread crumbs that, altogether, they weighed as much as the whole loaf of bread that little Inger had trod on so as not to soil her shoes. And when the very last bread crumb had been found and given away, the bird's gray wings turned white and spread out wide.

"A tern is flying over the sea!" said the children who saw the white bird. Now it ducked down into the sea, now it soared in the bright sunshine; it shone, it wasn't possible to see what had become of it. They said that it flew straight into the sun.

Pen and Inkwell

❖   ❖   ❖

THE words were uttered in a poet's chamber as someone was looking at his inkwell, which was standing on
the table: "It's remarkable, all the things that can come
out of that inkwell I wonder what will be next. Yes, it's
remarkable!"

"So it is!" said the inkwell. "It's incomprehensible! That's
what I always say!" it said to the quill pen and to anything
else on the table that could hear it. "It's remarkable, all

the things that can come out of me! Yes, it's almost incredible! And I don't really know myself what will be next, when the human being starts drawing from me. One drop of me is enough for half a page of paper, and what can't appear there? I'm something quite remarkable! All the poet's works emanate from me! These living beings that people think they know, these profound emotions, this good humor, these lovely descriptions of nature. I can't comprehend it myself, because I'm not familiar with nature. But after all it's in me. From me has originated—and does originate—this host of hovering, lovely maidens, gallant knights on snorting chargers! Indeed, I'm not aware of it myself! I assure you, I don't give it a thought!"

"You're right about that!" said the quill pen. "You don't think at all. Because if you did, you'd understand that you merely provide fluid. You provide moisture so that I can express and render visible on the paper what I have in me, what I write down. It's the pen that writes! Not a soul has any doubts about that, and most mortals have as much of an understanding about poetry as an old inkwell!"

"You have only a little experience!" said the inkwell. "You've scarcely been on duty a week, and already you're half worn out. Are you pretending that you're the poet? You're only hired help, and I've had many of that sort before you came—both of the goose family and of English fabrication! I know both the quill pen and the steel pen. I've had many in my employ, and I'll have many more when he, the human being who makes the motions for me, comes and writes down what he gets out of my insides. I wonder what will be the next thing he draws out of me!"

"Inkpot!" said the pen.

Late in the evening the poet came home. He had been to a concert, heard an excellent violinist, and was quite engrossed and entranced by his incomparable playing. He had produced an amazing flood of tones from his instrument; now they sounded like tinkling drops of water, pearl upon pearl, now like twittering birds in chorus as the storm raged through a forest of spruces. He seemed to hear his own heart crying, but in a melody, the way it can be heard in the lovely voice of a woman. It was as if not only the strings of the violin rang out but also the bridge, yes, even the pegs and the sounding board as well—it was extraordinary; and it had been difficult, but it looked like play, as if the bow could leap back and forth over the strings. You would have thought that anyone could imitate it. The violin rang out by itself, the bow played by itself; it was these two who did it all. The maestro who guided them, gave life and soul to them, was forgotten; the maestro was forgotten! But the poet thought of him; he named him by name and thereby wrote down his thoughts: "How absurd if the bow and the violin were to put on airs about their performance! And yet, that is what we mortals do so often: the poet, the artist, the scientific inventor, the general. We put on airs ourselves, and yet we are all merely the instruments upon which the Lord plays. To him the honor alone! We have nothing to put on airs about!"

Yes, this is what the poet wrote; he wrote it as a parable and called it "The Maestro and the Instruments."

"You had it coming to you, madame!" said the pen to the inkwell when the two were alone again. "I daresay you heard him read aloud what I wrote down!"

"Yes, what I gave you to write," said the inkwell. "After all, it was a dig at you because of your arrogance. You can't even understand when someone is making fun of you! I've made a dig at you straight from my insides. I daresay I should know my own malice!"

"Ink holder!" said the pen.

"Writing stick!" said the inkwell.

And they both had the feeling that they had answered well. And it's a good feeling to know that you've answered well. You can go to sleep on it, and they did sleep on it. But the poet didn't sleep. The thoughts poured forth like the tones from the violin, rolled like pearls, raged like the storm through the forest. He felt his own heart in there; he was aware of the glimmer from the eternal Master.

To him the honor alone!

The Barnyard Cock and the Weathercock

❖   ❖   ❖

There were two cocks, one on the dunghill and one on the roof; both of them arrogant; but which one accomplished the most? Tell us your opinion, we'll keep ours all the same.

A plank fence separated the chicken yard from another yard, in which there was a dunghill, and on it grew a huge cucumber that was fully convinced that it was a hothouse plant.

"One is born to that," it said deep down inside. "Not everyone can be born a cucumber. There must be other living species too! The hens, the ducks, and the entire stock of the neighboring farm are also creations. For my part, I look up to the barnyard cock on the fence. To be sure, he is of quite another significance than the weathercock, which has been placed so high. It can't even creak, much less crow! It has neither hens nor chicks. It thinks only of itself and sweats verdigris! The barnyard cock, now, is quite a cock! Look at him strut—that's dancing! Listen to him crow—that's music! No matter where he goes you can hear what a trumpeter is! If he were to come in here, if he were to eat me up—leaves, stalk, and all—if I were to enter his body, what a rapturous death that would be!" said the cucumber.

Later on in the night there was a terrible storm. Hens,

chicks, and even the cock sought shelter. The fence between the yards blew down with a great crash. Tiles fell down from the roof, but the weathercock was firmly fastened and not once did it turn around—it couldn't! And yet it was young, newly cast, but staid and sober-minded; it had been born old, and did not resemble the flighty birds of the air, the sparrows and swallows. It despised them, ". . . those dickybirds, small of size and *ordinaire*." The doves were big, glossy, and shiny, like mother-of-pearl; they resembled a kind of weathercock, but were fat and stupid. Their only thought was to get something in their craws, said the weathercock. They were bores to associate with. The birds of passage had also paid a visit and told of foreign lands and of caravans in the air, and dreadful cock-and-bull stories about birds of prey. It was new and interesting the first time, but later the weathercock knew that they repeated themselves, and it was always the same. And this is tedious. They were bores, and everything was a bore. No one was worth associating with, every last one of them was insipid and vapid!

"The world's no good!" he said. "Drivel, the whole thing!"

The weathercock was what is known as blasé, and this would have made him decidedly interesting to the cucumber had she known. But she looked up only to the barnyard cock, and now he was in the yard with her.

The fence had blown down, but the lightning and thunder were over.

"What do you have to say about that cockcrow?" said the barnyard cock to the hens and chicks. "It was a bit unpolished. The elegance was lacking."

"Garden plant!" he said to the cucumber, and in that one expression all his extensive breeding was revealed to her, and she forgot that he was pecking at her and eating her.

"Rapturous death!"

And the hens came and the chicks came. And when one comes running, the others run too! And they clucked and they "cheeped." And they looked at the cock and were proud of him. He was one of their kind.

"Cock-a-doodle-do!" he crowed. "The chicks turn at once into big hens when I say that in the hen yard of the world."

And hens and chicks clucked and "cheeped" behind him.

And the cock proclaimed great news: "A cock can lay an egg! And do you know what lies in that egg? A basilisk! No one can bear the sight of it. The human beings know that, and now you know it too—know what's inside me, know what a terribly fine barnyard-cock-of-the-walk I am!"

And then the barnyard cock flapped his wings, lifted his comb, and crowed again. All the hens and little chicks shuddered, but they were terribly proud that one of their kind was such a terribly fine barnyard-cock-of-the-walk. They clucked and they "cheeped" until the weathercock had to hear it, and hear it he did. But he wasn't impressed by it!

"It's all nonsense!" he said to himself. "The barnyard cock will never lay an egg, and I can't be bothered to! If I wanted to, I could certainly lay a wind egg, but the world's not worth a wind egg! It's all nonsense! I can't even be bothered to sit here."

And then the weathercock broke off, but he didn't kill the barnyard cock.

"Even though that's what he counted on doing!" said the hens.

And what does the moral say? "Indeed, it's better to crow than to be blasé and break off!"

The Dung Beetle

❖   ❖   ❖

THE emperor's horse was getting golden shoes, a golden shoe on every single foot.

Why was he getting golden shoes?

He was the loveliest animal, had fine legs, the most intelligent eyes, and a mane that hung about his neck like a silken veil. He had borne his master through clouds of gunpowder and a rain of bullets, heard the bullets sing and whistle; he had bitten, kicked, and fought when the enemy pressed closer; with his emperor he had sprung over the fallen horse of the fiend, saved his emperor's crown of red gold, saved his emperor's life, which was worth more than red gold, and for this reason the emperor's horse was getting golden shoes, a golden shoe on every single foot.

Then the dung beetle crawled out.

"First the big, then the small," it said. "After all, it's not the size that counts." And then it held out its thin legs.

"What do you want?" asked the smith.

"Golden shoes!" replied the dung beetle.

"You're certainly not very bright!" said the smith. "Do you want to have golden shoes too?"

"Golden shoes!" said the dung beetle. "Aren't I just as good as that great beast who is to be waited on, groomed,

looked after, and given food and drink? Aren't I a part of
the emperor's stables too?"

"But why is the horse getting golden shoes?" asked the
smith. "Can't you understand that?"

"Understand? I understand that it's an affront to me!"
said the dung beetle. "It's an insult! So now I'm going out
into the wide world!"

"Scram!" said the smith.

"Vulgar oaf!" said the dung beetle. And then it went
outside and flew a little way, and then it was in a beautiful
little flower garden where there was a scent of roses and
lavender.

"Isn't it lovely here?" said one of the little ladybugs that
flew about with black dots on its red shieldlike wings.
"How sweet it smells, and how beautiful it is here!"

"I'm used to better things!" said the dung beetle. "Do
you call this beautiful? Why, there isn't even a dunghill
here!"

And then on it went, into the shade of a big cabbage. A
caterpillar was crawling on it.

"How glorious the world is!" said the caterpillar. "The
sun is so warm! Everything is such a delight! And one day,
when I go to sleep and die, as they call it, I will wake up
a butterfly!"

"Don't give yourself ideas!" said the dung beetle. "Now
we're flying about like butterflies! I come from the emper-
or's stables, but no one there—not even the emperor's
favorite horse, who, after all, wears my cast-off golden
shoes—has such delusions! Get wings! Fly! Yes, now we'll
fly!" And then the dung beetle flew. "I will not be vexed,
but it vexes me all the same!"

Then it plumped down on a big plot of grass. Here it lay
for a little while, then it fell asleep.

Heavens, how the rain poured down! The dung beetle
was awakened by the splashing and wanted to burrow
down in the ground at once, but couldn't. It overturned; it

swam on its stomach and on its back. Flying was impossible! It would never come away from here alive! It lay where it lay, and there it stayed.

When it had cleared a bit, and the dung beetle had blinked the rain out of its eyes, it caught a glimpse of something white. It was linen spread out to bleach. It went over to it and crawled into a fold of the wet cloth. It certainly wasn't like lying in the warm heap in the stable, but there was nothing better; so here it stayed for a whole day and a whole night, and the rainy weather stayed too. Early in the morning the dung beetle crawled out. It was so vexed by the weather.

Two frogs were sitting on the linen; their bright eyes beamed with pure joy. "What delightful weather!" said the first. "How refreshing it is! And the linen holds the water so wonderfully! My hind legs tickle just as if I were swimming!"

"I wonder," said the other, "if the swallow—who flys so far and wide on its many journeys abroad—has found a better climate than ours: such a drizzle, such humidity! It's just like lying in a wet ditch. If that doesn't make one glad, then one doesn't really love one's country!"

"Then you've never been in the emperor's stables?" asked the dung beetle. "The moisture there is both warm and spicy! That's what I'm accustomed to! That's my kind of climate, but you can't take it with you on your journey. Isn't there any hotbed in the garden where persons of rank, such as myself, can put up and feel at home?"

But the frogs didn't understand him—or else they didn't want to understand him.

"I never ask a second time," said the dung beetle after it had asked three times without receiving an answer.

Then it walked a bit; there lay a fragment of a flowerpot. It shouldn't have lain there, but lying where it did, it provided shelter. Several earwig families were living there; they don't insist upon a lot of room, only company. The females are especially endowed with maternal love, and for this reason the youngsters of each were the prettiest and the most intelligent.

"Our son has become engaged," said one mother, "the sweet innocent! His highest ambition is to crawl, once, into a clergyman's ear! He's so adorably childish, and the engagement keeps him from running wild! That's so gratifying to a mother."

"Our son," said another mother, "was up to mischief the moment he came out of the egg. He's bubbling over! He's sowing his wild oats! That's a tremendous consolation to a mother! Isn't it, Mr. Dung Beetle!" They recognized the stranger by its figure.

"You're both right," said the dung beetle, and then it was invited inside—as far as it could come under the fragment of pottery.

"Now you're also going to see my little earwig," said a third and a fourth mother. "They're the most lovable children, and so entertaining! They're never naughty—except when they have a pain in their stomachs, but one gets that so easily at their age!"

And then each mother talked about her youngsters, and the youngsters talked along with them and used the little fork they have on their tails to tug at the dung beetle's whiskers.

"They're always up to something, the little rascals!" said the mothers, reeking of motherly love. But the dung beetle was bored, and so it asked if it were far to the hotbed.

"It's a long way out into the world, on the other side of the ditch," said the earwig. "I hope none of my children will ever go that far, for then I would die."

"All the same, I'm going to try to go that far!" said the dung beetle, and left without taking its leave. That's the most polite thing to do.

By the ditch he met several of his kin, all dung beetles.

"Here's where we live!" they said. "It's quite cozy. May we invite you down in the rich dirt? No doubt the journey has worn you out."

"So it has," said the dung beetle. "I've been lying on linen in the rain, and cleanliness in particular takes a lot out of me! I've also got rheumatism in the joint of my wing from standing in a draft under a fragment of pottery. It's really quite refreshing to find oneself among one's own kind."

"Are you by any chance from the hotbed?" asked the oldest.

"Higher up," said the dung beetle. "I come from the emperor's stables, where I was born with golden shoes on. I'm on a secret errand that you mustn't pump me about, as I'm not talking!"

And then the dung beetle crawled down in the rich mud. There sat three young female dung beetles. They snickerered, because they didn't know what to say.

"They're not engaged," said the mother, and then they snickered, because they didn't know what to say.

"I've never seen them prettier in the emperor's stables," said the traveling dung beetle.

"Don't lead my girls astray! And don't speak to them unless your intentions are honorable. But so they are, and I give you my blessing!"

"Hurrah!" said all the others, and then the dung beetle was engaged. First engagement, and then the wedding. After all, there was nothing to wait for.

The next day went quite well, the second dragged along, but on the third day one had to think of food for wife and perhaps tots.

"I've allowed myself to be taken by surprise!" it said. "So now I must take them by surprise in return!"

And it did. Gone it was. Gone the whole day, gone the whole night. And the wife was left a widow. The other dung beetles said they had taken a regular tramp into the family; the wife was now a burden to them.

"Then she can become a maiden again," said the mother, "remain my child. Fie on that dastardly wretch who abandoned her!"

In the meantime it was on its way, having sailed across the ditch on a cabbage leaf. Early in the morning two people came. They saw the dung beetle, picked it up, and twisted and turned it. They were both very learned, especially the boy. "Allah sees the black dung beetle in the black stone in the black mountain! Isn't that the way it's written in the Koran?" he asked. And he translated the dung beetle's name into Latin and gave an account of its genus and nature. The older scholar voted against taking it home with them. The examples they had there were just as good, he said. The dung beetle didn't think this was a polite thing to say, and so it flew out of his hand and flew a good distance—its wings had become dry—and then it reached the hothouse. One of the windows had been pushed up, so it could pop in with the greatest of ease and burrow down in the fresh manure.

"How luscious it is!" it said.

Soon it fell asleep and dreamed that the emperor's horse had fallen and that Mr. Dung Beetle had been given its golden shoes and the promise of two more. That was a pleasure, and when the dung beetle awoke it crawled out and looked up. How magnificent it was in the greenhouse. Enormous fan palms spread out overhead, the sun made them transparent. Beneath them was a luxuriance of greenery, and flowers glowed as red as fire, as golden as amber, and as white as the driven snow.

"What wonderfully magnificent plants! How marvelous it all will taste when it starts to rot!" said the dung beetle. "This is a fine dining room. No doubt some of the family dwells here. I will track them down and see if I can find anyone worth associating with. I have my pride and I'm proud of it!" Then off it went, thinking of its dream about the dead horse and the golden shoes it had won.

All at once a hand grabbed the dung beetle. It was squeezed and turned over and over.

The gardener's little boy was in the hot house with a friend; they had seen the dung beetle and were going to have some fun with it. It was wrapped in a grape leaf and put down in a warm pants pocket. It wriggled and crawled until it received a squeeze from the hand of the boy, who went quickly over to the big lake at the end of the garden. Here the dung beetle was placed in a broken old wooden shoe with the instep missing. A stick was made fast for a mast, and the dung beetle was tied to it with a woolen thread. Now it was a skipper and was going out sailing.

The lake was very large. The dung beetle thought it was the ocean, and it was so astonished that it fell over on its back with its feet kicking in the air.

The wooden shoe sailed, for there was a current in the water; but if the ship went too far out, one of the boys rolled up his pants right away and went out and fetched it. But the next time it drifted, the boys were called—called in earnest—and they hurried away, leaving the wooden shoe a wooden shoe. It floated farther and farther from land. It was terrifying for the dung beetle; it couldn't fly because it was tied fast to the mast.

A fly paid it a visit.

"What glorious weather we're having," said the fly. "Here I can rest and sun myself. You are quite comfortable."

"You're talking as if you were not in possession of your senses! Don't you see I'm tied up?"

"I'm not tied up!" said the fly, and then it flew away.

"Now I know what the world is like," said the dung beetle. "It's an ignoble world! I'm the only respectable soul in it. First I'm refused golden shoes, then I have to lie on wet linen and stand in a draft, and in the end they foist a wife upon me. Then, when I take a quick trip out in the world to see how it is, and how it should be for me, along comes a human whelp and ties me up and puts me in the raging sea! And in the meantime the emperor's horse goes about with golden shoes on! It's enough to make one croak! But one can't expect sympathy in this world. The story of my life is quite interesting, but what's the good of that when no one knows about it? Nor does the world deserve to know about it, otherwise it would have given *me* golden shoes in the emperor's stables when the steed held out its feet and was shod. Had I been given golden shoes, I would have been a credit to the stables. Now it has lost me and the world has lost me. Everything is finished."

But everything wasn't finished yet. A boat came along with some young girls in it.

"A wooden shoe is sailing there," said one.

"A little bug is tied fast to it," said the other.

They were right alongside the wooden shoe. They picked it up, and one of the girls took out a pair of scissors and cut the woolen thread without harming the dung beetle, and when they came ashore she put it in the grass.

"Crawl, crawl! Fly, fly if you can!" she said. "Freedom is a wonderful thing."

And the dung beetle flew right in through the window of a large building and sank exhausted in the fine, soft, long mane of the emperor's charger, who was standing in the stable where he and the dung beetle belonged. It clung fast to the mane and sat for a while to collect its thoughts. "Here I sit on the emperor's charger, sit like a rider. What am I saying? Yes, now it's clear to me! It's a good idea and a correct one at that. Why did the emperor's horse get golden shoes? The smith asked me about that too. Now I see it! The emperor's horse was given golden shoes for my sake!"

And now the dung beetle was in good spirits.

"Travel clears one's head!" it said.

The sun shone on it, shone very beautifully. "The world hasn't gone so mad yet," said the dung beetle. "You just have to know how to take it." The world was lovely: the emperor's charger had been given golden shoes because the dung beetle was to be its rider.

"Now I'm going to climb down and tell the other beetles how much has been done for me. I'll tell of all the pleasures I've indulged in on my journey abroad, and I'll say that now I'm going to remain at home until the horse has worn out its golden shoes!"

What Papa Does
Is Always Right

❖   ❖   ❖

NOW I'm going to tell you a story I heard when I was a boy, and every time I've thought of it since, it struck me as being much nicer, for it's the same with stories as with many people: they grow nicer and nicer with age, and that's so delightful!

Of course you've been out in the country! You've seen a really old farmhouse with a thatched roof. Mosses and herbs are growing on it of their own accord. There's a stork's nest on the ridge—you can't do without the stork. The walls are crooked, the windows low—indeed, there's only one that can be opened. The oven juts out just like a little pot belly, and the elder bush hangs over the fence, where there's a little puddle of water with a duck or ducklings on it, right under the gnarled willow tree. Yes, and then there's a dog on a chain that barks at each and every one.

Just such a farmhouse was out in the country, and in it there lived a couple: a farmer and the farmer's wife. No matter what little they had, there was still one thing they could do without: a horse that grazed in the ditch by the side of the road. Papa rode to town on it, the neighbors borrowed it, and one good turn was repaid by another. But I daresay it was more profitable for them to sell the horse or swap it for something or other

that could be of even more use to them. But what was that
to be?

"You'll be the best judge of that, Papa!" said the wife.
"Now, there's a fair on in town. Ride there and get money
for the horse, or else make a good bargain. Whatever you
do is always right! Ride to the fair!"

And then she tied his neckerchief, for after all she knew
how to do that better than he did; she tied it in a double
bow—it looked so perky—and then she brushed his hat
with the flat of her hand, and she kissed him on his warm
lips. And then he rode off on the horse that was to be sold
or swapped. Yes, Papa was the best judge of that.

The sun blazed down; there wasn't a cloud above. The
dust whirled up from the road, for there were so many
people on their way to the fair—in carts, on horseback,
and on their own two feet. It was sizzling hot, and there
wasn't a bit of shade along the way.

A man was walking along driving a cow; it was as pretty
as a cow can be. "I daresay that cow gives delicious milk!"
thought the farmer. "It could be quite a bargain to get
that!" He said, "Look here, you with the cow! Shouldn't
the two of us have a little chat together? Here's a horse,
which I do believe costs more than a cow, but it doesn't
matter! A cow is of more use to me. Shall we swap?"

"I'll say!" said the man with the cow, and so they
swapped.

Well, that was settled, and now the farmer could have
turned back. After all, he'd done what he'd set out to do.
But as long as he'd made up his mind to go to the fair,
then to the fair he wanted to go, just to have a look at it.
So he went on with his cow. He walked along at a good
clip, and the cow walked along at a good clip, and soon
they were walking alongside a man who was leading a
ewe. It was a fine ewe, with plenty of meat and plenty of
wool.

"I'd like to own that!" thought the farmer. "It'd never

be without something to graze on by the side of our ditch, and in the winter we could bring it into the house with us. As a matter of fact, it would be better for us to keep a ewe than a cow. Shall we swap?"

Well, the man with the ewe was only too willing, and so this swap was made, and the farmer went on down the road with his ewe. There by the stile he saw a man with a big goose under his arm.

"That's a big fellow you've got there!" said the farmer. "It has both feathers and fat. It'd look good tethered by our pond. This is something for Mama to gather peelings for! She's often said, 'If only we had a goose!' Now she can have one—and she shall have one! Do you want to swap? I'll give you the ewe for the goose, and thanks into the bargain!"

Well, the other man was only too willing, and so they swapped. The farmer got the goose. He was close to town; the crowds on the road increased. It was teeming with men and beasts. They walked on the road, and in the ditch, all the way up to the tollman's potato patch, where his hen stood tied, so that she wouldn't run away in her fright and get lost. It was a bobtail hen that blinked with one eye and looked good. "Cluck! Cluck!" it said. What it meant by that I cannot say. But when the farmer saw her, he thought: "She's the prettiest hen I've ever seen. She's prettier than the parson's sitting hen. I'd so like to own her! A hen can always find a grain of corn. She can almost look after herself! I think that would be a good bargain if I got her for the goose." "Shall we swap?" he asked. "Swap?" said the other. "Why, yes, that wasn't such a bad idea!" And so they swapped: the tollman got the goose, the farmer got the hen.

He'd done quite a lot on that journey to town, and it was hot and he was tired. A dram and a bite to eat were what he needed. Now he was by the inn. He wanted to go in, but the innkeeper's hired hand wanted to go out. He met him right in the doorway with a sack heaping full of something.

"What have you got there?" asked the farmer.

"Rotten apples!" answered the fellow. "A whole sackful for the pigs."

"Why, that's an awful lot! I wish Mama could see a sight like that. Last year we had only a single apple on the old tree by the peat shed. That apple had to be kept, and it stood on the chest of drawers until it burst. 'There's always plenty!' said Mama. Here she could really see plenty!"

"Well, what'll you give?" asked the fellow.

"Give? I'll give you my hen in exchange!" And then he gave him the hen for the apples and went into the inn and right over to the bar. He leaned his sack of apples up against the tiled stove. There was a fire in it, but he didn't give that a thought. There were lots of strangers here in the room: horse traders, cattle dealers, and two Englishmen—they're so rich that their pockets are bursting with golden coins, and they love to make wagers!

Now you shall hear.

"Sssssssss! Sssssssss!" What was that noise over by the stove? The apples were beginning to roast.

"What's that?" Well, they soon found out about the whole story—about the horse that had been swapped for the cow, all the way down to the rotten apples.

"Well," said the Englishmen, "you'll be getting a cuff from Mama when you come home! There'll be the devil to pay!"

"I'll get a kiss and not a cuff!" said the farmer. "Our Mama's going to say, 'What Papa does is always right!' "

"Shall we wager?" they said. "A barrelful of gold coins! A hundred pounds to a ship's pound!"

"A bushel is enough," said the farmer. "I can put up only the bushel of apples—and myself and Mama into the bargain! But that's more than a level measure; that's a heaping measure!"

"Heaping! Heaping!" they said, and then the wager was made.

The innkeeper's wagon was brought out, the Englishmen got in, the farmer got in, the rotten apples got in, and then they came to the farmer's house.

"Good evening, Mama!"

"Same to you, Papa!"

"Well, I've made a swap!"

"Yes, you're the best judge of that," said the wife, putting her arm around his waist and forgetting both the sack and the strangers.

"I've swapped the horse for a cow!"

"Heaven be praised for the milk!" said the wife. "Now we can have milk dishes and butter and cheese on the table. That was a lovely swap!"

"Yes, but I swapped the cow for a ewe!"

"That's decidedly better too!" said the wife. "You're always considerate. We've plenty of fodder for a ewe. Now we can have ewe's milk and cheese and woolen stockings— yes, even a woolen nightshirt. The cow doesn't give that. She loses her hair. You're the most considerate man!"

"But I swapped the ewe for a goose!"

"Are we really going to have a goose this year for Martinmas, little Papa? You're always thinking up ways to please me! That was sweet of you. The goose can stand tethered and grow fatter by Martinmas."

"But I swapped the goose for a hen!" said the husband.

"A hen! That was a good swap," said the wife. "The hen lays eggs; it hatches them out—we'll have chickens, we'll have a hen yard! That's just what I've always wanted!"

"Yes, but I swapped the hen for a sack of rotten apples!"

"Now I've got to give you a kiss!" said the wife. "Thank you, my own husband! Now I'm going to tell you something. While you were gone I thought I'd make a really good meal for you—an omelet with chives. I had the eggs, but no chives. So I went over to the schoolmaster's. They have chives there, I know. But the wife is so stingy, that sweet she-ass! I asked if I could borrow! 'Borrow!' she said. 'Nothing grows in our garden, not even a rotten apple! I can't even lend you that!' Now *I* can lend her ten—yes, a whole sackful. What a joke that is, Papa!" And she kissed him squarely on the mouth.

"Now you're talking!" said the Englishmen. "Always down and out, and always without a care! That's certainly worth the money!" And so they paid a ship's pound of golden coins to the farmer, who received a kiss instead of a cuff.

Yes, indeed, it always pays for the wife to realize and

explain that Papa is the wisest, and whatever he does is right.

See, that's a story! I heard it when I was a boy, and now you've heard it too and know that What Papa Does Is Always Right.

The Snowman

❖ ❖ ❖

I'M fairly creaking inside, it's so delightfully cold!" said the snowman. "The wind can really bite life into one! And how that glowerer there can glower!" This was the sun that he meant; it was just about to go down. "She's not going to make me blink! I daresay I can hang onto the fragments!"

He had two big triangular fragments of tile for eyes; the mouth was a piece of an old rake, and so he had teeth.

He had been born to the cheers of the boys and greeted by the jangle of bells and the crack of whips from the sleighs.

The sun went down; the full moon came up, round and big, bright and lovely in the blue air.

"There she is from another angle," said the snowman. He thought the sun was showing itself again. "I've made her stop glowering! Now she can just hang there and shine so I can have a look at myself. If only I knew what one does to move! I'd so like to move! If I could, I'd go down now and slide on the ice, the way I saw the boys doing it! But I don't understand how to run!"

"Gone! Gone!" barked the old watchdog. He was somewhat hoarse. He'd been that way ever since the time he was a house dog and had lain under the tiled stove. "The sun'll soon teach you how to run! I saw it with your predecessor last year, and with *his* predecessor. Gone! Gone! And they are all gone!"

"I don't understand you, friend!" said the snowman. "Is that one up there going to teach me how to run?" He meant the moon. "Well, of course she can run. She ran before, when I glared at her. Now she's sneaking around from another side."

"You don't know anything!" said the watchdog. "But then you've only just been made! The one you're looking at now is called the moon; the one that left was the sun. She'll be back tomorrow. I daresay she'll teach you how to run down in the moat. We'll soon be getting a change in the weather. I can tell by my hind leg—it's aching. The weather's going to change."

"I don't understand him," said the snowman, "but I've

got a feeling that he's saying something unpleasant. That one who glowered and went down—the one he calls the sun—she's not my friend, either. I can feel it."

"Gone! Gone!" barked the watchdog, turning on his tail three times and lying down in his house to go to sleep.

There really was a change in the weather. Early in the morning a thick, clammy fog settled over the entire countryside. At daybreak the wind started to blow. It was biting cold; the frost really nipped. But what a sight to behold when the sun rose! All the trees and bushes were covered with rime. It was like an entire forest of white coral, as if every branch had been heaped with sparkling white blossoms. The myriads of delicate twigs, which cannot be seen in summer for the many leaves, now came into their own—each and every one. It was like lace, and as shining white as if a radiant white light were streaming from every branch. The weeping birch stirred in the wind; it seemed to be as alive as the trees in summer. It was incomparably lovely; and when the sun shone—my, how it all sparkled! It was as if it had been powdered over with diamond dust, while the big diamonds glittered on the earth's blanket of snow. One might even believe that myriads of tiny candles were burning, whiter than the white snow.

"How incredibly lovely!" said a young girl who came out in the garden with a young man, and stopped close to the snowman to look at the glittering trees. "There's no lovelier sight in summer," she said, and her eyes beamed.

"And there aren't any fellows like this one at all," said the young man, pointing to the snowman. "He's splendid!"

The young girl laughed, nodded to the snowman, and danced on with her friend across the snow, which creaked beneath them as if it were starch.

"Who were those two?" the snowman asked the watchdog. "You've been here in the yard longer than I have. Do you know them?"

"That I do!" said the watchdog. "After all, she has petted me and he has given me a bone. I don't bite them."

"But what are they supposed to be?" asked the snowman.

"Sweeeeeeethearrrrrrrts!" said the watchdog. "They're going to move into a doghouse and gnaw bones together. Gone! Gone!"

"Are those two just as important as you and I?" asked the snowman.

"Why, they belong to the family," said the watchdog. "I must say, there's very little one knows when one was born yesterday. I can tell by the way you act! I have age and knowledge; I know everybody here. And I've known a day when I didn't stand outside chained up in the cold! Gone! Gone!"

"The cold is delightful!" said the snowman. "Tell! Tell! But you mustn't rattle your chain, for it makes me crack inside."

"Gone! Gone!" barked the watchdog. "I was once a puppy—tiny and sweet, they said. Then I lay on a velvet stool inside the house, lay on the lap of the head of the family. I was kissed on the chaps and had my paws wiped with an embroidered handkerchief. I was called "the most delightful" and "cuddly-wuddly." But then I grew too big for them, so they gave me to the housekeeper. I came down to the basement! You can see in there from where you're standing. You can look down into the room where I was lord and master, for that's what I was at the housekeeper's. It was probably a humbler place than above, but it was more comfortable here. And I wasn't mauled and hauled about the way I was by the children upstairs. The food I got was just as good, and there was more of it! I had my own pillow, and then there was a tiled stove—the most wonderful thing in the world at this time of year. I crawled all the way in underneath it until I was out of sight. Oh, I still dream about that tiled stove! Gone! Gone!"

"Does a tiled stove look so lovely?" asked the snowman. "Does it look like me?"

"It's the very opposite of you! It's as black as coal and has a long neck with a brass drum. It eats wood until the flames pour out of its mouth. You have to stay beside it, close up to it, underneath it; it's an infinite pleasure! You must be able to see it through the window from where you're standing!"

And the snowman looked, and he really did see a black highly polished object that had a brass drum. The fire shone out at the bottom. The snowman felt very queer. He had a feeling that he was unable to account for; something had come over him that he had never known before, but which everyone has known who isn't a snowman.

"And why did you leave her?" said the snowman—he felt that it had to be of the female persuasion. "How could you leave such a place?"

"I had to," said the watchdog. "They threw me outside and put me here on a chain. I'd bitten the youngest Junker in the leg for kicking away the bone I was gnawing on. And bone for bone, I thought. But they took exception to this, and I've been chained up out here ever since. And I've lost my clear voice. Listen to how hoarse I am. Gone! Gone! That was the end of that!"

The snowman was no longer listening. He gazed steadily into the housekeeper's basement, down into her parlor, where the stove stood on its four legs and seemed to be as big as the snowman himself.

"I'm creaking so strangely inside," he said. "Will I never come in there? It's a harmless wish, and our harmless wishes ought to be granted. It's my greatest wish, my only wish, and it would almost be unjust if it weren't granted. I must come in there, I must lean up against her, even if I have to break the window."

"You'll never get inside there," said the watchdog. "And if you did get to the tiled stove, you'd be gone! Gone!"

"I'm as good as gone!" said the snowman. "I think I'm breaking in two!"

All day long the snowman stood gazing in through the
window. In the twilight the room was even more inviting.
From the tiled stove came a gentle glow, as could never
come from the moon or the sun; no, it glowed as only a
tiled stove can glow when it has something inside it. If the
door was opened, the flames shot out as they were in the
habit of doing. The snowman's white face turned a scarlet
hue, he was red all the way down to his chest.

"I can't stand it," he said. "How it becomes her to stick
out her tongue!"

The night was very long, but not for the snowman. He
stood deep in his own lovely thoughts, and they froze so
they creaked.

In the early-morning hours the basement windows were
frozen over; they were covered with the loveliest flowers
of ice that any snowman could wish for, but they hid the
tiled stove. The panes wouldn't thaw; he couldn't see her.
It creaked and it crunched; it was just the sort of frosty
weather to satisfy any snowman, but he wasn't satisfied.
He could and he should have felt so happy, but he wasn't
happy: he had what is known as the "tiled-stove-yearning."

"That's a bad sickness for a snowman to have," said the
watchdog. "I've had a little of the same sickness myself,
but I've got over it. Gone! Gone! Now we're going to have
a change in the weather."

And there was a change in the weather: a thaw set in.

The thaw increased, the snowman decreased. He never
said a word, he never complained, and that's a sure sign.

One morning he fell over. Something like the handle of
a mop was sticking in the air where he had been standing.
This is what the boys had built him around.

"Now I can understand his longing," said the watchdog.
"The snowman had a poker inside him. That's what has
affected him; now it's over! Gone! Gone!"

And soon the winter was over too.

"Gone! Gone!" barked the watchdog.
But in the yard the little girls sang:

> "Hurry forth woodruff, fresh and fair,
> Willow, hang your woolen tassels there,
> Come cuckoo, lark! Sing, be merry,
> Spring has come in February.
> Cuckoo! Tweet-tweet! I sing too!
> Come, dear sun, the way you often do!"

So no one is thinking about the snowman!

In the Duck Yard

❖   ❖   ❖

A duck came from Portugal, some said from Spain. It makes no difference—she was called "The Portuguese." She laid eggs, was butchered and served for dinner; that's the course of her life. All those who crawled out of her eggs were called "The Portuguese," and that meant something. Now, of the entire stock only one was left in the duck yard—a yard to which the chickens also had access, and where the cock behaved with infinite arrogance.

"That violent crowing of his outrages me!" said The Portuguese. "But he is handsome. That cannot be denied, despite the fact that he is no drake. He should control himself, but controlling oneself is an art. It reveals breeding. That's what the little songbirds up in the linden tree in the neighboring garden possess. How sweetly they sing! There's something so moving in their song. I'd call it *Portugal!* If I had a little songbird like that, I'd be a mother to him, affectionate and good. It's in my blood, in my Portuguese!"

And at the same moment as she was speaking, a little songbird did come. It came headlong down from the roof. The cat was after it, but the bird escaped with a broken wing and fell down in the duck yard.

"That's just like the cat, the scoundrel!" said The Portuguese. "I know him from the time I had ducklings myself! That such a creature is permitted to live and walk about on the rooftops! I don't believe it would happen in Portugal!"

And she took pity on the little songbird, and the other ducks, who weren't Portuguese, took pity on him too.

"The poor little mite," they said, and came one after the other. "It's true that we're not singers ourselves," they said, "but we do have internal sounding boards, or something like that; we feel it even if we don't talk about it."

"Then I want to talk about it," said The Portuguese. "And I want to do something for it, for that is one's duty!" And then she went up to the drinking trough and flapped in the water, so that she almost drowned the little songbird in the deluge he received. But it was well meant. "That's a good deed!" she said. "The others can look at it and follow its example."

"Peep!" said the little bird; one of his wings was broken. It was hard for him to shake himself, but he quite understood that well-meant deluge. "You're so tenderhearted, madame!" he said, but he insisted on nothing more.

"I've never given the tenderness of my heart a thought!" said The Portuguese. "But I do know that I love all my fellow creatures with the exception of the cat. But then no one can ask that of me! I myself am from foreign parts, as you probably can tell by my carriage and my feathered gown. My drake is a native, doesn't have my blood, but I don't put on airs! If you're understood by anybody in here, then I daresay it's by me."

"She was a *portulaca*[1] to the craw," said one ordinary little duckling who was witty, and the other ordinary ducklings thought that *portulaca* was quite splendid—it sounded like Portugal; and they nudged one another and

[1] Purslane.

said, "Quack!" He was so incomparably witty. And then they took up with the little songbird.

"True, The Portuguese has the language at her command," they said. "Our bills are not given to big words, but we participate just as much. If we don't do anything for you, we keep quiet about it, and we find that to be most agreeable."

"You have a sweet voice," said one of the oldest. "It must be delightful to be aware that one gives so much pleasure to so many, the way you do. Of course I don't know anything about that! And so I keep my mouth shut, and that's always better than saying something stupid, the way so many others say to you."

"Don't pester him!" said The Portuguese. "He needs rest and care. Little songbird, shall I splash you again?"

"Oh, no, let me stay dry!" he begged.

"The water cure is the only thing that helps me," said The Portuguese. "Diversion is also quite good! Now the neighboring hens will be coming soon to pay a visit. There are two Chinese hens. They wear pantaloons and have considerable breeding, and they've been imported—which elevates them in my esteem."

And the hens came, and the cock came! He was so polite today that he wasn't rude.

"You're a real songbird," he said, "and with your little voice you do as much as can be done with such a little voice! But something more locomotive is needed for it to be heard that one is of the male sex!"

The two Chinese hens stood enraptured over the sight of the songbird. He looked so disheveled from the deluge he had received that they thought he resembled a Chinese chicken. "He's lovely!" And then they took up with him. They spoke in whispers, and the *p*-sound in proper Chinese.

"Now, we belong to your species. The ducks—even The Portuguese—belong to the web-footed birds, as you no doubt have observed. You don't know us yet, but how many do know us or take the trouble to! No one, not even among the hens, even though we're born to sit on a higher perch than most of the others. Of course it doesn't matter—we go our silent way among the others whose principles are not our own. But we look only at the good qualities and talk only about the good, despite the fact that it's hard to find where none exists. But with the exception of the two of us and the cock, there's no one in the hen house who is gifted. But they are respectable. You can't say this about the occupants of the duck yard. We warn you, little songbird, don't believe the one there with the short tail—she's perfidious! That speckled one there, with the uneven wing bows, she loves to argue and never permits anyone to have the last word. And then she's always wrong! That fat duck talks badly about everybody, and that's contrary to our nature. If you can't say something nice, then you should keep your mouth shut. The Portuguese is the only one who has a little breeding, and with whom one can associate. But she's passionate, and talks too much about Portugal!"

"What a lot the two Chinese have to whisper about!" said a couple of the ducks. "They bore me; I've never talked with them!"

Now the drake came. He thought the songbird was a house sparrow. "Well, I can't tell them apart," he said. "And besides, it makes no difference! He's one of the mechanical musical instruments, and if you've got them, then you've got them."

"Pay no attention to what he says!" whispered The Portuguese. "He's worthy of respect in business, and business is everything! But now I'm going to lie down to rest. One owes it to oneself to be nice and fat until one is ready to be embalmed with apples and prunes."

And then she lay down in the sunshine, blinking one eye. She lay so well, she behaved so well, and then she slept so well. The little songbird pecked at his broken wing and lay down next to his protectress; the sun shone warm and delightful; it was a good place to be.

The neighbor hens continued to scrape. As a matter of fact, they had come there solely for the sake of the food. The Chinese left first and then the others. The witty duckling said, about The Portuguese, that the old one would soon be going into her "Duckage." And then the other ducks cackled, "Duckage! He's so incomparably witty!" And then they repeated the first witticism: *"Portulaca!"* That was very funny. And then they lay down.

They lay there for a while, then all at once some slops were thrown down in the duck yard. It made such a splash that the entire sleeping company flew up and flapped their wings. The Portuguese woke up too and fell over, crushing the little songbird quite dreadfully.

"Peep!" he said. "You tread so hard, madame!"

"Why are you lying in the way?" she said. "You mustn't be so thin-skinned! I have nerves too, but I've never said 'Peep'!"

"Don't be angry," said the little bird. "That 'Peep' slipped out of my beak."

The Portuguese paid no attention to this, but flew to the slops and had her good meal. When it was over and she had lain down, the little songbird came and wanted to be pleasant:

> "Twittery-twing!
>   About your heart
>   I'll always sing,
>   Far, far, far on the wing!"

"Now I'm going to rest after the food," she said. "You've got to learn the house rules in here! Now I'm going to sleep."

The little songbird was quite taken aback, for he had meant so well by it. When madame later awoke, he was standing in front of her with a little grain of corn he had found. He put it in front of her, but she hadn't slept well and of course she was cross.

"You can give that to a chicken!" she said. "Don't stand there and hang over me!"

"But you're angry with me," he said. "What have I done?"

"Done!" said The Portuguese. "That expression is not of the finest sort, I'll have you know!"

"Yesterday there was sunshine here," said the little

bird, "but today it's dark and gray! I'm so deeply grieved."

"You certainly don't know enough about measuring time," said The Portuguese. "The day isn't over yet, so don't stand there and pretend to be so stupid."

"You're looking at me so angrily, the way those two evil eyes looked when I fell down here in the yard."

"Impudence!" said The Portuguese. "Are you comparing me with the cat, that beast of prey? There's not one drop of evil blood in me. I've taken care of you, and I'm going to teach you how to behave!"

And then she bit off the songbird's head. He lay dead.

"Now what's that?" she said. "Couldn't he take it! Well, he certainly wasn't much for this world, then! I've been like a mother to him, that I know, for I do have a heart."

And the neighboring cock stuck his head into the yard and crowed with the power of a locomotive.

"You'll be the death of somebody with that crowing!" she said. "It's all your fault! He lost his head, and I'm about to lose mine!"

"He doesn't take up much room where he lies," said the cock.

"Talk about him with respect!" said The Portuguese. "He had manners and song and good breeding! He was affectionate and softhearted, and that's just as becoming to the animals as to those so-called human beings."

And all the ducks gathered around the little dead songbird. The ducks have strong passions, no matter whether it's envy or compassion. And as there was nothing here for them to be envious of, they were compassionate. And so were the two Chinese hens.

"We'll never have a songbird like that again! He was almost Chinese!" And they cried so they clucked, and all the hens clucked. But the ducks went about with the reddest eyes.

"We have heart," they said. "There's no denying that!"

"Heart!" said The Portuguese. "Yes, that we have—almost just as much as in Portugal."

"Now let's see about getting something in the carcass!" said the drake. "That's more important! If one of the mechanical musical instruments breaks down, we'll still have enough."

The Butterfly

❖ ❖ ❖

THE butterfly wanted to have a sweetheart. Naturally he wanted one of the pretty little flowers. He looked at them; each one was sitting so prim and proper on its stalk, the way a maiden should sit when she is not engaged. But there were so many to choose from that it proved irksome. The butterfly couldn't be bothered, and so he flew to the daisy. The French call her Marguerite. They know that she can foretell the future, and she does it when sweethearts pick petal by petal off her, and with each one they ask a question about the beloved: "Loves me? Loves me not? Loves me a lot? A teeny-weeny bit? Not at all?" Or something like that. Each one asks in his own language. The butterfly also came to ask. He didn't nip off the petals, but kissed each one—it being his opinion that one comes the farthest without resorting to force.

"Sweet Marguerite!" he said. "Of all the flowers, you are the wisest woman! You understand how to foretell the future. Tell me, am I to marry this one or that? When I find it out, I can fly straight over and propose!"

But Marguerite did not reply at all. She could not bear his calling her a woman, for of course she was a maiden, and then one is not a woman. He asked a second time and he asked a third. And when he didn't get a single word out

313

of her, he couldn't be bothered with asking her anymore and flew off to woo without further ado.

It was early spring. There were snowdrops and crocuses in abundance.

"You are quite nice!" said the butterfly. "Lovely, small candidates for confirmation! But a bit green!" Like all other young men, he was looking for older girls. Then he flew to the anemones. They were a little too tart for him, the violets a little too soulful, the tulips too gaudy, the white narcissus too bourgeois, the lime blossoms too small— and they had so many kinfolk. To be sure, the apple blossoms looked like roses, but they stood today and fell off tomorrow—all according to the way the wind blew.

That was too short a marriage, he thought. The sweet pea was the most pleasing: she was white and red, pure and delicate—one of those homey maidens who look good and yet are cut out for the kitchen. He was just going to propose to her when, at the same moment, he saw hanging close by a pea pod with withered flowers on the top.

"Who's that?" he asked.

"That's my sister," said the sweet pea.

"Well, that's the way you're going to look later!" This frightened the butterfly, and so he flew away.

The honeysuckles were hanging over the fence. There were plenty of those maidens—with long faces and sallow complexions. They weren't his type at all.

Well, what was his type? Ask him!

Spring passed. Summer passed, and then it was autumn. He had made just as much headway. And the flowers appeared in the loveliest garments. But what good was that? The fresh, fragrant lightness of heart was lacking. Fragrance is just what the heart needs, and there is not very much fragrance to dahlias and hollyhocks. So the butterfly turned to the mint.

"Now it has no flower at all. But it is all flower, gives off a fragrance from root to top, and has a flower scent in every leaf. She is the one I will take!"

And so he proposed at last.

But the mint stood still and stiff, and at last she said, "Friendship, but no more. I am old and you are old. We could quite well live for each other. But marry? No! Let us not make fools of ourselves at our great age!"

And so the butterfly got no one at all. He had searched too long, and one should not do that. The butterfly became a bachelor, as it is called.

It was late autumn, with rain and drizzle. The wind sent cold shivers down the spines of the old willow trees, making them creak. It was not good flying outside in summer clothes—you'd be in for an unpleasant surprise, as they say. But the butterfly did not fly outside, either. By chance he had come indoors, where there was a fire in the stove. Indeed, it was as warm as summer. He could live.

"But living isn't enough!" he said. "One must have sunshine, freedom, and a little flower!"

He flew against the pane, and was seen, admired, and stuck on a pin in the curio chest. More could not be done for him.

"Now I too am sitting on a stalk, just as the flowers do!" said the butterfly. "But it is not very pleasant. Indeed, it is like being married—one is stuck!" And then he consoled himself with that.

"That is poor consolation," said the potted plants in the parlor.

"But one cannot quite believe the potted plants," thought the butterfly. "They associate too much with people."

The Snail and
the Rosebush

❖ ❖ ❖

AROUND the garden was a hedge of hazlenut bushes, and beyond it were fields and meadows with cows and sheep. But in the middle of the garden stood a flowering rosebush, and under it sat a snail. It contained a lot: it contained itself.

"Wait until my time comes!" it said. "I shall accomplish something more than sending forth roses, bearing nuts, or giving milk, as cows and sheep do."

"I'm expecting a great deal from you," said the rosebush. "May I ask when it's coming?"

"I'm biding my time," said the snail. "You, now, are in such a hurry! It doesn't raise one's expectations."

The next year the snail was lying in just about the same spot in the sunshine, under the rosebush, which was budding and sending forth roses—always fresh, always new. And the snail crawled halfway out, stretched out its horns, and drew them back again.

"Everything looks the way it did last year! There has been no progress. The rosebush keeps on sending forth roses; it makes no further headway."

The summer passed and autumn came. The rosebush kept on sending forth flowers and buds until the snow fell. The weather turned raw and wet. The rosebush bent down to the ground; the snail crawled into the earth.

Now a new year began, and the roses came forth and the snail came forth.

"Now you're an old rose stock!" it said. "You must soon see about dying. You've given the world everything you had in you. Whether it was of any consequence is a question I haven't had time to think over. But still it's clear that you haven't done the slightest thing about your inner development, or else you would have produced something else. Can you justify that? Soon you'll end up as kindling. Can you understand what I'm saying?"

"You frighten me," said the rosebush. "I've never given it a thought."

"No, I daresay you never were much prone to thinking. Have you ever figured out for yourself why you put forth flowers and how the flowering came about? Why this way and not another way?"

"No," said the rosebush. "I flowered for the joy of it. I couldn't help myself. The sun was so warm, the air so invigorating. I drank the clear dew and the strong rain. I breathed, I lived! A force came up in me from the earth and from above; I sensed a joy always new, always great, and for that reason I had to blossom. That was my life—I couldn't help myself."

"You have led a very easy life," said the snail.

"Assuredly! Everything has been handed to me!" said the rosebush. "But even more has been given to you! You are one of those thoughtful, profound natures, one of the highly gifted who wants to astound the world."

"That has never crossed my mind at all," said the snail. "The world is of no concern to me! What have I to do with the world? I have enough with myself and enough in myself."

"But shouldn't each one of us here on earth give the best we have to others, bring what we can? To be sure, I have only given roses—but you, you who have received so much, what have you given to the world? What are you giving to it?"

"What have I given? What am I giving? I spit at it! It's no good! It is of no concern to me! You send forth roses. You can go no further! Let the hazelnut bush bear nuts. Let cows and sheep give milk. They each have their public; I have mine in myself! I withdraw into myself, and there I stay. The world is of no concern to me!"

And then the snail went inside its house and sealed it up.

"It's so sad," said the rosebush. "As much as I'd like to, I cannot crawl inside. I must always come out, come out in roses. The petals fall off; they fly about in the wind. And yet I saw one of the roses being put in the house-wife's hymnbook; one of my roses was placed on the breast of a lovely young girl; and one was kissed by the lips of a child in blissful joy. It did me so much good! It was truly a blessing. This is my reminiscence, my life!"

And the rosebush bloomed in innocence, and the snail languished in its house. The world was of no concern to him.

And the years went by.

And the snail was dust in the earth. The rosebush was dust in the earth; even the keepsake rose in the hymnbook had withered away. But in the garden new rosebushes bloomed; in the garden new snails grew; they crawled into their houses and spit—the world was of no concern to them.

Shall we read the story again from the beginning? It will be no different.

The Teapot

❖   ❖   ❖

THERE was a proud teapot—proud of its porcelain, proud of its long spout, proud of its broad handle. It had something in front and something behind, the spout in front and the handle behind, and it talked about that. But it didn't talk about its lid; that was cracked and had been riveted. It had a flaw, and one is not fond of talking about one's flaws—the others are sure to do that. Cups, cream pitcher, and sugar bowl, the whole tea service, would be sure to remember more the frailty of the lid, and to talk about it, than about the good handle and the excellent spout. And the teapot was aware of this.

"I know them!" it said to itself. "I am also well aware of my flaw, and I acknowledge it. Therein lies my humility, my modesty. We all have flaws, but one also has talents. The cups were given a handle, the sugar bowl a lid. I, of course, was given both, and one thing in front that they will never receive: I was given a spout. That makes me the queen of the tea table. The sugar bowl and the cream pitcher have been granted the privilege of being hand-maidens of palatability. But I am the dispenser, the mistress. I diffuse the blessing among thirsting humanity. In my interior the Chinese leaf is prepared in the boiling, tasteless water."

All this the teapot said in its intrepid youth. It stood on

the ready-laid table. It was lifted by the most delicate hand. But the most delicate hand was clumsy: the teapot fell, the spout broke off, and the handle broke off. The lid is not worth mentioning—enough has been said about that. The teapot lay in a swoon on the floor, the boiling water running out of it. It had received a hard blow. And the hardest blow of all was that they laughed at it, and not at the clumsy hand.

"That memory I will never lose," said the teapot when it later related the course of its life to itself. "I was called an invalid and put over in a corner, and on the following day I was given away to a woman who came begging for drippings. I sank down into destitution, stood speechless, both inside and out. But as I stood there my better life began. You are one thing and turn into quite another. Dirt was put inside me. To a teapot this is the same as being buried, but a flower bulb was put in the dirt. Who put it there, who gave it I do not know. It was given a compensation for the Chinese leaves and the boiling water a compensation for the broken-off handle and spout. And the bulb lay in the dirt, the bulb lay inside me. It became my heart, my living heart. I had never had one like that before. There was life in me, there was vigor and vitality; the pulse beat, the bulb sprouted. It was bursting with thoughts and emotions. It bloomed. I saw it, I bore it, I forgot myself in its loveliness. How blessed it is to forget oneself in others! It did not thank me. It did not think of me: it was admired and praised. I was so happy because of that: how happy it must have been then. One day I heard someone say that it deserved a better pot. I was broken in two. It hurt terribly, but the flower was put in a better pot—and I was thrown out in the yard, to lie there like an old fragment. But I have a memory that I cannot lose."

The Candles

❖   ❖   ❖

THERE was once a big wax candle that was well aware
of itself.

"I am born of wax and cast in a mold!" it said. "I shine
better and burn longer than any other candle! My place is
in a chandelier or a silver candlestick!"

"That must be a delightful existence," said the tallow
candle. "I am merely of tallow, only a taper. But I take
comfort in the thought that it's always a little more than
being a tallow dip! It is dipped only twice, whereas I am
dipped eight times to arrive at my proper thickness. I am
content! To be sure, it is finer and more fortunate to be
born of wax and not of tallow, but after all one doesn't put
oneself into this world. They go into the parlor in a crystal
chandelier; I remain in the kitchen. But that is a good
place too. From there the whole house is fed!"

"But there's something far more important than food!"
said the wax candle. "Festivity! To see the radiance and to
be radiant oneself! There's going to be a ball here this
evening. Soon my whole family and I are going to be
fetched!"

The words were scarcely uttered before all the wax
candles were fetched. But the tallow candle came along
too. The mistress herself picked it up in her delicate hand
and carried it out into the kitchen. A little boy was stand-

ing there with a basket. It was filled with potatoes, and a few apples had been added. All this the good woman gave to the poor boy.

"Here's a candle for you too, my little friend!" she said. "Your mother sits working far into the night; she can use it!"

The little daughter of the house was standing nearby, and when she heard the words "far into the night," she said with heartfelt joy, "I too am going to stay up until far into the night. We're going to have a ball, and I'm going to wear my big red bows!"

How her face shone! This was happiness! No wax candle can shine like the two eyes of a child!

"What a blessed sight!" thought the tallow candle. "I will never forget it, and I daresay I will never see it again."

And then it was put in the basket under the lid, and the boy left with it.

"Where am I going now?" thought the candle. "I'm going to poor people. Perhaps I won't even be given a brass candlestick, whereas the wax candle is sitting in silver and looking at the most fashionable people. How wonderful it must be to shine for the most fashionable people. After all, it was my fate to be of tallow and not of wax!"

And the candle did come to poor people, a widow with three children in a lowly little cottage right across from the house of the rich family.

"God bless the good mistress for her gift," said the mother. "Why, there's a lovely candle! It can burn until far into the night!"

And the candle was lighted.

"Sputter, phooey!" it said. "What a nasty, smelly match she lit me with! Such a match would hardly have been offered to a wax candle over in the rich family's house!"

There too the candles were being lighted; they shone

out into the street. The rumbling carriages brought the elegantly clad ball guests. The music rang out.

"Now they're beginning over there!" observed the tallow candle, and thought of the little rich girl's radiant face, more radiant than all the wax candles. "I'll never see a sight like that again!"

Then the youngest child of the poor family came, a little girl. She flung her arms around the necks of her brother and sister—she had something very important to tell them and it had to be whispered: "This evening . . . Imagine! . . . This evening we're going to have hot potatoes!"

And her face shone with bliss. The candle shining there saw a joy, a happiness, as great as that it had seen over in the house of the rich family, where the little girl had said, "We're going to have a ball, and I'm going to wear my big red bows!"

"Is having hot potatoes equally as important?" thought the candle. "The children here are just as happy." And then she sneezed; that is to say, she sputtered, a tallow candle can do no more.

The table was set; the potatoes were eaten. Oh, how delicious they tasted! It was quite a feast! And afterward each child received an apple, and the youngest child recited the little verse:

> "Again, dear Lord, my thanks to thee,
> For giving so much food to me! Amen!"

"Wasn't it nice of me to say that, Mother?" the little one now cried.

"You must neither ask nor say such a thing," said the mother. "You should think only of the good Lord, who has given you enough to eat."

The little ones went to bed, received a kiss, and fell asleep right away, and the mother sat sewing until far into the night to earn a livelihood for them and for herself. And from the house of the rich family, the candles shone and the music rang out. The stars twinkled above all the houses, above those of the rich and those of the poor, just as bright, just as lovely.

"Come to think of it, this was a strange evening," thought the tallow candle. "I wonder if the wax candles were any better off in silver candlesticks. I wish I could find that out before I burn down."

And it thought of the two children—equally as happy—one illuminated by wax candles, the other by a tallow candle!

Yes, that's the whole story!

The Most Incredible Thing

❖   ❖   ❖

WHOEVER could accomplish the most incredible thing was to have the king's daughter and half the kingdom. The young people—indeed, the old ones too—strained all their thoughts, tendons, and muscles. Two ate themselves to death and one drank himself to death to accomplish the most incredible thing—each according to his own taste—but that wasn't the way in which it was to be done. Little street urchins practiced spitting on their own backs—they considered this to be the most incredible thing.

On a given day each one had to show what he considered to be the most incredible thing. Children from the age of three to people in their nineties had been appointed as judges. There was a whole exhibition of incredible things, but everyone soon agreed that the most incredible thing of all was a huge clock in a case, remarkably contrived inside and out. At each stroke of the clock appeared living pictures that depicted the hour. There were twelve performances in all, with movable figures and with song and speech.

"This was the most incredible thing!" people said.

The clock struck one, and Moses stood on the mount and wrote down the First Commandment on the Tables of the Law: "Thou shalt have no other gods before me."

The clock struck two: now appeared the Garden of Paradise, where Adam and Eve met, both happy without owning so much as a clothes closet, nor did they need one, either.

On the stroke of three, the three Wise Men appeared, one as black as coal—he couldn't help that, the sun had blackened him. They came bearing incense and precious objects.

On the stroke of four came the Seasons: Spring with a cuckoo on a beech branch in full leaf; Summer with a grasshopper on a ripe sheaf of grain; Autumn with an empty stork's nest—the bird had flown away; Winter with an old crow, which could tell stories and old memories in the corner by the tiled stove.

When the clock struck five, the Five Senses appeared: Sight came as an optician, Hearing as a coppersmith, Smell sold violets and woodruff, Taste was a chef, and Touch was an undertaker with mourning crepe down to his heels.

The clock struck six: there sat a gambler casting a die. The highest side turned up and on it stood six.

Then came the Seven Days of the Week or the Seven Deadly Sins—people couldn't agree. After all, they belonged together and weren't easy to tell apart.

Then came a choir singing matins.

On the stroke of nine followed the Nine Muses: one was employed in Astronomy, one at the Historical Archives, and the rest were in the theater.

On the stroke of ten, Moses again appeared with the Tables of the Law. There stood all of God's Commandments, and there were ten of them.

The clock struck again: now little boys and girls were hopping and jumping. They were playing a game, and with it they sang: "Digging, delving, the clock's struck eleven!" And this is the hour it had struck.

Then it struck twelve. Now the nightwatch appeared in

a fur cap and with a spiked mace. He sang the old night-watch cry:

> " 'Twas at the midnight hour
> Our Savior, Lord was born."

And as he sang roses sprang up, and they turned into the heads of cherubs borne by rainbow-hued wings.

It was a delight to hear, it was a joy to behold. The entire clock was such an incomparable work of art—the most incredible thing, all the people said.

The artist was a young man, tenderhearted, fond of children, a loyal friend, and helpful to his poor parents. He deserved the princess and half the kingdom.

The day of decision was at hand, the entire city was decked out, and the princess was sitting on the throne of the land—it had been given a new horsehair stuffing, but this didn't make it any more comfortable or any easier to sit on for that. The judges on all sides stole sly glances at the one who was going to win, and he stood confident and happy—his success was assured: he had accomplished the most incredible thing!

"No! That's what I'm going to do now!" cried a tall, rawboned, strapping fellow at the same moment. "I'm the man to accomplish the most incredible thing!" And then he swung a huge ax at the work of art.

CRASH! SMASH! SHATTER! There it all lay. Wheels and springs flew about. The whole thing was destroyed!

"I was capable of doing that!" said the man. "My deed has surpassed his and overwhelmed you all. I have accomplished the most incredible thing!"

"To destroy such a work of art!" said the judges. "Yes, that was the most incredible thing!"

The entire populace agreed, and so *he* was to have the princess and half the kingdom! For a law is a law, even if it is the most incredible thing.

From the ramparts and from all the city towers it was proclaimed: "The wedding is to be solemnized!" The princess wasn't at all pleased with it, but she looked lovely and she was richly dressed. The church was ablaze with light—it looks its best late in the evening. The noble maidens of the city sang and ushered in the bride. The knights sang and accompanied the bridegroom. He was swaggering as if he could never be brought to his knees.

Now the singing stopped. It grew so quiet that you could have heard a pin drop on the ground. But in the midst of all that silence the church doors flew open with a rumble and a bang, and BOOM! BOOM! The entire timepiece came marching down the middle of the aisle and lined up between the bride and bridegroom. Dead people cannot come back again—we know this very well—but a work of art can come back again. The body had been smashed to bits, but not the spirit. The Art Spirit had returned as a ghost, and this was no joke.

The work of art stood there as lifelike as when it had been whole and untouched. The strokes of the clock rang out, one after the other, all the way to twelve, and the figures swarmed in. First came Moses. Flames seemed to flash from his forehead. He threw the heavy Tables of the Law onto the bridegroom's feet, pinning them to the floor of the church.

"I cannot lift them again!" said Moses. "You have broken off my arms! Remain now as you are!"

Next came Adam and Eve, the Wise Men from the East, and the Four Seasons, and they all told him unpleasant truths: "Be ashamed of yourself!"

But he wasn't ashamed of himself.

All the figures that had been revealed with each stroke of the clock stepped out of the timepiece, and they grew to a terrible size; it was as if there weren't room for the real people. And when the nightwatch stepped out on the stroke of twelve, with fur cap and mace, there was a strange commotion. The nightwatch went straight over to the bridegroom and struck him on the forehead with the mace.

"Lie there!" he said. "One good turn deserves another! We are avenged and the master too! We are disappearing!"

And then the entire work of art vanished. But all the candles around the church turned into huge flowers of light, and from the gilded stars under the roof were shining long bright shafts of light. The organ pealed by itself. All the people said that this was the most incredible thing they had ever experienced.

"Then, will you summon the right one?" said the princess. "The one who constructed the work of art—he is to be my husband and my lord!"

And he was standing in the church. The entire populace was his retinue. Everyone rejoiced, everyone gave him his blessing. There wasn't a soul who was envious.

Indeed, *that* was the most incredible thing!

The Gardener and
the Lord and Lady

❖ ❖ ❖

A BOUT four or five miles from the capital stood an old
manor house with thick walls and towers and a corbie
gable.

Here there lived—but only during the summer—a rich
lord and lady who belonged to the high nobility. This
manor was the best and finest of all the manors they
owned. It looked like new on the outside and was cozy
and comfortable on the inside. The family coat of arms had
been carved in stone above the gate; beautiful roses twined
about the shield and the bay; a whole carpet of grass
stretched out in front of the manor; there were red haw-
thornes and mayflowers; there were rare flowers even
outside the greenhouse.

The lord and lady also had a clever gardener. It was a
delight to behold the flower garden, the orchard, and the
kitchen garden. Adjoining this was what was left of the
original old garden of the estate, with several box hedges
trimmed to form crowns and pyramids. Behind these stood
two enormous old trees. They were almost always bare of
leaves, and it was easy to believe that a gale or a water-
spout had strewn them with big clumps of dung. But each
clump was a bird's nest.

From time immemorial, swarms of shrieking rooks and
crows had built their nests here: it was a complete bird

city, and the birds were the aristocrats, the landed propri-
etors, the oldest stock of the family seat, the real lords and
ladies of the estate. None of the human beings down
below was any concern of theirs, but they put up with
these low-flying creatures even though they banged away
with guns now and then, sending chills up the spines of
the birds, so that each one flew up in fright, shrieking:
"Caw! Caw!"

The gardener often spoke to his lord and lady about
having the old trees chopped down; they didn't look good,

and once they were gone, in all likelihood, they would be
rid of those shrieking birds, which would go somewhere
else. But the lord and lady had no desire to be rid of the
trees or the swarm of birds. This was something the estate
couldn't be without; it was something from bygone days,
and that shouldn't be wiped out at all.

"Those trees, after all, are the inheritance of the birds. Let them keep it, my good Larsen!"

The gardener's name was Larsen, but that is of no further consequence here.

"Isn't your sphere of operation big enough, little Larsen? The entire flower garden, the greenhouses, the orchard, and the kitchen garden?"

Those he had; those he tended, looked after, and cultivated with zeal and skill. And the lord and lady admitted this. But they never hesitated to let him know that, while visiting, they had often eaten fruit or seen flowers that surpassed those they had in their own garden; and this distressed the gardener, for he wanted to do the best and he did the best he could. He had a good heart and did a good job.

One day the lord and lady sent for him and told him blandly and superciliously that on the previous day, while visiting distinguished friends, they had been served a species of apples and pears so succulent and tasty that they and all the guests had expressed their admiration. To be sure, the fruits were not domestic, but they ought to be imported, made to thrive here if our climate permitted it. It was known that they had been purchased from the first fruit dealer in the city. The gardener was to ride in and find out where these apples and pears had come from and then write for cuttings. The gardener knew the fruit dealer well. It was to this very dealer that, on behalf of the lord and lady, he sold the surplus of fruit that grew in the garden of the estate.

And the gardener went to the city and asked the fruit dealer where he had gotten these highly praised apples and pears from.

"They're from your own garden!" said the fruit dealer, and showed him both apples and pears, which he recognized.

My, how happy this made the gardener; he hurried

back to the lord and lady and told them that both the apples and the pears had come from their own garden.

The lord and lady couldn't believe this at all. "It's not possible, Larsen! Can you obtain a declaration in writing from the fruit dealer?"

And this he could; he brought back a written attestation.

"How very extraordinary!" said the lord and lady.

Every day now bowls of these magnificent apples and pears from their own garden appeared on the table of the lord and lady. Bushels and barrels of these fruits were sent to friends in the city and beyond, yes, even abroad. It afforded them great pleasure! And yet they had to add that, after all, there had been two remarkably good summers for tree fruit. These had turned out well everywhere in the land.

Some time passed. The nobility dined at the court. On the following day the gardener was summoned to his lord and lady. At the royal table they had been served such luscious, tasty melons from their majesties' greenhouse.

"You must go to the court gardener, my good Larsen, and obtain for us some of the seeds from these priceless melons!"

"But the court gardener has got the seeds from us!" said the gardener, quite pleased.

"Then that man has discovered a way of bringing the fruit to a higher stage of development," replied the lord and lady. "Each melon was excellent."

"Well, then, I can be proud!" said the gardener. "You see, my lady and my lord, this year the court gardener hasn't had any luck with his melons, and when he saw how splendidly ours were standing, and tasted them, he ordered three to be sent up to the castle."

"Larsen! Don't get the idea into your head that they were the melons from our garden!"

"I think so!" said the gardener, and went to the court

gardener and obtained from him written proof that the melons on the royal table had come from the manor.

This was really a surprise to the lord and lady, and they did nothing to keep the story quiet. They showed the attestation; indeed, melon seeds were sent far and wide, just as the cuttings had been sent previously.

They received word that the seeds took and bore quite excellent fruit, and it was named after the lord and lady's family seat, so that this name was now to be read in English, German, and French. This had never occurred to them before.

"As long as the gardener doesn't get too many big notions about himself!" said the lord and lady.

It affected him in another way: now he made every effort to make a name for himself as one of the best gardeners in the land, to try each year to produce something outstanding from every garden variety; and this is what he did. And yet he was often being reminded that the very first fruit he had raised, the apples and the pears, had really been the best; all later varieties were quite inferior. To be sure, the melons had been very good, but after all they were of an entirely different sort. The strawberries could be called excellent, but still they weren't any better than the ones grown on the other estates. And when the radishes failed one year, then only those unsuccessful radishes were mentioned, and not the other good things that had been raised.

It was almost as if the lord and lady found relief in being able to say, "It didn't turn out well this year, my little Larsen!" They were quite happy in being able to say, "It didn't turn out well this year."

Once or twice a week the gardener brought fresh flowers up to the drawing room, always tastefully arranged; it was as if the colors grew stronger by being placed side by side.

"You have taste, Larsen," said the lord and lady. "That is a gift that has come from Our Lord, not from yourself."

One day the gardener brought a big crystal bowl. In it was lying a water lily leaf. On top of this, with its long thick stalk down in the water, had been placed a dazzling blue flower as big as a sunflower.

"Hindustani lotus!" exclaimed the lord and lady.

They had never seen such a flower before, and during the day it was put in the sunshine and in the evening in reflected light. Everyone who looked at it found it to be remarkably lovely and rare; indeed, the highest young lady of the land said so, and she was a princess; she was wise and tenderhearted.

The lord and lady took pride in making her a present of the flower, and it went with the princess up to the castle.

Now the lord and lady went down in the garden themselves to pick a flower just like it if there were any more left. But it was nowhere to be found, so they called the gardener and asked where he had got that blue lotus from.

"We have searched in vain!" they said. "We have been in the greenhouses and all around the flower garden!"

"No, it's not there, all right!" said the gardener. "It's only a lowly flower from the kitchen garden! But how beautiful it is, isn't it! It looks like a blue cactus, and yet it's only the blossom of the artichoke!"

"You should have told us so right away!" said the lord and lady. "We were convinced that it was a rare foreign flower. You have made fools of us in the eyes of the young princess! She saw the flower here and found it to be quite lovely. She didn't recognize it, and she is well versed in botany. But that science has nothing to do with vegetables. What on earth were you thinking of, good Larsen, to put such a flower in the drawing room? It makes us look ridiculous!"

And the magnificent blue flower, which had been taken from the kitchen garden, was thrown out of the lord and lady's drawing room, where it didn't belong. Yes, the lord and lady apologized to the princess and told her the flower was only a vegetable and that the gardener had taken it into his head to display it. But for that reason he had been severely reprimanded.

"That was a shame and an injustice!" said the princess. "Why, he has opened our eyes to a magnificent flower that we would never have noticed at all. He has shown us loveliness where it didn't occur to us to look for it! Every day, as long as the artichokes are in bloom, the castle gardener shall bring one up to me in my drawing room."

And this was done.

The lord and lady informed the gardener that he again could bring a fresh artichoke blossom to them.

"As a matter of fact, it is pretty," they said. "Highly unusual!" And the gardener was praised.

"Larsen likes that!" said the lord and lady. "He's a pampered child!"

In the autumn there was a dreadful storm. It started during the night and was so violent that many big trees on the outskirts of the forest were torn up by the roots. And to the great sorrow of the lord and lady—sorrow as they called it, but to the gardener's delight—the two big trees with all the birds' nests blew down. The shrieking of the rooks and the crows could be heard above the storm. They beat on the panes with their wings, said the servants at the manor.

"Well, you're happy now, aren't you, Larsen!" said the lord and lady. "The storm has blown down the trees, and the birds have taken to the forest. Not a vestige remains of bygone days; every sign and every trace are gone! We are grieved!"

The gardener didn't say anything, but he was thinking of what had been on his mind for a long time: the best way of utilizing the splendid sunny spot, which had not been at his disposal before. It was going to be the pride of the garden and the joy of the lord and lady.

The huge, blown-down trees had crushed and broken the old box hedges, with all their fancy shapes. Here he raised a thicket of plants, domestic plants from field and forest.

What no other gardener had thought of planting in the garden of an estate he planted here in profusion, in the kind of soil each one was to have, and in shade and in sunshine, as each species required. He tended them with affection, and they grew in splendor.

The juniper bush, from the heath of Jutland, rose, in shape and color like the Italian cypress; the shiny, prickly Christ's-thorn, always green in the cold of winter and in the summer sun, was a beautiful sight. Many different species of ferns were growing in front, some looking like the offspring of palm trees and others as if they were the parents of that delicate, lovely plant that we call Venushair. Here stood the despised burdock, which, in its freshness, is so pretty that it would enhance a bouquet. The burdock grew in dry soil, but farther down in moister earth grew the dock plant—a plant also held in low esteem, and yet, with its height and its enormous leaf, so picturesquely beautiful. Waist-high, with flower upon flower like a mighty many-armed candelabra, soared the great mullein, replanted from the meadow. Here stood woodruffs, primroses, and hellebore, the wild calla lily and the delicate three-leaved wood sorrel. It was a delight to behold.

In front, supported by strings of steel wire, growing in rows, were quite small pear trees from French soil. They received sunshine and good care, and soon bore big, juicy fruits, as in the country from which they had come.

In place of the two leafless trees, a tall flagpole had been erected, from which Dannebrog[1] waved, and nearby

[1] The Danish flag.

yet another pole, around which, in summer and autumn, twined the hop with its fragrant, conelike catkins, but on which in winter—according to ancient custom—was hung a sheaf of oats so that the birds of the air might have their feast in the joyous Yuletide season.

"Our good Larsen is growing sentimental in his old age!" said the lord and lady. "But he is faithful and devoted to us!"

Around the beginning of the New Year, in one of the illustrated periodicals of the capital, a picture of the old manor appeared. One could see the flagpole and the sheaf of oats for the birds in the joyous Yuletide season. And it was referred to, and emphasized, as a lovely thought that such an ancient custom had here been restored to such prominence and veneration, so characteristic of precisely this old family seat.

"Everything Larsen does," said the lord and lady, "they beat a drum for! What a happy man! Why, we should almost be proud to have him!"

But they weren't proud at all. They felt that they were the master and mistress. They could give Larsen notice, but they didn't do it. They were good people. And there are so many good people of their sort, and that is gratifying to every Larsen.

Well, that's the story of "The Gardener and the Lord and Lady."

Now you can think it over!

The Flea and
the Professor

❖ ❖ ❖

THERE was a balloonist who came to grief. The balloon burst; the man dropped down and was dashed to smithereens. Two minutes earlier he had sent his boy down by parachute. This was the boy's good fortune. He was unharmed and went about with considerable knowledge for becoming a balloonist. But he had no balloon, nor had he any means of acquiring one.

He had to live, and so he went in for legerdemain and talking with his stomach—this is called "being a ventriloquist." He was young and easy on the eyes, and when he had acquired a goatee and put on fashionable clothing, he could be mistaken for the offspring of a count. The ladies found him handsome. Indeed, one maiden was so taken by his good looks and his legerdemain that she accompanied him to foreign lands and cities. There he called himself "professor"; nothing less would do.

His constant thought was to get hold of a balloon and go aloft with his little wife. But they did not yet have the money.

"It will come!" he said.

"If only it would!" she said.

"After all, we're young, and now I am a professor. Crumbs are also bread!"

She helped him faithfully, sat by the door, and sold

343

tickets to the performance—and this was a chilly pleasure in the wintertime. She also helped him in one of his tricks. He put his wife in the drawer of a table, a huge drawer. There she crawled into the back drawer, and then she could not be seen in the front drawer. It was a kind of optical illusion.

But one evening, when he pulled out the drawer, she had disappeared from him too. She was not in the front drawer, not in the back drawer, not anywhere in the house, nowhere to be seen or heard. This was her leger-demain. She never came back again. She was tired of it all, and he grew tired of it all; he lost his good humor and could not laugh or perform tricks any more, and then no one came. The earnings became poor, the clothes became shabby, and at last the only thing he owned was a big flea—an inheritance from his wife, and for this reason he was quite fond of it. So he trained it, taught it tricks; he taught it to present arms and shoot off a cannon—but a tiny one.

The professor was proud of his flea, and the flea was proud of itself. It had learned something and had human blood in its veins. It had been in the greatest cities, had been seen by princes and princesses and won their highest acclaim—this stood in print in newspapers and on plac-ards. It knew it was a celebrity and could support a professor, indeed, even a whole family.

It was proud and it was famous, and yet, when the flea and the professor traveled by railway, they went fourth class. It arrives just as quickly as first. There was an unspoken promise between them that they would never be parted, never marry. The flea would remain a bachelor and the professor a widower. It all adds up to the same thing.

"One should never revisit the scenes of one's greatest success!" said the professor. He was a judge of human nature, and that too is an art.

At last he had traveled to every land except the land of the Wild Men, and so he wanted to go to the land of the Wild Men. The professor knew, of course, that they ate Christian people there. But he wasn't really a Christian, and the flea wasn't really a person, so he thought they could risk journeying there, for they could make a good profit.

They traveled by steamship and by sailing ship. The flea performed its tricks, and so they had a free passage on the way and came to the land of the Wild Men.

A little princess reigned there. She was only eight years old, but she reigned. She had taken the power away from her father and mother, for she had a will of her own and was so adorably sweet and naughty.

At once, when the flea presented arms and shot off the cannon, she fell so in love with it that she said, "Him or no one!" She became quite wild with love, and indeed, she was already quite wild to begin with.

"Sweet little sensible child," said her father, "if only one could first make a person out of it!"

"You just leave that to me, old boy!" she said, and that wasn't a nice thing for a little princess to say to her father. But she was wild.

She put the flea on her little hand.

"Now you're a human being. You'll rule with me. But you will do as I wish, or else I'll kill you and eat the professor."

The professor was given a big hall to live in. The walls were of sugarcane. He could go and lick them, but he didn't have a sweet tooth. He was given a hammock to sleep in; it was as if he were lying in a balloon—the one he had always wanted and which was his constant thought.

The flea remained with the princess and sat on her little hand and on her delicate throat. She had taken a hair from her own head. The professor had to tie it around the flea's leg, and then she kept the flea tied to the piece of coral she wore in the lobe of her ear.

What a wonderful time for the princess, and for the flea too, she thought. But the professor didn't like it there. He was a traveling man, was fond of going from city to city and reading in the newspapers about his wisdom and patience in teaching human tasks to a flea. Day in and day out he loafed in the hammock and received his good food: fresh birds' eggs, elephant eyes, and roast thigh of giraffe. The cannibals do not live on human flesh alone—that's a delicacy.

"Children's shoulders with piquant sauce," said the princess' mother, "are the tastiest!"

The professor was bored and only too willing to leave the land of the Wild Men, but he had to have the flea with him. It was his prodigy and his livelihood. How was he going to capture it and get hold of it? That was not so easy.

He strained all his powers of concentration, and then he said, "Now I have it! Princess' Papa, permit me to do something! May I train the inhabitants of the land in the art of presentation? This is what, in the biggest countries of the world, is called breeding."

"And what can you teach me?" said the princess' father.

"My greatest skill," said the professor, "is to fire off a cannon so the whole world trembles, and all the most delicious birds of the skies fall down roasted! That's quite a bang!"

"Out with the cannon!" said the princess' father.

But in the whole land there was no cannon except for the one the flea had brought, and it was too small.

"I'll cast a bigger one!" said the professor. "Just give me the means. I must have fine silken cloth, a needle and thread, rope and string, and stomach drops for balloons: they inflate, alleviate, and elevate! They give the bang to the cannon stomach!"

He was given everything he asked for.

The entire population gathered to see the great cannon. The professor didn't send for them before the balloon was all ready to be filled and sent aloft.

The flea sat on the princess' hand and watched. The balloon was filled; it swelled out. It was so uncontrollable that it could hardly be held down.

"I must have it aloft so it can cool off," said the professor, and seated himself in the basket that hung below it.

"I can't possibly manage to steer it alone. I must have an expert companion along to help me. There's no one here who can do it except the flea."

"I'd rather not allow it!" said the princess, but still she handed the flea to the professor, who put it on his hand.

"Let go of the string and the ropes!" he said. "Here goes the balloon!"

They thought he said "the cannon!"

And then the balloon went higher and higher, up above the clouds, away from the land of the Wild Men.

The little princess, her father and mother, the entire population, stood and waited. They are waiting still. And if you don't believe it, just go to the land of the Wild Men. There every child speaks of the flea and the professor and believes they are coming back when the cannon has cooled off. But they are not coming. They are back home with us. They are in their native land, riding on the railroad—first class, not fourth; they earn good money; they have a large balloon. No one asks how they got the balloon or where it came from. They are prosperous folk, esteemed folk—the flea and the professor.

The Gate Key

❖   ❖   ❖

EVERY key has its story, and there are many keys: the chamberlain's key, the watch key, St. Peter's key; we could tell about all the keys, but now we're just going to tell about the Civil Servant's gate key.

It had been made by a locksmith, but it could very well believe it had been a blacksmith, the way the man took hold of it, hammering and filing. It was too big for a pants pocket, so it had to go in a coat pocket. Here it often lay in the dark—but, come to think of it, it did have its fixed place on the wall beside the silhouette of the Civil Servant from his childhood. There he looked like a dumpling in shirt frills.

They say that every human being acquires in his makeup and conduct something of the sign of the Zodiac under which he is born: Taurus, Virgo, Scorpio, as they are called in the Almanac. Madame Civil Servant mentioned none of these. She said that her husband had been born under the "sign of the Wheelbarrow": he always had to be pushed ahead.

His father had pushed him into an office, his mother had pushed him into matrimony, and his wife had pushed him up to the rank of Civil Servant; but she never mentioned the latter. She was a level-headed, good wife, who hauled in the right places, talked and pushed in the right places.

Now he was well on in years, "well proportioned," as he said himself, a well-read, good-natured man, who was as "bright as a key" to boot—something we will be able to understand later on. He was always in good spirits; he liked everybody and was only too fond of talking to them. If he were walking in the town, it was hard to get him home again if Mama wasn't along to give him a push. He had to talk to everyone he knew, and the dinner suffered.

From the window Madame Civil Servant kept watch. "Now he's coming!" she would say to the maid. "Put on the pot! Now he's standing still, talking to somebody, so take off the pot, or else the food will be cooked too much! Now he's coming, so put on the pot again!"

But still he didn't come.

He could stand right under the window of the house and nod up; but then if somebody he knew happened to come by, he couldn't help it, he had to have a few words with him. And if another acquaintance came along while he was talking with this one, then he would hang onto the first by the buttonhole and take the second by the hand while he shouted to a third, who wanted to go by.

It was enough to try the patience of Madame Civil Servant. "Civil Servant! Civil Servant!" she would shout. "Yes, that man is born under the sign of the Wheelbarrow: he can't budge unless he's given a push ahead!"

He was very fond of going to bookshops and browsing in books. He paid his bookseller a tiny fee for permitting him to read the new books at his home, that is to say, for being allowed to cut open the pages of the books lengthwise, but not across the top, for then they couldn't be sold as new. He was a walking newspaper, though an inoffensive one, and knew all about engagements, weddings, and funerals, literary gossip and gossip of the town; indeed, he would let drop mysterious hints that he knew of things that no one else knew. He had got it from the gate key.

Even as newlyweds the Civil Servant and his wife were

living in their own home, and from that time they had had the same gate key. But they were not aware then of its remarkable powers; they found out about those later.

It was during the reign of King Frederick the Seventh. At that time Copenhagen had no gas, it had train-oil lanterns: it had no Tivoli or Casino, no trolley cars and no railroads. There were few diversions as compared with what there are now. On Sunday one went for a walk out of the city gate to the churchyard, read the inscriptions on the graves, sat down on the grass, ate from one's lunch hamper, and drank one's schnapps with it; or else one went to Frederiksberg, where there was a regimental band in front of the castle and crowds of people to look at the royal family rowing about in the tiny narrow canals, where the old king steered the boat; he and the queen nodded to everyone without making any distinction in rank. Well-to-do families went out there from town to drink their afternoon tea. They could obtain hot water from a little farmhouse beyond the gardens, but they had to bring their own samovars with them.

The Civil Servant and his wife took a trip out there one sunny Sunday afternoon; the maid went ahead with the samovar and a hamper of provisions and "a drop to wash it down with."

"Take the gate key," said Madame Civil Servant, "so we can get in our own gate when we come back. You know it's locked here at dusk, and the bellpull has been broken since this morning! We'll be late getting home! After we've been to Frederiksberg, we're going to Casorti's Theater at Vesterbro to see the pantomime: 'Harlequin, Foreman of the Threshers,' where they come down in a cloud; it costs two marks per person!"

And they went to Frederiksberg, listened to the music, watched the royal family go bathing with banners waving, saw the old king and the white swans. After drinking a cup of good tea, they hurried away, but still they didn't get to the theater on time.

The tightrope walking was over, the stilt walking was over, and the pantomime had begun. As always, they had arrived too late, and for this the Civil Servant was to blame; every moment along the way he had stopped to talk to someone he knew; inside the theater he also met good friends, and when the performance was over, he and his wife had to accompany them to a family on the bridge to have a glass of punch; it was only going to be a ten-minute stop, but this, of course, stretched out to a whole hour. They talked and talked. Especially entertaining was a Swedish baron—or was he German? The Civil Servant didn't remember exactly; but on the other hand, the trick with the key—which the baron taught him—he retained for all time. It was extraordinarily interesting; he could make the key reply to everything it was asked about, even the most secret.

The Civil Servant's gate key was especially suited for this purpose. The bit was heavy, and it had to hang down. The baron let the bow of the key rest on the index finger of his right hand. It hung there loosely and lightly; each beat of the pulse in the tip of the finger could set it in motion, so that it turned—and if it didn't, then the baron knew very well how to make it turn as he wished. Each turning was a letter of the alphabet, from A and as far down in the alphabet as one cared to go. When the first letter had been found, the key turned to the opposite side; in this way one sought the next letter, and thus one arrived at complete words, complete sentences—an answer to the question. It was all a fraud, but always an amusement. And that was precisely what the Civil Servant thought at first, but he didn't stick to it: he became completely wrapped up in the key.

"Husband! Husband!" cried Madame Civil Servant. "The

West Gate closes at twelve o'clock! We won't get in; we have only a quarter of an hour left in which to hurry!"

They had to get a move on; several people, who wanted

to go in the town soon passed them by. At last they reached the outermost guardhouse. Then the clock struck twelve and the gate slammed shut, a large number of people stood locked out, and among them stood the Civil Servant and his wife, with maid, samovar, and empty lunch hamper. Some standing there were thoroughly frightened, others were irritated; each one took it in his own fashion. What was to be done?

Fortunately it had been decided of late that one of the city gates, the North Gate, was not to be locked; here the pedestrians could slip through the guardhouse into the town.

The way was not at all short, but the weather was fine, the sky was clear with stars and shooting stars, the frogs were croaking in ditch and marsh. The party began to sing, one ballad after the other; but the Civil Servant didn't sing, nor did he pay any attention to the stars—no, not even to his own two feet; he fell at full length right by the side of the ditch. One would have thought he'd had too much to drink, but it wasn't the punch, it was the key that had gone to his head and was turning there.

At last they reached the guardhouse of the North Bridge; they went across the bridge and entered the town.

"Now I'm happy again!" said Madame Civil Servant. "Here's our gate!"

"But where's the gate key?" said the Civil Servant. It was in neither the back pocket nor the side pocket.

"Good gracious!" cried Madame Civil Servant. "Haven't you got the key? You've lost it doing those key tricks with the baron! How are we going to get in now? You know the bellpull has been broken ever since this morning. The nightwatch hasn't got a key to the house! Why, this is a desperate situation!"

The maid began to wail; the Civil Servant was the only one who maintained his composure.

"We must break one of the windowpanes at the sausage-monger's," he said. "Get him out of bed and come in that way."

He broke a windowpane; he broke two. "Petersen!" he shouted, and stuck the handle of his umbrella in through the opening. Then the daughter of the family in the base-ment gave a loud shriek. The sausagemonger threw open the door to the shop, crying, "Nightwatch!" And before he'd rightly seen the family, recognized them and let them in, the nightwatch was blowing his whistle, and in the next street another nightwatch answered and started blowing. People came to their windows. "Where's the fire? Where's the riot?" they asked, and were asking still when the Civil Servant, who was already in his parlor, was taking off his coat—and in it lay the gate key, not in the pocket but in the lining. It had fallen down through a hole that shouldn't have been in the pocket.

From that evening the gate key acquired a singularly great importance, not only when they went out in the evening but also when they stayed home and the Civil

Servant showed off his sagacity by letting the gate key provide answers to questions.

He made up the most plausible answer, and then let the gate key supply it. At last he believed in it himself; but not the apothecary, a young man closely related to the Civil Servant's wife.

This apothecary had a good head on his shoulders, a critical head; already as a schoolboy he had written reviews of books and plays, but without his name being mentioned—and that means such a lot. He was what is called a *belesprit*, but he didn't believe in spirits at all—least of all key spirits.

"Of course I believe, I believe," he said. "Blessed Mr. Civil Servant, I believe in the gate key and all the key spirits just as firmly as I believe in the new science that is beginning to make itself known: table-turning, and the spirits in old and new furniture. Have you heard about that? I have! I've had my doubts. You know I'm a skeptic, but I've been converted after reading a frightful story in a quite reputable foreign publication. Mr. Civil Servant! Can you imagine! Yes, I'll tell you the story the way I read it; two bright children have seen their parents arouse the spirit in a big dining table. The little ones were alone, and now they wanted to try to rub life into an old chest of drawers in the same fashion. It came to life; the spirit awoke, but it couldn't tolerate the commands of children. It got up—the chest of drawers creaked—it shot out its drawers—and with its chest-of-drawer legs it put each of the children into a drawer. And then the chest of drawers ran out through the open door with them, down the stairs and out in the street, over to the canal, where it threw itself in and drowned both the children. The tiny bodies were placed in consecrated ground, but the chest of drawers was brought to the town hall, convicted of infanticide, and burned alive in the square! I've read it!" said the apothecary. "Read it in a foreign publication. It's not something I've made up myself; I swear by the key that it's true! Now I swear by all that's holy!"

The Civil Servant found such a tale to be too coarse a jest; the two of them could never talk about the key—the apothecary was "key-stupid."

The Civil Servant made progress in key wisdom; the key was his entertainment and his enlightenment.

One evening, as the Civil Servant was about to go to bed, he was standing half undressed when someone knocked on the door to the entryway. It was the sausagemonger in the basement who had come so late; he too was half undressed; but, he said, a thought had suddenly occurred to him, which he was afraid he couldn't keep overnight.

"It's my daughter, Lotte-Lene, who I must talk about. She's a pretty girl; she has been confirmed and now I want to see her make a good marriage!"

"I'm not yet a widower," said the Civil Servant with a chuckle, "and I have no son that I can offer her!"

"You understand what I mean, Civil Servant!" said the sausagemonger. "She can play the piano and she can sing— you must be able to hear it up here in the house. You have no idea of all the things the girl can do. She can mimic the speech and walk of everyone. She's made for playacting, and that's a good career for pretty girls of good family—they could marry into a family with an estate, although such a thing has never entered my mind or Lotte-Lene's! She can sing and knows how to play the piano! The other day I went up to the Song Academy with her. She sang, but she doesn't have what I call a 'beery-bass voice' in ladies or a canary-bird screech up in the highest registers, which so many songstresses are required to have now. And so they advised her not to choose this career at all. Well, I thought, if she can't be a singer, then she can always be an actress, for a voice is the only thing needed for that. Today I talked about it to the director, as he's called. 'Is she well read?' he asked. 'No,' I said, 'not in the least!' 'Reading is necessary for an artist!' he said. 'She can still acquire that,' I thought, and then I went home. 'She can go to a rental library and read what is there,' I thought. But this evening, while I'm sitting and getting undressed, it occurs to me: why rent books when you can borrow them? The Civil Servant has lots of books; let her read those. There's enough to read there, and she can have it free!"

"Lotte-Lene is a strange girl," said the Civil Servant, "a pretty girl! She shall have books to read! But does she have what is called 'get-up-and-go,' ingenuity, genius? And if she does, what is equally as important, is she lucky?"

"She has won twice in the Merchandise Lottery," said the sausagemonger. "Once she won a wardrobe and once six pairs of sheets! That's what I call luck, and that's what she has!"

"I'll ask the key!" said the Civil Servant.

And then he placed the key on the index finger of his right hand and then on the index finger of the sausagemonger's right hand, and let the key turn and supply letter after letter.

The key said, "Triumph and happiness!" And so Lotte-Lene's future was decided.

The Civil Servant gave her two books to read right away: *Dyveke*[1] and Knigge's *Associating with People*.

From that evening a closer acquaintanceship of sorts grew up between Lotte-Lene and the Civil Servant and his wife. She came often to the family, and the Civil Servant discovered that she was a sensible girl—she believed in him and in the key. Madame Civil Servant found, in the openness with which every moment she revealed her extreme ignorance, something childish and

---

[1] A tragedy by Ole Johan Samsøe.

innocent. The married couple, each in his own fashion, was fond of her, and she was fond of them.

"It smells so delightfully up there!" said Lotte-Lene.

There was an odor, a scent, a fragrance of apples in the hall, where Madame Civil Servant had stored a whole barrel of Gravenstein apples. There was also a smell of rose and lavender incense in all the rooms.

"It produces an atmosphere of quality!" said Lotte-Lene. And then she feasted her eyes upon all the beautiful flowers that Madame Civil Servant always had. Yes, even in midwinter, lilacs and cherry blossoms were blooming here. The cut, leafless branches were placed in water, and in the warm room they soon bore leaves and blossoms.

"You'd think there was no life in those bare branches, but see how they rise up from the dead."

"It has never occurred to me before," said Lotte-Lene. "Why, Nature is lovely!"

And the Civil Servant let her look at his "Key Book," in which had been written down remarkable things said by the key, even about half an apple cake that had disappeared from the pantry on the very evening the maid's sweetheart came calling.

And the Civil Servant asked his key: "Who has eaten the apple cake, the cat or the sweetheart?" And the gate key replied, "The sweetheart." The Civil Servant believed it even before he asked, and the maid confessed—why, that damned key knew everything!

"Yes, isn't it remarkable!" said the Civil Servant. "That key! That key! And it has said 'triumph and happiness' about Lotte-Lene. Now we'll soon see! I'll vouch for that!"

The Civil Servant's wife wasn't so confident, but she didn't express her doubts when her husband was listening. But later she confided to Lotte-Lene that, as a young man, the Civil Servant had been completely addicted to the theater. If someone had given him a push then, he would decidedly have appeared as an actor. But the family dismissed the idea. He wanted to go on the stage, and in order to get there he wrote a play.

"This is a great secret that I'm confiding to you, little Lotte-Lene. The play wasn't bad. It was accepted by the Royal Theater and booed off the stage, so it has never been heard of since, and I'm glad of it. I'm his wife and I know him. Now you want to follow the same career. I wish you well, but I don't think it'll work. I don't believe in the gate key!"

Lotte-Lene believed in it, and in that belief she and the Civil Servant found each other.

Their hearts understood each other in all propriety.

Moreover, the girl had other skills that Madame Civil Servant set store by. Lotte-Lene knew how to make starch from potatoes, sew silk gloves out of old silk stockings, recover her silk dancing slippers—even though she could afford to buy all her clothes new. She had what the sausagemonger called "shillings in the table drawer and bonds in the safe." This was really a wife for the apothecary, thought Madame Civil Servant. But she didn't say so, nor did she let the key say so, either. The apothecary was soon going to settle down and have his own pharmacy in one of the larger provincial towns of the land.

Lotte-Lene was constantly reading *Dyveke* and Knigge's *Associating with People*. She kept these two books for two years, and by then she had learned one of them—*Dyveke* —by heart, all the roles. But she wanted to perform only one of them, that of Dyveke, and not in the capital, where there is so much envy—and where they didn't want her. She wanted to start her artistic career, as the Civil Servant called it, in one of the larger provincial towns. Now it happened, by a strange coincidence, that this was in the very same town in which the young apothecary had settled down as the town's youngest, if not only, apothecary.

The great evening of expectation was at hand: Lotte-Lene was to perform and win triumph and happiness, as the key had said. The Civil Servant wasn't there; he was in bed and Madame Civil Servant was taking care of him. He was to have hot napkins and chamomile tea—the napkins on his tummy, the tea inside his tummy.

The couple didn't attend the *Dyveke* performance, but the apothecary was there, and he wrote a letter about it to his relation, Madame Civil Servant.

"Dyveke's collar was the best!" he wrote. "If the Civil Servant's gate key had been in my pocket, I would have taken it out and hissed through it! That's just what she deserved and just what the key deserved for having lied so shamefully to her about 'triumph and happiness'!"

The Civil Servant read the letter. It was all spite, he said, a "key hatred" with that innocent girl as the victim.

As soon as he was out of bed and human again, he sent a short but venomous letter to the apothecary, who wrote a reply as if he had interpreted the whole epistle as nothing more than a high-spirited joke.

He expressed his thanks for this, as well as for every well-meant contribution in the future to making public the key's incomparable value and importance. Then he confided to the Civil Servant that, in addition to his profession as apothecary, he was working on a long "key novel," in which all the characters were keys and keys alone. The gate key, of course, was the leading character and had been patterned after the Civil Servant's gate key—it had the gift of prophecy; all the other keys had to revolve around it: the chamberlain's old key, which had known the pomp and festivity of the court; the watch key, tiny, elegant, and important, at four shillings from the iron-monger's; the key to the box pew, which counts itself as one of the clergy, and which, after sitting all night in a keyhole in the church, has seen spirits; the keys to the pantry and to the fuel and wine cellars all make their appearance, curtsying and circulating around the gate key. The sunbeams make it shine like silver; the wind—the spirit of the world—flies into it and makes it float. It is the Key of all Keys, it was the Civil Servant's gate key, and now it is the key to the Pearly Gates, it is a papal key, it is "infallible"!

"Gall!" said the Civil Servant. "Unmitigated gall!"

He and the apothecary never saw each other again. Oh, yes, except at Madame Civil Servant's funeral.

She died first.

She was mourned and missed in the house. Even the cut cherry branches, which sent out fresh shoots and blossoms, grieved and withered away; they stood forgotten, for she no longer took care of them.

The Civil Servant and the apothecary walked behind her coffin, side by side as the two oldest relations.

There was neither the time nor the mood here for bickering.

Lotte-Lene tied a band of mourning around the Civil Servant's hat. She had long since returned to the house, without winning triumph and happiness in an artistic career. But it could come; Lotte-Lene had a future. The key had said so, and the Civil Servant had said so.

She came to see him. They talked about the deceased and they wept—Lotte-Lene was soft; they talked about the arts, and Lotte-Lene was strong.

"The life of the stage is lovely," she said, "but there's so much unpleasantness and envy! I shall go my own way instead. First myself and then the arts!"

Knigge had told the truth in his chapter about actors; she realized this. The key had not told the truth, but she didn't speak of this to the Civil Servant. She loved him.

As a matter of fact, during his entire period of mourning, the gate key had been his consolation and encouragement. He asked it questions and it gave him answers. And when the year was up, and he and Lotte-Lene were sitting together one sentimental evening, he asked the key: "Shall I get married and whom shall I marry?"

There was no one to give him a push, so he gave the key a push and it said: "Lotte-Lene!"

Now it had been said, and Lotte-Lene became Madame Civil Servant.

"Triumph and happiness!"

These words had been said in advance—by the gate key.

Afterword

❖ ❖ ❖

WE start on a journey. The journey teaches us and we teach the journey, and slowly, unalterably, the journey changes and then the destination changes. Andersen began his professional life as a novelist and he continued writing novels and plays until his death—thirty plays and six novels. Even with all that energy expended, his name would never have left Denmark but for the short folk tales he used to bridge the childhood and grown-up worlds, in neither of which he felt he belonged. He yearned to explain what of himself he could. There were traditional tales recast, written between his serious professional works, and other stories of his own. The plays, on which he spent so much energy and for which he had so much hope, weren't popular and few were produced. The novels earned him praise when they were published and are now almost all out of print. The "fairy" tales . . .

It's difficult to think of childhood without them. The stories have been told and retold, translated into dozens if not hundred of languages. They have been bowdlerized, modified, made into ballets, modern dances, poems, cartoons and animated films, children's plays, and holiday costumes. Andersen himself has been represented as part of a folk tale, a happy-go-lucky wanderer and lover of children, and luckiest of all, well loved and famous in his own lifetime. That part is true.

Andersen was following a trend, a watershed in Victorian literature: the mining of the vast treasures of the oral tale. The brothers Grimm had published *Kinder- und Hausmärchen* in 1812–15, and the English soon followed, recognizing the depth and psychological penetration of many of these previously neglected tales. In Denmark, the trend had been begun by N.F.A. Grundtvig (1783–1872). It's worthwhile to take a moment to look at the work of this extraordinary man.

Grundtvig, a Lutheran minister, composed most of the hymnody used to this day in Danish churches. He was an enthusiastic reader of Kierkegaard and worked for a revival of Christianity that would ease the dry rationalism of its former expression. This trend was widespread in Europe and in America was expressed in the spiritualism that produced the Christian Science, Seventh Day Adventist, and Jehovah's Witness movements. Grundtvig also wrote poetry and in 1820 translated *Beowulf* into Danish. In 1832, he published *Nordens Mytologi*, which introduced many Danes to their own superb heritage of myth. Andersen had certainly been exposed to this trend and to Grundtvig's work. Kierkegaard said, "Reasoned philosophy fails to account for the depths and tragedies of human existence." The Norse classics harked back to an older age, one of violence and bloodshed but one also of feeling and an open-eyed assessment of human possibilities of courage, heroism, pain, and loss.

The Teutonic folklore gathered by the brothers Grimm shared many stories and much tradition with the Norse tales. Their work was translated and read with great interest. Andersen, one of the most traveled men of his time, was exposed to these trends all over Europe as well as in Denmark. "The Tinderbox," "Little Claus and Big Claus," "Cloddy Hans," "The Girl Who Trod on a Loaf," and "What Papa Does Is Always Right," among others, are folk tales familiar at all European hearths. Andersen didn't copy these tales; he retold them.

There are two conflicting philosophies in storytelling, especially in the oral form. One is that the ancient tale or myth must be told exactly as heard, being borne as an almost sacred responsibility from generation to generation. Modification or elaboration of any kind is a violation of the story's provenance. The story is preeminent; its power is enhanced by its purity, even though it may, over centuries, cease to be understood by its ordinary hearers, and be available only to the specialist or dedicated student.

The other is that each teller understands the story differently, comes to it from a different background and point of view, and therefore makes modifications to explicate and clarify it to himself before presenting it to his hearers. The teller interacts with his audience and, if he is good at what he does, brings forth elements of the story that may have been hidden. The story does change, but its basic elements remain in place.

The danger in the first case is that the living story may become "classic," removed from the ordinary audiences for whom it was first created. The danger in the second is that, in attempting to make it relevant, its point may be changed beyond recognition over time, or it might become so chatty and forced that its magic is lost and its informality of speech dates it almost before it's out of the teller's mouth.

Andersen, in translation, has been subjected to excesses on both sides. I've been reading these tales since I was a child, and I've come on both the stuffed nightingale and the pop version. The new translation is, I think, a middle way. Andersen adopted an informal, oral style, which was later gussied up by many of his translators in a desire to make the work classic and to clean it up for Victorian children's ears. The work here gets much of the spirit back. "In China, you know, of course, the Emperor is Chinese," and "A duck came from Portugal, some said from Spain. It makes no difference. She was called The Portuguese." There's a Dickensian love of little details, flourishes or grace notes that add a hominess to what builds the story. "Here they lived—but only during the summer."

Andersen used details and an easy style, but he walked a narrow line and never went over it into the kind of pandering to kid vocabularies and pop slang that Disney movies do. Compare the language used in *The Little Mermaid* animated film with the language Andersen used in the story itself. "Wow, cool," the fish tells the mermaid, who says, "My father's gonna kill me." "She's got it bad," another mermaid observes, trivializing a yearning that in the Andersen story is tragic.

When Andersen's stories are serious, the language used to dress them is serious, and when the story is lighter, the language lightens and the characters pay homage to the form that surrounds them. In one, a proud princess renounces her unfit suitors. Princesses and unfit suitors abound in all European traditions of storytelling. Andersen's princess looks at one of them: "Won't do," she says, "scram."

Hans Christian was anything but the simple teller of childhood tales his readers imagine, or perhaps want him to be. He never married; he had no children. He was a shy man, easily depressed, but convinced by a hard childhood that it was a desperate necessity to proclaim and exalt himself, to work against the odds, and he expected very long odds indeed.

He was born in Odense, in 1805. Odense was then the second largest city in Denmark, but it was on an island, Furen. In 1807, Denmark joined the Napoleonic War, siding with Russia. After being defeated by Sweden, it was forced to give up its rights to Norway. The loss caused great poverty in the cities of this primarily agricultural country. Hans Christian's father was a cobbler, a man embittered by his low status, poor education—although he could read—and scant prospects. He married Hans Christian's mother two months before her son was born. This casual approach to the calendar wasn't uncommon in the class to which the family belonged.

Hans Christian's mother was illiterate, but a loving presence. His father was also devoted to him and tried to give him the education he had been denied. The couple was ill-matched—he, a rationalist-atheist, she, a superstitious theist. These trends were never resolved in the family or in Hans Christian. I think the paradoxes and ambiguities of the home situation provided the motive force for the flowering of his gifts and prepared the arena in which the gifts would find their expression.

Hans Christian's grandfather was mentally ill, and Hans Christian was both ashamed and terrified of the inheritance. His grandmother tended the garden of the mental hospital and Hans Christian was in touch with the inmates there and other old people in the area who provided him with every kind of verbal expression. He was used to conundrums, metaphor, personification, and a slipping away of reality against which the rationalist part of his nature supplied the necessary corrective.

The island was also a bit of a cultural backwater, removed from the more sophisticated world of Copenhagen. Many of the old styles of speech and folkways had been preserved there, as well as the best-maintained Renaissance castle in Europe, where it can still be seen, with its moat, battlements, and perfect fairy tale setting.

In the class in which Hans Christian was raised, children were worked long and hard. Even though he was allowed to go to school, he must have seen children at brutal and backbreaking labor in long hours of unskilled work. In none of his stories is childhood romanticized as it is by other writers. Seldom is it made wonderful. "The Little Match Girl" is only one of the visions we have of childhood as cold, lonely, and treated with offhand cruelty and rare sympathy.

To the extent that he was a schoolboy, Hans Christian was privileged. The schooling itself was marginal, a charity affair, but he did have time to play and dream, rare for poor children in those days. He seldom made his games with other children. His father gave him a puppet theater and he spent hours constructing lives for his characters.

When he was seven, his father gave up the cobbler shop and went into Napoleon's army, hoping to better himself and return a war hero. The elder Andersen never saw action, but the two years he was away must have been very hard on his wife and son. He came home broken in health and died in 1816. His widow supported herself and Hans Christian by cleaning houses and taking in washing.

It was a custom among the titled nobility of the time to sponsor or promote one or two of the gifted sons of the poor. Someone would notice or recommend a musical or literary prodigy, and he would be invited up to the castle to perform. My grandfather had been such a boy and to the end of his life he would describe the wonder of being sent for by the baron on the hill on various occasions to sing, recite, or supply wit for the parties at the castle, away from the mud and ugliness of the village. Not only was the performance paid for with food or money enough to feed the family for a week, but the culture shock provided a valuable experience. The gleaming floors of the reception hall, the rooms on rooms, the heavy velvet drapes, and the profusion of lamps, food, and warmth were a world away from his familiar dirt floor, the single room odorous with the sweat, cooking, closeness of the whole family, the freezing privy.

Hans Christian drew the interest of such people in Odense's upper class and was often asked to perform, singing and declaiming. He had a high, clear soprano voice, a joke to his schoolfellows, a boon to his starving mother.

She married again to another cobbler and apprenticed Hans Christian to a tailor, but that ended in failure. Her second husband died several years later, leaving the widow in the starkest circumstances.

When Hans Christian was thirteen, a repertory company came to the theater in Odense and he got a job as an extra. His short stint convinced him that the theater was his calling. That meant Copenhagen. Over his mother's objections, he left home.

That road was (and is) rocky, full of failure and rejection. The letter of introduction he had led nowhere. The Royal Theater manager told him that with no more than his rudimentary schooling, he had no place there. After a dozen fits and starts he began to submit plays.

These plays were refused, but a member of the theater's board became interested in Hans Christian. Such an interest seems as miraculous as the transformations in one of his stories. By all accounts, Hans Christian was at that time all bumptious boy-man, a callow show-off, using big words incorrectly, demanding attention, all persistence and no experience. He was every mentor's nightmare: the writer with true talent and deep gifts he wasn't showing and who comes on like a steam calliope at a funeral.

Luckily for the world, James Collin, the board member, saw past this desperate overreaching of an essentially reclusive person who was trying too hard and ruining his own chances. Collin arranged for schooling and a stipend.

Hans Christian graduated in 1829, at the age of

twenty-four, and must have felt like a battle-scarred veteran whose best years had been spent getting to the place to which everyone else in his world had already been given easy access years before.

He had written a poem about a dying child, one of the earliest of the flood of that genre, echoed in Dickens, Harriet Beecher Stowe, Louisa May Alcott, and dozens of photographers who made endless studies of dead children. Although written for himself, the poem became an instant worldwide success, printed and reprinted. There were no laws or copyright controlling the artistic product at the time. Hans Christian would have fame, but not money.

The poem was a beginning, but seemed an ending. The second beginning was *A Walking Tour from the Holman Canal*, a comic, satirical fantasy, a bit like *The Pickwick Papers* in its approach, but without Dickens' sure hand. The elements were there: fantasy, concern with the life-death divide, a sense of the absurd. The work did very well and gave Hans Christian enough money to send some to his mother. He was, by then, light-years separated from the class in which he had been raised. That summer he passed two university degree exams and bid good-bye to the schoolroom.

Here began the travels that would take him all over Europe and last on and off for the rest of his life. He had fallen in love, faithful to the ideal of the German Romanticism he was adopting as his own—hopelessly. All of his loves would be hopeless. She married. He suffered and wrote and saw himself very much in the Goethe-Heine tradition. Of course, his first big trip outside Denmark would be to Germany. He visited all the major cities there.

Then he went to Italy in 1833, north to Prague, Bohemia, Austria, and back to Denmark, where he began the first of his stories, a book of four: "The Tinder Box," "Little Ida's Flowers," "Little Claus and Big Claus," and "The Princess and the Pea." Three were folk stories, "Little Ida's Flowers," his own. The book was an immediate success. The tales were newly approached:

> A soldier was marching along, left, right! Left, right. He had his knapsack on his back and a sword at his side, for he had been to the wars and was going home. And on the way he met an old witch. Oh, she was horrid: her bottom lip came right down to her chest.

In those days, tales for children were for the purpose of moral instruction and no extras. These stories in which flowers talked and toys and figurines came to life were brand-new and a window flung wide-open on the way children actually think and feel.

By 1836, Hans Christian was an established writer with a novel and two volumes of tales. He was working on a second novel. The next years would be prolific, adding to his fame, which was, even then, international, but Andersen wasn't a man destined for happiness. Ambition, self-doubt, and an almost childish self-centeredness crippled his relationships and chilled the delight he might have felt with his gifts and his fame.

He traveled constantly in those years: Greece, the Balkans, and Constantinople, at a time when travel was difficult and often dangerous.

All of Hans Christian's loves were hopeless, all importunate, passionate, self-defeating, and doomed. Now it was Jenny Lind.

She was very like him: poor, orphaned, gifted, and able to catch the interest of exalted patrons at an early age. She was needy, neurotic, and terrified of losing the gift on which she and her family depended, a gift like mercury in the palm.

She became an icon, a rage. Barnum brought her to America; she was the toast of Europe. Her relationship with Hans Christian was hopeless. Labile, highstrung individuals with intangible gifts usually need the presence of stable, reasonable, and balanced friends and lovers who moderate their excesses and smooth their feathers. Whom do they pick? She realized the impossibility of a more than friendly relationship. He didn't. As with his other loves, he suffered loudly and publicly. Such effusions went with the romantic bravura of the time, and so they didn't do him much harm.

Andersen's libido was more erotic than sexual, anyway. He courted both genders and established triangles with both, but the objects of his desire were always unattainable. His relationship with Jenny, if doomed, resulted in his emergence from being a refashioner of folk stories to a creator of his own best tales, using the children's story form without its content, so as to make a new genre. "The Ugly Duckling," "The Nightingale," "The Snow Queen," and "The Fir Tree" were all written under the Jenny spell, and the content was that of transformed autobiography, his own life made metaphor. "The Nightingale" is a direct tribute to Jenny, who was, after all, the Swedish Nightingale.

"The Snow Queen" is Andersen's longest and most involved tale: love and loss. The characters are children: Kay and Gerda, who are best friends. Kay receives the splinter of a broken Devil's mirror in his eye. This renders the world and all its creatures ugly and evil. Later, he is kidnapped by the ice-hearted Snow Queen and driven into the lands of ice. Gerda sets out to rescue him. After great dangers, she almost loses hope, but never quite. The story is pervaded with a homesick anguish that is almost palpable. That emotion is at its most intense in childhood and is seldom captured by an adult writer. The closest description of it is in *Heidi*, by Johanna Spyri. A gift Andersen shared with Dickens was his ability to remember childhood in all its intensity and all its pain. Anyone who remembers childhood as a golden time has memory loss. We seal those years off not because of their irrelevance but because of their anguish. "The Snow Queen" ends with Gerda finding Kay and her tears flushing away the hateful shard in his eye, but Andersen is no fool. There is a huge price to pay. The two have lost their childhoods. He tells us that they remain children at heart, but all that means is that the homesickness has gone soul-deep in both of them. You don't make up lost years, he says. Andersen's fantasy is grounded with both feet in the hard facts of reality, which is what makes it so compelling. The Little Mermaid is told:

The very thing that is so lovely here in the sea, your fishtail, they find so disgusting up there on earth. They don't know any better. Up there they have to have two clumsy stumps, which they call legs, to be beautiful!

Andersen's later life was one of travel and stay-overs at the homes of the rich and famous, of universal fame and adulation, but his joy was marred by his self-centered blindness and straitjacketed by the persona he had made for himself. He wrote autobiographies that concealed more than they showed. Dickens prepared his way and fame in England, where he traveled in triumph and he, in turn, paved the way for Lewis Carroll, Charles Kingsley, and George McDonald. His work succeeded in English in spite of awful translations and Victorian bowdlerizations. The dying Elizabeth Barrett Browning made him the hero of her last poem.

The European revolutions of 1848–51 changed the cultural climate there, but these washed over Andersen, who saw his reputation outlive the chaos. He traveled widely for the rest of his life and his talent matured in later tales. "The Marsh King's Daughter" and "Anne Lizbeth" are products of this later, wider style.

As egocentric and eccentric as Hans Christian was, he continued to be welcome in the homes of wealthy and generous families. Happy families gave him the security at the end of his life that he lacked at the beginning. He continued to have crushes on members of both sexes, but the Victorian talent for overlooking the specific while damning the general came to his rescue. Even when his behavior was indiscreet, it was never a public trouble to him. In his last years, he was able to discuss his bisexuality, and to write of it, more freely than he had before. His final stories produce overtly effeminate men and mannish women.

He also continued to travel, although with age's

complaints, including fear of the poverty that was long years past. Dickens died, other friends and contacts died, but his support system to the very end was chrome steel. He died in the presence of loving and caring friends, at five past eleven in the morning, the fourth of August 1875.

> And it was summer—the warm, glorious summer. —"The Snow Queen"

—JOANNE GREENBERG